P9-CCP-204

Also by Elizabeth Aston

Mr. Darcy's Daughters

The Exploits & Adventures of Miss Alethea Darcy

The True Darcy Spirit

The Second Mrs. Darcy

A NOVEL

ELIZABETH ASTON

A TOUCHSTONE BOOK
PUBLISHED BY SIMON & SCHUSTER
New York London Toronto Sydney

TOUCHSTONE
Rockefeller Center
1230 Avenue of the Americas
New York, NY 10020

This book is a work of fiction. Names, characters, places, and incidents either are products of the author's imagination or are used fictitiously. Any resemblance to actual events or locales or persons, living or dead, is entirely coincidental.

For information regarding special discounts for bulk purchases, please contact Simon & Schuster Special Sales at 1-800-456-6798 or business@simonandschuster.com.

Designed by Davina Mock

Manufactured in the United States of America

1 3 5 7 9 10 8 6 4 2

Library of Congress Catalog Card Number: 2006052586

ISBN-13: 978-0-7432-9729-5
ISBN-10: 0-7432-9729-6

For Jessica Buckman
with love

The Second Mrs. Darcy

Chapter One

"It is a truth universally acknowledged, that a single woman in possession of a good fortune must be in want of a husband."

Lady Brierley made this pronouncement in booming tones that brooked no disagreement. "Of course you will marry again."

Octavia smiled at Lady Brierley, a woman all nose, but despite her Roman appearance, very good-hearted.

They were sitting on the verandah of the Thurloes' house in Alipore, a suburb of Calcutta, making the most of a pleasant breeze which ruffled the huge leaves of the banana tree near the house. The hovering bearer came forward on silent bare feet to fill their cups with more fragrant Darjeeling tea.

"I am sure you are right," said Octavia, "but, however, I am not in possession of a good fortune. I am in possession of virtually no fortune at all."

"No fortune? Of course you have a fortune. Your late husband was certainly well-to-do; he had a good income, a good estate, a first wife brought him a handsome portion—and then he won a considerable amount in prize money; it was known throughout the service that Captain Darcy was a lucky captain in the matter of prizes."

"That is true, but he put a lot of that money into his house and estate, and both are entailed."

Lady Brierley narrowed her eyes. "I had heard that was the case, but I did not believe it. He had no brothers, no close relations at all; pray, who will inherit?"

"A man called George Warren, a distant cousin."

"George Warren! I have heard of him, he is the son of Lord Warren, who— Well, it is all most irregular, and I am sorry for you, my dear, if you are not left in as comfortable circumstances as you might have expected."

"I shall have a small income, on which, with care and good management, I shall be able to live."

"That is hardly—" began Lady Brierley.

Octavia smiled. "It is not as though I was brought up in affluence, I am used to making do on little."

"Before your marriage, you were a Melbury. Your brothers and sisters may not rank among the very rich, but they hardly have to watch every penny."

Which was true enough, but they certainly grudged every penny that had to be spent on Octavia. Octavia disliked her brothers and sisters—half brothers and sisters—in fact, quite as much as they disliked her. There were five of them, three sisters and two brothers. One sister married and—thankfully—living in Yorkshire, two others married and living in London—married well, by the standards of the world, although Octavia didn't care at all for Lord Adderley, and knew Mr. Cartland to be quite under her sister's forceful thumb.

Her eldest brother, Sir James, the Squire of Melbury, lived in the country, at Melbury Hall, rarely left his land and stables and hounds to visit London, and took no interest in his young half sister; a person of no fortune, no consequence, no account, he would have said, if asked. Her next brother, shrewd, ambitious Arthur, always ready to point out Octavia's failings and defects, spent most of the year in London. He was a rising politician, who sat for the family parliamentary seat of Melbury.

Her brothers and sisters had never forgiven their father, the late Sir Clement Melbury, for remarrying, several years after his first wife had died, when he was well advanced in years. He had seven children, of whom her five half brothers and sisters were the survivors; two more children had died in infancy. What need had he to disgrace them, caught by a pretty face and a well-turned ankle, choosing to marry the daughter of a man who was hardly more than a tradesman, not even a successful London merchant, not in any great line of business, and his mousy, ill-bred wife? The daughter had been attractive, in an insipid, ordinary way, but their father had made a fool of himself, of course he had; what folly to marry a girl less than half his age, a nobody.

They had felt nothing but relief when the second Lady Melbury died in childbirth, leaving a baby daughter, whom he had named Octavia. The name annoyed them, as suggesting that this child was one of them, which, of course, in their opinion, she wasn't.

Lady Brierley was busily arranging Octavia's future for her. "Well, my dear, we must think of what is to be done. You will return to England, I dare say, there will be legal matters to be dealt with, and this cousin of yours must be persuaded to give you an annuity, he will not wish to appear mean in the eyes of the world, and Captain Darcy was a man with many friends and of standing. He was liked by everyone, so amiable as he was. No, that is the best course for you, the voyage to England will take you several months, so your period of mourning will be almost over by the time you arrive, and then, you know—"

Octavia could finish the sentence for her. *And then, you know, you might be so lucky as to find yourself another husband.*

Lady Brierley's mind was indeed still running on husbands. "On the other hand, such matters can be dealt with by lawyers, and with the Ninth Foot due to be posted here, although of course soldiers are careful whom they marry—but still, even with a very modest portion, you are a Melbury by birth, and that does count for something. You were fortunate before; where so many girls return to England still unmarried, you quickly found a husband, and I don't see why that should not be the case again."

What a lottery marriage was, Octavia reflected. Her father had married again, within ten months of being made a widower for the second time, and this time he chose better, in the eyes of his older children; the third Lady Melbury, herself a widow, was the placid daughter of a respectable squire, and her first husband had been a man of position and wealth. She had brought Octavia up without enthusiasm or much kindness, but she had a strong sense of duty, so that when Sir Clement was carried away by an inflammation of the chest, and his heir and his siblings made it quite clear they had no wish to take responsibility for their half sister, Lady Melbury had taken the eight-year-old Octavia to live with her in a pleasant house near Weymouth, in Dorset.

Octavia's half brothers and sisters had paid their younger sister little attention for the succeeding seven years, hoping merely that a fever or some childish complaint such as a virulent attack of measles would carry her off. But Octavia survived the dangerous early years of infancy and had grown into a tall girl, taking after her despised mother, with very few graces about her and a distressing tendency to speak her mind.

Then, at the age of thirty-nine, Octavia's stepmother had announced her intention to marry a Dublin physician, which was all very well for her, the Melburys said, quite good enough, and would mean that there was no longer any danger that a dowdy Lady Melbury might turn up unexpectedly in town and want to be introduced to their circle. But not even a mere half sister was going to be allowed to go and live in Dublin in such a household, not while she bore the name of Melbury.

Since her brothers were Octavia's legal guardians, they could impose their will on their despised half sister. Lady Melbury would have taken Octavia with her to Ireland, but she accepted the family's ruling without argument and set off to her new life in Dublin as wife to Dr. Gregory without Octavia. After all, she told her stepdaughter, she was a great girl now, fifteen was nearly grown up. She would do better to keep up her connections with her father's family than languish in Dublin.

Octavia fought the decision, but Arthur was absolute, and so she stayed on in Dorset, in the company of a woman who wasn't well educated enough to be called a governess, a woman of indeterminate age who drifted around the house in a cloud of melancholy and with a perpetual sniff that drove Octavia to leave the house and saddle her horse and gallop the fidgets out of herself on long solitary rides.

When her brother Arthur found out about the rides, he put a stop to them by the simple expedient of selling her horse and leaving her with one old pony who could be used in the trap to take them to and from the nearby village when required.

"One is expected to marry, of course," said Octavia, watching a mynah bird with its comical yellow eye hopping about on the sparse grass in search of insects. "It's considered the natural state for any young woman. And yet, do I want to marry again? I am not so sure that I do."

Lady Brierley pursed her lips. "You are still grieving for your husband, of course it is too soon to be making any plans of that sort, any definite plans, that is. However, one must look ahead, you will come out of your blacks, and you know, once a woman has been married, she is accustomed to the state. Even women with husbands a great deal less amiable than poor Captain Darcy find themselves wishing to marry again."

"Only I am tall, you know, and that does limit the possibilities."

Lady Brierley looked sharply at Octavia; was there a hint of laughter in her voice?

"Nonsense, height has nothing to do with it. You are graceful, you carry your inches with style, and there are shorter men who prefer—"

"Oh, I think I could only like a man I could look up to," said Octavia gravely.

At eighteen, Octavia had been summoned to London from Dorset, whisked away from one day to the next by an impatient Arthur, to be inspected and made ready for marriage by her sisters.

One look at her, and they despaired. "She's taller than most men, which is a grave handicap," complained Augusta.

"Built like a cart horse," said Theodosia.

"You'll have to do your best to make something of her," said Arthur with a shrug. "She is as ill bred as her mother, and you must break her of this habit she has of speaking her mind; that will never do."

And they tried, in their ruthless way. Muslined and crimped and scolded and directed as to just how to behave, Octavia must be meek, men didn't like any forwardness in a woman, particularly not in one who resembled a bean pole. She must laugh, but softly, nothing merry or uproarious, at whatever jokes or pleasantries her partner might make; she must listen; she must hold her tongue and keep her thoughts to herself, no one was interested in her except as a wife of more or less suitable breeding and the possible mother of future sons.

"At least she looks healthy enough," said her brother disparagingly. "Perhaps some country fellow in town for the season might take a fancy to her, some man who is not averse to an Amazon for a wife."

Privately, her half sisters laughed at her prospects. "If she had a fortune . . . but even then, she is so very *rustic.*"

Neither of them had had any great fortune, but they had been so beautiful as girls that each of them had swept more than one eligible man off his feet the moment she had come out, and had married, in turn, the richest and most influential of her suitors.

At first, Octavia felt sorry for their husbands, at least for Theodosia's husband. Augusta's spouse, Lord Adderley, was a dark, brooding, unpleasant man, who looked at Octavia as though she were an insect; he and Augusta deserved each other, she soon decided. But Henry Cartland, Theodosia's husband, was a kinder man, who seemed to have a gleam of sympathy in his eye when he heard her being harangued by one or other of her family. However, he made no attempt to intervene or stand up for her; he had been married to Theodosia for long enough to know that it would be a wasted effort.

The season had passed in a whirl of dances and parties, with Octavia hating every moment of it, making no friends, and certainly attracting no parti, eligible or otherwise.

"Perhaps we should have sent her to Dublin after all," said Theodosia, in irritated tones. "Perhaps she would be better off in Ireland."

"In that company, in the house of a mere physician? She is our half sister, and is known to be so. No, no," said Augusta. "I shall get Adderley to see about a passage to India, where let us hope she may snare a Company man or an army officer."

"Augusta is right, it's the only thing to do with her," Arthur had said. "The girl's a liability. She'll never get herself a husband here in England, unless some curate can be persuaded to take her on, to help in the parish. She may have an honourable name, but everyone knows her mother was a nobody; she can't expect a good match, no looks, no fortune, nothing to recommend her to any man. And she makes no effort to attract, she is a hopeless case."

"And there is one great advantage to this plan," Octavia overheard Theodosia say, "at the very least she will be gone two years, for the voyage takes many months, and we shall oblige her to spend at least a year there, to give herself a chance of finding a husband."

"The voyage may be dangerous, severe weather, you know, many ships are lost at sea in bad weather."

"And there are pirates, I believe, in some parts of foreign oceans."

"Yes, although it is not so hazardous a journey as it was during the war."

The sisters thought with regret of the years when enemy frigates bearing down on the East Indiaman, guns firing, passengers taken away and never seen again, were a common occurrence.

It had indeed been a long and often stormy crossing, the voyage out, but the ship had suffered neither shipwreck nor attacks by pirates, and the time at sea had brought Octavia a kind of happiness. The routine of the ship suited her; it allowed her to grow back into her own skin after her disastrous season in London. She made one or two friends among some of the girls in the fishing fleet, as they were uncharitably known, although her frank ways earned disapproval from others, and from most of the mamas who were accompanying their daughters.

One of the girls had become engaged on board, to a ship's officer, and had indeed been married by a disapproving captain. As they had anticipated the wedded state, it was uncertain whether the fruit of their love would arrive before the vessel sailed into harbour in Bombay, a topic that kept all the female passengers agog with interest, and among the men, led to a book being opened as to the chances of the baby being born on board or ashore—despite the often expressed disapprobation of a clerical gentleman on his way to convert the heathen of Bengal.

Octavia had gone overland to Calcutta, where a distant cousin had agreed to look after her and launch her into such society as existed in that crowded, noisy, lively city. He and his wife had turned out to be pleasant enough people, and, to Octavia's joy, Harriet Thurloe was a keen horsewoman, with whom she could go out riding every morning on the Maidan, before the scorching heat made any outdoor activity impossible.

And then a Royal Navy frigate had called at Calcutta, on an unscheduled visit for urgent repairs: spars broken, a mast sprung in a gale. A dance had swiftly been arranged for the naval officers, and Octavia had found herself partnered in the quadrille by a handsome man in his early forties, a Captain Darcy, who wasn't in command of the *Wentworth* moored at Howrah, but on his way out to his own commission.

They were eye to eye in height, and he was a grave man, but with a sense of humour that Octavia appreciated. A week after they had met, and a week before he was due to sail, he had proposed, and Octavia, liking him, if not swept off her feet, had accepted.

It had been the talk of the town: all the young ladies and their mothers or aunts or cousins had had their eye on Captain Darcy.

"He is very well connected," Harriet had said. "Of an excellent family. The Darcys are very rich; his cousin, Fitzwilliam Darcy, is Mr. Darcy of Pemberley, you know."

"Christopher Darcy has a neat estate in Wiltshire," Mr. Thurloe added.

"He is a widower," Harriet told Octavia. "His first wife was a great beauty, and the granddaughter of an earl. He was heartbroken when she died. It was an accident of some kind, I seem to remember, her horse bolted, and she was thrown. Or did her carriage overturn? I can't exactly remember. That was five years or so ago, and people said he was so grief-stricken he would never marry again. However, once a man has had a wife, I find he likes to have another, so I'm not surprised that he wishes to marry again. Although . . ."

She didn't finish the sentence, but Octavia knew what she was thinking. Why should a well-bred, well-off man, formerly married to the descendant of earls, pick Octavia for his second wife?

Captain Darcy told her why. "You laugh a lot," he said, after giving her an affectionate kiss. "You have a smile on your lips, and your eyes dance. We naval men have a hard time of it at sea, and it will be a joy to come home to a warm smile and laughter."

In the brief time they had together, it had been a happy marriage. He wanted a son, he made no bones about that, but he was kind and considerate when she lost a child early on, more concerned for her than for the loss of his hopes. "It's difficult in this climate," he said, having decided to leave her in Calcutta with Harriet while he was on his commission. "Plenty of time yet."

Only he hadn't had time. A keen botanist, he had taken the opportunity on his next visit to Calcutta to go up country with a naval friend. There, he had been bitten by an insect, a poisonous insect, and had, so the stricken lieutenant reported on his return to Calcutta, died soon afterwards.

Lady Brierley rose to take her leave. "You must take care of yourself, my dear, and if there is anything we can do—the Admiral was an old friend of Captain Darcy, as you know; they served together in the war on several occasions, and we in the service do not forget the families of our fellow officers."

Octavia was touched by her kindness, and indeed by the kindness of her cousins, the Thurloes, who had taken her back into their household and were concerned for her future.

"It is all round Calcutta," Harriet exclaimed, when she came in from a drive out to Tollygunge.

"What is?" said Octavia, helping her cousin with the ribbons of her straw hat. "You have just missed Lady Brierley."

"No doubt calling to find out if it is true that you are penniless, thanks to that dreadful entail! To think of George Warren inheriting!"

"Not quite penniless."

"As good as."

The Thurloes returned to the subject of Octavia's fortune that evening at dinner. Octavia, feeling hot in her black dress, although it was made of muslin, fanned herself vigorously. She wished that the *punkah wallah,* sitting peacefully in his corner and working the overhead fan by means of a string attached at one end to his big toe and at the other, via some pulleys, to the centre of the revolving wings, were more energetic in his task.

Although why should he be? It was one of the unexpected pleasures of India, she had found: the contrast between the cool mornings, the time for brisk exercise, for riding and for clear thinking, and the languorous heat of the day, giving way to the ease of the evening.

The weather was cooler now, in September, with the hot season and the rains over; the monsoon had come late that year, meaning that the baking sultry days of the early summer months had seemed to go on for ever, finally breaking in a stupendous thunderstorm which sent sheets of water on to the dusty streets, transformed in a flash into foaming streams and even rivers, causing many of the inhabitants to be virtual prisoners in their houses until the floods subsided, leaving a muddy, stinking detritus beneath still-brooding skies.

Octavia loved the drama of the weather, she loved the energy and vitality of a city thronged with people, mostly desperately impoverished, but still loud with talk and colour and life. How dull distant England seemed, although she knew that the Thurloes were endlessly homesick for green fields and hedges, for villages with church spires, for the mists of autumn mornings when the huntsman's horn rang out over the fields.

"Or London, how much I envy you returning to London!" said Harriet. "And you will be pleased to see your brothers and sisters again," she added, without conviction, having a very good notion of just how pleased they would be to have Octavia turning up on their doorstep again.

"It is such a pity that Darcy's heir should turn out to be George Warren," Robert Thurloe said, not for the first time, as he ate a mango and then dipped his fingers into the water bowl. "No one, except his mother and the Prince Regent, with whom he is on very good terms, one understands, has a good word to say for the fellow.

My advice, Octavia, if you decide to return to England, is to write to Mr. Darcy, Mr. Darcy of Pemberley, in Derbyshire. He is not a close connection of your late husband's, but he is a man of considerable wealth and influence. He has a fine estate, and has done very well out of mineral rights, I understand. He may be able to advise you as to the best course with regard to approaching George Warren."

Octavia had no intention of contacting any of her Darcy connections, however rich and influential. She suspected that their reaction to the arrival of an impecunious widow, even one bearing their name, would be much the same as that of her own family. They would compare her unfavourably with that paragon of breeding and beauty, the rich, aristocratic first Mrs. Darcy, whose memory had haunted her marriage. And from all she had heard of George Warren, the chances of his providing for her in any way seemed remote; he was not that kind of a man.

The lawyer in Calcutta who had laid out for her just how Captain Darcy's affairs were arranged had expressed his own doubts about Mr. Warren in no uncertain terms. Mr. Dyer was a small man with round, red cheeks, which he blew out in a disparaging way when the subject of George Warren came up. "Mr. Warren has a reputation for doing nothing which is not of immediate benefit to himself. You must make the attempt, of course, I would not advise otherwise, but you should not hang any great hopes on a favourable outcome."

Well, she, Octavia, wasn't going to go cap in hand to any George Warren. She would ask Christopher's lawyers in London to write to him, and if, as she expected, the answer was a flat refusal, then she would take it no further.

"Have you made up your mind when you will return to London?" Harriet enquired, as she and Octavia left the table and went to sit on the verandah.

Octavia listened to the sounds of an Indian night, the yelps and yowls of the pi dogs, the unearthly howls of the hyenas, a baby in a neighbouring house crying, then being hushed, the hoot of an owl, that harbinger of doom, according to the Indian servants, although Octavia liked those big birds of the night, with their huge, unblinking eyes and feathered wings. She didn't care so much for the bats, visible against the last trails of yellow left from the abrupt tropical sunset, squeaking and flitting to and fro. And the frogs had started up in their steady nighttime chorus.

How she would miss it all; how would she cope with life in Cheltenham or Bath, or whatever genteel town her tiny income would take her to?

"The *Sir John Rokesby* sails on the twenty-fifth, and I dare say you could get a cabin. Oh, how I envy you, how I wish we were going back to England."

Harriet's plump face looked quite distressed, and Octavia leant over to pat her hand. "Well, you will be returning in two years, will you not?"

"Two years! Two more years of this, I do not know how I will bear it."

"You could return sooner."

"And leave Robert on his own? That would be unkind, unchristian, unwifely. And besides," she added wisely, "it is never a good idea to leave one's husband on his own in such a place, there are temptations, and I have seen it all too often, the handkerchief waved at a departing wife, and within hours the desolate husband has found comfort in a pair of willing arms. For the women here are uncommonly beautiful, and Robert is no different from any other man in that. No, I must serve my time out, but you—I cannot imagine why you hesitate. Time has passed, you know, I dare say you will find yourself on better terms with your family than you imagine; it is different, being a married woman—that is to say, a widow, but it is not the same as when you were a girl."

Better terms? Well, she could hope so, but she had a strong suspicion that none of her family would be pleased to see her. Had she been a rich widow, the case might be different, but she knew they would be annoyed by her circumstances.

Chapter Two

"A caller, at this hour?" said Harriet.

She and Octavia had just returned from their morning ride, and were still in their riding habits.

"Tell him to return later," Harriet said to the bearer.

The bearer looked grave. "It is a lawyer sahib, for Mrs. Darcy. Upon an urgent matter."

"Oh, well, in that case."

"Mr. Dyer?" said Octavia. "What can he want that is urgent? Ask him to come in, Chunilal."

But it was not Mr. Dyer who came into the room. This was a stranger, a perspiring, red-haired, red-faced young man, freckled and hot.

"Beg pardon, ma'am, for calling so unconscionably early in the day," he said. "However, this news has just reached us, it came overland, you know, and London never sends overland unless it's urgent. I thought you might be out later on, so I took the liberty of calling early. If it is inconvenient, I shall return later, at any hour you care to name; however, I believe you will wish to hear what I have to say."

Octavia was intrigued. Overland from London? "I assume it is to do with the estate of my late husband, Captain Darcy."

"Late husband . . . ? Captain Darcy? Oh, no, not at all, nothing to do with Captain Darcy."

"Are you not a colleague of Mr. Dyer, who handled my husband's affairs here in Calcutta?"

"No, not at all, nothing to do with Mr. Dyer, I know him, of course, it is a small world, but this is an entirely separate matter."

"Well, then," said Octavia, gesturing to the harassed-looking young man to take a seat. "What has it to do with, Mr. . . . ?"

"Oh, Lord, I never introduced myself, and I do not think your servant caught my name. I am Mr. Gurney, Josiah Gurney."

Mr. Gurney had a sheaf of papers with him, and he began to sort through them in a hasty way. "Yes," he said. "Now, your mother was Susannah Worthington before her marriage, is that correct?"

"My mother?" Octavia was nonplussed. Her mother, the woman she had never known, who had died when she was born? What had she to do with anything, let alone urgent missives from London?

"Daughter of the late Mr. Digby Worthington, of Yorkshire? Who was your grandfather?"

"Yes, he was my grandfather."

"And you have papers to prove it, I suppose."

"I have some papers—but what is all this, Mr. Gurney? You are nothing short of mystifying, and I do not see what my mother's family nor my grandfather can have to do with anything here in Calcutta."

"Ah, what it has to do with is you, Mrs. Darcy. You were the only child of the late Lady Melbury, she was the second Mrs. Melbury, I think?"

"Yes."

"And she was an only child, she had no brothers or sisters?"

"No."

"Exactly so. That is exactly the case as stated here."

Octavia didn't know whether to laugh at this absurd parade of paper shuffling and the air of suppressed importance evident in Mr. Gurney's freckled face, or whether to ring the bell for the bearer to escort him out. She decided on a compromise. "It is growing warmer and you have had a hot journey, I think. Allow me to call for refreshments."

The bearer arrived with tall glasses of *nimbu pani,* a refreshing drink made with fresh limes and sugar. Mr. Gurney mopped his brow with a large spotted handkerchief.

"I am afraid I am not making myself clear, but I am obliged to ascertain the facts, to make sure that everything is as is stated in these papers from London. It has all taken a deal of time, but with her passing away in India and her lawyers in London, it doesn't make for easy communication."

"What are these papers you mention? Who has passed away?"

Mr. Gurney looked surprised. "Did I not say? I refer to the estate of the late Mrs. Anne Worthington, who died, I regret to say, some months ago. In Darjeeling. She lived in England, had done so since she became a widow, but she had made the trip to India to visit her tea plantations." His cheerful face assumed a look of sudden gravity, then he brightened. "She was, however, a very old lady, well into her eighties, a remarkable age, you will agree."

"And a redoubtable woman, to be making the journey to India at that age. But there is some mistake," said Octavia calmly. "I'm not related to this Mrs. Worthington. There is obviously some confusion because the name is the same as my mother's. My grandfather was Mr. Digby Worthington, as we have agreed, but his wife, my grandmother, was an Amelia Worthington, who died many, many years ago. I have no other Worthington relations; my grandfather was an only son."

"Ha!" exclaimed Mr. Gurney. "Not so, Mrs. Darcy, not so. If you are unacquainted with the fact that your grandfather had a younger brother, then I can understand your confusion."

"A younger brother?" said Octavia; this really did startle her. "You are mistaken, I would have known about it had such a person existed."

"Would you? He was, perhaps, something of a black sheep, a ne'er-do-well, in the eyes of his family, and when he left the shores of England never to return . . . Such people often drop from memory, and I believe that your grandfather died before you were born. Exactly so. Your mother, sadly, died when you were born, and as you yourself said, you have no other Worthington relatives, so how should you be aware of the existence of this other brother, who left England so many years ago?"

"I still find it impossible that there could be any such person."

"Ah, you find it hard to believe, but I assure you, Mrs. Darcy, the papers are all in order, there is no question about it. I represent a firm of lawyers in London, Wilkinson and Winter, a firm of the very highest repute, anyone will vouch for them. If they say a thing is so, with regard, that is, to wills and ancestors and descendants and so forth—then you may take it that they are right. And since this is no mere trifling legacy at stake, they will have been most particularly careful to ascertain—in short, you can take it that you had such a great-uncle, that his widow was Mrs. Anne Worthington, of Leeds in Yorkshire, who recently left this mortal round."

"Yes, very well, I believe you, but what has it to do with me? I never knew Mrs. Worthington; as I did not know of her existence, I scarcely could have known her. I am sorry to hear of her death, but it hardly seems an urgent matter. Has she no other living family? I assume there is some problem to do with her estate, and you seem to think that I may be able to assist you in some way, but you have come to the wrong person, I cannot help you at all."

"No, no, I do not ask for your help, except in the matter, the pure formality, of my needing to see that you are indeed who you are. No, I have the honour of being the bearer of what I am sure you will find good tidings, for Mrs. Worthington names you in her will as her sole heir; you inherit everything she owns."

"But I am no blood relation of hers! She never knew me, how can this be?"

"She had no family of her own, you are her husband's closest living relation, and since her fortune came to her from him, on his death, it is quite right and proper that it should come to you."

Octavia's head was in a whirl. She closed her eyes for a moment and then opened them again. No, she wasn't dreaming. She was sitting here, with this strange young man, in Harriet Thurloe's large drawing room, with its double doors leading on to the verandah beyond. There, outside, just whisking out of sight was Ferdie, the mongoose, encouraged to live in the garden as a deterrent to and scourge of snakes . . . She pulled herself together. "Precisely what, Mr. Gurney, do I inherit from this supposed great-aunt of mine?"

Mr. Gurney looked alarmed. "As to precisely, that is something I can't say. These are confidential matters, and the overland route, although swifter than the sea journey, is fraught with potential hazards. I merely have the information I have given you. However, I think I may say that it will be a substantial inheritance, Mrs. Worthington had property in India, and . . ."

"Tell me, how came she to have property in India?"

"Did I not explain? Mr. Worthington made his fortune in India, so I am informed. He was a nabob, as we say, and he never returned to England once he had quit the country of his birth, when he was a young man of twenty or so. He was sent out to India by his family. He met his wife here, and they lived in Darjeeling. After her husband's death, Mrs. Worthington returned to England. To the north of England; there is, I understand, a property in the north of England, in Yorkshire. Again, I have no details."

Octavia could hardly believe her ears. A house? Yorkshire was the county where her third half sister Drusilla resided, but it was a large county, there was no likelihood of her having been a neighbour of the late Mrs. Worthington's. Not that, from the sound of it, her great-aunt would have been the kind of person that Drusilla would call upon.

"In the circumstances," said Mr. Gurney, frowning, "of course, I do not know what your plans are, but I would urge you to consider returning to England as soon as it can be arranged. There is a vessel, an East Indiaman, the *Sir John Rokesby,* which is due to sail; it might be difficult to obtain a passage at this late stage, but if it were possible, I most strongly advise you to make the voyage to England. You need to consult with our firm in London, that will be much the best thing for you to do."

"My cousin, Mr. Thurloe, is with the Company. I think there would be no problem with obtaining a berth. I was contemplating going back to England in any case, it was only the expense—"

"Oh, Mrs. Darcy, expense is no consideration at all. I am empowered—directed, I should say—to make available to you whatever sums you might need to defray the expenses of the journey—of any expenses you might incur. You have only to name a sum; there is no problem with that, none at all."

Octavia smiled, and Mr. Gurney blinked. The tall young woman suddenly looked years younger, not that she could be so very old, and there was a colour in her cheeks; he had thought she looked sad and pale when he arrived, but now she was transformed.

"May I take it that you will go to London?" he asked, after several minutes' silence.

"Yes. If I could have some money, that would be . . ." She hesitated, fearful of asking too much. "Perhaps fifty pounds."

"Fifty? Let us say a hundred, or more if you wish it. I assure you, you can draw on us for a much larger sum than that."

"No, no thank you, I shall need very little on the voyage, and I should not like to carry too large a sum on my person."

"Very wise, very wise. I shall send a clerk round with it this afternoon."

He rose, perspiring more than ever; however did he manage in the really hot weather?

"One thing, Mr. Gurney, I would request of you."

He looked enquiringly at her.

"Pray, can you keep the news of this inheritance to yourself? Calcutta is a small place, and until I have the details—well, I would prefer that no one knows about it."

"Of course, of course. No, I am as capable of discretion as the next man, more so, for in my profession one has to keep mumchance, you know. No danger of this getting out, I assure you."

He bowed himself out, the door closing behind him as Harriet, looking cool and neat in a pale green dress, came in through the other door.

"Was that Mr. Dyer? What did he want?"

"It was a colleague of his, some papers that needed attending to."

"Is it something that Robert can help with?"

"Oh, no, it is nothing, nothing at all."

Why didn't she want to tell Harriet, to spill out the good news that she knew would delight her friend? Was it caution, for after all, she had only Mr. Gurney's word that there was any substantial inheritance? The house in Yorkshire might be a tumbledown cottage, and the fortune in the end a few hundred pounds. Or the will might be disputed, some natural child of her great-uncle might appear to make a claim on the estate; her great-uncle must have been a wild young man to be packed off to India in such a fashion.

"Did you ever hear of a Mr. Worthington, Harriet? He lived in India, in Darjeeling, but died some years ago. He was survived by his wife."

Harriet shook her head. "We have only been here for six years, you know. I do remember someone talking of a Mrs. Worthington, perhaps that was his widow. I believe she was very rich, and went back to England. Why do you ask?"

"Oh, merely that Mr. Gurney wanted to know if I had been acquainted with either of the Worthingtons."

"Her money came from tea, I seem to remember."

Before Harriet could ask any more questions, Octavia told her that she had decided to go back to England on the *Sir John Rokesby*. "If Mr. Thurloe can arrange it for me."

"My dear, of course he can. How I shall miss you! But it is for the best, I truly think so, you must go back before you lose your looks in this horrid climate, and then you may see if anything can be got out of Mr. Warren." She paused. "I know you will accept nothing from us, but it did occur to Robert and me that perhaps the cost of your fare was a concern to you. We should be so happy if—"

"No, no, it is not a consideration, I have the money for that and a little more besides. Which reminds me, I shall need some clothes, some half-mourning for when I arrive back in England. Will you please send a servant to Madame Duhamel for me?"

Madame Duhamel was a Frenchwoman who had come to Calcutta with her husband, only to be left a widow when he was carried off by the cholera. She had set to making her own living, and employed several local derseys to make up the fashionable clothes she designed. With good contacts in Paris, she had the fashion dolls and the plates only a few months behind the modistes in London; Octavia knew she would dress her in style.

"Madame Duhamel!" exclaimed Harriet. "She is wickedly expensive, you know."

"But I shall not need so many clothes, and it will not do for me to arrive in London black and dowdy; my sisters are very smart, and will abuse me for a provincial if I do not take care."

"Oh dear, you are quite right, first impressions are so important. Well, if you have the wherewithal, you cannot do better. I shall send to Ballygunge at once, there is no time to be lost. Indeed, I may ask her to make a gown for me, my blue is looking sadly shabby, I thought, when I wore it to the Lawrences the other night."

When Octavia retreated to her room that night, lying under the muslin draped over the posts of the bed to keep insects at bay, she found sleep elusive. In a day, her world had been turned upside down. Hope sprang in her breast, hope that Mr. Gurney had not been exaggerating, that her inheritance would provide her with at least a modest independence. In which case she would no longer be a poor relative, no longer obliged to put up with her sisters' patronising ways. Perhaps there would even be enough money to rent a house in a quiet part of town; if the house in Yorkshire could be sold, she had no desire to live in Yorkshire . . .

Fortune, Mr. Gurney had said. What constituted a fortune? To her, an income of a few hundred a year would be a fortune beyond her wildest dreams. How pleased Christopher would have been for her. Dear Christopher, with his kindness and sense of amusement. Tears slid through her closed eyelids as she finally fell asleep, her mind filled with memories of her husband, and the inheritance quite forgotten.

Chapter Three

Octavia lay in her narrow berth in the tiny cabin she occupied on the *Sir John Rokesby*. She wasn't asleep, but listening to the sounds around her that had become so familiar to her over these last six months: the creak of the ship as it hit the waves and rolled up and then back, the shrill bosun's pipe, the noise of the sails and rigging singing in the wind, running bare feet on the deck, orders bellowed out, the slap of halyards against the three masts, and, more often than she would have liked, the scuttle of rodents' feet as these unwelcome fellow passengers went about their ratty business.

Tonight, even in the early hours that were the quietest on board, the hours she had come to know as the dog watch, there was an expectancy in the air. The long voyage was nearly at an end. Today, with the wind in the right quarter, which the captain had assured her it would be, the ship would be making land, and then it would sail up the Thames to berth at Tilbury docks, in the heart of London.

It was more than five years since she had sailed from Tilbury, on a soft June day, alone; none of her half brothers or sisters had felt inclined to take the time to see her off.

Her brothers and sisters. Half brothers and sisters; at least she had some hope of not turning out like them. She shifted in her bunk, too short for her long legs, and gazed into the darkness, seeing them in her mind's eye.

Octavia heard the sounds of the morning watch going on deck, followed by the steady thump as the lascars washed and dried the decks, the sound of the chants as sails were furled or unfurled. She sat up, shivering slightly. She missed the warmth she had grown used to in India; a voyage that had started in brilliant sunshine was ending on a chill March day.

The *Sir John Rokesby* slid up the grey Thames in the mist. They could have been coming into port anywhere; for a wild moment Octavia imagined they had taken a wrong turn and were arriving in America, or Canada. Anywhere but London, where she would be greeted without enthusiasm by her brothers and sisters, a black sheep making an unwelcome return.

There was no one waiting for her on the dockside; of course there wasn't. She looked out at the forest of masts around her, for a moment wishing she was setting sail and not arriving. Then she squared her shoulders and, wrapping her cloak about her as a gust of cold air struck her, snatching at her hat, walked down the gangplank to set about the business of making sure her few boxes and trunk were despatched to Theodosia's house in Lothian Street. A kindly officer helped her into a hackney carriage, and she was off along grey London streets.

Home, Octavia said to herself. All the passengers had talked enthusiastically of coming home, even the disappointed girls for whom a season or two or three in India had failed to produce the requisite husband. They had families, she supposed, people who might even be glad to see them, whereas she— Well, she wasn't going to allow herself to fall into a fit of the dismals. This might turn out to be a far different homecoming from any she had imagined, should what Mr. Gurney had told her in Calcutta turn out to be even half true.

She stared out at the warehouses, a hive of industry as goods were loaded on and unloaded from the immense number of ships in this busiest of ports, and drew her cloak more closely about her.

Harriet, kind Harriet, who had made sure that she had warm clothes for her return to England: "One forgets how cold it is at home." They were, thankfully, the clothes of a matron, of a married woman, velvets and silks; even though in mourning colours, they suited her much better than the light dresses of her girlhood.

She sincerely mourned her late husband. She had never been deeply or passionately in love with him, but she had liked him, found comfort and even pleasure in his arms and bed, and had enjoyed his company. Had they been given more time together, it might have grown into a very happy marriage.

What was to become of her? What kind of a life could she make for herself? If she had money, then the prospects were far more cheerful, the choices greater. It would be hard to make decisions for herself, after the in-between time of her early widowhood, and the out-of-times days on board. She hadn't been bored on the *Sir John Rokesby;* with far more assurance than she had had on the voyage out, she had found it easier to make friends and play her part in the social round of the small world of a ship.

She had her sketchbooks with her, and paints, and had whiled away many hours building doll's houses. That was something that happened by chance, when the small daughter of a fellow passenger, fretful after an illness, had wanted something to play with. Octavia, remembering how much pleasure she had had as a girl from the doll's house that she had made with the help of a friendly joiner, acquired some balsa wood from the ship's carpenter and set about modelling a stately home for little Emily. The carpenter had offered to do it, he could run her up a house in a jiffy, but Octavia was eager for an activity to soothe her restless mind. Busy fingers were, she had long ago discovered, a very good remedy for troubled spirits, and so she had set about it herself, creating a fine Palladian house which was the admiration of her fellow passengers.

"Amazingly clever," said one of the officers. "And you a woman, I'd hardly have believed it possible."

The doll's house had aroused suspicions in some of the less amiable among her fellow passengers. Did they imagine she didn't hear their whispers?

"She was lucky to catch Captain Darcy, she was indeed, a very good catch for her, if not for him, poor man."

"Wasn't she a Melbury before her marriage?"

"Yes, indeed, but only a half sister to the baronet and his brother and sisters. Her mother was a nobody, daughter of a tradesman."

"Only imagine, and when you think who the first Mrs. Darcy was."

"Oh, perfection, such a beauty and a handsome fortune with her, which, however, they say he went through in no time."

"You'd think he'd have found himself another rich wife, of equal standing, instead of marrying Miss Octavia Melbury, who after all has no looks, is far too tall for a woman, and has no fortune, and if you say she's of low origin, too—Well!"

Octavia couldn't help feeling a spurt of temper when she heard people singing the praises of the first Mrs. Darcy. Christopher never spoke of her after the time when Octavia had asked him, hesitantly, whether he had, as the saying went, buried his heart with his first wife. He had looked startled, and then laughed.

"No, indeed, I did not, no such thing. Don't listen to what all the old tabbies have to say about the first Mrs. Darcy, it is none of their business, nor, indeed," he added, more serious now, "of yours. I don't mean that in any unkind way," he said quickly, seeing the look on her face; she was all too used to rebukes from her family, but not from Christopher. "I merely mean that all that is in the past, and to tell you the truth, I do not care to remember my first marriage. I assure you I am as happy now as I ever was then, more so."

His words were meant to reassure her, and she had been grateful for them, although she didn't believe him. How could she compare to the first Mrs. Darcy, the rich, well-born, beautiful Mrs. Darcy?

Unwanted tears prickled Octavia's eyes as his voice came back to her, as though he were with her, speaking those words. She was going to miss him, she wished he were here at her side, rejoicing in her sudden increase of fortune, making plans for the future.

All too soon, the hackney cab was turning into Lothian Street.

The cab driver drew up outside the familiar house with its red-brick façade and handsome front door; she had arrived. She opened her purse for the coins to pay the cab driver, then stepped down on to the pavement. She paused, looking up at the windows of the house, then took a deep breath, went up the three shallow steps, and lifted the knocker.

Chapter Four

The door was opened by the butler, Coxley, whom Octavia disliked, not merely because he had a face like a fish, but because he had always shown his disdain for her. He recognised her, welcomed her with chilly civility, and said that he would inform her ladyship that Miss—that Mrs. Darcy had arrived.

A cold kiss from Theodosia, accompanied by an uncomplimentary, "How tanned you are," and then, "I've told them to put you in the Blue Room on the second floor, I am sure you will be comfortable there."

Octavia went unsteadily up the familiar stairs, finding, as she had done from the moment she stepped ashore, that the ground under her feet seemed to be swaying. The Blue Room was on the second floor up a further flight of stairs, and as she went into the familiar room, she felt as though she had never been away. It was far from one of the best bedchambers in the house; it had been considered quite good enough for a mere Miss Octavia Melbury, and was clearly still good enough for a widowed Mrs. Darcy. The carpet was a little worn, the furniture made up of items that had done earlier duty elsewhere, the curtains the same as when she had inhabited the room before, only a little more faded.

A maid had been sent to wait on her, a country girl judging by her rosy cheeks, not yet grown pale in the sooty, dank air of London.

Upon enquiry, Octavia discovered that the girl's name was Alice, she was fifteen last month, and had newly come up from Wiltshire, where her mother was in service on Sir James Melbury's estate.

Octavia washed her hands and face in the water that Alice brought up. She stood in front of the glass to tidy her hair. Yes, she was slightly tanned, no surprising consequence of a long sea voyage, but fair as she was, she had kept her complexion, the worst effects of the sun being a few pale freckles across the bridge of her nose. She had never gone very brown in India and hadn't been there long enough to take on the sallow look that so many English people had, nor had her skin ever burned in the hot sun.

"We dine at home tonight," said Theodosia when Octavia went downstairs. From the sound of her voice, she considered this a great condescension. Octavia felt a flash of anger; her sister might at least put on an appearance of welcome. There were no enquiries about the voyage, nor condolences for the loss of her husband. At least her brother-in-law Henry Cartland seemed glad to see her, welcoming her with something like affection, and even venturing a few words of sympathy on her recent loss.

His wife swiftly put him in his place. "Don't be absurd, Henry. Octavia had hardly been married five minutes when she lost her husband"—she made it sound as though the loss had been due to some carelessness on Octavia's part—"she can really have barely known him. Wasn't he away at sea for most of your married life?" she went on, addressing Octavia.

"Yes," said Octavia.

"It is the most unfortunate thing you didn't bear him a son," her sister said in her forthright way. "It is a thousand pities that his heir should be George Warren, you can expect nothing from him, he is an out-and-out Whig and will grudge you a single penny."

"Entailed estates make for many problems," Mr. Cartland said with a sigh.

"It is a most unfortunate arrangement in this case," said Theodosia. "Quite unnecessary, in my opinion; what business had Captain Darcy to have an entail?"

It had never occurred to Octavia, when she accepted Captain Darcy's hand, to enquire about his fortune or estate. But Mr. Thurloe had done so, and, on the whole, he said, it was quite satisfactory. "He has a good estate in Wiltshire, worth some two or three thousand a year, and then there is his navy pay, although of course these days there are not the opportunities for prize money as there used to be; why, in the war, a mere master and commander could sail away in penury and come back a rich man after a lucky encounter, able to set up his carriage and buy himself a house and land. Of course, those days are behind us, but still, Captain Darcy does not do so badly. However, the estate is entailed, you understand the nature of an entail?" he had added, seeing Octavia's puzzled look.

He had explained it to her. Captain Darcy's estate was entailed upon the male line. He could not leave it to her, nor to anyone else; it would pass, in the absence of an heir of his loins, into the hands of a second cousin. "A man with no very good name, a rakish fellow," Mr. Thurloe said with a frown. "It is your duty to be brisk about breeding, my dear, because then your own future is secure in the case—well, that is, life at sea is always uncertain, and should anything befall Captain Darcy, if you have a son, you will be provided for, you will be able to live on the estate in comfort during the boy's minority, and then of course, he will take care of you."

"And if I don't have a son, but only daughters, or no children at all?"

"Then, my dear, you will have nothing but whatever the captain should leave as his personal fortune. Which is nothing very much; it seems that the fortune his first wife brought with her was unwisely invested. I did hear she was an expensive creature, so maybe that was the truth of it. However, let us be sanguine, he is a healthy man who has no idea of taking risks at sea, and the entail will be soon cut off by the birth of a son, if you do your duty."

The marriage had taken place quickly, in light of the captain's imminent departure. Octavia had hesitated, feeling it might be wiser to postpone the ceremony until Captain Darcy's return, but Robert Thurloe would have none of it. "A bird in the hand, my dear," he said bluntly to Harriet, who was inclined to agree with Octavia. "Who knows whom Captain Darcy may not meet on his travels? No, no, they must tie the knot as soon as may be, and then Octavia will be sure of him."

"So is it true that his private fortune was practically nothing?" Theodosia said now.

Her husband attempted to remonstrate with her. "My dear, here is Octavia only just arrived, tired after her long journey; it is hardly the time to ply her with questions of this nature."

"Nonsense," said Theodosia. "There is no point in beating about the bush. We are all family here, we dine alone, and the sooner we know just what Octavia's circumstances are, the better."

"I was left enough to buy some clothes and to pay my passage and a little put by," Octavia told her sister. "When everything is settled, I shall have an income of about a hundred and fifty pounds a year."

"Well, that is something, in any case," said Mr. Cartland, who would have found it hard to manage on less than his own income of fifteen thousand a year.

"It is barely enough to live on. I am really annoyed with Captain Darcy for having so little foresight, for making so little provision for her." And then, to Octavia, "Why did you come back? I should think it was easier to live in India on very little money, surely everything is cheaper there."

Her husband made a tsking noise and shook his head at his wife's ill breeding.

"I had no particular reason to stay in Calcutta."

"No reason? You had every reason; in London you were unable to find a husband, whereas in India you made a perfectly respectable match—except for this tiresome entail, of course."

"Mr. Thurloe felt that my best course would be to return to England and approach Mr. Warren, to see if he can be persuaded to give me an annuity, or an allowance. I know he has a reputation of being a close man—"

"He is simply a man who knows how to take care of his money," said Theodosia. "Which is more than can be said for your late husband, I might point out. Yes, Warren must be approached, must be made to see that he has to do his duty by you. And meanwhile, we must put our heads together and decide what is to be done with you."

Octavia caught Mr. Cartland's shocked eye, and had to make an effort not to burst out laughing. She knew whose heads were to be brought into service on this matter, and it would not include her own; her views were of no interest to Theodosia, nor would they be to Augusta and Arthur.

"Naturally, you are our guest here," Henry Cartland said quickly. "You are welcome to stay for as long as you like."

"Be quiet, Henry," said Theodosia. "Octavia is my sister, this has nothing to do with you." She looked at Octavia with narrowed eyes. "I will say that you are improved in looks since you went away, despite being burned by the sun. It is an extraordinary thing; for the most part women return from India with any trace of beauty gone."

Octavia was startled at this compliment, coming as it did from such an unexpected quarter; she was used to nothing but criticism from her sisters.

"It is all to the good. One marriage can lead to another, even though you are now past your prime, at four or five and twenty you have lost your bloom—but even so, it may be possible. It will be best for you to stay in London, I think, and we shall see if we can find you another husband."

"But I don't want to marry again!" exclaimed Octavia, furious at the heartlessness of her sister's words. "It is less than a year since Christopher died, I am in mourning, I have no wish to be looking for another husband."

"You can't pretend any great grief for a man you hardly knew. You did very well to catch him, very well indeed, and it is a great pity that things turned out as they did; whatever did the man have to go plunging into the jungle for?"

"He was very interested in natural philosophy, and he had heard news of a rare plant that he had long wanted to see—"

"Natural philosophy, my—" Theodosia caught her husband's eye, and the words died on her lips. "Well, as to that, the past is the past, and we must look to the future, and since you have no fortune, just as you didn't have when you left, the only course open to you is marriage."

"Or I could seek employment as a governess," said Octavia, still angry, and yielding to an impulse to annoy her sister.

As soon as the words were out, she regretted them. Her sister's eyes flashed, and Mr. Cartland, after giving her a quick, despairing glance, fixed his gaze on the ceiling.

The abuse washed over all, all her sister's pent-up rage: the disgrace. Octavia was born a Melbury, even if she had never been worthy of the name; what would people say if her sister went out to be a household drudge; how could she, on her first day home, come up with such a crack-brained scheme and upset her own sister so greatly?

Mr. Cartland called for his wife's smelling salts; Icken, her maid, stalked into the room and waved a vinaigrette under Theodosia's nose. Octavia could hear her hissing under her breath, "Shameful, upsetting the mistress like that, her own sister, she should know better."

"Theodosia suffers from her nerves," Mr. Cartland said, a smile flickering to his face and then vanishing again.

It was as though the intervening years had never happened, as though Octavia were a nineteen-year-old girl once again, expected to be obedient and to listen to her elders and betters.

She had had enough of this. She was a grown woman, a married woman, if now a widow; what right had her sister to treat her in this way and lay down the law about what she should and shouldn't do?

She rose from the table. "Theodosia is unwell, I think my presence upsets her, I shall go to my room," she said, flashing a smile at her brother-in-law before she fled upstairs.

It was inevitable that Theodosia, when she had recovered from her equanimity to some degree, should send for her other sister and brother. "Let us see if they can talk sense into the wretched woman, let us see if they can't make Octavia see reason," she said to her husband with grim satisfaction.

Mr. Cartland, who knew that the combined forces of his wife and her sister and his brother-in-law were more than he could stomach, beat a hasty retreat to his club, murmuring that he had business to attend to in town, might not be back for some hours.

Octavia wasn't at all surprised, as she sat sipping a cup of chocolate the next morning, to be told by a bright-eyed Alice that she was wanted downstairs as soon as ever might be, that Mr. Melbury and Lady Adderley had called and were waiting to see her.

Octavia had heard the door knocker, knew perfectly well that it was far too early for any but members of the family to be at the front door, and had correctly guessed what was in store for her.

She didn't hurry her toilette, and indeed took unusual care over it. She put on a dark grey bombazine morning dress, trimmed with black silk rosettes on a flounced hem, which the clever fingers of Madame Duhamel's derseys had made for her from a not-too-out-of-date pattern in the book of plates which had arrived in Calcutta on the last ship. It was modish enough, if not bang-up-to-the-minute—her sisters' sharp eyes would at once spot last year's trimming and the set of the sleeve that no modish London lady would dream of being seen in, but Octavia knew it suited her. The awareness of looking her best heightened her courage, so that, with the tinge of colour in her cheeks from the apprehension that she was trying so keenly to quell, she made a striking picture as she entered the room.

Her brother Arthur rose from his seat. "Well, upon my word," he exclaimed. "I never saw you in better looks, Octavia. I should have thought—"

A formal kiss from Augusta. "That's as may be, Arthur," she said in her brisk way, "and we must be pleased to see Octavia looking tolerably well, but nothing alters the fact that she is several inches taller than any woman has any right to be, and what is more, several inches taller than any Melbury female has ever been. Of course, she gets her height from her mother."

From the contempt in her voice, you would have thought Octavia's mother had been a giantess; it was a familiar insult, and one that Octavia knew how to ignore. She was, in some obscure way, proud of her height; it was an inheritance from her despised grandfather and as such, she treasured it. If it set her apart from her brothers and sisters, so much the better.

"Now," said Theodosia. "We have been discussing your situation while we were waiting for you to come down—what an age it took you to dress—and this is what is to be done."

Octavia listened with half her mind. Did her sisters and brother imagine she would have nothing to say in the matter? Did they expect her to accept being treated simply as an object to be dealt with as they might a horse or a long-standing servant who had become a problem?

Their decision was clear cut. Arthur was to approach Warren and represent to him in the most forceful and persuasive terms how very bad it would look for his late cousin's widow to be seen to be destitute. By this means, it was to be hoped, they might squeeze some money out of him, which would go towards Octavia being able to support herself, if not in comfort, at least not in penury.

"Until such time as we can find you another husband," Augusta finished in a definite voice.

"You weren't able to when I was last in London, why should it be any different now?" said Octavia.

"Well, upon my word, Octavia," said Arthur, looking down his long nose at her. "If you are going to take that tone with us, I shall consider you ungrateful. Your sister is only—"

"Meanwhile," went on Theodosia, as though Octavia hadn't spoken, an old trick and one that always reduced Octavia to seething if helpless fury, "you will go down to Hertfordshire, where you may stay with our cousins, Mr. and Mrs. Ackworth. I wrote to them first thing this morning, so it is all arranged. We don't want you drooping about town in your weeds, there is nothing more depressing or off-putting to the male sex than a widow in her weeds. Your year of mourning will shortly be over, fortunately before the end of the season. You are no longer a green girl; we shall see if there is not some older man, a widower who wishes for more sensible company than a debutante would provide. You do not want for sense, when you are not being wilful and obstinate, and some country squire, who is not too nice in his . . ."

Octavia considered. Her first reaction was to refuse all their suggestions, to insist that she was going to make her own way in the world and that they need not bother themselves with her at all. On the other hand, almost anything would be preferable to spending these next few weeks in London, in Lothian Street, incarcerated within doors except when her sister condescended to take her out in the carriage, or demanded her company while she took her morning constitutional in the park.

"Very well," she said. "I shall go to the Ackworths, if they will have me."

"No question of that," said Theodosia.

"Not for a few days, however. I have a few things to attend to, lawyers to see—"

"Oh, as to that, you are not to be dealing with lawyers, I shall arrange all that," said Arthur.

"No," said Octavia. "I will not authorise you to act on my behalf, indeed, I shall write to the lawyers and say quite clearly that they are to deal with no one but myself. And don't puff up like that, Arthur. I am of age, well past my majority, as you all remind me, a married woman, and more than capable of seeing a lawyer, any number of lawyers."

"Hoity-toity," said Arthur. "You may write to them—who are they, by the way?—and tell them to call at Lothian Street. Of course you cannot see them by yourself, it is out of the question, quite improper, in fact. Theodosia will tell me when the man is to call, and I shall make myself available."

There was no point in arguing with Arthur, he never took any notice of any view that was not his own, and considered that nothing Octavia said was worth listening to. She would counter his interference with cunning, it was the only way.

That settled to his satisfaction, he took his leave, his sister Augusta staying behind to support Theodosia in her attack on Octavia for showing herself, yet again, to be the most obstinate, unnatural creature in the world.

"I wish the Ackworths joy of you," were Augusta's parting words.

"And I hope they talk some sense into you, so that we see an improvement when you return to London."

To the best of Octavia's recollection, she had never met the Ackworths, who were her cousins on her father's side of the family. Perhaps she had done so when she was an infant, when her father was still alive, but Augusta's assurance that they were sensible people and her confidence that they would be in agreement with the rest of the Melburys made her fear the worst.

Chapter Five

The next morning Octavia received an early visitor. She was still in bed, drinking a bowl of thick hot chocolate while Alice bustled about laying out her clothes for the day. Her visitor was a lively young woman, with a head of dark curls, roguish brown eyes, and a determined little chin.

"Do you remember me?" she said, swirling into the room and perching herself on Octavia's bed. "I'm your niece, Penelope."

"Heavens," said Octavia, looking at the modish young lady. The last time she had seen Penelope was when she was a baby.

"When you were in London doing the season, I was away in the countryside at a stuffy old boarding school," said Penelope. "I'm eighteen now, and this year is my come-out, did Mama tell you?"

Theodosia had mentioned it, saying that it was going to be a busy season for her and Augusta, with daughters to bring out. Where was Penelope? Octavia had enquired, to be told that she was paying a brief visit to the country, staying with Lord and Lady Osterby, in fact, whose daughter was Penelope's friend. And now here she was, very grown up and assured.

"Lady Adderley's daughter Louisa is coming out as well, is she not?"

Penelope frowned. "Yes. It's a pity, since she is a great bore, apart from being so very beautiful, which I am not. That annoys Mama, although not Papa"—her face lit up—"who says he likes me just as I am, and so will any man of discernment and sense. Only," she added, "I'm not sure I want to marry a man of discernment and sense. Your husband was a naval officer, was not he? It must be so exciting to go to sea!"

"Yes, however I never did so, except to and fro across the ocean to India on East India Company vessels, which is not quite the same."

"I am sorry you lost Captain Darcy," said Penelope, suddenly serious. "And when you had been married only two or three years, Mama said, and hardly seeing him all that while; that is the disadvantage of being married to a naval man, of course, although I know that Admiral Verney's wife goes everywhere with him, she says her sea legs are better than her land ones. Oh dear, there I go again, mentioning legs, which Mama says I ought not to do."

"Why ever not?"

"There are all kinds of things I mustn't say and subjects I may not talk about. You're going to stay with our cousin Ackworths, are not you?"

"I am."

"I was there, in the autumn."

She fell silent, and Octavia wondered whether her experience of Hertfordshire had been a good or a bad one.

Penelope soon told her, her face alight with the memory. "Oh, it was the greatest fun, although I had been ill and that was why I was sent there, to recover my health and spirits; Mama thought I would simply sit indoors and do nothing and go nowhere until my cough went. It was a shocking cough which irritated Mama's nerves; in fact, that was why I was sent away, not really from any concern for my health. Mr. and Mrs. Ackworth are excellent people, very kind and not at all stuffy." She gave Octavia a swift look from beneath her eyelids. "You do not know them, Papa says, and I dare say you are wondering if they are like—well, like Uncle Arthur or Aunt Augusta, but you need not fear, they are not. They go about a good deal, they know everyone, and I met . . . oh, such interesting people."

"In a small town in Hertfordshire? Is not society there somewhat— I should have thought it would be a limited circle."

Penelope was blushing. "Oh, there were not so many people there, but it was agreeable company, and I went to the assembly ball, which made Mama extremely cross when she heard of it, for I was not officially out, however Cousin Jane said a small-town assembly was neither here nor there and it would do me good to practise my dancing in company, for it is not the same as with the dancing master, not at all. And I danced every dance, it was delightful."

"So your cousins—our cousins—do not lead such a quiet life as your mama supposed?"

"Oh, well, in comparison to London, of course—but I prefer the country. I would rather live in the country than in town." She paused, biting her lip, then smiled. "Cousin Jane was used to be fond of dancing when she was young. She took me through the steps of the quadrille, again and again, so that I am now quite an expert. She said she and Cousin Hugh loved to dance, and she only wished they had had the waltz when she was a girl, as she thought it looked most exhilarating, much more enjoyable than minuets and country dances."

Octavia blinked. Why was Theodosia suggesting she go to Hertfordshire, to be out of the way, if the Ackworths were as Penelope said?

"Mama and Aunt Augusta have no notion of what they are like," Penelope confided. "They never visit there, for they think Meryton provincial and our cousins countrified and unfashionable. They are useful, to send us young ones down into the country when our mamas want to be rid of us, but they don't realise what fun it is there. Louisa only went once, and she didn't like it at all, she says the cousins are provincial, but I do not think they are, not at all."

So Penelope had a mind of her own, did she? And, although she said nothing that went beyond the line of what was acceptable, she clearly had no illusions and judged for herself. Octavia warmed towards her niece, with her blushes and her eyes bright with the memory of dancing and pleasure.

Penelope slipped off the bed. "I can hear Grindley's steps, she's my maid. I expect Mama wants me to go out shopping or some such thing, and has left instructions as to what I am to wear. I have a new hat I bought myself, which I like very well, but she will say it is hideous, I dare say, and will be angry for me spending my allowance without her permission."

She whisked herself out of the room, leaving Octavia with her chocolate grown cold and her thoughts in a whirl. That chit had met someone she cared for in Hertfordshire, that was obvious, although she doubted if Theodosia had any inkling. But what she had to say about her cousins cheered her no end; she had been afraid of another Augusta, another Theodosia, and was relieved that they sounded quite unlike her sisters.

Octavia rose and dressed, and before she went downstairs, she sat down at the rickety writing table under the window and penned a letter to Messrs. Wilkinson and Winter, informing them of her arrival in London and requesting them not to attempt to contact her in Lothian Street; she would come herself to their premises in King's Bench Walk as soon as possible.

How to post the letter, that was the question. Normally, she would have asked one of the footmen to take it for her, or handed it to the butler to post, but she knew Theodosia made it her business to inspect all the post, inwards and outwards, and as soon as her sister saw the name on the letter, her suspicious mind would tell her these were Octavia's lawyers and the information would be passed to Arthur. Then goodbye to any hopes Octavia had of keeping her inheritance secret.

No, she would have to contrive so that she went out alone. If Theodosia and Penelope were going out shopping, it was unlikely that Theodosia would ask her to accompany them, so if she lurked in her room until she heard the sounds of their departure, then she might slip out without being interrogated.

Half an hour later, she heard the sound of a carriage drawing up outside, the front door opening, Theodosia's imperious voice telling Penelope she looked a fright in that hat, the door closing, hooves clattering away down the street. In a moment she had her pelisse on and was running down the stairs to the hall.

Coxley was still there. "Are you going out, ma'am? Shall I call a footman to accompany you, or your maid?" he enquired in what Octavia considered a most officious way.

"No thank you, I am perfectly all right on my own."

"Mrs. Cartland would prefer—"

"Yes, but I would not."

"Shall I tell Mrs. Cartland where you are gone?"

"I shall no doubt be back before Mrs. Cartland returns, but should anyone enquire for me, I am gone to the circulating library."

And before he could ask which of the several libraries patronised by the upper echelons of society she intended to visit, she was out of the house and walking rapidly away down the street.

Like the admiral's wife mentioned by Penelope, it had taken her a while to find her land legs after being so many months at sea, but she thankfully noticed that the pavement no longer seemed to be coming up to meet her, and she relished the chance to stretch her legs in a brisk walk. She had taken endless dutiful turns around the deck of the *Sir John Rokesby,* whenever the weather permitted, but it was not the same as walking in London; she had not realised until now how much she had missed London, with its bustle of traffic, the shops, the noise; even though the day was grey, there was a hint of spring in the air.

She was acutely aware of all the smells and sounds around her, so different from her surroundings of the last few years. Instead of the streets crowded with bullock carts and rickshaws, with the slap of the rickshaw *wallah*'s bare feet on dusty ground, here were elegant curricles and a footman walking a pair of pugs. The pungent odours and vivid colours of a hot Indian city, of spices and sweating bodies, of ebullient vegetation and fetid water, were replaced by the evocative smell of rain on paving stones, and the scentless yellow petals of the early daffodils planted in a window box.

She was used to hearing the endless chatter of a dozen different languages, of women dressed in bright silk saris, men in turbans, robes, dhotis, or swaggering in white uniforms. Here the cockney cries of London sounded in her ears, "Carrots and turnips, ho! Sweet China oranges, sweet China! Fresh mackerel, fresh mackerel!" Newsmen bawled out the latest scandal, muffin men held their trays about their heads, shouting their wares, while the road was busy with carriages dashing past, men on horseback trotting by, carts and drays rumbling along at a slower pace.

People in this smart part of town were dressed in the height of fashion, the men in long-tailed coats, pantaloons, and tall hats, the women in morning dresses of muslin and fine silk, with deep-brimmed hats decorated with flowers. She noticed that the women wore no pelisses; how did they not feel the cold? Well, she would have to pass as dowdy, her blood was thin after her time in a hot climate, she thought it folly to shiver for the sake of a fashionable appearance.

She had not forgotten her geography, and she went first to the post-office in North Audley Street, where she entrusted her letter to the two-penny post. She came out from the receiving office, and hesitated. She had intended to go to Hookham's library, which was in Old Bond Street, but it now occurred to her that Theodosia might be in that area, since she had taken Penelope shopping, and if so, she might be seen . . .

She laughed at herself and set off down the street. What if Theodosia did see her? She might go where she chose and do what she chose, within the bounds of common civility owed to one's hosts, and these would not be one whit transgressed by her visiting a circulating library. She would not allow herself to be oppressed by Theodosia's habit of wanting to take charge of everyone's doings and movements; she was no longer a girl under her sister's care. She would go boldly to Old Bond Street, and let Theodosia mind her own business; it was hard on Penelope, who was the business of the moment, but there was nothing that she, Octavia, could do to alter that.

It didn't take her long to reach Hookham's library. She had inscribed her name there when she was in London for her season, and now she wrote down her married name, Mrs. Darcy, paid her subscription, and was free to choose her books.

This was a special delight; she had been starved of new books in India, and had promised herself a subscription as soon as she reached London. It was an indulgence, circumstanced as she was, but she must just hope that the Worthington inheritance would be enough that she could spare the trifling sum.

Of course, it might be that her cousins, who sounded modern in their outlook, from what Penelope had said, had plenty of books, including the newest novels, but she would take a good selection with her, in case their taste didn't coincide with hers, or perhaps they might not be great readers. Her stepmother hadn't been, she took an age to read even a single volume, and complained that reading made her head ache and her eyes water; now, no longer a child, Octavia suspected that Lady Melbury's indifference to books probably had more to do with poor eyesight than anything else. Perhaps her physician husband would notice and obtain a pair of spectacles for her; Octavia tried to visualise her stepmother with spectacles, but couldn't; she had always been a trifle vain about her appearance and youthful looks.

Octavia spent longer than she had intended at the library, and when she got back to Lothian Street, it was to be greeted by the information that Mrs. Cartland was awaiting her return in her private sitting room.

Octavia went upstairs to take off her hat and pelisse, and then went to see what Theodosia wanted. She found her sister was seated with a tray of cold meats and fruit on one side of her, and on the other a small table with a letter placed exactly in the centre of its round top.

"This came for you," said Theodosia, picking it up.

"Thank you," said Octavia.

"Not so fast, if you please. Who is writing to you?"

"Until I open the letter, I have no idea. And whoever it may be, it is no business of yours, Theodosia." Before Theodosia realised what her sister's intention was, Octavia had tweaked the letter from her fingers.

"Upon my word!"

Octavia glanced at the letter. It was addressed in a man's hand, but not one she recognised. It bore a frank, so it wasn't likely to have come from Christopher's lawyer, nor yet from Wilkinson and Winter. She was as mystified as Theodosia, but wasn't going to say so. She would take it upstairs and open it in private, she decided, but then, seeing the steely look in her sister's eye, she sighed and reached for the paper knife which was on Theodosia's writing desk.

"It is from a Mr. Portal," she said, turning the page over to read the signature.

"Well, that is something to have the great Mr. Portal write to you, a mere relict—"

Octavia knew she was about to add "a person of no account," but for once her sister restrained herself.

"Why, what is so strange about it?" Octavia had turned to the beginning of the letter and was running her eyes down the page. "It appears that he knew my husband and wishes to express his condolences."

This was true enough, but there was more to the letter than that, some sentences which she did not quite understand, but which she wasn't going to pass on to Theodosia. Mr. Portal, it seemed, had also been acquainted with her great-uncle and -aunt, and from what he wrote, although it was couched in discreet terms, he was well aware of her inheritance. Presently in France, he looked forward to having the honour of meeting her on his return to England, and meanwhile she could have every confidence in Mr. Wilkinson.

How odd, what did it mean? Who was this Mr. Portal?

"I suppose you have no idea who the great Mr. Portal is, being away so long, and not moving in quite those circles when you were a debutante. He is known everywhere as Pagoda Portal, you may have heard the name."

"Like the tree in India?"

"I have no idea why he is called Pagoda, it is an outlandish name, although I believe it is something to do with his having made a great deal of money in India. He is a nabob, but a well-born, extremely well-connected nabob; nobody can say he is any kind of a mushroom."

"So he is great because he is rich?"

"Now, do not be putting on those false missish airs. You have lived long enough and enough in the world to know that a great fortune commands a good deal of wholesome respect. Especially, as I say, when combined with belonging to such an ancient family—the Portals have been landowners and members of Parliament for ever, and they are related to quite half the House of Lords."

She hesitated for a moment, seeking her words with care, which was unusual for her.

"However, his life is somewhat irregular, it would not do for you, in your position, to become more than a mere acquaintance, it would do your reputation no good at all if you were to be drawn into his set."

"What set is that?"

"Oh, a very ramshackle, mixed set of persons, artists and poets; here a banker and there a politician, and women novelists and musicians, not at all the kind of people who would be admitted into my drawing room."

Octavia thought they sounded rather charming.

"However, that is part of his eccentric way, a man so rich may be as eccentric as he wishes, you know. The difficulty comes in his—what shall I call them? His domestic arrangements. Now you are a married woman I can speak freely: Mr. Portal is not married, and it seems has not the least intention of entering that happy state. Instead, it is openly known that he and Henrietta Rowan, a tiresome woman if ever I knew one, have a liaison that goes far beyond what is proper. She is a widow, who seems to think that such a state allows her perfect liberty; she declares she will never marry again, and certainly there appears to be no inclination on either party to regularise their union."

"Have they set up house together?"

"Good gracious no, whatever are you thinking of?"

"From the way you spoke—"

"It is a liaison, as I said, and one of which the whole polite world is aware. Mrs. Rowan, who is very well off in her own right, has her own house, done up in the most extraordinary style, I have to tell you, in the Turkish mode; it is a fancy of hers to admire the Turks, and therefore she has carpets and cushions and all kinds of hangings which are entirely unsuitable for one in her position. And in London! She spent years abroad, in Turkey, which is where she acquired the taste for such nonsense."

Theodosia looked around her own sitting room with great complaisancy; in Octavia's opinion, the room was overfilled with furniture, much of it downright ugly.

"However, Mr. Portal seems to like it well enough, one cannot expect a man who has made his own fortune to have much taste, perhaps. Mrs. Rowan holds a salon there in the afternoon, and soirées, and I don't know what else. I admit that society flocks to her parties, she is considered a notable hostess, although for the life of me—I consider that she is not quite the thing. But since it appears that you don't know Mr. Portal and this letter is written as a mere courtesy call, made as much on my account as yours, I dare say, then any question of you pursuing the acquaintance of either him or Henrietta need never arise."

How like Theodosia, laying down the law on whom Octavia might be permitted to know, and asserting the rightness of her own moral judgement.

Octavia returned to her letter. "Mr. Portal sounds an amiable man," she said. "He writes that he will do himself the honour of calling upon me when he is back in London."

"Oh, that is only form, simple politeness, it means nothing, why should he call on you?"

"If he should do so, do you wish me to say I am not at home?" Octavia asked with deceptive meekness.

"That will hardly be up to you. It won't arise, but if it did, it would never do to cross him, not with him being so rich and influential—

although he sits as a Whig, please remember that. Your brother Arthur will hardly speak to him, they have crossed swords in the House too often for him to find Mr. Portal in the least bit agreeable. No, he must always be accorded every courtesy, but it is quite unnecessary for you to pursue the acquaintance."

Which opinion made Octavia determined to become acquainted with Mr. Portal, and also with the interesting Mrs. Rowan.

Chapter Six

Octavia had a swift reply from the lawyers: Mr. Wilkinson would be at her disposal whenever it were convenient for her. By great good luck, the letter had been delivered into Mr. Cartland's hand. "You will not wish everyone to be aware of your affairs," he said, with a kind smile, when he found her alone in the drawing room. Her sister would have demanded to know the contents of the letter, but he simply passed it to her and went back into his library.

Octavia decided that she would slip out to see the lawyers the very next morning. And she would have to exercise her skills of subtlety again; were she to announce that she was going into the city, there would be questions and deep disapproval—a woman on her own to venture into that part of London, it was not to be thought of. There would follow disagreeable, probing questions as to what business she had there. She could lie, which she found hard and disliked, but any hint of the truth would bring the conclusion she most feared: her sister or brother summoning the lawyers to Lothian Street, where Arthur or Mr. Cartland or Lord Adderley must be present to take the entire business out of her hands and put to rest for once and for all her obstinate insistence on managing it for herself.

Theodosia had ordered the carriage for later that morning. She summoned Octavia to tell her that she was to accompany her. "For I am going to the library; you will want to join the library, if you can afford the subscription, and if not, you may take out a volume or two on my account. I shall have no objection to that."

"Thank you, Theodosia, but I took out a subscription at Hookham's library when I went out yesterday, and borrowed some books."

"I was told you had gone to the circulating library, but I did not realise you were entering your name there. You did not tell me that. You should have consulted me first; Hookham's is by no means the most fashionable library at present. I would have advised you to take out a subscription at Earle's, in Albemarle Street. However, you may wait while I change my books and then I shall pay one or two calls, on the Miss Watsons, for instance. Do you remember them from when you were last in London? No? Well, they are an unremarkable pair, to be sure, but their salon is fashionable, everyone goes there, and they know everything that goes on in town, one hears all the latest *on dits* there. They know you are staying in Lothian Street, they will expect me to bring you."

Why? Octavia wondered. What possible interest could they have in Theodosia's poor relation?

"And it is important that they like you, for in due course, not so long now, when you are out of mourning, and if something can be done about your clothes, you will be going to one or two parties, and they know just how everyone is situated, which eligible men are looking out for a bride. We cannot hope for too much, but they understand the situation, they will be inclined to help, not on your account, but because I and Augusta take care to remain on good terms with them, there is no one whose good opinion is worth more . . ."

Theodosia's voice tailed off, even her supreme self-confidence faltering in the light of the smile on Octavia's face, her half sister's look of amusement, of positive merriment.

"Well, you may find it amusing although I can't for the life of me think why you should do so, but let me tell you, the only hope for you, if you are not to live in genteel poverty, is to catch yourself another husband."

"Yes," said Octavia. "You have told me so."

"Then I tell you again, and will do so until you listen; you are so stubborn, there is no doing with you." Theodosia went towards the door. "Please be ready within half an hour, and you should wear that hat with the feather, it is the best of your hats."

"I have the headache," said Octavia. "I prefer not to go out in the carriage."

"Of course you do not have the headache, you are perfectly well." Any hint of an indisposition in anyone but herself always roused Theodosia's ire. "And if you think you do, all the more reason to come out in the carriage. It will do you more good than remaining cooped up indoors all day long."

"Perhaps I may take a walk later, but I assure you I would be dull company this morning."

Theodosia persisted for a while, but Octavia stood her ground, and had the satisfaction, an hour later, of seeing her sister and Penelope drive away in the open carriage. They would be gone at least two hours, with luck; now she must hurry about her own affairs.

She told the butler to call her a hackney, and for a moment it looked as though she was going to have a fight with him as well, but she looked him in the eye. "A hackney cab, if you please."

"And where shall I tell the jarvey you wish to go?" said Coxley.

"I shall give him my direction," said Octavia, knowing that her reticence would be reported back to Theodosia; she would have to concoct a good reason for her expedition, with all the necessary corroborative details; no, it was simple, she needed to see Christopher's lawyers; that would bring reproaches, but it would be believable.

The offices of Wilkinson and Winter were situated at the river end of King's Bench Walk, near the Temple. It was a handsome building of the last century but heavily begrimed with soot, and once admitted, Octavia found herself in a dimly lit passage, lined with boxes and papers. However, she was not kept waiting there for more than a few minutes before being ushered into the presence of Mr. Wilkinson, a cadaverous individual in sombre clothes as befitted his profession, who rose to his considerable height as she came into the room, offered her a chair, and said, in a gravelly voice, that he was honoured by Mrs. Darcy's visit.

"Do you come alone?" he said, looking at the door as though an entourage were lurking outside.

"Yes, I'm on my own."

He raised an eyebrow, and gave a thin smile. "I had expected your brother, Mr. Arthur Melbury, to accompany you."

"Mr. Melbury knows nothing at all about this."

"Nothing about your coming here?"

"Nothing about that, certainly." Octavia sat straight in her chair, a glint of defiance in her eyes. "Also, nothing about this inheritance. It seems so improbable that I have come into my great-aunt's fortune, if it is what might be called a fortune. Mr. Gurney, in Calcutta, spoke of a substantial inheritance, but, really, I am quite in the dark as to what it all means. So I prefer not to speak of it, to my family nor anyone else, until I have the truth of it."

Mr. Wilkinson gave her a look of approval. "You are perhaps right, although a brother— However, let us get down to details. A substantial inheritance is not quite how I would describe the estate of the late Mrs. Worthington."

Half an hour later Octavia came out of the lawyer's office, almost missing the two shallow steps down to the street in her agitation and excitement. Mr. Gurney had not been wrong when he had used the word *fortune.* Fortune! It hardly described the wealth that Octavia, in that brief time, had found herself to be in possession of.

The hackney cab that had brought her from Lothian Street drew up beside her; after taking another fare, the jarvey had returned, judging that Octavia would want to make the return journey, which might mean another good tip.

"Back to Lothian Street?" he asked as he shut the door on her.

"No," said Octavia. "I want to walk. Take me to— I shall go to Green Park."

She could not possibly go back to Theodosia's house yet, not until she had calmed her nerves and composed herself, and begun to come to terms with this extraordinary change in her circumstances.

She gave the hackney cab driver a tip that made him stare, and touch his forehead with a deeply appreciative "And a very good morning to you, ma'am," before whipping up his horse, and guiding it back into the traffic.

Unlike Mr. Gurney, Mr. Wilkinson had been precise, precise almost to the last guinea; his words were still ringing in Octavia's ears. "The house in Yorkshire, Axby Hall, is a considerable property, a fine building from the middle of the last century, in good order, and with the farms and land forms an estate altogether of some five thousand acres. It also includes most of the properties in the nearby village of Axby, which are all at present occupied by good tenants." There was no private house in London, the late Mrs. Worthington didn't care for London, but she had owned several commercial premises in London as well as in York and Leeds, which were bringing in rents that made Octavia stretch her eyes.

"However, that is the least of it," Mr. Wilkinson had continued. "There are the tea plantations in India, which bring in a considerable annual income, the figures are all here, and although of course the profits are dependent on the crop and the hazards of shipping, the plantations are well managed, and you will find the figures for the last five years on this sheet.

"In addition, there is the sum of ninety thousand pounds in gilts; Mrs. Worthington was always a conservative investor—and, held at the bank, there are her jewels." He lifted yet another sheet of paper covered in lists and figures. "This is the inventory with the valuation that was made a year ago."

Octavia's eyes flickered unbelievingly down the page: a diamond necklace, a pair of rose diamond drop earrings, a number of large uncut rubies, an emerald necklace with matching bracelets . . . It was a long list, and the words floated in front of her eyes.

"Good heavens, what use had she for all these?" she cried. "And what should I do with them all?"

"I do not believe she ever wore most of them," said Mr. Wilkinson, pursing his lips. "Although she may have done so when Mr. Worthington was alive, when they were in India. She kept them as an investment, I dare say, and a good one, for they are unquestionably worth a great deal more than she or Mr. Worthington paid for them, as you will see. The jeweller who valued them, who knew her and looked after her jewellery for her, remarked that she was extremely knowledgeable; they are all stones of the highest quality. Should you decide to sell any of them—although I hardly think you would need to—he would be glad to have the handling of the sale, he asked me to say."

Octavia looked down at the papers that Mr. Wilkinson had handed to her, barely taking in the columns of figures, still unable to comprehend the extent of her inheritance.

"And all this comes to me?"

"Yes. You are named in her will, there is no mistake. She left some small legacies, annuities for her servants, that kind of thing, but the rest comes to you—you see, born Octavia Susannah Melbury, daughter of the late Sir Clement Melbury and Lady Melbury, now Mrs. Darcy, of Alipore, Calcutta. Now, it is fortunate, extremely fortunate, that she died after your late husband—since that removes any complications that might otherwise have arisen."

"What complications?"

"As a married woman, your inheritance would have come under your husband's control, and could have formed part of his estate. I understand there was an entail? Yes. Well, it would not have formed part of the entailed property, and should have come to you in the event of your husband's death—but it might have been, as I say, a complication—not one we need consider in this case. I have from Calcutta copies of the documents relating to your husband's sad and premature demise, please accept my deepest sympathies—and I am sure everything will be quite in order with regard to that."

Christopher would have rejoiced in her good fortune, Octavia reflected, as she watched the cows who grazed in Green Park lying comfortably on the grass, chewing the cud, looking, she couldn't help feeling, very much like one or two of Theodosia's acquaintances, with their bland, bovine expressions.

Had Christopher survived, he would undoubtedly have put quite a lot of her inheritance into his house in Wiltshire, a place that seemed to eat up money. She went pale at the thought of the Worthington money passing into the grasping hands of Mr. Warren; well, there was no point in dwelling on might-have-beens; Christopher, God rest his soul, was gone, Mr. Warren had Dalcombe, and she had her own immense fortune from her mother's despised family. She gave a little skip, startling a stout man hurrying past.

She had pledged Mr. Wilkinson to secrecy.

"It will get about in due course," he said. "Such things always do, although not from me or anyone in my employ, we know our business too well for that, discretion is essential in our profession, Mrs. Darcy. Now, I am one of the executors of the will, and the other is a Mr. Portal—ah, I see you know the name. He is presently abroad, travelling in France, I believe, but that need not hold us up, although, as a lifelong friend of your great-uncle and -aunt, I know that he is very eager to make your acquaintance."

"He wrote to me, from France, but I did not quite understand his position. So he is an executor?"

"Yes. Meanwhile, you will want someone to advise you; your brother, Mr. Arthur Melbury, would be the proper person, for I understand that Sir James Melbury is rarely in town. I can be in touch with Mr. Melbury at his earliest convenience to discuss—"

Octavia cut in swiftly. "I forbid you, I absolutely forbid you to have any contact with Mr. Melbury about this or anything to do with me."

Mr. Wilkinson's grave face took on a look of astonishment.

"I am twenty-five, and as a widow I believe I have full control of my financial affairs, is not that so?"

"In law, yes, but as a practical matter, I beg of you to consider what a responsibility such a fortune is. Mr. Melbury is known as an astute man, he will be better able to—"

"No. If I decide to run wild and sell out of the gilts and gamble the money away at the card table, I shall do so; it is entirely my own business."

"But, Mrs. Darcy," he began in appalled tones.

"I joke, Mr. Wilkinson. I am not a gambler, and I have been too poor for most of my life not to know the value of large sums in gilts. But I mean what I say. Whom did Mrs. Worthington rely on to advise her?"

He looked doubtful. "We were her lawyers, and she had a man of business in Yorkshire, but as to investments and so forth, and the plantations—well, I believe she saw to all that herself."

"Then so shall I."

"But, Mrs. Darcy, the cases are quite different. Mrs. Worthington was a woman who—"

"I shall make mistakes, I am sure, but my mind is quite made up."

She could see that he was going to argue, and could watch his mental processes as he thought better of it. She knew just what was going through his mind, that in no time at all, she would be married again, and her fortune would pass into the hands of a man, someone who would take care of everything for her.

"Not so," she said to the nearest cow, who gazed at her with huge, soft eyes. "I am a woman of independent means, definitely in possession of a good fortune, but I am not in the least in want of a husband!"

Chapter Seven

Arthur called early the following morning, when his sisters and niece were still in the breakfast parlour. Penelope was toying with a piece of toast, looking out of the window, and, while her mother was attending to her morning coffee and arranging everyone's day for them, letting herself give way to a heavy sigh. She rose politely as her uncle came into the room, dropping a neat curtsy, and presenting a dutiful cheek for his avuncular kiss.

"You are not in looks, Penelope," he said. "You need to get some roses into your cheeks. I saw Louisa yesterday, and she is blooming, quite blooming; you will have to look to your laurels."

"What have Louisa's looks to do with me?" Penelope muttered as she sat down again.

Arthur greeted his sisters, Theodosia with enthusiasm, Octavia less so, and sat himself down, calling for a fresh pot of coffee. "I have just time for a cup, but I shan't stay. I have called on Octavia's account, as it happens. I met Lady Warren last night, at the Batterbys' rout—I didn't see you there, Theodosia. It was a sad crush, you did well to avoid it."

"We called in early, probably before you arrived, for we were going on to the Tollants' ball."

"Oh? Well, as I say, Lady Warren was there— Octavia, are you paying attention?"

"I?" said Octavia, who had been looking out of the window and watching a pair of quarrelsome sparrows perched on the parapet of the house opposite.

"You, ma'am. I said, I have taken the time out from my own affairs entirely on your account, the least you can do is to listen to what I have to say."

"I'm sorry, Arthur, but what have these routs and balls and Batterbys and Tollants to do with me?"

"Nothing at all, but Lady Warren does. She is George Warren's stepmother, as it happens. And a connection of your late husband's, now I come to think of it."

Another connection? What an entwined world it was, with the upper ten thousand woven into a spider's web of marriages and consanguinity. Here was she, with a large family of half brothers and sisters, cousins, now even more connections through Christopher's family—and yet, in truth, she was still an orphan, with no close ties of feeling to any of them.

Arthur's eyes narrowed; he loved tracing family links. "Caroline Warren was a Bingley before she married, and her brother married the eldest Bennet daughter, a family of no importance, it was not a good match, she brought him hardly a penny, but what is more to the point, her next sister, Elizabeth, had the very good luck to snare Fitzwilliam Darcy and so she became the mistress of Pemberley; my word, she did well for herself there! Now of course, Captain Darcy was a cousin of that family, not a close cousin, but the connection is there."

Octavia spread a generous portion of strawberry jam on a piece of toast. The connection seemed more remote than most, and while Lady Warren might be the most amiable creature, she had not heard a good word spoken about her stepson.

"And George Warren is, of course, unfortunately, Christopher Darcy's heir. So I took it upon myself to mention to Lady Warren that you were returned to England. She expressed surprise, had no idea of it, but at once said that she would call upon you at the first opportunity and knew that George would also do himself the honour of waiting upon you."

* * *

Lady Warren had lied to Arthur. Lady Warren knew perfectly well that Octavia was in England; she made it her business to know most of what was going on in London society, and in such a case, when the news was of direct interest to her or to her stepson, George, upon whom she doted, she made sure she had all the details. She had known to the day, almost to the hour when Octavia arrived in Lothian Street, and sent a note round to George's lodgings, summoning him to her house.

"You will call upon her, of course," she said, sitting at her elegant writing desk, while George lounged in the most comfortable chair near to the fire.

"The devil I will."

Caroline Warren knew him too well to pay any attention to this. "The widow of your cousin, from whom you have inherited a very pretty estate; of course you must call. It would look odd if you didn't, in the circumstances."

"What business had Christopher Darcy to be marrying again, at his age? And to pick a woman with no fortune, and from what I remember of her, nothing much else to recommend her. Regular maypole, ain't she? I never thought him to have a goatish disposition, he should have stayed a widower, or found himself a rich woman to marry if he had to put his neck into the hangman's noose a second time. Although his first marriage don't seem to have done him much good, for all she was considered a good catch; Lord knows what happened to the first Mrs. Darcy's fortune."

"I thought he ploughed every penny he had into his house and land, prize money, her portion, everything."

"Well, I shall find out by and by, now I'm installed there and have all the accounts and papers to hand. A few extra thousand would have been worth having, but you say the second Mrs. D is landed safely on these shores, so she lives to enjoy her share of the inheritance. I dare say I'll have her or that prosy brother of hers coming round begging me to give her an annuity or some such thing. I shan't, of course, that family of hers can't let her starve, and she's no responsibility of mine if she can't live on what her husband left her."

"Which was little enough. I suppose he expected her to bear him a son and heir, what a mercy he was carried off before that could happen. It is fortunate for you that India has such a very unhealthy climate, where insect bites and the like can finish you off; that doesn't happen in Wiltshire that I ever heard."

"No, down there you die of boredom instead." He raised a languid hand. "No need to remonstrate with me. It's a devilish neat property, and will bring me a tidy little income, which I can do with."

"Have a word with Arthur Melbury before you pay your duty call on Mrs. Darcy, so that she has no expectations of any kind, knows that your visit is purely a matter of form."

"Lord, how tedious duty is. She's only a half sister to the rest of that Melbury lot, ain't she?"

"Yes, Sir Clement married her mother in an aberrant moment; she was from a family in trade, not in any great way, neither. At least she had the grace to expire in childbirth, and the third Lady Melbury was unexceptionable, if dull."

George Warren was surprised by Octavia when he paid a visit to the house in Lothian Street. There was a glint in her eye, as though she were laughing at him, which he didn't care for, and an air of confidence about her; what right had a poor widow to look as though she hadn't a care in the world? And for all her half-mourning grey dress—not badly cut, either; George was a connoisseur of women's clothes—she looked far from full of grief. But she had the decency to look more sombre when he spoke of Christopher; in flattering terms, although the truth was that he and Captain Darcy hadn't got on well together, chalk and cheese.

The matter of money, of his inheritance, of her slight income, was not raised. And the only reference she made to Dalcombe House, the house where she might have expected to spend many years of her married life, was when she said that if she were at any time in Wiltshire, she would like to see the house where Christopher had been born and grew up, and which he loved so much.

He couldn't refuse, and, he consoled himself, he wouldn't have to put up with her company. He didn't intend to spend more than a few weeks there each summer; he was not planning to rusticate.

He rose thankfully as soon as the half hour was up. What a tiresome woman Mrs. Cartland was, eyeing him in that way; he knew that scheming look, the automatic assessment of every matron with a marriageable daughter. Well, he wasn't in the market for a bride, and if he were, Penelope Cartland, who was looking at him with a wide-eyed dispassionate stare that he found disconcerting, would not be on his list. Her mama had better teach her a few manners, or she'd end up on the shelf. Men did not care to be looked at in quite that way; what with her and Octavia's self-possession, he felt quite put out.

And Mrs. Darcy had nothing in the way of a pretty foot, he remarked to himself, as he walked off down Lothian Street, twirling his cane. That came of being so damned tall; whatever had Christopher Darcy seen in her to want to marry her?

Mrs. Cartland was not pleased with George Warren, and she expressed her dissatisfaction almost before the door had closed behind him. "He has a very insolent air to him, and after all, his father's title is a new one; he is only the second baron. However, I should like to see a little more civility from you, miss, when we have a gentleman to call"—this to her daughter.

"He is a horrid man, I do not like him at all," said Penelope.

"What is this word, *horrid*? Anyone would think you were living in the pages of those novels you read. And it is not for you to set up for liking or disliking anyone, let me tell you. You will be guided by your mama and papa as to whom you may like or dislike."

She turned to Octavia. "I think him very remiss not to— Well, I believe there is nothing to be got out of George Warren, he has the reputation of being very tight with his money."

Arthur called a few minutes after Warren's departure, and was shown into the room where the ladies were sitting. He pursed his lips and looked grave. "I have to tell you now, Octavia, that Theodosia is right. I took up the matter of an annuity for you with Warren, for your income is so very small, and in the light of what you might have expected, disappointing. However, he would have none of it, said the estate was encumbered, that the house and land are in a bad way, and will need a great deal spent on it to bring it into order, so that nothing can be spared for you. Nor does he feel any obligation to you."

"There was no point in your asking him, then, was there?" said Octavia, wishing Arthur would keep his long nose out of her business. "And you had no right to talk to him without consulting me first. I didn't want to ask George Warren for a single penny, thank you!"

Octavia spoke more sharply than she had intended, but she was alarmed. Arthur's interference now was as nothing compared to how he would behave when he knew about her inheritance; he would immediately do everything in his power to take control. He couldn't, in the eyes of the law, but where family was concerned, law didn't enter into it. Another dreadful thought occurred to Octavia. This Mr. Portal, so inconveniently travelling abroad, what if he were a crony of Arthur's, an habitué of the same clubs? Men were all the same; they all had the idea fixed in their minds that a woman, particularly a young woman, and one who had hitherto always been at the bottom of the family pile, would of nature be incapable of looking after money, land, or in any way taking care of her own affairs.

Mr. Portal and Arthur might very well be of one mind—although, how much power did an executor have? The lawyer had said executor, not trustee. Octavia tried to remember the lawyer's exact words, for there was a world of difference, she felt sure, between the one and the other.

"Tell me, Arthur," she said, cutting across his grumbles. "An executor is what, precisely?"

"An executor?" He stared at her. "There you are, fancying you can deal with things yourself, and as simple and basic a concept as that is beyond you. Who is the executor of Darcy's will?"

"It doesn't matter. He's a lawyer. I only want to know what the powers of an executor may be."

"Give me his name, and I will go and see him, as I already told you that I would."

"No, Arthur, you will not."

"I know what an executor is," said Penelope. "For a good friend of mine was left a legacy and the executor sorted it all out. But once it was done, he had no say in how he was to use the money, that was entirely up to him."

Arthur gave his niece a quelling look. "The word gives the meaning, Octavia. He executes, that is to say, carries out what is specified in a will. It will hardly be an onerous job in your case, with so very little— I dare say the lawyer's fees will swallow up more of the very little you have, that is why you need me to see to it all for you, I will make very sure they don't take a ha'pporth more in fees than is right."

"I wanted information, merely, Arthur, not assistance."

"If you are going to be so headstrong, then I shall take my leave. It was always the way, you have always been obstinate and difficult, refusing to see what is best for you. You do not deserve to have the family you do, taking care of you and looking out for your best interests."

"And he is quite right," said Theodosia. "Shocking behaviour, a shocking way to speak to your brother. Penelope, I did not like to hear you speaking up so pert just now, it is not for you to open your mouth on subjects about which you know nothing, less than nothing." Octavia, noting the stormy look in her niece's eye, quickly asked if she might be spared to help her with her packing.

"Packing? Alice will pack for you," said Theodosia.

"But Penelope knows the household in Hertfordshire, she will be able to advise me on what I shall need. In the way of evening dresses and so on."

"I do not think the advice of a girl can be of any use to you, and as to evening dresses, I hardly believe that there will be any need for anything special, and besides, what do you have?"

The change of subject had, however, as Octavia had hoped, taken the edge off her irritation at her sister's treatment of Arthur and reminded her that her tiresome guest would be departing in the morning.

"Go with your aunt, then, Penelope, and see if you may make yourself useful."

"Do you really require my services?" Penelope enquired, as they went upstairs.

"No, Alice will have seen to everything, but it occurred to me that you might have been tempted into an argument with your mother, and in her present mood, it would be unwise."

Penelope gave a rueful smile. "You are right, it never does to argue with Mama. Subtlety is the only way. If you don't need me, then I shall go to my room for a while, I have some letters to write, and Mama won't bother me if she thinks I am with you."

Once inside her own room, Octavia had to laugh at the duplicity of her niece. If only she'd ever learned to handle Augusta the way Penelope did, her time in London as a girl would have been much easier. The more she saw of Penelope, the more she liked her, and the more apprehensive she felt about Penelope's future. There was a resolution to the girl, a strength of character that meant she would fight for what she wanted, for what she thought was right, and how could she come off best in any such contest?

She'd need all Penelope's resolution herself once the family knew of her inheritance. It wouldn't be long now before she came into possession of her fortune. Mr. Wilkinson had given no precise date, but assured her that she might draw funds to the tune of whatever she wanted. A line to him at any time and he would be at her service. He thought she might reasonably expect everything to be settled soon after she was returned from the country, for by then Mr. Portal would be in London, and would finish off his duties as executor of the will.

Chapter Eight

Octavia enjoyed the first part of her journey, as the coach left the Spread Eagle in Gracechurch Street and made its way northwards through the busy London streets, even though her eyelids were drooping.

The night before, she had finally fallen into a fitful sleep shortly before dawn, to be roused after what seemed like minutes by her maid: the stagecoach left at eight o'clock, she must be up and about. Theodosia had almost brought herself to apologise for not sending her to Hertfordshire in one of their carriages; they would be needed, they could not spare the horses. Octavia was not to know that Mr. Cartland had expostulated with his wife.

"Damn it, you can't pack her off on the stagecoach! She is your sister, our sister, that is no way for her to travel. If she is not to travel in our carriage, then she should go post!"

"There is no point in her growing used to comforts which she will not be able to enjoy in her situation. I have paid for a good seat, and she is no miss to be frightened by the journey, she has travelled in India where there are bandits at every corner, I dare say, and snakes and who knows what other dangers besides; going on the stagecoach—and only as far as Hertfordshire—is a mere nothing in comparison."

Mr. Cartland gave up the argument as a lost cause. Once Theodosia had made her mind up, there was no dealing with her, particularly when, as in this case, she knew herself to be in the wrong.

"Mr. Ackworth will be very shocked when he discovers she is travelling on the stage," Penelope said to her father. "If he had known what Mama planned, he would have sent his own carriage all the way to London for her, you may be sure, but I suppose Mama took good care, when announcing the time of Octavia's arrival in Meryton, not to mention her mode of travel."

Octavia would have preferred to travel in her brother-in-law's carriage, as who would not, but going on the stage was not such an ordeal, and she was thankful for any conveyance that took her away from London and from Theodosia and Augusta. Augusta had called on the previous evening, to add her own instructions to her about how she was to behave and what she was to spend her time doing, which was polishing her social skills—"For what will pass in Calcutta will not do in London; to be a provincial is bad enough, but to have a strange foreign touch will not do at all. The Ackworths are sensible, practical people who know how things are; they will put you in the way of acquiring some polish before you return to town."

"And there is the matter of clothes," Theodosia said. "Perhaps there is a dressmaker, some local woman, who could provide the elements of a wardrobe, then I am sure Icken could add a touch of modishness as needed. You will want morning dresses and carriage dresses and two ball dresses. Riding clothes will not be necessary, you will not be riding, you do not have a horse."

"Surely such little money as I have must be carefully hoarded for other expenses than fashionable clothes, don't you think?" Octavia said drily.

Theodosia's mouth tightened, and she shot a meaningful glance at Augusta. "We are well aware of how you are circumstanced, but it is essential that you present a good appearance once you are out of mourning. It would reflect badly on Augusta and myself, and indeed on your brothers, were you to be seen to be poorly dressed. Your wardrobe, a minimum wardrobe, will be our present to you. And should you catch the fancy of a man of some fortune, well then, you may pay us . . . However, that need not concern us now."

Octavia had a corner seat and so could look out of the window. Once they reached the open country, and rattled past neat dwellings interspersed with market gardens, the sunny spring morning raised her spirits. She had forgotten how pretty the English countryside was, even in the frozen, pre-blooming stillness of March, with the trees still gaunt and leafless. The hedges and fields, the villages with the church and manor, the men and women working the land, were all so different from the landscape and colours she had grown used to in India.

Yet she felt a pang of loss for that hot and mysterious country. Would she ever return there? Would she ever again watch the sluggish, murky waters of the Hoogly slide past, enjoy the startling dawns and sudden sunsets, hear the endless cawing of the crows, watch the vultures and hawks circling overhead, taste the hot, spicy food that Christopher adored?

It was difficult to imagine that this English scene was part of the same world; that in Calcutta the bazaars would be alive with people and colour and sound, while here a housewife would be tripping through the door of a village shop, no bustle or noise or wandering cow to interrupt her leisurely purchases.

Her attention was caught by a fine modern house, situated half way up a hill, facing south, an elegant building with a Grecian façade, and the Indian scene faded from her mind.

"Mr. Mortimer's house," a burly man in a green coat sitting beside her said, with a nod towards it. "He's a gent who made a fortune in the city, and like all such, he wanted to buy a country estate. However, none was available, or none that took his fancy, so he set about building a house for himself. And a neat job he's made of it, too. Mr. Quintus Dance was the man who designed it, an up-and-coming young man, who will make a name for himself, I am sure."

Octavia, instead of quelling the man with a glance, as her sisters would instantly have done should they ever have had the misfortune to find themselves travelling on the stagecoach, at once entered into conversation with her fellow passenger, who was in the building trade, he told her. They discussed buildings, the modern as opposed to the classical style, and Octavia listened with lively attention to his disquisition on the importance of guttering and downpipes. "I take a keen interest in all aspects of building," he said apologetically, fearing he might be boring her.

But she wasn't bored, not at all. He was a most interesting man, an importer of fine marbles, and supplier to nearly all the great houses now building. "That house of Mr. Mortimer's," he said with a backwards jerk of his thumb, as the coach swung round a corner and the house disappeared from view. "I provided a mort of marble for that house, for fireplaces, panelling in the library, and even a bathroom. Very up to date is Mr. Mortimer, he has a contrivance for running water which is quite remarkable. Carrara marble for the pillars and travertine for the hall floor."

They chatted on; Mr. Dixon, as he turned out to be called, was a well-travelled man. "For we don't have much marble in this country, and that's a fact. And what there is isn't always of the best quality; no, I look to Italy for my best marble, and Turkey, too. During the war with France, when that Boney was rampaging about the Continent, well, I tell you, it was hard to keep my head above water. I inherited the business from my father, and he had it from his father before him, but with not being able to travel nor trade with Italy nor anywhere else in Europe, life was hard. I went further afield, to Greece, even, but bringing the marble back all that way is uncommon expensive, and then, with folk being so nervous about the outcome of the war, there wasn't as much building going on as one would like to see."

Mr. Dixon had travelled to India as well, and on the very vessel that Octavia had just sailed back to England on, the *Sir John Rokesby*.

"A commodious, comfortable vessel, and with a good turn of speed under a good captain."

Octavia was fascinated by what he had to say, and was soon questioning him eagerly about styles of architecture now in fashion—Mr. Dixon wasn't enthusiastic about the Gothic, not much call for marble in those kind of houses, and who in their right mind would choose to set up home in a place that looked like it was out of the Middle Ages?

"Give me a modern style any day, elegant lines, spacious, light, that's the kind of house a gentleman and his family can live in."

In no time at all, they had reached the first stage, at the Salisbury Arms in Barnet, and as soon as the coach turned into the yard, the passengers tumbled out to try to swallow a cup of coffee in the few minutes allowed to them while the horses were changed.

"I'll see to that for you," said Mr. Dixon, surging across the inn yard. "It's no place for a young lady like yourself to be jostling and shoving just to get a cup of coffee."

In fact they had a few minutes' grace, time for him to return with a cup of dark, steaming coffee and for her to drink it without scalding her throat, for a handsome equipage arrived at the inn, and the ostlers and boys leapt to the horses' heads. "A prime team," observed Mr. Dixon, watching with keen eyes.

The innkeeper came running out in his leather apron. "Good morning, my lord," he said to the tall man in a many-caped coat, who had swung himself to the ground from the curricle. A waiter hurried up with a pewter mug, which the driver of the curricle took with a smile.

He was a striking-looking man; Octavia, while trying not to stare, could hardly take her eyes off him. There was a vitality about him that almost seemed to crackle, and his lean face, with keen eyes set above a long, aristocratic nose and a mobile mouth, promised both intelligence and wit.

A new pair of horses were in the shafts, the man was back in the driving seat; he called to the ostler to let go of their heads, and with a swift manoeuvre he was out of the yard and bowling along the road.

Then the post boy was tootling his horn, the passengers scrambled back on board the stagecoach, the last of them only just making it before the powerful team of four fresh horses leapt forward, and they were on their way again.

"That was Lord Rutherford," Mr. Dixon said, settling himself into his place and saying politely that he hoped he wasn't taking up Octavia's room. "He has a house near Meryton, not his principal seat, of course. That's Rutherford Castle, up Richmond way, and a gloomy pile it is, to be sure. This house of his in Hertfordshire isn't much better, his mother lives there mostly. It's Elizabethan, all chimneys and fancy brickwork, and not worth the upkeep if you ask me. Still, his lordship is rarely there, spends most of his time in London. A Whig, you see, and the Whigs don't go in for being country gents, not like the Tories, who take their landowning very seriously."

"Does his wife also prefer to live in London, is she a political hostess?"

"He ain't married, though it's not for want of the young ladies and their mamas trying, from what I hear. He's as rich as can be, but he don't care for the married state too much. Likes the females, I beg your pardon, but not in the matrimonial way." He paused and shook his head. "His mama's not quite right in the head by all accounts, so perhaps he doesn't take too cheerful a view of the married state."

Mr. Dixon was going on to Grantham, and it was with real warmth that Octavia bid him good day as she jumped down from the steps of the coach at Meryton. He saw to her boxes, and looked about him with a worried air, even as the coachman was warning him to "Look lively there, if you don't want to get left behind."

"Where's this person who's meeting you?" he demanded, hesitating with his foot on the step.

"My cousins are sending a man and their carriage; look, I believe that is it over there. Thank you for your concern."

"That's all right, and remember, when you take it into your head to go building a fine new house, you just get in touch with Ebenezer Dixon of Grantham, you only have to mention my name, they all know me there, well, so do all the architects, and you'll have such marble as will make you stretch your eyes!"

Chapter Nine

Sholto Rutherford noticed Octavia as he swept in and out of the inn, but it was no more than a passing glance, his eye caught by her height and graceful carriage, rare for so tall a woman to hold herself with quite that pride, part of his mind noticed, but the rest of his mind was elsewhere, and the image of her was lost seconds later in the cloud of dust sent up behind his curricle as it sped on its way towards London, even as the slower stage was lengthening the distance between them, heading in the opposite direction.

Sholto was quite out of temper, unusual for him, but his mother, Lady Rutherford, was tiresome enough to try the patience of a man with twice as calm a temperament as his. The truth of it was that Sholto and his mother didn't get on, and had been at outs ever since he was a small boy. There was affection there, but such a vastly different outlook that they puzzled one another extremely.

Sholto sometimes wondered why his father had ever married his mother, for there again, there seemed little similarity in their characters. Of course, his mother had been a beautiful woman; the portrait of her painted by Romney when she was at the height of her looks showed that well enough. And his father had been an easy-going man, not much irritated by the little things of life—but had his mother's growing strangeness been such a little thing? Of course his father had the option of taking up his residence separately from his wife, which was what he had done, dividing his year between London, when the House was sitting, and Yorkshire, when it wasn't, while she lived the year round in Chauntry, the Hertfordshire house that had been in the family since the time of Queen Bess; a sprawling, inconvenient place with, Lord Rutherford had been heard to remark, more chimneys than bedchambers.

Sholto had long suspected that Lady Rutherford had never wanted children, and that the strain of having a twin son and daughter had in some way set her apart from them and from their father. As he grew up, he saw her drifting further and further into a world of her own, a world that his sister, Sophronia, seemed able to take in her stride, but which continued to irk him.

He didn't mind his mother being unconventional—his family came from that part of the aristocracy that never gave a moment's attention to what anyone else thought of them—but he did mind her refusal, once his father had died, to take any interest either in the vast northern pile which was the seat of the earldom or in the other family houses. Excellent stewards and housekeepers ran the Rutherford houses with perfect competence, but it was not the same as having a proper mistress for at least one of them.

And there was Sophronia, his twin, thirty-five years old and still unmarried, who resolutely declined to take on her mother's role. She lived in bickering amiability with Lady Rutherford at Chauntry, but was perfectly happy to leave all the details of looking after the house to the staff. "Running a house is nothing but a bore," she said. "I have no more desire to attend all day long to household trivia than you have. Simply being born a woman does not mean that I am naturally domestic, all women are not that way inclined, however convenient it is for the male sex to believe it is the case."

Sholto's father had died when he was sixteen and still at school. He finished his education at Cambridge, and had since then spent most of his time in London, at his large house in Aubrey Square.

He had driven out of London the day before with the purpose of informing his mother that she must move out of Chauntry while necessary repairs were carried out on the house.

"It is essential, Mama," he said for the tenth time, exasperation creeping into his deep voice, "that the hall chimney and several others be rebuilt."

"It is out of the question," she said, waving an airy hand at him. "I am not to be banished from my house on any whim of yours. I can see perfectly well what you are about, I am not so foolish as not to know what you want. You are attempting to edge me out of here, with this fanciful talk of brickwork and fire hazard. This house has stood perfectly well for more than two hundred years. I will not have the great hall pulled about and filled with workmen. I can imagine nothing more inconvenient than having a pack of stonemasons and carpenters in the house. They will upset the animals."

"I would postpone the works until the summer if I could, when you might go to Brighton; however, Mr. Finlay informs me that the matter has now become a matter of urgency."

"Mr. Finlay!" said Lady Rutherford, dismissing Sholto's estate manager with another wave of her hand. "What does he know about anything? I am not to be moving on the word of that man. Besides, I dislike Brighton, it has become unspeakably vulgar ever since our fat prince—oh, I beg his pardon, fat King—constructed his monstrous pavilion."

"You can go to Yorkshire if you prefer not to be here while the house is in the upheaval of building works, and if the Dower House—"

The mention of the Dower House seemed to bring her to the brink of a spasm, and her daughter, Sophronia, after exchanging a speaking glance with Sholto, waved a vinaigrette under her mother's nose, and begged her, in a brisk voice, not to upset herself, it was bad for her system.

"And what does Sholto care for that. I am not upsetting myself, he is upsetting me. Summon Dr. Gibbons this instant, he will tell Sholto that I am not to be teased in this way, that I shall be out of sorts for days as a consequence of his coming here with his mad schemes."

"If the chimneys are in danger of catching fire, Mama, you will possibly be more than out of sorts, you will be smoked out, kippered,

I dare say," Sophronia said. "Not all Dr. Gibbons's medical care will help you then."

Lady Rutherford gave her daughter a dark look. "How dare you use such language in my house, Sophronia, and to me."

Sophronia shrugged. "Have it your way, Mama. For myself, I should be quite happy in the Dower House, or Yorkshire. It is all one to me. Where I would most like to be is London, but of course you won't go there, and Sholto wouldn't have you if you wanted to."

"And of what importance is it where you want to be? Since when do your opinions and wishes have anything to do with anything?"

Sholto suppressed a grin. Sophronia was a constant source of delight to him. She had inherited none of her mother's faults, instead being blessed with her father's tolerant nature. Her mother's attempts to marry her off to a series of men she had taken in dislike had failed; what in her mother was obstinacy was in her resolution, and in the end, her mother had been obliged to give in.

A weaker character would have become her mother's slave, a mere footstool for such an imperious woman, but Sophronia had too much character for Lady Rutherford to care to have her dancing in attendance on her, her daughter's intelligence was too keen and her sense of humour and of the ridiculous too strong to make her comfortable company. So Sophronia spent her spinsterhood in her own way, painting and walking, and with her own circle of friends; Sholto liked her much the best of his family, and would have felt sorry for her, if she had not on more than one occasion informed him in her forthright way that he might spare himself the emotion, she was perfectly happy in the life she had made for herself.

But in this case, her tongue and her reasoning could not prevail against her mother's stubborn determination to thwart Sholto's plans. So he had ordered his carriage, and frowned at Sophronia when she came out to bid him farewell.

"There is no doing with her at present," Sophronia said. "I will try to make her see sense, and if the wind sets in the east, I may contrive to have the chimney smoke so badly that even she understands that something must be done."

"I doubt if you'll succeed," said Sholto, his frown giving way to his more usual smile.

"Damn it," he said aloud, as he passed through Meryton. "Let the house tumble about her ears, and I hope she may be buried in the rubble."

He had no great liking for Chauntry, and not just because his younger years there had not been altogether happy ones. He found the house uncomfortable. It had the reputation of being haunted, and although he didn't believe in ghosts, there was no question but that the house had an atmosphere. He had asked Sophronia if she felt it, and she had said at once that it was clearly a house where some very unpleasant things had happened, which seemed to linger in the rooms, but she wasn't especially affected by the supernatural, and since she contrived to spend a good deal of time out of doors, and had her own sitting room and bedchamber in the most recent part of the house, an addition made by his grandfather in the last century, she took no notice.

"Of course, it is difficult to keep servants, as you know, for they are very superstitious; however, any fear of ghosts is assuaged by the higher wages we pay."

Sholto arrived back at his London house in the early afternoon, thirsty and dusty after his drive, but with the fidgets shaken out of him by the cracking pace he had taken. The door opened as he drew up; a footman sprang forward to take his coat as he went into the house and his butler surged towards him with offers of refreshment, and the news that Mr. Poyntz was waiting for him in the library.

Sholto peeled off his gloves, handed them and his hat to the footman, and went directly to his library. Henry Poyntz was one of his oldest friends; they had been at Eton and the university together, and although their worldly fate was very different, they had remained fast friends. He greeted Henry with real affection, asked after his parents and numerous siblings, and told the hovering footman to bring a bottle of claret.

Henry was the youngest of five brothers, all exceptionally able men, the sons of a clergyman. His father had a good living, but with three daughters to provide for as well as his sons, the boys all had to find careers for themselves. And they had; choosing the army, the navy, the law, the academic life, and the Church. Henry had been in the army for the long war with Napoleon, serving in Spain and fighting at Waterloo. After he had recovered from the wound he had received on the battlefield, he decided he had had enough of war and killing and sold out, announcing his intention of taking holy orders.

Sholto sat down on the window seat and raised a glass to his friend. He was a good fellow, and Sholto was delighted to see him. Henry wasn't one of your puritanical, hellfire clergymen. Tall and handsome, with a witty tongue and a good deal of charm, he was liked by all his acquaintance; you would be hard put to find anyone with a bad word to say about him. His was just the company Sholto needed after his unsuccessful trip into Hertfordshire, he would rouse the dullest man out of the glooms, not that Sholto was gloomy, his was not a melancholy nature, as Henry told him when he recounted his mother's implacable refusal to see sense over the chimneys.

"Luckily," Henry added, "or you'd be in a constant state of the black dog, with Lady Rutherford to deal with. What a time Newsome has of it with her, I wouldn't be in his shoes for anything."

"I can't think what she wants with a chaplain in any case," said Sholto. "She never goes to church, nor attends household prayers; I never knew a more ungodly woman."

"The Reverend Newsome is useful to you," said Henry, suddenly serious. "He takes good care of your library there, and is bringing it into some degree of order, which it needs. Your ancestors not having been of a bookish disposition, it's gone to wrack and ruin."

Sholto raised his hand in a gesture of surrender. "I know, I know, and he has turned up some fascinating volumes, a first folio of Shakespeare, for example, apart from sorting out the family papers. You'd be surprised what he has dug up about the doings of the Rutherfords in the seventeenth century."

"No, I wouldn't," said Henry at once. "The house was besieged by Cromwell, wasn't it? I bet the Lord Rutherford of his day was just such a man as you. I can see you in a sash and a feathered hat, manning the cannons and defying the Roundheads."

"You are out there. My great-great-grandfather was away when the house was attacked, fighting with the King. It was his wife who defied the parliamentary forces." He paused. "I sometimes think it's a pity she was successful, it might have made my life much easier if the house had been slighted then. They nearly lost the place, of course, during the Commonwealth, and it fell into some disrepair; however the new King made amends, for once, and restored the family fortunes, and the house was put to rights. Now, though—"

"Is it so serious?" Henry asked. "These stewards can make a fuss about a small matter, blowing it up out of proportion to justify their wages."

"Finlay is not that sort of a man. I have looked at it with him, and talked to the builders; there is no doubt that it needs a great deal of work done on it, and soon. My mother should not be living there, she should not have roaring fires going day and night as she does; but there is no reasoning with her. Now you've put me back in a bad mood, thinking of the house and her. I looked for you in Meryton, by the way, but they told me you were in Lincolnshire."

"So I was, visiting the family, but now I plan to spend a few weeks in town, if you can put me up."

"Do your clerical duties permit you to be away so long?"

"Dr. Rawleigh is glad to see the back of me. He says I rattle through the services and he would prefer to manage on his own. He has no need of a curate, you know, he would not have one if you hadn't obliged him to take me on."

Dr. Rawleigh was the Rector of Meryton, a living in Lord Rutherford's gift, a living that he planned to present to Henry as soon as the Rector, an elderly scholar with more interest in books than people, saw fit to retire.

"What he means is that you are active in the parish, and show up his scholarly indolence to the parishioners. Once you are out of the way, it will be to the devil with the souls in his care and back to his books." Sholto rang the bell. "Berwick," he said to his butler, "Mr.

Poyntz will be staying for a while, he will have his usual room." He turned back to Poyntz. "So what brings you to London?"

"Family affairs. My mother wants me to attend my sister's ball—Georgiana is making her come-out this year, you know."

"Already?" said Sholto, who thought of his friend's youngest sister as a mere chit in the schoolroom.

"She is turned eighteen, and grown very pretty. I warn you, my mother has her eye on you as a suitable husband, although I have told her that I don't think you have any matrimonial inclinations. Or do you?" he said, cocking a knowing eyebrow.

"I suppose I shall have to marry one of these days, but don't let your mother try to push Georgiana in my direction, a charming girl, I am sure, but if and when I marry, it won't be to a girl of her age."

"Men do."

"Not I."

Henry Poyntz ran over in his mind the succession of elegant beauties whose names had been linked with Sholto's over the years, and was inclined to agree with his friend. "Marriage is different from a liaison, of course. One does not look for the same qualities in a wife as in a mistress, and a very young woman is likely to be more malleable, can be moulded . . ."

"You think so? You don't know much about women, Henry, which is probably as well, given your chosen profession. No, I shan't marry, not until I find some woman who doesn't get up to all the usual tricks of her sex, and that is not very likely to happen soon. Let Georgiana fall in love with some dashing young fellow, and I am sure she will be very happy."

It pained Henry to hear Sholto speak in that way. In everything else, Sholto was relaxed, amusing, an excellent companion, a fine swordsman, nothing stuffy or dull about him, and he'd spent many a merry evening in the company of his friend and his various mistresses—although not the current one, whom Henry Poyntz disliked. Many women were willing to find solace in the strong arms of Lord Rutherford, but when it came to anything that might touch his heart, a suggestion of love, of any more tender emotion, then Sholto was made of steel. He despised women for their wiles and guiles, he told Henry. "They pretend to love you, and the moment their fancy wavers, they are off after some juicier prey."

Poyntz knew that his friend regarded the whole marriage mart of London society—Almacks, the balls, the parties, the gossip, the pushy mamas—with bored contempt, although he was a good and graceful dancer when he could be prevailed upon to attend any of the season's functions.

Which he would, given the good nature that lay beneath his cynicism. Henry knew that he would respond to his mother's invitation to Georgiana's come-out ball, he would arrive in reasonable time, display perfect good humour and excellent manners, be affable and attentive to his partners, dance every dance, and leave every mother in the room sighing with vexation at the knowledge that it all meant nothing; they had long ago learned that it was a waste of any mother's time and effort to make any attempt to capture the rich and eligible Lord Rutherford for their daughters, no matter how lovely, how accomplished they were.

Henry's private opinion was that, in the end, needing an heir, Sholto would marry the daughter of a neighbour in Yorkshire, whom he would then install in his draughty ancestral home, leaving her with the castle and nursery to attend to, while he decamped back to London. There was no getting away from it, Sholto disliked and mistrusted most women. With his the way his mother was, his early view of the female sex had not been a fortunate one.

A successful falling in love when he was a young man in London might have set him upon a different path, but he had had the bad luck to fall head over ears in love with the beauty of her year, Miss Eliza Hawtrey. That had ended unhappy, which misfortune seemed to set the seal on Sholto's bitterness, and he'd embarked on a series of arm's-length attachments, all he would ever permit himself. And the moment he sensed that any high-born lady of the moment was growing fond of him, she would be ruthlessly cut out of his life.

Which was why Kitty Langton had lasted longer than the others; icy-hearted, was Henry's view of her, despite her luscious form and melting eyes. She was a harpy, and had her claws far further into Sholto than perhaps he was aware of.

Henry sighed, and stood up. "Let's dine at Pinks," he suggested, "and then we might call in at the Brindleys' ball."

"To support your sister?" said Rutherford, raising an eyebrow.

"I don't know who may be there," said Poyntz with a carelessness that didn't deceive Sholto for a moment. "I should just like to dance, it is a long while since I have enjoyed a waltz."

Chapter Ten

The journey from Meryton to Ackworth was only a matter of two miles or so. The carriage that Hugh Ackworth had sent to fetch Octavia drove along a deep lane and then came up to the brow of a hill, where a pleasing landscape lay before her. Her mind was on houses, and her eyes focused on a very large house set down in the valley, beside a winding river, a pretty spot and in a sheltered place, with the land rising behind it, although she suspected it would be both damp and also in shadow for most winter days. Built in red brick, with a great arched gateway, it had numerous chimneys, several of them with columns of smoke rising into the air; in the parkland around it, fat sheep grazed, and it presented a serene and tranquil scene.

A mile further on, the carriage turned in through a handsome pair of gates. Her cousins were waiting at the door of Ackworth Manor, an ancient house which had been extended and altered over the centuries, but still had pleasing harmony of scale to it.

Mr. Ackworth, as Penelope had suspected, was loud in his indignation that Octavia should have travelled on the stage. "That is Theodosia's doing, do not attempt to deny it, no, my dear"—this to his wife—"Mrs. Darcy is no fool, she can have few illusions about her sisters."

The Ackworths were in their forties, he a man of medium

height, with a well-bred if sardonic look to him, and she a lively, slender woman with a good-humoured mouth. They ushered Octavia into the house, saying that she must be tired after her journey.

"Especially jostling about on the stage, squashed up to all kinds of people you would rather not be in company with," put in Mr. Ackworth.

"In truth, I was sat next to a man who was very interesting, and we talked so much that the miles flew past."

Mr. Ackworth snorted, and Mrs. Ackworth said that Octavia was quite right to make the best of what had to be endured. She was to go upstairs this instant, to wash and change, and to lie down upon the bed if she felt in need of a rest. They dined at six, there was no need to hurry.

Octavia would have been ashamed to do any such thing, when it was obvious that her host and hostess were a tireless pair; she was sure that they would not have dreamed of resting in the day time.

The house smelt of beeswax and pot-pourri; it was a pleasingly mellow house, which had been in Mr. Ackworth's family for centuries. The dining room was hung with tapestries, woven, Mr. Ackworth told her, in the seventeenth century; he showed her how his ancestors had cut into the fabric to allow for the opening of a door which had been put in at a later date. The room was warm from a good fire, and the food, all their own produce, was substantial, well cooked, and more than welcome to Octavia, who found she was very hungry after her journey.

"Do you have a large circle of acquaintance here in Hertfordshire?" she asked. "My niece Penelope told me that she was never dull here."

"That girl is a joy," said Mr. Ackworth. "She takes after her father, but has more character than he does. I do hope her mother doesn't succeed in marrying her off to some bore with more money than sense."

"We dine with some five and twenty families," said Mrs. Ackworth. "The big house here is Chauntry, of course, you will have noticed it as you came in the carriage, a vast red-brick edifice dating from the age of Elizabeth."

"I saw it indeed, and meant to ask you about it."

"It belongs to Lord Rutherford, but he is rarely here. It is lived in by his mother, Lady Rutherford, whom we visit, but as seldom as possible, since she is a difficult woman."

"Mad, quite mad," said Mr. Ackworth dispassionately.

"Well, she is not quite in the ordinary way, but . . . her daughter, Lady Sophronia, is a different kind of creature, however, for whom we have a great affection; you will like her. She is not a young woman, of course, past thirty, but she is young at heart, with a sharp wit and a good eye for the comical. I feel you will get on together. She never married, which is a pity, for it would have got her away from her mother. She dines with us; without her mother, since, fortunately, Lady Rutherford never dines out. She summons people to Chauntry from time to time, and we feel obliged to go, in the interests of good neighbourliness, but we are always relieved when the evening is over, she is so odd."

For some reason, Octavia didn't want to tell her cousins of her glimpse of Lord Rutherford at the inn. So brief an encounter could hardly be worth a mention, and she had no desire to reveal what an impression the man had made on her. "Where does Lord Rutherford live, if not at Chauntry?"

"His seat is in the north, near Richmond, in Yorkshire, but he is not a country dweller. They are Whigs, you know, and he spends most of the year in London; he is active in politics and has a busy social life. He has no wife, the mamas say he is not a marrying man, although that may change. His single state does not mean he is indifferent to women, on the contrary, he has had a string of beautiful mistresses, but he is disinclined to put his head in any matrimonial noose. I can say these things to you, my dear, I can see you are not offended by my frankness, and you have been a married woman, I need not be careful of your morals, I think!"

Octavia laughed, liking her cousins more and more. Mrs. Ackworth had the outlook and attitude of the last century, when women were more outspoken and less constrained than her contemporaries; Octavia found her a breath of fresh air after the rectitude of her sisters.

"Chauntry is a large house for a solitary woman and her daughter."

"It is absurd her living there. There is a perfectly good Dower House, which would be much more convenient for her—but, as I said, she prefers grandeur and state to comfort and convenience."

"We can find you better company than Lady Rutherford, rest assured of that, Octavia," Mrs. Ackworth said. "Although you will not want to be going out to the assemblies and so on just yet, not while you are still in mourning, although your year will soon be up, and then you must make the effort to get out into the world. You do not look to be the moping kind; it will do you good to meet new people and have some enjoyment."

"I must not trespass on your hospitality for too long," said Octavia, and with a rueful smile. "My sisters expect me back before the season is over, as soon as I can put off my blacks. They have hopes of my finding another husband for me; as quickly as possible."

"Your sisters have some sense," said Mrs. Ackworth. "It is no secret that you have been left in straitened circumstances, and life isn't easy for a gentlewoman of slender means; you are too young, too good looking, to while away the years in some dismal spa. A good marriage—"

Octavia laughed. "Well, my sister Drusilla has a brood of children and is never in good health, so if I weren't to marry again, I dare say the family will try to pack me off there to do my auntly duty," Octavia said lightly, and, once again feeling guilty for not telling anyone about her inheritance, added, "It will not come to that, I have other plans."

Mr. Ackworth sent Octavia off to bed early. "For you are looking peaky, I dare say you found London tiring; a few days of country air will bring a bloom to your cheeks and take those dark circles from under your eyes."

The country air was one thing, but the quietness of the countryside was another. Not since she had left her home in Dorset had she spent a single night of such utter stillness, the only sounds those of a hunting owl, or the sharp, distinctive bark of a fox.

Octavia lay in the soft, comfortable four-poster bed, the sheets fresh and warmed by the pan of coals the maid had drawn across them before turning down the covers for her. She had pulled back one of the bed curtains, and opened the shutters at the window, so that she might look out at the clear, frosty sky.

She had grown used to the southern stars during her time in India, but these blazing stars, sprinkled across an inky sky, were the stars of her girlhood, old friends to a lonely child. She felt extraordinarily peaceful lying there, the sounds of Calcutta, of the creak and wind of the ship, of the constant blur of carriages and wagons and voices in London no more than a memory.

She found herself remembering her last night in Dorset, when her stepmother had already left for Ireland. Her elder brother had arranged her journey to London, the hired chaise would be at the door first thing in the morning, the governess had been paid off, and had left, sadly weeping, for a new position, and Octavia had spent a solitary evening drifting about the house, touching familiar objects, pulling out books she wanted to take with her and then putting them back on the shelves. She had no one to talk to except the housekeeper, never a great conversationalist, and a woman who did not bother to restrain her pleasure in Octavia's departure, when she would have even less work to do, and would have the house to herself except for the maid and the slow-witted boy who did the heavy work; Arthur had turned off all the other servants.

And here she was, more than five years older, once again to be put up for sale by her sisters like a horse to any man who would take her off their hands. How shocked they would be when they learned of her plans for an independent life, how furious that she were become so rich, how enraged that she had kept the fact to herself.

She slept soundly and deeply, waking long after the thin spring sun had risen over a landscape sparkling with frost, and was ashamed to find, as she entered the breakfast parlour, that Mrs. Ackworth had been up at first light, and had been busy ever since.

"I have to rise early, or the days are never long enough," she said, feeling the silver coffeepot to make sure it was hot before pouring Octavia a cup. "I write my letters and do accounts, and then there are so many tasks, I never have time for all I want to do."

After breakfast, Mrs. Ackworth took Octavia to see the rest of the house: the lofts, with the soft smell of apples laid up from the previous autumn; the dairy, where a large, cheerful dairymaid bobbed a curtsy to Octavia without stopping in her steady labour of churning butter. "We have a herd of Jersey cows, and make our own cheese, more than we can use, so we sell it round about; we are famous for our cream cheeses."

They came out from the dim coolness of the dairy and into a sunny yard, with hens scratching around, and in the poultry run itself, geese and two large turkeys set up a din when they saw Mrs. Ackworth.

"You would not think that birds who have no brain at all could become so friendly; it is always hard for me when the time comes for them to fulfil their destiny. I swear some of them are more intelligent than many humans, but that says more about our fellow beings than it does about the birds."

Mrs. Ackworth kept bees, and their hives were near her large herb garden, where green shoots were showing forth. "In the summer it is a delightful garden, with the scented air, and the hum and buzz of the bees. I like to sit here, although never for long, for there is always some duty calling inside or in the gardens."

The house had a sufficient staff, meagre in comparison to the large number of servants that even modest establishments maintained in India, but Octavia had a fair idea of how much work all this must entail.

"I am busy from dawn to dusk," said Mrs. Ackworth complacently. "It suits me. I was born a countrywoman, and keeping the house and my domain in order is a pleasure to me. And Mr. Ackworth is a keen farmer, and as occupied as I am, although in the evening he likes to come into his library and his books, while I find I nod off over my embroidery!"

The days, each one bringing new greenery and life to the countryside, slipped past. Octavia enjoyed helping her cousin, but knew that such a life would drive her to distraction. How odd, that in India she and Christopher had dreamed of such a life, the life they would one day live at Dalcombe, and had felt nostalgia for the scent of new-mown hay, for green fields, for misty dawns and long grey twilights. Yet Octavia was restless, and she was delighted when Mr. Ackworth offered her a mount. "It has not been a good weather this winter, with rain and then heavy frosts," he said. "All the horses need as much exercise as they can get, let us see which one will be best for you."

He put her up on a quiet hack, but as she rode round the paddock, and he saw with what ease and assurance she rode, he laughed, and told the groom to saddle Vagabond. Octavia was all admiration as a large black horse, ears pricked, was led out.

"He is a handful, but there is not an ounce of wickedness in him, he will be an excellent ride for you."

For the first few times she went out, she was accompanied by a groom, but she dispensed with his services as she grew to know the surrounding land. Mr. Ackworth was doubtful as to the wisdom of her riding out alone, but when she told him where she planned to go, he agreed that she would come to no harm. "You are on my land until you reach the crossroads," he said, "and then to the south is Rutherford parkland, there can be no objection to your riding there, nor to the west, which belongs to Squire Jervis; I am on good terms with all my neighbours, I am glad to say."

So Octavia rode out along the ridge, relishing the energy and strength of her horse, who felt the springy turf underfoot and snatched at the bridle, eager for a gallop. She pulled him up when she reached the crossroads, and then trotted down the deep rutted lane that ran past the Rutherford lands, looking for a gate where she might jump into the park. There was one a little further on; she put

Vagabond to it, and the big horse hopped neatly over. Once in the park, he pretended to take offence at the deer grazing and moving about the park, but Octavia chided him and told him not to be silly and he settled down to a steady canter along the perimeter by the fencing.

Octavia was startled by a shout; her horse shied violently, as startled as she was, and she only just managed to stop him kicking up his heels and galloping off. There was another shout, the words clearer now: "What is all this, who are you?"

An angular woman wearing an extraordinary turban on her head, adorned with feathers and coloured strips of silk, stepped briskly out from beneath the trees. She was accompanied by a younger woman, one, however, who was dressed in a perfectly normal blue gown, with a wide-brimmed hat.

Octavia stared, wondering who the older woman could be, dressed in such a very odd style. It was not only her headgear, her dress was a kind of Eastern robe in shades of vivid red, from scarlet to cherry pink; was she a foreigner?

"We startled you," said the younger woman. "I am sorry, you nearly came off."

"There is no need to apologise," said the turbanned woman, "since she stayed on, at least she can ride. Who are you, and who gave you permission to go galloping about in my park?"

"It is Rutherford's park," the younger woman put in quickly, "and you know quite well that our neighbours often ride here."

"This isn't a neighbour," said the woman, fixing a pair of blazing blue eyes on Octavia. "I have never seen her in my life. The Vicar of Stoke has a new bride, I am told, but you can hardly be she."

"Mr. and Mrs. Bolton are still away on their honeymoon, Mama," said the younger woman.

"I knew it could not be her, no Vicar's wife I ever heard of rides about on other people's land on a large black horse. Stay," she went on, raising her hand in a dramatic gesture. "I don't know you, but I know the horse!"

"Of course you do," said the young woman. "It's Vagabond, Mr. Ackworth's Vagabond."

"What, is she a horse thief as well as a trespasser? I never heard of such a thing." She stepped forward, and tugged at Vagabond's forelock before blowing gently into his nostrils, an activity of which the horse seemed greatly to approve.

"Pay no attention to Mama, she likes to joke. This will be Jane Ackworth's cousin, I told you she was coming to stay. Am I right?" the young woman said to Octavia.

Octavia leant down to shake hands. "I am Mrs. Darcy."

"Which of the many Mrs. Darcys?" said the older woman. "I know, you are Christopher Darcy's second wife. Ha," she said with a sudden, raucous laugh, which made Octavia jump. "I could tell you a thing or two about the first Mrs. Darcy."

"Mama is Lady Rutherford, and I am Lady Sophronia," said the younger woman, "since the normal methods of introduction seem to have been made superfluous."

Lady Rutherford was watching a bird hopping from twig to twig of a nearby tree. "A yellowhammer," she observed, and then went on. "And no groom with you? Mr. Ackworth is remiss. I should not allow my daughter to ride on her own."

"No chance of that," said Lady Sophronia with asperity, "since I never ride if I can help it." She smiled at Octavia. "I am fond of horses, indeed I am fond of most animals, but I have never been a keen horsewoman."

"You've come from India," said Lady Rutherford, who had been looking at Octavia as though she were another yellowhammer. "That accounts for the thin face, you need to eat up while you are at the manor, plenty of cream and good food there. The East saps the strength, I have often noticed it. Christopher Darcy's wife, and left in very reduced circumstances; it doesn't surprise me. Christopher always was a fool, a fool when it came to wives and a fool with his money. But there you are, that is what men are like."

"You are very welcome to ride in the park, Mrs. Darcy," said Lady

Sophronia, ashamed for her mother. "Will you not come into the house for some refreshment?"

"Not everyone wants to be sitting about maudling their insides with tea," pronounced Lady Rutherford.

Octavia certainly didn't want to. "Thank you," she said quickly, "but I must be riding back, or my cousins will be wondering what has become of me."

"What a strange pair Lady Rutherford and Lady Sophronia are!" said Octavia as she sat with her cousins that evening in the dining room at Ackworth Manor, the curtains drawn, a fire lit in the handsome old stone fireplace, and the soft flickering candlelight sending a warm glow on to their faces.

"I should have warned you," said Mrs. Ackworth, "only I had no idea of Lady Rutherford being out and about. It is unusually early for her to be abroad."

"She is a late riser, then?"

"No," said Mrs. Ackworth. "It is that she is an eccentric, a complete eccentric."

"I told you, mad as a hatter," said Mr. Ackworth, reaching for another helping of the duck in green sauce.

"Lady Rutherford believes in hibernation," Mrs. Ackworth told Octavia.

Hibernation? Octavia was so astonished that she forgot her manners and paused with her fork in the air, staring at her cousin.

"From late autumn, in about November, to spring, Lady Rutherford remains indoors, keeping almost entirely to her bedchamber, wrapped up in numerous garments, and sleeping a good deal. When she emerges, she declares she has had enough sleeping for the year, and so she spends hardly any time asleep, some two or three hours a night. She is a great bird-watcher, and we are quite used to hearing of her being out at all hours in pursuit of some owl or buzzard; stalking some feathery creature at two in the morning is nothing to her."

"And she lives alone with her daughter? It must be hard for Lady

Sophronia, come the winter, she must be left very much on her own. Or does she hibernate as well?"

"No, her mother wishes she would do so, she considers it the best and most healthy way to live for everybody, but Lady Sophronia has all her mother's strength of will and a good deal more sense, so she will have none of it. I do not think she is lonely, she has a fortunate disposition, she reads and sketches and, indeed, I sometimes suspect she prefers the winter, when she barely sees her mother at all. She goes out when she wants, she is a welcome guest at all the houses hereabouts, she has a large circle of friends."

"And I dare say she has to run the house while Lady Rutherford is—indisposed?"

"Not at all. Lady Sophronia is not inclined to domesticity, no more than her ladyship is. They have a good housekeeper and a steward, which is fortunate, for although Rutherford is hardly ever there, they still keep a large staff, and the house itself, which is very old, is always in need of care and attention."

Octavia helped herself to a portion of spiced parsnips. "It seems to me to be a badly situated house," she said. "It must be in shadow for much of the day, except in high summer, and surely, so near the river as it is, it must be damp."

"Damp, foggy, impossible to heat, great smoking chimneys, it is as impractical a house as any in the land," said Mr. Ackworth. "Rutherford always says if he had his way, he'd knock it down and build a modern house, further up the hill."

"That would be a very good position," said Octavia. "South facing, and with an excellent outlook."

"The Romans thought so, at any rate," said Mrs. Ackworth. "That is another one of Lady Rutherford's hobbies, she is up there every summer with men who can ill be spared from the estate work, digging and burrowing. She was in ecstasies last June when she unearthed a piece of leather which she said was a Roman shoe."

"She was right," put in Mr. Ackworth. "Our vicar is something of an antiquarian, and he says her knowledge is remarkable. If you ever go into the house you will see the collection her ladyship has made;

any number of pots and rusty buckles, all set out on shelves in glass cupboards."

"And I dare say the house has had many additions since it was built in Tudor times," said Octavia.

"It has," said Mr. Ackworth. "It has been added to each century, but in such a higgledy-piggledy way. There are more tall chimneys than a house can have any need of, and they all smoke, or have birds nesting in them—"

"And Lady Rutherford will not allow the nests to be removed," said Mrs. Ackworth.

"Well, if it were mine, I would do as Lord Rutherford wants to do, and take it down to build a new house further up the slope."

"It is all talk with him," said Mr. Ackworth severely. "Pass the sweetmeats to Octavia, Jane, she is still looking peaky, we cannot send her back to London so thin."

"All talk?" said Octavia.

"These Whig grandees have no interest in anything that happens beyond the bounds of London. They live on their rents and maintain their great houses and estates, but at a distance, or they will spend at the most a few reluctant weeks in the summer there. Whigs are London people, they like to breathe the sooty, foul air, and then to let it out again in Parliament. And Rutherford is your arch Whig, he is full of wicked Whiggery. He would never take the time or effort it would require to rebuild Chauntry."

"He could employ an architect, I suppose," said Mrs. Ackworth.

"Pooh, with an architect you have to spend even more time on your building scheme, or you will find yourself a good deal the poorer and with another house that no one would want to live in, turrets sprouting here, inconvenient kitchens there. That would not be Rutherford's way; what he does, he will keep under his direction. No, no, the house will moulder on, until one dark night a wind will blow the roof off or the chimneys away." He laughed heartily. "Probably bearing Lady Rutherford off with it; she would be perfectly happy to wake up and find herself lodged in a tree with some great owl hooting at her. She is like an owl herself with those immense eyes."

"Lady Rutherford always makes Mr. Ackworth feel uneasy," Mrs. Ackworth explained later as she and Octavia sat in the cosy drawing room, warm from the logs burning in the grate; Mr. Ackworth had stayed in the dining room to drink his port and read a book.

"The eyes *are* remarkable," said Octavia. "And her daughter has them, too."

"So does Lord Rutherford," said Mrs. Ackworth. "Only his are a darker blue, and he does not share his mother's temperament; in him, the eyes are formidable, a hawk rather than an owl."

"Why has Lady Sophronia never married?"

"She did a season or two in London, when she was a girl, but for some reason or other, did not marry. Rumour has it that she received one or two very good offers, for the Rutherfords, you know, may marry as high as they choose. But she did not choose, and now that she is the wrong side of thirty, it is unlikely that she will marry, despite having a handsome fortune."

"There are no other brothers or sisters?"

"No, just the two of them. People say that Rutherford must marry and get an heir; every season the mamas are agog with hope that he will cast his eye in the direction of one of the debutantes, but they are too young for a man of his age, he is the same age as Lady Sophronia, of course, and by the time a man has got to that age, you know, he is used to not having a wife."

"Lady Rutherford would have something to say if he cast his handkerchief in the direction of any woman," said Mr. Ackworth as he came into the room and stood before the fireplace, holding his hands to the flames. "She would not like to be the Dowager Countess, not at all. She has her vanities, for all her head is full of owls and Romans and those animals she has wandering about the house."

"Animals?" said Octavia.

"Animals everywhere," said Mr. Ackworth. "Dogs and cats are nothing to her, no, she must have a tame pig and a sheep and rabbits hopping here and there, and parrots screeching from the rafters."

"That is true, but she certainly has a knack with the creatures," said Mrs. Ackworth. "And you cannot criticise her way with horses."

"No, no. She breeds Arabians," Mr. Ackworth said to Octavia. "Best in the country, I give you that."

"Do not be standing there like that," said Mrs. Ackworth, "you are taking all the heat from Octavia, and she will feel the cold, coming from India, show some compassion."

Chapter Eleven

The moon was full, the weather had turned mild, and Octavia was invited with her cousins to dine with the Gouldings at Haye Park.

Mr. Ackworth was not a great diner-out, he claimed. "It takes away useful time when I could be gainfully employed on the farm or doing my accounts, instead of putting the horses to and driving for an hour or more in the carriage and then being obliged to sit on uncomfortable chairs and spend an afternoon and evening in the company of a great many people who have nothing new to say to one another. And I do not know why the Gouldings are not in town, for," he said to Octavia, "they are fashionable people, not at all like us. Surely that daughter of theirs, what is her name?"

"Charlotte, as you very well know," murmured his wife, adjusting the straps on the window of the coach.

"Charlotte, yes. Charlotte was to make her come-out, we heard all about the ball they were to give in their London house."

"You know perfectly well that they postponed Charlotte's London season for a year, after she was so ill with the chicken pox. She had it just before Christmas and it left her not in her best looks, and very tired," Mrs. Ackworth explained to Octavia. "Lady Goulding is a sensible woman. Charlotte is still very young and a London season is strenuous, even when a girl is completely well."

"They could have left her at Haye Park and gone to London.

Goulding should be there, he is an MP, he has no business being in Hertfordshire and dragging his neighbours out to dine."

"It is all humbug," Mrs. Ackworth said to Octavia. "You will see when we are there how much he enjoys being in company. And it will be the very thing for you. Mrs. Goulding keeps an excellent table, they have a French chef, and there are always a lively party of younger people invited, for Charlotte and her brothers."

Haye Park was an imposing, modern house built in the reign of George II, set in a well-landscaped park. Lady Goulding came out to greet them, a tall, kindly looking woman with fine, aristocratic features who was dressed in a most elegant gown of ruched green silk. Sir Joseph Goulding was a rubicund man in a dark blue coat, half a head shorter than his wife, with a cheerful expression and a ready laugh.

Charlotte Goulding might be pulled after her bout of chicken pox, but, Octavia said to herself, if this was how she appeared when not in looks, she must be an out-and-out beauty when she was quite well. She had a rare perfection of feature, and a tall slender figure, like her mother. She was dressed with charming simplicity in a yellow muslin gown with delicate roses on the flounces, a dress that suited her to perfection. Lady Goulding obviously had excellent taste.

Seeing the very evident affection her parents showed Charlotte, Octavia wondered if they were altogether sorry to have postponed their daughter's come-out. They might prefer to have her at home for a little longer, for, with what her cousins had said was a good fortune, she would surely be snapped up the moment she made her appearance in London, and her loving parents would in no time be waving her off from the church door on the arm of some eligible young man.

"Now, here is someone who is very anxious to meet you," said Lady Goulding, taking Octavia's arm. "How tall you are, we are used to think of Charlotte as a tall girl, but . . ." Her voice tailed away as she caught her words, fearing she might be suspected of a criticism.

"Miss Goulding is a perfect height, ma'am," said Octavia at once. "I find my own inches a sad trial, but your daughter's height suits her very well."

A lively looking young woman dressed in a dashing bronze gown was coming towards them, her face alight with smiles. She was pregnant, Octavia noticed, as the woman held out her hand in the friendliest way. "I have so looked forward to our meeting, I was delighted when Lady Goulding told me you were dining here tonight. Oh, don't look so startled, we have never met, that is what you are wondering, is it not? I am a Darcy, by birth, that is, I was Camilla Darcy, although I am now Mrs. Wytton—that is Mr. Wytton over there, casting admiring glances at Charlotte"—turning to Lady Goulding—"how well she looks, Lady Goulding, she will be a wild success when you take her to London, all the men will be sighing over her beauty."

Lady Goulding moved away, leaving Octavia with Camilla. "So you see, we are cousins by marriage. What a shocking thing to happen to Christopher; I have the fondest memories of him, he was a most amiable man, and I am sure you must miss him so much. Alexander," she called to her husband, "come over here, I want to introduce you to Mrs. Darcy, Captain Darcy's wife."

Alexander Wytton, a tall man with a handsome face and a pair of intelligent dark eyes, came over to his wife's side. He pulled out a chair. "I beg you will sit, Camilla, you must take care of yourself." He bowed over Octavia's hand. "I am honoured to make your acquaintance, Mrs. Darcy."

"Oh, that is all nonsense," said Camilla, but she accepted the chair. "I am breeding, as you can see," she said, giving her stomach a pat.

"Camilla!" said Alexander.

"Oh, don't be stuffy," said Camilla. "He is anxious as an old hen," she went on. "Now, don't give me one of your looks, Alexander, my dear. Since Mrs. Darcy—may I call you Octavia?—is kin, I may say what I like. And here comes the Gouldings' butler, who always makes me laugh, he is such a cadaverous individual, you would think he was going to announce the last trump, not dinner. Now, let Alexander take you in, and I shall sit near you, because I want to hear all about you."

Octavia was happy enough to sit next to Alexander, finding him to have a keen mind and a witty way with words. On her other side was a tall clergyman whom Lady Goulding had introduced her to earlier on, a Mr. Henry Poyntz, not the incumbent of the parish here, but the son of an old friend of Sir Joseph Goulding's. He and Camilla were clearly good friends, and their corner of the table was very lively, causing Charlotte to turn her lovely eyes in their direction, with some astonishment, and Sir Joseph to call down the table to them to keep up their high spirits, he liked nothing better at his table than the sound of people enjoying themselves. "And try the saddle of lamb, Wytton," he added, "I swear you will never have tasted a more tender joint."

So it was not until after the meal was over, and Lady Goulding had led the women from the table to amuse themselves in the drawing room, leaving the men to their port, that Camilla began her interrogation of Octavia.

"You are staying with your sister, are you not? Mrs. Cartland. Mrs. Cartland and I do not get on, she considers me fast. And I most heartily pity that girl of hers, what is her name?"

"Penelope," said Octavia.

"Yes, she takes after her father, who is an amiable man, but weak. Is Miss Cartland weak? I suspect she has something of her mother's strength of character."

Octavia laughed. "You seem to know them well."

"I do not move in that set," Camilla said frankly. "And if Alexander were here, he would wag his finger at me for abusing your relatives."

"One cannot choose one's family," Octavia said. "Theodosia and I have never been close, although," she added politely but without conviction, "I am sure she has always had my best interests at heart."

"Oh, as to that, let us not bite our tongues. She packed you off to India, did not she? And although it was a lucky circumstance, for you met Christopher, I cannot think it kind in your family to do that. You had only had one London season, I believe?"

"Yes, but I did not take, and clearly never would take, and

although they prize the Melbury name, my lack of fortune meant it was highly unlikely that I would find myself a husband."

"That is all in the past, and there is no need to remember those days at all. I hope that the time you had with Christopher was a happy one, that leaves you with good memories."

"It does indeed," said Octavia, furious with herself to find tears prickling her eyes.

Camilla thrust a wisp of lacy handkerchief into her hand. "I am sorry, Alexander would be right to rebuke me, here you are still in mourning, and I am insensitive."

"Not at all," said Octavia, giving her eyes a token dab before handing the handkerchief back. "It was just for a moment—you are very kind."

"And you aren't used to kindness, not at Lothian Street, I'll be bound."

"Everyone was very kind in India, and a naval officer, you know, always is part of a wider network of friends—it is in a way almost another family. I met with nothing but kindness from anyone associated with the service."

"That is quite as it should be, but tell me, what are your plans?"

For a moment, Octavia was tempted to tell Camilla of her inheritance, but no, this was neither the place nor the time. She had kept it to herself thus far, she would wait a little longer.

"I hope to spend a little while longer here in the country while I am still in mourning—"

"Forgive me," Camilla interrupted, "but I would not set you down as a country girl."

"No, indeed, I am quite sure after helping my cousin at the manor that such a life would not suit me at all. I prefer town life."

"Only town life is expensive," said Camilla. "Is George Warren going to do the decent thing and provide you with an annuity?"

"I do not think George Warren is the kind of man who would willingly part with any money, let alone with a regular drain on his purse such as an annuity would be," said Octavia drily.

"Ah, you have made his acquaintance, I see. Well, I think it a very shocking thing if he does not. I shall ask my papa whether he can bring his influence to bear; my papa has no opinion of Mr. Warren at all, I may tell you."

"My brother has approached him," Octavia said, the indignation she still felt showing through, "even though I expressly asked him not to."

"Oh, Arthur Melbury is the kind of man who will always do what he thinks is right, regardless of the trouble or inconvenience it may cause. But without money, with such a very small income, how will you manage?"

Octavia found herself blushing.

"I have some plans," she said, knowing how lame it sounded.

Camilla gave her a shrewd look. "In another woman, I would say there was a man in this, but with you—no, it is too soon for you to be interested in men."

"Everyone says I will marry again," said Octavia with some heat. "However, you may believe me when I tell you I have no wish to find myself a second husband. I was happy with Christopher, very happy; I might not have the luck a second time to marry another such a one."

"Yes, clever, amusing, kind men do not grow on trees," said Camilla. "I count myself fortunate indeed to be married to one myself, but there are not, as you say, so many of them, not enough to go round, in fact, which accounts for some of the dreadful husbands one meets."

The gentlemen came in soon after, and Octavia was touched to see how Alexander at once made his way to the sofa where Camilla was sitting.

"Alexander, you must mingle," said Camilla, with a merry smile. "It is quite Gothic, you know, to want to sit and talk to your wife."

"Oh, hang that," said Alexander. "Besides, why should I not talk to Octavia? It is not every day one acquires a charming new member of the family."

"I am talking to Octavia," said Camilla. "You may go and flirt with Charlotte."

Alexander cast the daughter of the house a quick glance. "Not to my taste," he said in a low voice, taking his place between Octavia and Camilla on the sofa. "She is a pretty enough girl, but—"

"Pretty enough!" cried Camilla. "Alexander, have you eyes in your head? You will not find a more beautiful girl anywhere."

Charlotte was smiling up at Mr. Poyntz, and wrinkling her brow at some droll remark he had made.

"You see, she does not have any great degree of understanding," said Alexander. "There's Poyntz, as amusing a man as ever lived, and she does not know what to make of him; there, she looks to her mother, to see if she should laugh or turn the jest off, she works her fan. She is well enough, but I am happy with my company here."

Camilla was watching Charlotte with a little frown. "Lady Goulding does not like to see Mr. Poyntz paying Charlotte so much attention. That's a match that wouldn't do."

"Oh, a man only has to smile at a pretty girl—all right, Camilla, at a beauty—and all her acquaintance have them married. Poyntz's tastes don't lie in that direction, he will prefer a woman with some thoughts in her head."

Camilla said, in a confidential way, "The Gouldings hope that Charlotte will make a match with Sholto Rutherford."

Alexander let out a crack of laughter, earning himself a look of rebuke from Camilla.

"Rutherford has far too much sense to fall for a dewy young creature like that."

"She would make an excellent countess," said Camilla.

"Oh, she would look the part, I grant you, but there is more to being the wife of a man like Rutherford than merely looking the part. Can you see Charlotte as a political hostess, and can you imagine Rutherford having a wife who could not play that role? Far more important than the title are his political ambitions. Charlotte is shy, however much her mama and governess's careful training have hidden it. It appears as a pleasing modesty, but it is deep seated, and it is not something that will easily be changed."

"A season in London, some polish, and she will be much more assured," said Camilla.

"For many young women, that would be true, but I think it is an essential part of her nature and will not change. She would find the demands of the kind of life Sholto leads quite insupportable. If she married such a man, she would retreat, under pretence of ailments or breeding, to the country, and join him in London as seldom as possible. No, no, it would not do. Besides," he added, "Rutherford shows no more sign of hanging out for a wife than he ever did, which is to say, not at all."

Octavia was smiling. "Now tell me, Mrs. Darcy, what amuses you?" said Alexander.

"It is just that on all hands I hear people discussing Lord Rutherford and whether he will or will not marry."

"Oh, there's always gossip about Sholto," said Alexander. "Much he cares. At the start of every season, the question is, will Rutherford bestow his hand, his title, and his immense fortune on some lucky damsel? And the answer these many years has been that he won't. And I think the matchmaking mamas should watch what they wish for, at least those who care for their daughters should."

"Alexander, what are you saying?" exclaimed Camilla. "Lord Rutherford is no ogre."

"No, but he's got a devilish sharp tongue, and I never knew a man who suffered fools less gladly. Life with Rutherford would be lively, I grant you, but with a woman who could not stand up to him, was not nearly his equal in quickness of mind and wit—well, it could be a very unhappy household and a poor life for the unfortunate woman. Charlotte would be eaten alive, and there'd be nothing left for her but the vapours."

"You are severe on Lord Rutherford," said Octavia.

"Oh, I say nothing behind his back that I would not say to his face. He is the best of fellows. We are related, through my mother's side of the family, and I have known him all my life. He is excellent company—for me, and for Camilla, but not for a Charlotte."

"And he is a man who doesn't like to settle for second best," said

Camilla. "He would not want an unequal match, he would expect any marriage he made to be a source of pleasure—no, don't look at me like that, Alexander. Sholto would want to take pleasure in his wife's company, to find that his life was enhanced by the married state. That is a high ideal for a state that, although the lot of most of us, often falls short of what might be wished for."

"Oho," said Alexander. "Now we hear some news."

"I do not speak of us, wretch," said Camilla, laughing. "I think Rutherford is such a man. There, that is all I have to say on the matter. Now, Octavia, this is very dull, for I do not believe you have met his lordship. Tell me about your family, for although we are kin, I know next to nothing about you."

Tea was brought in, carriages were called for, Sir Joseph bustled around his parting guests, assuring them that it was a fine night, no hint of frost, with the moon shining clear and bright in a cloudless sky.

"Very pleasant weather for the time of year," he added. "Positively balmy, with just the hint of a breeze."

"Goulding's breeze is a stiff southerly," said Mr. Ackworth, once he and his wife and Octavia were seated in the carriage, and bowling down the long drive of Haye Park, the full moon glinting between the leaves of the oak trees set along the drive.

Mrs. Ackworth was concerned that Octavia was not warm enough. "Put this sheepskin across your knees. Sir Joseph may say it is balmy, and it is mild for the time of year, but you, used as you are to the extreme heat of the East, you will be glad of a sheepskin."

Octavia sat back, marvelling at how the brilliance of the moonlight drained the countryside of colour.

Mr. Ackworth sniffed, leant forward, and let the window down, despite the outraged protests of his wife. "Hugh, what are you thinking of, put that glass up directly, we will all catch our death of cold." He took no notice, instead leaning his head further out of the window before turning back into the carriage and saying, "Can you not smell it?"

"It is smoke," said Octavia.

"A chimney has caught fire, that is all," said Mrs. Ackworth. "Do shut that window, Hugh." At that moment, the carriage rounded a bend and a gust of acrid-smelling smoke came into the carriage. Now Mrs. Ackworth was looking alarmed. "That is more than a chimney, my dear, can they be burning ricks?"

"More than a rick," said Mr. Ackworth grimly, and putting his head out of the window once more, he called to the coachman to stop.

The coachman drew up, and Mr. Ackworth leapt down to the lane. Octavia heard the coachman say, "Looks like Chauntry's on fire, sir. That's a fair old blaze, and no mistake. Shall I go back and take the Leythorpe road, it's a long way round, but—"

"Good God, no," said Mr. Ackworth. "Drive on, we must see if we can help." He jumped back in, the coachman whipped up his horses, fretful now with the smoke in their nostrils, and pressed on.

Octavia was peering out of the window; the coachman was right, below them was the shadowy outline of Chauntry, its chimneys stark against the moon, and clouds of dark smoke billowed from several of the windows.

"The west wing is on fire," muttered Mr. Ackworth. "Not ablaze yet, but it soon will be!"

"Dear God," said Mrs. Ackworth, "let us pray that Lady Rutherford and Sophronia and all the servants were wakened in time."

"It looks to me as though most of the household is out on the lawn," said Mr. Ackworth. "I reckon it's been burning for quite a while." The carriage turned in through the gates and rattled up the drive, until the coachman brought it to a halt, calling down that he couldn't trust the horses any nearer.

The poor animals were in a lather, and the coachman jumped down and went to their heads, patting them and calming them as they rolled frightened eyes and moved restlessly in their traces.

"Take them over to that tree," said Mr. Ackworth. "And turn the carriage so that it faces the other way. They will be upwind of the smoke there, they will be less distressed."

Mrs. Ackworth was down on the grass. "Let John Coachman go with you, Hugh," she said. "Octavia and I will hold the horses." She spoke soothingly to the horses and stroked the nose of the offside one, telling him not to be such a booby.

"If you can manage them," said Octavia, looking after Mr. Ackworth and the coachman, who were running towards the house, "perhaps I can go with them, there might be something I can do."

"Yes, yes, you go," said Mrs. Ackworth. "The horses know me, they will be all right."

Octavia gathered up her skirts and set off at a run.

"And tell Lady Rutherford and Sophronia that there is a bed for them at the manor," Mrs. Ackworth called after her. "They cannot stay here unless the fire is swiftly extinguished."

"And there seems little hope of that," said Octavia, holding her skirts in one hand as she plunged down a bank and came level with the house.

It was an extraordinary scene. The area just beyond the great gateway was strewn with furniture and carpets and pictures, and more things were being carried out of the house in a steady stream. A tall figure was calling out commands and advice in a loud, unpanicked voice; Lord Rutherford—how must he feel, to see his home burn?

Octavia looked about her to see what she could do. A capable-looking woman was tending to a man sitting on the ground, who seemed to have sustained a blow to his head; she was stanching the blood from a cut and issuing brisk orders to a couple of scared-looking maids. Clearly any necessary womanly succouring was well in hand; Octavia had the use of her limbs, she would help in another way.

She saw Lady Sophronia, dragging out a wicker basket, and ran over to her. "Rescuing the puppies," said Lady Sophronia, coughing furiously. "The bitch just whelped, couldn't leave them in there."

"Is everyone out? How is your mother?"

"At the moment it is the west wing that is on fire, and Sholto fears the whole house will go up, although there is a chain of men with buckets from the river, and there is a pump round at the back—it will not do, the fire has too strong a hold."

Octavia headed for the front door in the central part of the house and went in, holding her skirt over her mouth and nose. The smell of smoke was strong in the air and she could see sparks and hear the ominous crackling of flames. Servants were throwing down all manner of things from the upper landings, tapestries and more pictures, and to the left, an anguished-looking man in clerical dress with a black smudge on his nose was hurrying to and fro with armfuls of books.

Tapestries she could not help with, but she could carry books. She followed the clergyman into what turned out to be the library, a room shelved from floor to ceiling, complete with disdainful-looking Romans and other worthies looking down from their pedestals.

"Which ones first?" she demanded.

"The ones at the far end, those nearer the door may all be replaced, oh, dear, I do not know—"

Octavia didn't wait for him to finish his sentence, but went rapidly to the shelves at the far end and pulled down an armful of books. Out through the hall and down the steps—where were they putting the books?

"Over there, over there," a smoke-smudged man in footman's livery shouted to her.

A carpet had been spread at some distance from the house, and the volumes were piling up on it.

It was on her third trip that Octavia, head down, a wet rag now wrapped around her face, intent on her purpose, ran smack into Lord Rutherford, who seized her roughly by her arm.

"Who the devil are you? What do you think you are doing? Are you mad?"

"The fire is not yet in this part of the house," she said, breaking free. "You should be grateful for another pair of hands."

"But—" And she was gone, back towards the house. Coughing

from the smoke, terrified by the growing proximity of the flames, Octavia nonetheless felt more alive than she had done in her life. She was not at all chastened by Lord Rutherford's outburst, dismissing him as merely another man who assumed that women were frail creatures, fit for nothing but to watch and be fearful.

Chapter Twelve

What the devil was that woman doing?

Sholto's mind had little room for exasperation or anything beyond watching the steadily increasing flames; trying to keep the more dim-witted of the servants from panicking, running into each other, or dashing into the smoke after some forgotten item; and directing the removal of the more valuable items from the house. Yet, in the midst of the turmoil and the smoke, there was room for annoyance that to add to his concerns, here was some woman heaving books around, damn it, she was as bad as Sophronia, who paid no attention at all to his commands to go away, far out of reach of the fire, and take care of her mother.

"Mama is very well able to take care of herself," Sophronia retorted. "She has her menagerie out of the house and is tending to them, the horses are all safe, and she doesn't give a button about anything else." With which she darted off to help an elderly footman, staggering under the weight of a hideous epergne.

"Pollet, you should have left that to melt," he heard her say. "It is a hideous thing, now go over there and let Mrs. Glimmit see to your arm, which is burnt."

And now this tall woman, in evening dress, forsooth, a complete stranger, was heading back towards the house.

"Stop!" he cried, aware that his voice was growing hoarse; in any case, she appeared not to hear, instead plunging in through the door; how he hated a mannish woman.

His mother's butler was at his side. "My lord, the roof has gone on the east wing, I fear there is little more we can do."

And then Sholto had no time for anything else but driving the servants and helpers away from the house—for people had come hurrying up from the village as the flames soared into the sky—commanding everyone to stand back, to get well away. He ran back into the hall, calling out, just as that woman appeared again, her face sooty, clutching a large tome.

"For God's sake, put that down and run," he said, taking three swift steps forward and attempting to take the book from her.

"No, I can manage," she said, but without further ado, he swept her up, over his shoulder like a large bolster, and carried her out of the house, dumping her unceremoniously on the grass in front of Sophronia.

She was flushed and indignant, and, superbly unaware of the smuts on her face, she gave him a contemptuous look.

"I never saw such foolhardy stupidity," he began.

"I think intrepidity is the word you mean," said Sophronia, still as calm as though her house burning down were an everyday occurrence. "What book have you gone to such lengths to rescue?" she asked Octavia.

"A first folio of Shakespeare," said Octavia, overcome with a fit of coughing. "It would be a tragedy were it to have been burnt."

"Not so much of a tragedy as if you had gone up in flames," said Sholto, then turned as a shout went up, and with a roar and a dreadful rumbling, the roof of the main part of the house caved in in a shower of flames and sparks, and the fire, unquenchable, spread with terrible rapidity.

Sholto stood, hands on his hips, his face impassive as he watched the flames engulf his house.

"It was a chimney that caught fire," Sophronia said calmly. "It was bound to happen."

Sholto moved towards her and put an arm around her. "It is more your home than mine, do you care very much?"

"Not at all," she said as he looked down at her with a glinting smile. "My eyes are red from the smoke, not from any sadness. It was a terrible old house. I am sorry that you have lost so many of your possessions, but then you have plenty more, do you not? And I think you owe Mrs. Darcy here an apology."

The tall woman was standing very straight, staring at the blazing house, and it wasn't smoke that was causing tears to cut a channel through her dirty cheeks.

"Why on earth are you weeping?" Sholto said.

"To see a house that has survived so long destroyed like this. Only think of the people who built it, men in ruffs and doublet and hose, women in farthingales, and then all through two or three long centuries, the men and women and children who made their lives here—"

"Sheer sentimentality," he said. "It is—was—my house, and you don't see tears pouring down my face. It was inconvenient, and beyond repair, and although I would rather it had been demolished brick by brick, which would be of some use for the future, this fire has saved me a heap of trouble."

"You have no imagination, brother," said Sophronia. "Mrs. Darcy, I think your cousin is looking for you."

"Thank God, there you are, Octavia," exclaimed Mr. Ackworth, who came up to her. He was in even a worse state than she was, in his shirtsleeves and with a livid mark on his cheek. "Good evening, Rutherford. I am deeply sorry to see Chauntry burn. Octavia, what have you been doing? I left you with Jane to mind the horses, and they tell me you have been running in and out rescuing books from the library—what folly."

"Folly indeed," said Rutherford furiously. "She could have been killed."

"But as it happens," said Octavia, rubbing her cheeks with the back of her hand, and laughing, "I was not. I am perfectly all right, and I am glad I brought out the books, I do not care to see books burn."

"Lady Sophronia, if there is anything we can do, my wife says that of course you must come to the manor . . ."

"My mother and sister will come back to London with me, Ackworth," said Sholto.

"Good," said Sophronia. "I shall enjoy that." She held out a hand to Octavia. "Thank you. I hope we meet again in happier circumstances."

Sholto watched as Ackworth hurried the tall woman away. "Who exactly is she?" he demanded of Sophronia.

"She is a cousin of the Ackworths, a widow, a Mrs. Darcy."

"Oh, she's the second Mrs. Darcy, is she? Melbury's sister. I hate an interfering woman, what business was it of hers what became of my books?"

"How ungenerous you are, Sholto. We women are not so helpless as you men would have us believe. I for one am grateful to her, and I think she showed great good sense in helping Mr. Newsome bring books out; she was giving him directions most competently, and I dare say saved his life, making him attend and set to going to and fro with the more valuable folios instead of standing in the library wringing his hands until he went up in smoke."

"What nonsense. Go and find Mama."

"It will take her a while to arrange what is to be done with all her animals. I am sure you will not mind if she brings one or two with her to London."

"I do mind. Oh, very well, if it keeps her quiet she may bring one or two of her dogs, but not that damned parrot. I will not have that parrot in my house. The horses are being stabled in the village, the grooms may take care of her zoo."

Some two hours later, when the moon was setting in the eastern sky, Sholto set off for London, his mother fast asleep in the corner of the carriage, snoring gently, his sister looking out of the window as though she were off on a pleasure outing. In the other corner, a large parrot gave a dismal squawk, and ruffled its bright green plumage.

Chapter Thirteen

Octavia slept late, and woke to find the day well advanced. "Mrs. Ackworth is in the breakfast parlour," said the maid who came in with the water.

"Good heavens," said Octavia, jumping out of bed. "What time is it?"

"Past ten o'clock."

A mere quarter of an hour later, Octavia was downstairs. Jane was sitting at the breakfast table, reading a letter.

"How long have you been up?" Octavia asked her.

"Oh, I rose at my usual time; despite all the excitement of last night, my duties are still to be done."

"You should have sent a servant to wake me."

"Not at all. For I merely had a late night, and some excitement, whereas you had an exhausting one, being in the thick of it. I am afraid your dress is ruined, quite beyond any mending or cleaning."

"I thought it would be so," said Octavia, longing for the coffee she could smell.

"They have made a fresh pot for you," said Mrs. Ackworth.

"And Mr. Ackworth is also up, I am sure."

"He does not need a great deal of sleep. He rode over to Chauntry first thing to see if there was anything he can do to help. Some of Rutherford's horses are to come here until he can make arrangements for them. I am thankful to say that they were all got out safely, horses panic most dreadfully in the face of fire, you know, and it can be impossible to get them to safety, but Rutherford's grooms all know what they are about."

"Lady Sophronia said she was glad to be going to London."

"I expect she is. She loves London, and it is only her sense of duty that has kept her at Chauntry, to take care of her mama. Although I am not sure that she needs to. Lady Rutherford is a great deal more capable than she appears, and I believe she would hardly notice if her daughter were not there. I cannot imagine what Rutherford will do with Lady Rutherford, send her to Yorkshire, perhaps, if she will consent to go, for it will be impossible for her to stay in London. They cannot live under the same roof, they will do nothing but argue. She irritates him intensely, and I believe she takes a delight in doing so."

Octavia thought about this as she ate her toast. They seemed an extraordinary family, but then, were not all families extraordinary? She was no judge; never having had what she could call a normal family life, she was in no position to ascertain if Lord Rutherford and his sister and mother were quite in the usual run of family relationships, just one of many patterns which worked more or less, but which were only comprehensible to those within the family circle.

"I cannot really say what is what, even within my own family," she said to her cousin. "For as you know, they are only half my family, as it were, and I grew up apart with them. I stay with them as a guest, or as a poor relation, and I may guess how things are, but that is all it is, guesswork."

"It is a shame you never knew your mother, no, nor your father, him dying when you were still a child."

Sir Clement Melbury had been Mrs. Ackworth's first cousin. "I knew him well," she said. "My father was the younger son of old Sir Arthur Melbury, your grandfather, and he was Vicar of Melbury. So we were close neighbours, and although Clement was much older than me—he was at Cambridge when I was learning my letters—I counted myself his friend. As I grew older, he would pull my pigtails and tell me terrible stories, and then, when I went to London, he looked out for me in a most brotherly fashion; I had no brothers of my own, we were a family of five girls."

Her voice grew quieter, and Octavia could see that she was looking back into the past.

"I was in love with him," she said in a matter-of-fact way. "Despite the disparity in our ages; of course that counts for little in affairs of the heart, and I always preferred men who were older than me."

"Was he in love with you?" Octavia ventured to ask.

"It would never have done," Mrs. Ackworth went on, still in the same reflective voice. "Not that it came to that. I believe he was growing fond of me, but I was never a beauty, you know. I had my admirers, but I was never anything out of the ordinary. And then Clement met Miss Valeria Smith, and that was that."

"He married her, and had all those children, my brothers, half brothers, I should say, and half sisters."

"They call you sister, and you are very insistent on these *halves*. But they have not treated you well. I dare say that you blame your father, thinking that they are his children, that he was as cold and heartless as they often appear to be—"

"What they have done for me, they did from duty, not affection."

"It is easy enough to neglect duty, although I admit the lack of affection. It was Valeria who made them the way they are, since by some freak of nature, they all turned out to take after her, and not your father. Although there are traces of Clement in Sir James, for your father was at heart a country man. He loved Melbury Hall, and hunting and shooting and looking after the land, he was never happier than when he was on the back of one of his rangy hunters, for he rode nearly eighteen stone, you know."

"Yes, I remember him as a big man."

"Valeria, on the other hand, was a townee through and through. She loved London, and detested the country. She didn't pine or mope when she had to be at Melbury, for Valeria wasn't ever one to do anything so weak, but she complained, and made life unpleasant for herself, and even before she died, she and your father were spending much of the year apart. She caught a cold, you know, which I always hold was entirely her fault, going out in April on a bitterly cold night—the weather was unusually harsh that year—clad in a light gown, with no proper warmth about her. She was fashionable, you see, and would not dream of being seen in anything so unmodish as a wrap or a pelisse, not in April. The cold went to her lungs and a week later, she was gone."

"Poor woman," said Octavia. "Leaving such a brood."

"Indeed, but the girls had an excellent governess, and by that time the boys were away at school, in Arthur's case, and James was sowing his wild oats—a lot of wild oats—in Oxford."

"Then a few years later, my father met my mother—"

"Another lovely woman, and fell in love all over again," Mrs. Ackworth finished for her. "Of course her dying when you were born was another tragedy for Sir Clement; I am pleased he found some degree of happiness, however, with the third Lady Melbury. She was kind to you, was she not? She brought you up with never a murmur, although of course there was no real obligation upon her to do so."

"She was one of those women who didn't ever seem to be entirely present," said Octavia dispassionately. "Nothing made her angry or happy, she seemed to mind about nothing very much."

"Oh, what a happy disposition," said Mrs. Ackworth, getting up from the table.

"Did you ever meet my mother?" Octavia asked, as she followed her cousin out of the room.

"I did, on the occasion of her marriage. For your papa asked me to be there; none of his children would attend, and he said, a little wistfully, I remember, that he would like to have at least one member of his family present. So I went for the ceremony, and saw them off at the church door, and very happy and pleased he looked, but I never saw her again. Within the year you were born and she was gone."

Mrs. Ackworth was walking briskly towards the herb room, where, in keeping with an earlier age, she dried and preserved the many fragrant products of her garden. "Does it distress you, to talk of your mother?"

"Not in the least. Since I never knew her, I am curious, but I can have no feeling for her." Octavia sniffed the aromatic air appreciatively, as her cousin opened the door to the herb room.

"It is old-fashioned of me to keep up the herb garden, I know, but I was brought up to do it," said Mrs. Ackworth. "My mother's herb garden was famous throughout Somerset, and I like to keep up the tradition, for all you can buy everything now in a shop."

Octavia sank her fingers into a pile of rose petals that Mrs. Ackworth had tipped on to the well-scrubbed table which ran down the centre of the room. Above their heads bunches of herbs and dried flowers hung from metal rails.

"I need to make pot-pourri, the bowl in the drawing room has quite lost its scent, and although I can refresh it, I will put that upstairs and put a new bowl in there."

Octavia let the dried petals slip through her fingers, admiring the shades of pink and blush white and deepest red.

"I know next to nothing about my mother's family. I was brought to realise that recently, when—when I met someone who had known my grandfather."

"There was no one to tell you about them, of course. Your grandparents were long gone, your mother an only child. It is a shame you have no connections on that side of your family."

"Not a shame as far as Augusta and Arthur and Theodosia are concerned!" said Octavia. "They see me tarnished by my low origin. When I first went to London, Arthur informed me, in the most serious tones, that my grandfather was a grocer. Even then it made me want to laugh, to hear him talking as though my grandpapa had been in the pay of Satan, as though there was no more terrible thing to be than a shopkeeper. I have no objection to grocers, where would we be without them?"

"Yes, your grandfather was indeed a grocer, Clement told me. He was in a good line of business, more than a humble shopkeeper. It was in Leeds or York, or one of those northern towns. But he speculated, on one thing and another, and I believe he lost most of his fortune on the stock exchange during the first French war, when everything was so uncertain. He certainly lost a good deal more than he could afford, and the business began to suffer. Your mother said that he died a poor man, a disappointed man."

She took out a little glass vial and removed the stopper, releasing a rich scent. "This is the essence of rose, an oil that I put in the pot-pourri," she told Octavia, adding two drops. "Stir it in with your hands for me."

Octavia did as she was bid, swirling the petals into an aromatic cloud.

"Now I need to add orris root, lavender, some orange peel and cinnamon bark," said Mrs. Ackworth, suiting the action to the words. "I am proud of my pot-pourri, I make it to a mixture handed down from my great-grandmother. Who was your great-great-grandmother, of course. I shall give you the receipt."

"I should like that," said Octavia. She raised a handful to her nose and took a deep, appreciative sniff. "Although I don't think I am likely ever to have a herb garden, I fear I do not take after my father in that. Like Valeria, I prefer town life."

"So you think, but I assure you a busy life in the country is the happiest one for most women. When—that is, should you marry again, you may well find yourself with a house and a garden and poultry yard, and then you will gather your own rosebuds and make your own pot-pourri."

For a moment Octavia's fancy was caught by this picture, an image of tranquillity and restfulness.

"Only I do not think I am a very restful person," she said. "I think I would startle the hens and alarm the pigs and send all the bees buzzing away, and the milk would curdle, and everything would be ahoo."

"How ridiculous you are," said Mrs. Ackworth, laughing. And she added, without a hint of reproof but with a world of warning in her words, "Of course if you do go to your sister in Yorkshire, she will keep you so busy in the house and with the children that I dare say you would never set foot out of doors."

Octavia's conscience attacked her again. Here was Mrs. Ackworth, and Mr. Ackworth, so concerned for her future, and she still could not bring herself to tell them that she had other plans, and plans that were perfectly possible, indeed which were certain to be fulfilled. Why was she so intent on reticence, why did she have this urge to keep it all secret? The Ackworths were not like the Melburys, who would at once leap in and interfere. Nevertheless, she was not going to confide in them. Once the news was out, her life would be so much more complicated. For the moment, she would simply cherish the peace of being in this manor house, and let the future see to the revelations and reactions that must come.

"You are a good creature," said Mrs. Ackworth. "I will say that for you, if you will take the compliment. I know that you grieve for Mr. Darcy, and you face a very uncertain future, but you keep always in a good humour, and it is remarkable that you are able to laugh at your brothers and sisters, not merely condemn them, which, were I in your shoes, I would certainly be tempted to do."

"It is not because I have a sweet nature, I assure you," said Octavia, taking the great silver bowl from Mrs. Ackworth, now filled with pot-pourri.

"Let me take that," said Mrs. Ackworth, as Octavia gave an involuntary wince. "You hurt your arm last night, I knew it, I saw you in the carriage, holding it, for all you denied that it gave you pain."

"It does hurt a little," admitted Octavia, relinquishing the bowl. "It is bruised, or a slight sprain. No kind of burn, merely that some of the books were very heavy."

"And did you get any thanks for your efforts from Lord Rutherford? I saw him talking to you when you were standing with Sophronia."

"On the contrary," said Octavia, laughing. "He was extremely rude and not at all grateful. He disapproves of females acting in such an unseemly way, and no doubt would rather have lost a quarter of his library than have my assistance. Men are so foolish."

"Lord Rutherford is not one to mince his words, although he can be as gallant and charming as any man when he chooses. It is only that he does not choose very often."

"Last night was a trial to test any man's temper," said Octavia.

"For all he said the fire had saved him a deal of trouble, I imagine he must have been greatly alarmed and shocked."

"I wonder if he will build new," said Mrs. Ackworth. "It is all the rage, these days, building houses, so perhaps he will. If only to provide a house for his mother, in which he does not have to live himself."

It was a week after this that Mr. Ackworth joined the ladies in the dining room for a cold nuncheon. "I am delighted to see you," said Mrs. Ackworth, surprised, for Mr. Ackworth rarely stopped to take any refreshment in the middle of the day.

"Ha," he said, carving a slice of ham and offering it to Octavia—"Our own ham, you will find it very good"—before piling several more slices on to his own plate. "Mr. Bennet called today. He is a neighbour of ours," he explained to Octavia. "A dry man, a widower, who has a house near Meryton. Longbourn, a neat little estate. But of course you met his granddaughter the other evening at the Gouldings'—on the fateful evening when Chauntry went up in flames."

Octavia looked surprised. "Did I?"

"Of course you did. Camilla, now Mrs. Wytton. Her mother was Elizabeth Bennet, one of Mr. Bennet's five daughters, before she married Mr. Darcy, so Mr. Bennet is a connection of yours also."

"A remote one," said Octavia, working it out.

"I should have asked him to stay, so that I could introduce you to him, but he was in a hurry, off to look at a prize bull, a great hefty fellow, over at Ludlett's farm."

"What has Ludlett's prize bull got to do with anything?" said Mrs. Ackworth. "Is this the news you promised us, that Mr. Bennet is going to see a bull?"

"No, no. The news he brought is that Netherfield House is let at last."

"No!" said Mrs. Ackworth. And then, to Octavia, "Netherfield House is a fine place, it belongs to a family in the north who never come here, have never been near the house, and it is let out. The last tenant left a year ago, and it has been empty ever since. Who has taken it, did Mr. Bennet say?"

"This will amuse you, I am sure you would never guess. Lord Rutherford is the new tenant."

"Lord Rutherford! Oh, I suppose for his mother, how cunning of him."

"I rather think he plans to install his mother in the Dower House, at Chauntry; he has been trying to persuade her to move in there this age—if he had succeeded, Chauntry would not have burned, for it would have allowed him to do the repairs on that chimney. However, be that as it may, Rutherford has taken the house to be near at hand while he rebuilds Chauntry."

"And I suppose he will have no more sense than to employ an architect whose head is full of the Gothic, arches and pointed windows and crenellations, and he will build a vast house, far bigger than he needs, to replace Chauntry, and within ten years will wish that it, too, could burn down," said Octavia.

"Lord Rutherford does not lack for sense, and he does not seem to me to have a Gothic frame of mind," said Mrs. Ackworth. "Perhaps something in the Grecian style, that would look very well on the hillside there; I assume he will move the house up the hill and avoid all the dampness and darkness which made Chauntry so difficult to live in."

"Whatever he does, he will not consult any of us," said Mr. Ackworth, reaching for his mug of ale.

"How much I should like to build a house," said Octavia, laying down her fork.

She spoke with such enthusiasm that her cousins paused, one with his ale halfway to his lips, Mrs. Ackworth with her spoon in a dish of relish.

"Build a house," said Mr. Ackworth, putting down his pewter mug and staring at her. "Why?"

"I have a great liking for houses, and how they are built. It has always seemed to me that to build a house of one's own, determining exactly how everything should be, would be a great pleasure. I met a man in the coach coming to Meryton—"

"—and I haven't forgiven Theodosia, sending you on the common coach where you were obliged to rub shoulders with all kinds of undesirable people," interjected Mr. Ackworth.

"Yes, but it gave me a chance to talk to this most interesting man, an importer of marble."

"What?"

"He was a most amiable person. We fell into conversation, and had a long discussion about current styles of building and the use of marble, and which architects are fashionable and which, in his opinion, knew their job. I was used to make doll's houses when I was a girl, I built several fine mansions for myself, and a mediaeval castle, a grim place with a ghost on the northern staircase."

"Ghost? What ghost? What are you talking about?"

"It is imagination, my love," said Mrs. Ackworth. "It is all in Octavia's imagination."

"Well, Octavia, be wary of filling your mind with ghosts, there's no knowing where that kind of thing can lead to. Haunted houses, ghosts, you've been reading too many novels. Let me recommend a volume of dull sermons, just the thing to bore you to death and then you won't have the energy for imagining ghosts or anything else."

He left the room, humming cheerfully to himself, a Clementi sonata that Octavia had played long ago, in her other life. The sudden realization that now she would be able to buy herself a pianoforte, a good one, brought a thoughtful look to her face, and earned her a knowing glance from her cousin.

"What are you up to, Octavia? I feel sometimes you are laughing at us all, that you have some scheme in view of which we know nothing."

"No, not at all," said Octavia, hastily and untruthfully. "Today it is a twelvemonth since Captain Darcy died, you know. Of course I was not there, but the lieutenant who was with him said that was the day."

"My dear, and here we are, joking and talking quite as normal; a year marks a turning point, even though it was so very far away."

"Does distance make a difference?" Octavia asked, amused.

"Here the seasons pass in their familiar way, marking the year, but in India it is all different, not at all the same, from what one hears. No chilly wintry mornings, no fresh spring days, no hay ripening in the fields."

"You are right," said Octavia, much struck by this observation. "And it has been such an odd year, first in Calcutta, and then the long voyage back to England."

In some ways it seemed longer than a year, and yet it had passed in a flash, as though it were only yesterday that she'd been in Calcutta, shocked and grieving. What a lot had happened in that year! Her life in India now appeared to be no more than a dream.

"And we shall lose you, just as we are getting to know you," said Mrs. Ackworth. "For now you will be leaving off your mourning, and returning to London."

Octavia thought of the difficulties that lay ahead, and for a moment wished she could stay at Ackworth Manor, enjoying the gentler round of country life. But it was impossible, and in truth, she missed the bustle of London. Besides, the prospect of beginning a new life as a rich, independent woman was an enticing one.

"I believe I must return to London. Theodosia expects me, and I will need to have new clothes made, and then there are the lawyers to see—" she hesitated, on the verge of telling her cousin everything, but no, she had told herself that she would wait until she had seen Mr. Portal. "And—and various practical matters to be dealt with," she finished.

Chapter Fourteen

Octavia returned to London in Mr. Ackworth's carriage, a very different journey from on her way out to Hertfordshire. They made a halt in Hampstead Village, safely past the heath with its threat of highwaymen, where the coachman had a package to deliver for Mr. Ackworth.

Stretching her legs for a few moments, relishing the feel of spring in the air, Octavia looked out over London, a dark patch of life in the distance, smoke from thousands of chimneys rising into the still air, a contrast to the rural scene around her, with a cowman leading his herd to the village pond where busy ducks swam. A comely young woman hurried past with a shopping basket over her arm; newly wed, Octavia decided, with her young husband coming home to a neat supper and domestic bliss in a snug parlour in one of those pretty cottages. Or, just as likely, to a cross wife and a brood of screaming children, drooling and fixing him with glares of hostility.

Octavia often made up these pictures of life behind other people's doors; she was, experience had taught her, almost invariably wrong, but it still gave her pleasure. With some families, there was no fathoming what went on within the domestic reaches of the house; take a family like the Rutherfords, enough to make the most acute observer or commentator on family life tear his hair out in disbelief and dismay. Who knew what grim secrets lurked behind these fresh-painted front doors, who knew what unexpected happiness might also lie within?

And then the carriage was making the descent towards London, and in no time they were drawing up in Lothian Street, and she was back in the bosom of her own family. She reminded herself that it was not to be for long, and with this happy thought in her mind, greeted her sister with perfect goodwill.

"Whose carriage is that?" demanded Theodosia, looking beyond her to where the carriage was standing, John Coachman at the horses' heads. "How came you to travel in a private carriage? And I was not expecting you until tomorrow."

"Mr. Ackworth kindly sent me in his carriage. May I tell the coachman to take the horses round to the stable?"

"It is not at all convenient," she began, and then realising that her ill nature would undoubtedly be reported back to Mr. Ackworth, who was on ridiculously easy terms with his servants, and being rather afraid of her cousin's tongue, Theodosia agreed, and told Octavia to come in or they would all take cold.

"I do not know why you were at the door," said Octavia. "Is Coxley not here?"

"Of course he is, you could have seen him standing there if you had used your eyes. I was just going out to take a turn in the park. My physician, Dr. Molloy, who is a great man—he is called in to treat the King—has told me I must take some gentle walking exercise every day for the sake of my health. Penelope, who is in a very disobliging mood, would not come with me. I despair of that girl. However, now that you are here, you had better come upstairs. And you can walk with me each morning, it will do you good."

Octavia followed her inside, and Coxley stepped forward to shut the front door. Walk in the park with Theodosia? She thought not; it would bore her extremely, as she would doubtless be expected to hear about Theodosia's delicate constitution, and how well this Dr. Molloy understood her delicate nerves. Octavia was of the opinion that her sister was as strong as a horse, and had nerves of steel, but she knew a feminine weakness was the fashion among Theodosia's set, and so Theodosia would sigh and try to look pale, complain how exertion of any kind was fatal to her nerves, and how the strain of a London season was almost too much for her.

Octavia suspected that her sister was more than willing to dispense with her stroll, for once inside, she told Icken in brisk tones to take away her pelisse, and to see that Mrs. Darcy's boxes were taken up to her room and unpacked.

Icken was a grim-visaged party of some forty years, who sniffed at the order and cast Octavia an unfriendly look; she was very top-lofty, and thought it beneath her to have to do anything for such a lowly creature as Octavia.

"I will see to it, and will tell Alice that Mrs. Darcy is returned."

"Icken is in a disagreeable mood," said Theodosia. "She does not care to walk out with me either, although I am sure it does her as much good as it does me."

She now took in the details of Octavia's dress, and let out a cluck of impatience. "Here you are still in grey, it is a most depressing colour and does not suit you at all with your insipid colouring—grey eyes, grey gown, grey cloak, it is like a shadow standing here. How are you to go about—or, no, you have been travelling, you chose to wear that shabby old thing because journeys can be so dusty, and one always arrives creased. Tell me that you have other clothes with you."

"I do not, at least no more than I went away with. I did not choose to have my clothes made in Hertfordshire, I shall see to that now I am back in London."

"It is very inconvenient, and thoughtless of you. There is a dress party on Tuesday, and I thought you might very well go; there will be a lot of people there, it is a chance for you to mingle in society, to polish up your London manners a little. In such a crowd, you know, you will hardly be noticed—however, if you have nothing to wear, you cannot go."

"I shall visit Madame Lilly this very afternoon."

"Well, I do not know how you will get there, for I shall need the carriage, and besides, the horses are not to be—"

"I shall take a hackney cab."

"A hackney cab! A fine thing for a Melbury to be cavorting about town in hackney cabs," she said unreasonably.

"It is the Darcy name that will be dishonoured," Octavia pointed out. "And as no one knows me, it will scarcely matter."

"That is true. Madame Lilly, you say?" The gleam of one keen to spot a bargain came into Theodosia's eye. "Pray, is she a Frenchwoman, or some Englishwoman taking on a French name? You must tell me how she does, because—where does she have her establishment?"

"In Pimlico."

"In Pimlico?" Theodosia lost interest, no good could come of any dressmaker who had an establishment in that unfashionable part of London.

Octavia was disconcerted to find that Madame Lilly of Pimlico and Madame Duhamel of Calcutta were not only sisters, but twins, and despite the differences that the climate of Calcutta as opposed to the moist air of England had wrought on their faces, the likeness was remarkable: the same determined jaw, beady eyes, and little rosebud mouth, pursed now in a moue as Madame Lilly took stock of her new client.

"Bien," she said, "I would have known the dress you are wearing anywhere for one of Hortense's, for the cut and line and finish are unmistakable. However, it is very plain, but then for a mourning dress, it is better to go for simplicity, in the case of a young woman, and if madame is in modest circumstances . . ." Her sharp eyes asked a question, and Octavia responded with frankness.

"I am not in such very modest circumstances, but I do not wish to go to Bond Street to some expensive modiste. And since I wish to renew my entire wardrobe"—Madame Lilly's eyes gleamed at this information—"and your sister made so well for me in India, it is natural that I should come to you."

"Eh *bien,* and you will do the better for it. For I tell you, that if I had the capital, I would hang out my sign in Bond Street and the *haut ton* would flock through my doors, for although I say it myself, few of my compatriots and none of your English dressmakers can compare with what I can do for you. My sister, in India, is a little behind the times, but I have contacts in France, I do not need to wait for the dolls to come over, or for plates to appear in *La Belle Assemblée,* for I already know the precise number of flounces, the correct trimming, the perfect velvet for the season, before your Bond Street modiste has a whisper of it."

They settled down to details, Madame Lilly summoning a drab little girl to assist her with samples of fabric; sketches were quickly made, plates brought out to show an underdress, the line of a cape, the trimming on a pelisse.

"With madame's height and figure, she can wear as many flounces as she likes without appearing squat, and there is nothing more flattering than rows of flounces, especially for a ball dress, when the movement is so important."

The introduction of a ball dress into the conversation was, Octavia knew, another question. Yes, she would want a ball dress, more than one. And other evening dresses, as well as morning dresses, walking dresses, carriage dresses.

"This will take some time to make," said Madame Lilly.

"I do not need them all at once, in fact it is better not," said Octavia, realising that Theodosia would want to know the contents of every box brought home to her.

"If it is a matter of payment . . ." The Frenchwoman's shrewd dark eyes grew suspicious.

"No, it is not. It is that I shall not be going about a great deal in society immediately, my life will be quiet at first."

"Of course, because mourning is put off, it does not mean that the spirits are not drooping," said Madame Lilly with sympathy. "I know what it is to be a widow. I lost my husband five years ago, that is why I have returned to dressmaking, to keep myself, but I was not a merry soul for many, many months. However, it is all for the best, for I find I would rather be a dressmaker than a wife, and

I build up my clientele, little by little. If you go into society, for I can see that you are well born, then people will ask you where you had your gown made, and you will perhaps tell them, and so I gain new business."

Octavia mentioned a riding habit. Her one from India had seen too much wear to be suitable for London, and in due course, sooner rather than later, now that she had the means, she had every intention of buying herself a horse.

Madame Lilly shook her head. "Riding habits I do not undertake to make. That is a special skill, and in that, as for men's clothes, the English tailor is supreme. You shall go to Fenniman's, providing money is not an object. For a riding habit, it is my belief that only the best will do, and Monsieur Fenniman is the best."

And so the next day Octavia went out once more, but this time no hackney cab was necessary; she could walk to Dover Street, where Fenniman's was to be found.

It had been more difficult than she thought to avoid accompanying her forceful sister on her morning constitutional, and Octavia had at last resorted to an underhand trick, looking at the threatening sky and remarking that Theodosia did not appear to be at her best, was she sickening for a cold, did she feel perfectly well?

It was decided that, rather than take her walk, Theodosia would summon Dr. Molloy, and while instructions were being given to a footman, Octavia slipped out unnoticed except by Penelope, who met her on the stairs. "You have a secretive look about you, Aunt Octavia. Are you by any chance doing something of which Mama would disapprove?"

"Not at all," said Octavia. "Your mother is indisposed, she finds, this morning, and I am going out for a walk."

"Indisposed! That means Dr. Molloy with his cold, pale eyes will be calling on her. I hate him. I shall go and practise the harp, anything is better than having to talk to him, he eyes one in such a way!"

Penelope pulled a very ungenteel face, making Octavia laugh, and her niece flitted away towards the music room.

More than the visit to Madame Lilly's, her trip to Fenniman's brought home to Octavia just how much her circumstances had changed; before her inheritance, she would never have ventured into such an establishment. Prices were not mentioned, but Octavia knew they would make her stretch her eyes, and she threw caution to the winds, ordering not one but two riding habits, "a wise decision," Mr. Fenniman noted, for in the summer, on warmer days, the lighter habit will be so much more comfortable."

When she left the tailor's premises, Mr. Fenniman himself escorted her into the street, assuring her that they would make every effort to deliver the first of her outfits within days, they quite understood that so recently arrived from India, she had little suitable to wear for riding in London.

She would need boots for riding, and shoes for everyday wear. Hats, too, and here Madame Lilly had been a mine of information, advising her to eschew the most fashionable milliners in favour of Millicent, who had an establishment off Montague Street. "Be bold in your choice of hats and bonnets," Madame Lilly had advised. "With the clothes I shall make for you, you will need hats that speak of drama, that are striking, not these dowdy fashions the English love, or the whimsical styles they favour for the summer."

It was by sheer luck that the first delivery of clothes from Madame Lilly, sooner than she would have believed possible, came while her sister was out of the house, and although Octavia knew perfectly well that the arrival of the boxes would be reported to Theodosia by the butler and by her maid, it meant that, with Alice's help, she could put some of the clothes away before Theodosia demanded to see what she had. Alice exclaimed with delight at the new finery, and whisked most of it into presses and closets, giving Octavia a knowing look when she said only to leave out two of the gowns.

"Well, that is better than I expected," said Theodosia, looking over the evening gown and the morning dress which the maid presented for her inspection. "Although the style is rather more flamboyant than I would have considered suitable. You are hardly setting up for a lady of fashion, you do not want people to think your circumstances are better than they are."

Penelope was allowed to see more of Octavia's new finery, and she exclaimed, "Oh, how I envy you, not having to wear pale colours all the time."

She was fair, like Octavia; they both owed their colouring to Sir Clement Melbury. "When you are fair, pale clothes make one look washed out and insipid, but Mama insists on my only wearing white and yellow and pale blue, none of which suit me. When I am married"—she flushed—"if I marry, then I shall wear these kinds of colours, richer and darker."

"Of course you will marry," said Octavia. "There can be no if about it."

"I am not so sure," said Penelope, suddenly serious. "Suppose one never fell in love—or did so, but could not marry the object of one's affections. I would prefer to stay single all my life, rather than be forced to marry a man I did not care tuppence for!"

Octavia had suspected as much. Penelope had undoubtedly lost her heart to an unsuitable man, or thought she had. Octavia hoped that this would be no more than a youthful fancy, for she couldn't imagine Theodosia, or indeed Mr. Henry Cartland, agreeing to a love match that was not also a good match in their sense of the word, meaning, a man who was of their world, wealthy, and well born.

But this was Penelope's first season, and she was very young, and she might be one of those girls whose fancies were volatile, for whom the young man who was everything to her this week would be dismissed the next with a toss of her pretty head and a shrug of her white shoulders, and an "Oh, him, I care nothing for him."

Penelope might be as heartless in her own way as her mother was, although Octavia felt this would not be so. There was a strength to her niece that didn't bode well for her future, at least, not if it were a different future from the one laid down for her by her mother.

With Alice's assistance, Octavia likewise managed to smuggle in the parcels from the bootmaker and shoemaker, and she herself came home in a hackney cab with two hatboxes from Millicent's. She was a milliner Theodosia had never heard of, no, she had no wish to see the hats, she was just on the point of going out, where was Penelope, why was that girl never there when you wanted her?

"Here, Mama," said Penelope, eyeing the hatboxes and whispering to Octavia as she went past that she was sure they were monstrous smart hats, and she would want to see them when she came in.

Unfortunately, it was a different story with the riding habits. The man from Fenniman's arrived with the first of Octavia's habits in the middle of a windy afternoon, when Theodosia was attending to her correspondence in her private sitting room.

She heard the footman say to Octavia, "This has come from Fenniman's," and was at the door of her room in a trice, looking out and catching Octavia just as she was about to go up the stairs to her own room.

"Fenniman! Did I hear Fenniman? What has come home from Fenniman's, I should like to know?"

"It is for me," Octavia said.

"For you? And what, pray, can you have ordered from Fenniman?"

"It's madam's riding habit," said Icken with a sniff.

Theodosia looked at the box, eyebrows raised, mouth pursed in disapproval. "A riding habit! You ordered a riding habit from Fenniman? Whatever can you be thinking of, do you have any idea of his prices? And what need have you of ordering a riding habit from anyone? When are you going to ride? For do not be expecting that Henry will be lending you a mount, no, nor Arthur neither. And to go to Fenniman's, whose prices are the highest in London, you cannot possibly afford half what it will cost."

"I am aware of the cost, Theodosia, and I have the money put by. I like to ride, and—"

"Like to ride! Well, there are many things we all like to do, but it does not mean that it is possible to do so."

"Please do not distress yourself so," she said with considerable dignity. "I have no intention of asking either Mr. Cartland or Arthur to provide me with a horse." And she whisked herself into her room, her heart thumping in a very uncontrolled way. She pressed her hands to her hot cheeks, and found she was trembling. It was all so unnecessary, she had only to tell Theodosia—but no, she would not do so. Not yet, not until the moment was right, until she had made her plans and knew she could carry them out. Tomorrow she would go to the lawyer, and put in train the finding of a house for herself.

As for a horse—there she was at a stand. Single women did not buy horses, she would hardly know where to begin. She would have to have a man's help with that. But who? Even when the news was out, she would hardly trust Arthur to find her a suitable horse, nor Mr. Cartland.

That would have to wait for the moment. Meanwhile, she would sit down and take several deep breaths and regain her composure. Then she would try on the new riding habit, midnight blue with extravagant froggings à la Hussar. Fenniman had sent a sample of the velvet for her to take to Millicent's for a hat to complete the outfit; how dashing it was.

Habit, hat, boots. She must make a visit to the glove maker for riding gloves as well as evening gloves and gloves to go with all her other ensembles—then all she would lack was a horse.

Which thought kept her amused through a difficult dinner, with Penelope unusually subdued, Mr. Cartland glancing anxiously at his wife, who was clearly not in a good mood; Theodosia still much annoyed with Octavia over the riding habit.

"Tomorrow you may come with us to the Barchesters' soirée, and this time I will accept no excuses," she said to Octavia, as she rose from the table. "It is time for you to be seen about, there may be some people there you know from when you were previously in London, but in any case it is an opportunity—there are some people Arthur would like you to meet."

Potential husbands, Octavia said to herself. Sound Tories, men of a certain age, men who might not be too particular as to height and fortune. She was sure Arthur would present her to at least one middle-aged widower who was looking out for a suitable wife.

Yet she found herself looking forward to the soirée. Penelope had whispered to her that the Barchesters were very smart, not at all stuffy, and although there would be dull people there, there were sure to be others who were not. Octavia came to the conclusion that she had a frivolous nature; after her time in the country, she was more than happy to plunge into a livelier social scene.

Chapter Fifteen

It was worse than she had expected, far, far worse. Only the knowledge that she was elegantly dressed, indeed a great deal more elegantly dressed than most of the women there, gave her any cause for feeling pleased.

It was a squeeze, a fashionable squeeze, and a political squeeze. Arthur was a Tory since his circle of friends tended to be of the same political persuasion. The Tories had just won the recent general election, Lord Liverpool was still in office as Prime Minister—and he was there, his eye twitching, his rather bland countenance displaying no emotion at his success. He looked dull, Octavia decided, not that she was given any opportunity to discover if this were the case, for she was far too unimportant to be honoured with the acquaintance of a Lord Liverpool. Instead, she was introduced to a large man in corsets, with an opulent air and breeches straining over wide thighs. Not a stupid man, but a deeply unpleasant one, a roué by the hot look in his eyes, and a rich one, or Arthur would not have been so obsequious when he made the introduction.

And then, when Octavia would have smiled and edged away, Arthur manoeuvred her into a corner, her escape blocked by the large man, and her brother hissed in her ear that she was to mind her manners, that this was Sir Willoughby Granston, a man of influence in the Party, a widower. "And rich," he said, before moving away, leaving her marooned and angry.

Sir Willoughby knew that she had been in India, he had interests in India, about which he was preparing to bore her. Annoyed, she raised her voice, and asked him what was his opinion of the subsidies to the maharajahs.

Ha, that silenced him, although it earned her several curious glances and not a few turned heads. "For some of them most supported by the government are of a tyrannical disposition," she continued.

His eyes grew cold. "You set yourself up to have an opinion on matters about which you know nothing." And then, mercifully, he edged away, saying in an audible voice that he deplored a clever woman, a woman who expressed her views on subjects about which she knew nothing, less than nothing.

Across the room, Snipe Woodhead was watching Octavia. Not that he found her interesting in herself, but she was a newcomer, and he was a gossip to his fingertips, a man who had to know everything that was going on.

"Who is that woman?" he said to his neighbour. "The tall one, who has just offended Willoughby?"

"Who do you mean? Oh, the lanky female in blue. That will be Mrs. Darcy, the second Mrs. Darcy, Christopher Darcy's wife. She was a Melbury before she married, been in India for years."

That was enough for Snipe. "Arthur Melbury's half sister. No fortune when she married Darcy, and no fortune now he's gone, the estate went to Warren, of course. Wonder what she's doing in London?"

"Oh, on the lookout for another husband, no doubt about it."

"What possessed Darcy to marry her? When you think what the first Mrs. Darcy was, bit of a comedown, ain't she? A Melbury's all very well, but isn't to compare with an earl's granddaughter."

"No, and I have heard that her grandfather was a haberdasher or a grocer or some such thing. On her mother's side; Sir Clement made a shocking misalliance there."

"Doesn't look as though she's overwhelmed Sir Willoughby with her charms," said Snipe with a mirthless laugh.

"No, she's missed her chance there, he likes big women, although she's probably too thin for him."

"Do the Darcys acknowledge her?"

"Haven't a clue, dear boy. Shouldn't think so, the relationship wasn't a close one, and she's no more than a distant connection. No, Melbury will have his work cut out if he's going to get rid of her. A country clergyman would be about the extent of her hopes, I should say."

Some extra sense told Octavia that the two fashionably dressed men were talking about her, and she held her chin a little higher as she edged her way through the throng, hating the braying voices, the smell of overheated bodies, the watchful eyes, the scent of ambition in the air. This was a gathering of men on the make, men hungry for advancement and a taste of power.

Would Arthur rise high in his Party, and in office? She doubted it. He was a shrewd man, but not a cunning one, and his eagerness to please and defer might flatter, but it surely couldn't help him up the political ladder, more than that must be needed.

Except, looking about her, perhaps it wasn't.

Arthur was displeased with her, and told Theodosia so, which meant that Octavia was lectured all the way home. Mr. Cartland was silent, in the carriage and when they were back in Lothian Street, only casting her an occasional swift glance of sympathy when he thought his wife wouldn't notice.

"That any sister of mine could be so rude to such a charming and influential man!" Theodosia was saying yet again. "If you behave in such a boorish way, you will never find yourself another husband."

Octavia sighed. "Theodosia, he may be influential, but he is not charming. He is also twice my age, and Arthur is losing his wits if he imagines that we could be in any way suited."

"It is for Sir Willoughby to decide what might or might not suit him, it is not up to you."

Octavia went upstairs, melancholy threatening to overwhelm her as she looked back on a most disagreeable evening. In the morning, she decided she would put an end to this charade, she would tell Theodosia and Arthur—

There was a knock at the door, and Penelope's head came round it. "Oh, good, you are still up." She advanced into the room. "Do you have the headache? You look as though you do. Shall I ring for your maid, would you like a tisane, or there are pastilles Mama burns when she has the headache? Did you not have a good time?"

"It was a dreadful party," said Octavia. "Where were you this evening?"

"At a dance," said Penelope without enthusiasm. "It was crowded and no one interesting was there. I went with my Cousin Louisa and Aunt Augusta, that is why Mama could go with you this evening, they do not take me to political parties." She let out a tremendous yawn. "I am so tired of dances and balls and parties and routs and all the rest of it."

"You should enjoy your season, most girls do."

"Do you think so? So do not I. There is such desperation to find a husband, the right husband, you know. The girls who are engaged may enjoy it, but I find it a very empty-headed way to pass the time."

Octavia sympathised, but what else was there for a girl in Penelope's position except to be thrust into society and to marry as quickly as possible?

"The men are all so young, or they are old and ogle one, I do not know which is worse," Penelope went on in tones of dissatisfaction.

Ah, so the man who had caught her fancy was older than her.

"And they have nothing to say which is of any interest, it is all insipid stuff, and gossip and the weather, you cannot have a proper conversation. If you try, they look at you as though you were an eccentric, and then Aunt Augusta comes zooming down on me, to tell me to mind what I am about. Of course Louisa is fascinated by whatever a man has to say, she listens, all agog, all attention, even if it is the most arrant nonsense. If I were a man, it would annoy me, but they do not seem to mind it at all. She has the nastiest temper of any girl I know, but of course they are unaware of that, she takes good care that she appears sweetness itself."

"Shall I pour you a bowl of milk?" said Octavia.

"You mean I am a cat," said Penelope, with perfect good humour. "Where Louisa is concerned, yes, I am. I pity her future husband, whoever it is, for he will soon find out what she is like. Or perhaps not, he will take no notice of anything she says, and spend most of his time with his horses or at his club. That is what men do, they are so much luckier than we are, do not you think so?"

"I do indeed," said Octavia, with a fervour that surprised her niece. "But not all your parties can be so very dull, you must enjoy some of them."

Penelope sighed. "The ones I might enjoy, I am not permitted to go to. In three days time there is a dance given by the Wyttons, and I should dearly love to go. However, it is the same evening as Mama has accepted an invitation to Vauxhall. Do you like Vauxhall?"

"I never went there above once, and it rained."

"It is all very well in its way, but it depends on the company, and . . . Well, I would rather go to the Wyttons', do you know them?"

"Mrs. Wytton is a cousin of my late husband; I met them in Hertfordshire, they seem a most agreeable couple."

"Oh, they are, the nicest people in the world. Only Mama does not think so, and Mr. Wytton is a Whig, you know, and quite Radical in his views, which makes Uncle Arthur fret and fume, and my uncle Adderley goes quite red in the face whenever his name is mentioned." She gave a wide yawn, and got up from the chair by the meagre fire. "Are you warm enough? I do wish Mama had put you in a nicer room." Then, with another yawn, she bade Octavia good night and left for her own bedchamber.

The next morning came an invitation for Octavia, a note from Camilla Wytton, saying that she and Mr. Wytton were just returned to town from Hertfordshire, that they were giving a small dance two nights from now, would Octavia forgive the short notice and informality of the invitation and honour them with her presence?

"What is that you have there, who is that from?" said Theodosia, who enacted a role as postmaster general in her house.

"Mama!" said Penelope in protest.

Octavia handed her the note.

"Not very civil, to ask you as an afterthought, I cannot see why they are asking you in any case—oh, I suppose your husband was related to them, that will be it. A duty invitation, a small affair, you may be sure that will be the beginning and end of the attention you will get from them, all as proud as can be, those Darcys, although I do not know why they hold themselves so grand, when you think what those girls got up to . . ."

Penelope was listening with keen interest. "What was that, Mama?" she said.

"Never you mind; you won't hear from me about how they ran off with this man and that man. And the eldest girl married to a clergyman, you'd think Mr. Darcy would look higher than that for his daughter! I suppose you must accept, Octavia, you will find note paper in the little parlour, you may use that, and Suky can take it round for you."

"I've been invited, too," said Penelope.

Theodosia raised her brows and gave her daughter a quelling look. "I cannot imagine why they sent an invitation, we do not move in their circle. And we are otherwise engaged."

"It is a pity," said Penelope innocently. "For some friends of mine will be there, and Lord Rutherford is invited. He is a cousin of Mr. Wytton's, you know."

"Lord Rutherford? Well, well, it is indeed a pity—however, you cannot go."

But luck was on Penelope's side. The hostess of the party arranged for Vauxhall sent a note, desolate to have to cancel, stricken with a sore throat, no voice, the doctor had forbidden her to set foot outside the house . . .

Theodosia reluctantly agreed that Penelope might go to the Wyttons' party. "Since Octavia can accompany you . . ."

Penelope danced up the stairs beside Octavia. "She means that if you take me, she can invite some cronies round for cards, which is what she likes best. She plays very high, you know, it annoys Papa dreadfully, but he cannot stop her. Oh, what fun. Shall you wear the dress you wore the other night?"

"No, I have a new one sent home, and I shall wear that." And she had to laugh at herself, aware that she wanted to show Lord Rutherford that she could look as elegant as any female in London—he had, after all, only seen her with her hair awry, her gown dishevelled, and sooty marks on her face.

Chapter Sixteen

The Wyttons' house was in Harte Street, a good-sized town house with an elegant hallway and a staircase rising to the next floor in a swirl of mahogany banisters. Upstairs were two drawing rooms, and as Octavia and Penelope reached the landing, they heard musicians tuning their instruments: fiddles, and the deep plangent sounds of a cello and a bassoon.

"It is not a formal dance, but it is always the greatest fun at the Wyttons'," Penelope told her aunt. "Mr. Poyntz likes going there the best of anywhere in London; he is a particular friend of Mr. Wytton's, of both the Wyttons. I dare say he will be here. You will like to meet him, he is a most interesting man, and he resided in India for some years when he was a child."

"I believe I have met the gentleman," said Octavia, not deceived by Penelope's attempt to sound casual. Good heavens, if that was the young man on whom her fancy had alighted, then she would have a difficult job of it; she could not see Theodosia countenancing such a match under any circumstances.

"Met him?" cried Penelope, as they went towards Camilla Wytton, who was standing in the doorway, greeting her guests. "How? Where?"

"In Hertfordshire; he is in holy orders, is he not?"

"Yes, he is, but—" Penelope remembered her manners, and

dropped a curtsy and said a pretty thank you to Camilla for inviting her. "Is Belle here?" Penelope asked, Belle being one of Camilla's younger sisters.

"Not yet, but she will be here, all my sisters are here tonight, except for Mrs. Barcombe."

"Which is as well," said Penelope, going further into the room with Octavia, who had in turn received a kind welcome from Camilla. "Have you met Mrs. Barcombe? She is the oldest of them, there are five sisters, but you will know that."

"No, indeed I do not, I was unacquainted with the family until I was introduced to Mr. and Mrs. Wytton at Haye Park; I never met any of my late husband's family or connections, since we were only together in India."

"Mrs. Barcombe is very disapproving, one of those people who is always right. I do not think she and Mrs. Wytton get on so very well together. Belle is a younger sister; I was at school with her and Georgina, her twin, although they are a little older than me. Georgina married Sir Joshua Mordaunt, she ran away with him in fact, but I am not supposed to know that was the case. They live in Paris, but they must be visiting London. So you were at Haye Park, was that where you met Mr. Poyntz?"

"Yes, it was."

"And I dare say Charlotte was talking to him a good deal," said Penelope in discontented tones. "It is always the same, she makes sheep's eyes at every young man, although she must know that her parents will consider nothing less than a great match for her. They say she is to marry Lord Rutherford, he is a particular friend of Mr. Poyntz's, you know, but I do not think there's any truth in it; why would a man like Lord Rutherford want to marry a goose like Charlotte Goulding?"

"You seem very up on everything," she observed.

"Is that a criticism? Do you think I should be missish and pretend not to know what is going on? That is how Mama would like me to be, but I think it is all nonsense. One cannot help noticing people, and there is no point in pretending that Charlotte Goulding is not a goose, for you only have to spend five minutes with her to know that is the case."

"She is very beautiful."

"Oh, quite lovely," said Penelope blithely. "A nonpareil, and when she makes her come-out, she will have the men flocking around her, until they discover she has no conversation, that is."

Octavia laughed. "Do the young men care for conversation, when there is a pretty face and a title in the background and a good fortune?"

"Some do," said Penelope. "You are right, however; most of them like a woman to smile and simper and look pleased to be spoken to. And Charlotte is not a flirt, I will grant her that. I am more of a flirt than she is, only not when Mama is present, naturally, for if she sees me behave in a way she thinks not suitable for one of my upbringing, she frowns and shakes her head and glares."

"I know exactly what you mean, but she does it from care for you, I am sure; she will want you to present yourself in the best way."

"She wants to sell me off like a Circassian slave, or some prize horse," said Penelope.

This was exactly how Octavia had felt, those long years ago, when she was doing her wretched London season under Theodosia's eagle eye. But Theodosia had had no affection for her, and she must have affection for Penelope. She said so.

"Do you think so?" said Penelope. "I do not. She wants me to make a remarkable match, the kind that makes all the other mamas mutter and feel envious. Most of all she wants me to marry someone of higher rank than Louisa. But it is easier for her, because she is the daughter of a nobleman, and Papa's family is an old one, but not aristocratic. They are gentry, landowners, and he is rich, richer than many members of the House of Lords, but it is not the same. Mama dearly wants me to be a peeress, she wants to be able to talk of my daughter, the Countess of this or the Marchioness of that. I don't care a button for all that, do you?"

Octavia said that there was no question of her caring or not caring, there was no possibility of her marrying anyone from among the peerage.

"I do not see why you should not, as well as anyone," said Penelope. "As long as he were tall. You would not do to set your cap at Lord Silloth, for example, for he is barely as tall as I am, and would not come up to your shoulder."

"I am not a girl in my first season, I don't have to find myself a husband," said Octavia. She was looking around the room, filling up fast with the Wyttons' friends, lively looking people with intelligent faces; how different from the dull politicians of her last party.

"Mama says you should," said Penelope, who was anxiously watching the door for every new arrival. "She says it is the only hope for you, with no money and no means of making a living for yourself. And Aunt Augusta says in the end you will have to go for a governess, but I took no notice, she is always making extravagant remarks—oh."

Mr. Poyntz came into the room, side by side with Lord Rutherford. They paused to exchange some words with Camilla and with Alexander, who was by her side, but Mr. Poyntz's eyes were looking round the room and he at once came over to join them. Penelope was in a glow; she should take care, Octavia thought, suddenly worried. Her niece was very matter-of-fact about her mama's ambitions, but did not perhaps comprehend how ruthless Theodosia might be in carrying them out.

Rank held such sway in London. Everyone was either up or down, or ascending and descending. Most anxious and nervous were those among the gentry who were looking upwards, keen to leave behind the quieter world of the country estate for the headier circles of the nobility. Of course, they might not aspire to marry sons and daughters into the very highest ranks; the Cavendishes and the Spencers, the Howards and the Churchills, tended to marry among themselves as they had always done. But an attractive daughter might catch a lesser peer, the son of a first baron or viscount or earl. Hadn't she heard that Lord Liverpool was the son of a physician who had been raised to the peerage? And there were others, such as Henry

Brougham, who had made their way into the upper House through the law or a dazzling career in the House of Commons.

Theodosia was aiming high if she had her eye on such as Lord Rutherford for her daughter. And Penelope, though brimming with vitality, was not a beauty like Charlotte Goulding or half a dozen other of the young ladies who were here tonight. Lord Rutherford, with an ancient title and a family line stretching back into the mists of the mediaeval age, might look as high as he wished for a bride—when and if he wanted one.

Mr. Wytton was at her side, wanting to introduce her to some friends, "For I do not believe you will have so many acquaintances here in London."

Sholto Rutherford, who had been watching Poyntz and Penelope with a thoughtful expression, saw Wytton taking Octavia over to join a little bunch by the window. "You are watching the maypole," said Snipe Woodhead, materialising at his elbow, and holding up a quizzing glass to take a better look at Octavia. "She annoys me with her air of self-possession, I cannot think why the Wyttons have invited her."

Rutherford rather wondered why they had invited Snipe, who was answering his own question. "Oh, of course, she is a connection by marriage of Mrs. Wytton's. Mrs. Wytton does not seem in looks, and that yellow dress gives her a very off appearance, do not you think so?"

"I am an admirer of Mrs. Wytton's," said Rutherford repressively. "She is breeding, and is tired, I dare say. It is foolish of her to entertain in this way," he went on, speaking to himself rather than to Snipe. "Wytton is not happy about it, but she laughs at him and says she is not going into purdah on account of her condition."

"She always was headstrong," said Snipe. "She is obstinate, like all the Darcys."

"Or you could say she knows her own mind, just as her father does."

"Well, this Mrs. Darcy, this gawky female from India, appears to be just as obstinate as her Darcy connections; she has a determined look to her chin."

Rutherford rather agreed with him, but he was not going to give him the satisfaction of knowing it. He moved away, spying Pagoda Portal, who had entered the room a few minutes ago and was standing by the fireplace in earnest conversation with Camilla Wytton and Henrietta Rowan.

"So you are back from France," said Lord Rutherford, joining their little group, and making a graceful bow to Henrietta.

"Ha, Rutherford," said Portal. He was a large man, with a gorgeous waistcoat stretched over a generous stomach, but he had an air of benevolence and shrewd eyes that looked his lordship up and down. "You have the air of a harassed man," he said, with a twinkle.

"You have heard that my mother is in residence in Aubrey Square," said Rutherford. "The house is filled with creatures that caw and yap and snarl and nip at one's heels. It is no wonder that I look harassed."

"Papa tells me you have taken Netherfield House," said Camilla. "Will Lady Rutherford move there? Or is she to live in the Dower House at Chauntry; it was untouched by the fire, was it not?"

"A dreadful business, that," said Portal, shaking his head. "I was in Paris when I heard the news, and I was shocked."

"Perhaps Lord Rutherford does not find it altogether a misfortune," said Henrietta.

"Yes, Lord Rutherford," said Camilla. "You have always complained about how inconvenient and damp it was."

"Whether I liked it or not, it is gone, beyond rebuilding. So I plan to start afresh, that is one reason for my taking a lease on Netherfield House; however, it will also be a more suitable home for my mother and sister. My mother will not move into the Dower House; she says she is not the Dowager Countess, which is, strictly speaking, true, and that the house is haunted."

"Haunted?" said Henrietta.

"By whom?" said Camilla.

"By no one and nothing. There is a legend that the wife of the ninth earl walks the rooms there; she fell out of a window or some such thing, and left behind an uneasy spirit, according to the locals."

"Lady Rutherford is a sensitive woman," said Camilla.

Lord Rutherford would not say aloud what his opinion was of his mother's sensitivity, so he merely smiled.

"Portal," he began. "Have you heard about Urquhart?"

"What about Urquhart?"

Robert Urquhart was the MP for a rotten borough in Yorkshire, one not in Lord Rutherford's control, but near where his seat, Rutherford Castle, was situated.

"He got so drunk after his victory at the polls that he fell in a ditch, and was not discovered until the next morning, dead."

"Good heavens, the unfortunate man," said Camilla.

"Not at all," said Portal calmly. "A fitting end for a disagreeable man. So there is to be a by-election, Rutherford; who is to take the seat?"

"I shall have to go up there in a little while to discuss it. Mr. Septimus Stanley is our man, I believe, he will be a thorn in the government's flesh, especially with regard to finance, on which he is something of an expert. He missed a seat at the election, and will be glad to have this one."

"An excellent man," said Portal. "If you set aside that he is pompous and humourless, I grant you his intelligence and ability." He turned to Camilla. "Tell me, is Mrs. Darcy here? I refer to the wife of the late Captain Darcy; she is newly arrived from India, and since her husband was a connection of yours, and she must now be out of mourning, it occurs to me that she might be here."

"Indeed she is. Do you know her? No, of course not, or you would have seen her at once, she is that tall, fair, striking-looking woman talking to Alexander. Let me take you over and introduce you; did you know her husband?"

"Yes, and I was acquainted with her great-uncle and -aunt. I should be honoured to make her acquaintance."

Lord Rutherford watched as Camilla led Mr. Portal through the room, which had filled up rapidly. He saw Octavia break off her conversation with Alexander and give her hand to Portal; tall she might be, but there was a certain grace to her. Still, Snipe was right, she was too sure of herself for a penniless widow who had never held any position in London society, nor ever would. Arthur Melbury might be looking out for a second husband for her, but he would look in vain; she was too tall, too out of the fashion, and made no effort, from what he could see, to charm or attract. She hadn't shared the good looks which had allowed her older sisters to make such good marriages; he supposed that she took after her mother.

Then he was greeted by another friend, and at once forgot about Octavia and the Melburys, finding his friend's account of a pair of carriage horses he had just bought much more interesting.

Octavia was alarmed, as soon as she realised who Mr. Portal was; this was the man Mr. Wilkinson had mentioned, the lawyer's fellow executor. He had known the Worthingtons in India, and she was eager to talk to him, but not here, and her heart was in her mouth lest he make any reference to her inheritance. He bowed over her hand, before looking at her with appraising eyes, and she thanked him for his letter.

"I was acquainted with your father and with your grandfather, on your mother's side, and I also knew your late husband, as I told you when I wrote," he said. "Christopher Darcy was an admirable man, and an honour to his profession."

"Thank you," said Octavia. "I miss him," she added simply.

"Of course, of course you do."

"You said you were acquainted with my grandfather, my mother's father."

"Ah, it was years ago, when I was a young man. It was but a slight acquaintance. I really knew his brother, your great-uncle, much better."

"You knew him in India?"

"Yes, he was kind to me when I first went out there. Then he went to the north and we didn't see much of one another, although we kept in touch. He was an excellent man; I understand you never knew him?"

"No, I didn't. Were you in India long?" she said, hoping to steer the conversation away from her family to that interesting country.

"Oh, for many years," he said.

Camilla, who had been standing nearby, was intrigued, and too openly curious for Octavia to be comfortable. "This is an uncle on your father's side or a relation of your mother's?"

"Mr. Worthington was a younger brother of Mrs. Darcy's maternal grandfather," said Mr. Portal. "That is right, is it not, Mrs. Darcy?"

At that moment, Alexander called Camilla away, saying that the musicians were playing in the other room, the young people might like to start the dance, here was Poyntz, with a partner standing by, and half a dozen other couples longing to indulge in a waltz.

Octavia seized her chance, and in a low urgent voice said to Mr. Portal, "Pray do not mention that I have inherited anything from my great-aunt. I do not wish it to be generally known at present, or indeed known at all to anyone except Mr. Wilkinson and yourself."

"My dear, you can trust me, I have not lived as long as I have without knowing when to be discreet. Henrietta, Mrs. Rowan, you met her just now, is aware of the position, she knows all my secrets, but you need have no worries on that score, none at all. I never knew anyone, man or woman, better able to keep a secret than Henrietta!"

As though she had heard her name, Henrietta Rowan looked in their direction, and Octavia was struck by the look of warm affection that passed between her and Mr. Portal. So this was the woman Theodosia had spoken of in such disparaging terms. Octavia took an immediate liking to her, and she was full of admiration for her clothes, which were dramatic, outré, and suited her very well.

"There are some matters to be discussed and arrangements to be made, however," said Mr. Portal. "If you will honour me with your trust, I can give you some advice, for it is my responsibility, you know. I could call round, you are staying in Lothian Street, but perhaps—"

"That would never do," said Octavia. "My sister, Mrs. Cartland, has to know everything, and we could not be sure of not being overheard; her servants are all ears in that house."

"In which case, since you cannot come to my house, I shall ask Henrietta to invite you to her apartments. She will name a time when no other callers will be present, and then we may talk about what needs to be done. She will write to you tomorrow—will your sister have any objection? They do not call on each other, they do not move in the same set, will she question the invitation?"

"Certainly she will; if she knows I have received any kind of missive she will interrogate me as to its contents," said Octavia. "Does Mrs. Rowan perhaps patronise Hookham's library?"

"She does indeed, she is a great reader. That is a good notion, she may meet you there, as one meets all one's friends, and then she will tell you when you are to come. You will like to know Henrietta better, I have a feeling you will have much in common. She is a remarkable woman, you will find."

Penelope talked about Mrs. Rowan when they went downstairs for supper in the Wyttons' handsome dining room, done out in distinctive classical style, with Pompeiian red walls and classical figures painted in the niches.

"She is Mr. Portal's mistress," she confided in a whisper. "I am not supposed to know such things, let alone to mention it, but it is so, and everyone knows it. She is a widow, and in control of her own fortune; she does not choose to marry Mr. Portal, and he is a single man and seems perfectly happy with the arrangement. It encourages immorality, Mama says, although not to me, of course. I like Mrs. Rowan."

Octavia drank some of her soup, while Penelope and Poyntz chatted together. Then, when he was distracted by the man on his other side, Penelope edged her chair closer to Octavia's. "Mr. Portal is not the only man here with a mistress."

"I do not suppose for a moment that he is," said Octavia, outwardly calm, but inwardly rather startled by this fresh evidence of the worldliness of her niece.

"Lord Rutherford has a mistress as well, Lady Langton. Only it is an adulterous connexion, which of course Mr. Portal's is not, for Lady Langton has a husband. He is never in town, he cares nothing for society, and she is always in London. And mostly in the company of

Lord Rutherford. That is why I am sure he will not marry, not Charlotte Goulding nor anyone else; she would not countenance it."

"Is he so much under her thumb?" said Octavia, startled by this artless confidence.

"Oh, my goodness, yes, she is a truly terrifying woman. She is not here, or you would see for yourself. I am surprised he is here, but of course he is a great friend of Alexander Wytton's, besides being a cousin of some kind. And Poyntz. I like Lord Rutherford when he is with the Wyttons, for he is at his ease and friendly. Look at him now, flirting with Miss Hartlesham, see how she colours up and laughs. It is all fun, there is nothing serious about it, she is engaged to Tom Kidlington."

"Is Lord Rutherford much given to flirting?"

"Only when he feels safe, as with Maria Hartlesham, and she is related to him, you know."

"He is an attractive man, does he not risk breaking hearts?"

"Oh, not Maria's, her heart belongs to Tom, they have been in love with one another for ever." She paused. "Do you think Lord Rutherford is too old for someone of Maria's age, for instance? He is past thirty-five."

"Hardly in his dotage."

"No, but there is an age difference." She gave Octavia a quick look from beneath her long eyelashes. "Some people might say eighteen and thirty-five should have nothing to do with one another."

"Oh, as to that, what is right for one couple is wrong for another. I would say there are many more important factors to a happy marriage."

She was rewarded by a glowing look from Penelope, and felt her heart sink. For it wasn't the age difference between Poyntz and Penelope that would bother the Cartlands, it was the lack of fortune and the clerical dress.

Chapter Seventeen

Henrietta Rowan lived in Bruton Street, in the most extraordinary set of apartments. Octavia exclaimed with pleasure as she took in the rich, sumptuous surroundings. Turkey rugs, brilliant hangings, comfortable sofas with fat cushions, miniatures and paintings and mirrors adorning the walls—it was a feast for the eyes, she told her hostess.

"I am so pleased you like it, it isn't to everyone's taste."

Pagoda Portal arrived soon afterwards, apologising for being behind his time. "I have come from Wilkinson and Winter, we were looking through all the papers, and there is a veritable heap of them, I may tell you."

Mrs. Rowan rose, and was about to leave, saying that they would have private matters to discuss, but Octavia said quickly, "Mr. Portal has told me that you know something of my circumstances, I would be happy for you to stay, I am sure what is said will go no further than this room."

"You may rely on Henrietta for that," said Mr. Portal. "And she may give you good advice, my dear, for while your money is in good hands with Mr. Wilkinson and, if I may say so, myself, it is no easy thing for a young woman to find herself suddenly in possession of so large a fortune. When news gets about, as in the end it will, do what you may to restrict the information, then it will be all over London, it will be the news of the moment, a point of discussion on every Tom,

Dick, and Harry's lips, until some new scandal or excitement drives it away."

"Pagoda is right," said Henrietta. "And you will become the target for the advances of many men; such a fortune as yours will make you the most eligible woman in London."

"Despite the low origins of the fortune?" said Octavia with a wry smile.

"Oh, my dear, when a fortune is as huge as yours, no one minds in the least where it came from. It was not got dishonestly, you have not become rich trafficking in human misery, the money is the product of hard work and great capacity on your great-uncle's side, and you must also thank your great-aunt, for taking such good care of her inheritance that it comes to you even larger than before."

"Mr. Wilkinson took me through the figures," said Octavia to Mr. Portal. "I confess my head was in a whirl, I could hardly take in what he was saying."

"The details are complex, and it will take you time to become familiar with them, as you must, unless you care to hand the authority for dealing with it to your brother, or Lord Adderley, a worthy man."

"On no account," said Octavia. "If my great-aunt could manage her fortune, then I can learn to do the same."

Mr. Portal's eyebrows rose. "I am not among those who assume a woman cannot manage money, but this is more than money, and it will take you time to master the details."

"To begin with," said Octavia, "I shall go north. I would like to see Axby Hall, and meet my tenants—"

"Mr. Forsyte is a first-rate man, an excellent tenant. Unless you intend to live there yourself, I would advise you to stay with him; his lease runs for another year, and you would be well advised to renew it, perhaps even for a longer term than his last one. I believe he would welcome a long lease."

"I do not care for Yorkshire," said Octavia, recalling a bitterly cold visit to her sister's draughty mansion one December. "But I should like to see where my mother's and my grandfather's family came from, which was originally York, was it not? I have never been to York. You know that I had never heard of my great-uncle's existence until the lawyer in Calcutta told me of the inheritance and how it was to come to me? I know practically nothing about that side of my family."

"Dick Worthington was a good man, and a very successful one," Mr. Portal said. "He was a nabob; he went to India in some disgrace—he was a much older man than me, very much established by the time I first went to India, but he made no secret of it. He arrived on those shores with nothing but a post as clerk in the Company's service—and how he obtained that I do not know, I think your grandfather must have contrived it."

"It must have been hard for a young man to be sent away like that."

"It was the making of him, I cannot imagine he would have thrived in England. However, he found that working for other people was not to his liking, and on expeditions about the country he fell in with a tea grower, and discovered that he had a real flair for the business. His mother, your great-grandmother, came from a family of farmers, he told me, and perhaps that was where he had his love of growing things, and his understanding from the agricultural point of view of cultivation of the plants, for there is a considerable science to that. Then he had a nose, he could tell you with a single sniff where a tea was grown, when it had been plucked, how it had been stored. All that was of inestimable value to him, and combined with a knowledge of trade and markets, from the family grocery business—you knew your grandfather was in the grocery line?"

"Yes."

"Combined with that, he soon established a name for himself and the beginnings of a flourishing concern. And his flair went for other things than tea: he had an eye for jewels, and for land which might increase in value. Wealth multiplies, you know, once you reach a certain point, then unless you are very unlucky or foolish, it is difficult for one's fortune not to grow."

"My grandfather did not die a wealthy man," said Octavia, fascinated by this account of a relative she had never known.

"That was a sad business, and it upset Dick Worthington very much, for all he'd been packed off in disgrace, no doubt in the expectation of his not surviving for long, for many people don't; you don't need me to tell you what a harsh and unhealthy climate it is. No, the thing is, your grandfather was a gambler. He could not resist a gamble. At first it was cards, with friends, and so his losses were no more than he could sustain, but then the habit grew upon him, and he bet upon horses—there is a race course in York, you know—and on sporting events, prize-fights, cricket matches, and finally, most dangerous of all, the stock exchange. One debt led to another, and in the end he drained all the money out of the business, and it failed. He was a broken man, and he died soon afterwards."

So it was true, what Mrs. Ackworth had told her about her grandfather. Two gambling brothers, Octavia thought: one gambling in business, giving up a secure post to take great risks, the other with a well-established firm, gambling it all away; two sides of the same coin.

"What makes one man prosper leads another to ruin," said Mr. Portal soberly, as though he had read her thoughts.

"However," said Henrietta cheerfully, "it all happened a good while ago, and you never knew any of the parties concerned, for all they were your blood, so I don't think there is any cause to fall into a melancholy fit over it. The upshot is that you are a very wealthy woman, a widow, in control of your fortune, and while the amount may be so large as to be alarming, in principle, a woman may live a very happy life when she is in such a position. My dear, when you return from Yorkshire, what then are your plans?"

"Providing I do not fall in love with York and decide to live there, which I do not think is very likely, I intend to take a house in London, a small house, nothing extreme, but a place where I may be my own mistress. Of course, I shall have to tell my family how it is that I am able to afford such a thing, and I fear there will be a good deal of anger in that quarter once I own up to my inheritance."

"And a great reluctance to see you looking after your own affairs, as you mentioned," said Henrietta. "Mr. Arthur Melbury has the reputation of being an obstinate man."

"He may be as obstinate as he chooses, he will have to accept the situation and my decision, however little he likes it."

"Where shall you have a house?" said Henrietta. "You may choose anywhere in London, you know, there is nowhere that will be beyond your means."

"You will want to be in a good part of town," said Mr. Portal. "I will ask about, if you wish, to see what is available."

"But will you live by yourself?" said Henrietta. "Just you and the servants, I do not think that is wise, a companion makes all the difference to your comfort. Have you no friend you could ask to share the house with you, no relations?"

"All my living relatives are Melburys. There are various aunts dotted about the countryside, I believe, my father's sisters, but I don't know them, and they have never made any effort to know me, so I shall not invite any of them into my house. No, I shall do very well on my own."

Brave words, for Octavia remembered all too well the loneliness of those years when her stepmother had gone to live in Dublin. However, London wasn't Dorset; in London she would find a circle of friends. She could ride, set up her carriage, go to concerts and the opera and the play; no, she would not let herself be lonely. In any case, if the alternative were to stay with Theodosia, or be shunted off for a turn with her other sisters, then there was no choice.

Chapter Eighteen

Octavia came to the conclusion that she was lacking in moral fibre; she stood self-convicted of cowardice and was also turning into an unblushing liar. She had put off yet again breaking the news of her inheritance to her family; she would, she decided, tell them when she came back from her journey north. And that meant she had to find a reason for her visit to Yorkshire, one that would satisfy Theodosia. She was ashamed of how readily the falsehoods came to her lips.

"Relations of Mr. Darcy, you say? They have invited you for a visit? Pray, what are they called? Perhaps Drusilla knows them."

Since Octavia had just made up the entire family, this was unlikely. "They live near York," she said. Drusilla's house was in the South Riding, she could not be expected to be on visiting terms with a family in the North Riding.

"Oh, York. Nettleton, you said? I do not know the name, they do not come to London, I suppose?"

"He is a lawyer," said Octavia, improvising rapidly.

"Married, I dare say, or he could hardly invite you to stay."

"Married with several young children."

"Oh, children. Well, if you feel you must go, but it is very odd to be leaving London now, with the season in full swing. I had several parties to which I was going to take you—however, you will not be gone long. You will travel on the mail, you will not be comfortable, it is a long journey."

"I go post," said Octavia boldly. "It is all arranged, the Nettletons are being very kind."

"What, paying for your coach travel, and post? He must be a very successful lawyer, or is he a man of property as well?"

"I believe they have a good income."

"Strange that they do not come to London."

Octavia packed quickly and discreetly, with Alice's help. The maid had become much attached to Mrs. Darcy, "such a pleasant-spoken, agreeable person," she told the other servants. "She treats you like you was a human being, not something brought in on the sole of a shoe."

So only Alice knew that Mrs. Darcy had packed more clothes than Theodosia was aware that she possessed and also a riding habit; Octavia hoped she might have a chance to ride while she was away.

She had written to Mr. Forsyte, the tenant of Axby Hall, saying that she was coming north and would be calling upon him. He had replied by return, writing in most cordial terms and inviting her to stay.

Which she intended to do, but she would go first to York, and put up at an hotel, and take time to explore that ancient city.

"The Minster?" said Mr. Cartland, who was fond of the north of England. "A fine cathedral, although rather large." He recommended, when his wife was out of hearing, that she put up at the White Swan. "It is not the smartest hotel in York, but it is clean and comfortable and quiet." He hesitated. "Their charges are not high, but if you find yourself . . . I would be most happy to . . . I should not like you to find yourself short of money."

"You are very kind," said Octavia warmly. "But I assure you I can well afford a few nights at the White Swan."

He gave her one of his sideways glances, and a quick, sly smile. "It occurs to me, sister, that your situation is not quite what it seems."

"I—that is . . ."

"Oh, I do not mean to pry. What you do not tell me, I cannot find myself passing on to your sister. I am glad for you if you are better circumstanced than appears, very glad. A woman on her own should not have to scratch for every penny."

Well, reflected Octavia, as she settled back into the comparative comfort of the hired chaise, there was one member of her family who wouldn't huff and puff when the story of her fortune came out. He would be pleased for her, and take no offence that he hadn't been told the instant she knew.

The journey was a long one, as Theodosia had pointed out. Octavia travelled swiftly, spending only two nights on the road, and arrived at York tired and stiff, glad to be out of the carriage, even though she had taken some pleasure in the changing scenery and sights along the way.

The next day she set out to explore the city, going first to the bookshop suggested by the hotel, where she purchased a guide-book to the city. She spent an hour in the cathedral, which was big, as Mr. Cartland had said, looking up at the rose window and imagining the Minster as it must have been on the day when Henry Tudor, recently crowned as Henry VII, had married the last of the York family, Elizabeth, uniting the white rose of York with the red rose of Lancaster. History was vividly in her mind as she walked along the line of Kings at the entrance to the choir; she herself had always held by the missing Richard III, having taken all the Tudors in strong dislike.

A pause for refreshments in a tea-room near the cathedral and then she wandered through the old part of the town, with its narrow, crowded streets. This was what London must have been like, before the Great Fire, but York also boasted fine modern houses, like those where her hotel was situated, near Bootham Bar. Altogether an agreeable city, if provincial, and she had an idea that the lowering grey skies might be a regular and unwelcome feature of the place.

In the afternoon, she set out to find Caper Street, and stopped, amazed, in front of a large establishment that proclaimed itself to be WORTHINGTON'S, GROCERS, SUPPLIERS TO THE GENTRY. She pushed open the door, the bell clanged, and a man in black came hurrying forward to attend to her.

"I do not wish to buy anything," she said. "I was interested—that is, my attention was caught by the name of the shop. I—I know someone by that name, you see. Is it the name of the present proprietor?"

"No, madame, it was the name of the original grocer who set up business here, in the last century. There has been no one of that name for many years, but the present owner, Mr. Maudlin, kept it on, for the reputation, you know. Worthington is a name that means quality and service in York to this day. Perhaps you would like to speak to Mr. Maudlin?"

He bowed her towards a chair set by the broad mahogany counter. It was a large shop, a very large shop, in immaculate order, everything arranged just so, attentive assistants scurrying to and fro, and seemingly carrying a wide range of goods. Minutes later a little round man, balding, with spectacles perched on his broad nose, came out of a door behind the counter and towards her.

"Good day, madame, Mr. Timley tells me you are enquiring about the name above the door."

He looked a question.

"My name is Mrs. Darcy," Octavia said, with a friendly smile. "Worthington was my mother's name, and I believe that this was my grandfather's shop."

"Good heavens," he cried. "What an honour, indeed it is. You are Samuel Worthington's granddaughter, oh, he was a good man, such a sad . . ." His voice trailed into silence.

"I never knew him," Octavia said, wanting to spare him any embarrassment. "Did you know him well?"

"Oh, dear lady, he was a lifelong friend, lifelong. I was in tea, I was a tea merchant, and I supplied him for many years. Then when—In time, I took over the business, but I kept the name, I did not wish to change it."

Mr. Maudlin was hesitant, wondering how much Octavia knew about her grandfather's business and its failure.

He felt uneasy in her presence. Here was the granddaughter of one of his good friends, whose mother he had dandled on his knee when she was a child, whose failure, decline, and death had made him wretched—but she was a fine lady, everything about her proclaimed it, her air, her clothes, the way she spoke. She belonged on the other side of the counter from him.

Her mother, his own daughter's playmate and equal, had taken a leap out of the world into which she had been born when she married Sir Clement. He had seen her weep before her wedding, but he and all her friends had felt sure it was the right thing for her to do; Sir Clement might be a much older man, they might have few interests in common, but given her circumstances, it opened a new life to her, far away from the city where her family had known disgrace. At the moment at the altar when she uttered her "I do" and became Lady Melbury, all that was wiped out. She took her husband's rank, belonged in his world, was safe, and that was a cause of rejoicing to all her family and well-wishers, although the rejoicing might be muted by the knowledge that a lovely young woman was marrying a man old enough to be her father.

All this was running through his mind, and part of it, at least, Octavia could guess. He was uncomfortable, so was she, and yet she longed to talk more about her family.

The invitation was tentative. If Mrs. Darcy—it would do them great honour—he had to say that Mrs. Maudlin kept a good table, always, and if she would consent to dine with them, he would send this instant to his house, to expect them, they dined late, not from any wish to be fashionable, but to keep in with his shopkeeping duties.

Mrs. Darcy would be delighted, the honour would be all on her side, she would be very happy to meet Mrs. Maudlin, and to dine with people who had been such close friends of her grandfather's.

The gulf was bridged, Mr. Maudlin let out an audible pouf of breath, and Octavia left determined to pay another visit to the cathedral, perhaps to hear the evening service, at four o'clock. She would present herself at Mr. Maudlin's house—detailed directions were given—and they parted with mutual satisfaction.

It was a happy evening. Mrs. Maudlin was a well-looking, sensible woman, younger than her husband by several years. Their eldest son and his wife were at the table; he a prosperous merchant in his forties, she a goldsmith's daughter who would, so Mrs. Maudlin confided in her, inherit her father's substantial business in due course, for she was an only child, and the apple of her father's eye.

"Will she sell it, when that time comes?"

Mrs. Maudlin was shocked. Businesses were not lightly to be bought and sold. "She knows a great deal about the goldsmith's craft; were she a man—however, she will manage it, with John's assistance, of course, and do it very well. There are many people of our sort who want their daughters to grow up removed from trade, to go to genteel seminaries to learn French and play the piano, to live lives far removed from the world of their parents. But we do not hold with that. I come from a farming family, and when my father died, my mother ran the dairy side as well as any man, supplying cheese to all the towns roundabout. We women can be just as hard-working as our menfolk, if we are allowed to be. I want my daughters to grow up to be good wives and mothers, of course, but also to make themselves useful."

"My great-aunt," Octavia said, "took over my great-uncle's concerns when he died, tea plantations in India, and property and other interests. I believe she handled it all most capably."

"Aye, Mrs. Anne Worthington had a remarkably shrewd head on her shoulders."

Mr. Maudlin was looking across the table at her. "I did hear—nothing more than a rumour, perhaps—that Lady Melbury's daughter was old Mrs. Worthington's heir."

"She has left me an inheritance," Octavia said.

"Well, your mother was no fool, it was a sad day when she was taken away by the Lord, and I dare say you are like her. But now you have no husband to advise you and be at your side, that is hard on a young woman," said Mrs. Maudlin.

"It is, but I must contrive as best I can."

"Aye, as we women have always had to."

Octavia felt a surge of panic, hearing again how shrewd Mrs. Worthington was. It was all very well, supposing that she could pick up where her great-aunt had left off, all very well the assurances from Mr. Portal and Mr. Wilkinson that Mrs. Worthington had chosen sound men of business to manage her widespread affairs—but would they be impressed with her? And when, in time, new appointments had to be made, decisions taken, actions approved of, what made her think that she would be capable of acting wisely?

Mrs. Maudlin was quick to notice the troubled look in Octavia's eyes.

"Yes, we in our family have all been brought up to trade and business, and you have not, but it's in your blood. You'll make mistakes, but you'll learn from them; that's what mistakes are for."

Young Mr. Maudlin was a blunt man, with a dry way about him. He fixed her with a stern, level look. "Providing, that is," he said, "that Mrs. Darcy is not tempted by the card table, not inclined to participate in gaming, which is, I know, fashionable among ladies in London, in the circles where I dare say Mrs. Darcy moves."

That at least she had no doubts about. "I do not have a gambler's nature," she said. "I do not bet on cards, in fact I seldom play cards, nor can I see that speculation or wild risks are in my nature. My father was a sound man, and I hope that is an inheritance I have from him."

On the other hand, Theodosia was more than a little inclined to gamble, and to bet far more than she ought. She had married a man with a pocket deep enough to sustain her losses, but . . . Might she be more like Theodosia than she knew, could she find the lure of a sudden win too great to resist? Since she had never had much money to risk—but no. The biggest gamble she would make would be to take the reins of her inheritance into her own hands, instead of relying on her brothers to manage it for her, or instead of at once looking out for a husband, to whom, under law, the whole of her fortune would then belong.

Mrs. Maudlin was alive to that risk. "You will marry again, no, you say you will not, and that is only right, with your poor husband not long gone, but it is in the nature of things, and then you need to choose well; if you have even a part of Mrs. Worthington's estate, then you will be a rich matrimonial prize."

"Lord, yes," said young Mrs. Maudlin, looking at Octavia with interest. "They will buzz around you like bees to the honey-pot. It was the same with me, but"—she stretched out her hand to her husband—"my dearest John was never a buzzer nor a fly. There are good men in the world, many of them, if you know where to find them."

Octavia was touched by the very real affection between them, and indeed between the older couple. It was the same easy trust and liking that she had found at the Ackworths', marriage as a partnership, not a constant imposition of authority or superiority, an equal match, one where the moral advantage did not fall too heavily on one side nor the other.

Altogether it was a most agreeable evening. The table was laden with Yorkshire food of the best kind, not ostentatious, but full of flavour; if Mrs. Maudlin was a farmer's daughter, then no doubt her family's farm provided the best of everything for the Maudlin household.

After they had dined, the younger granddaughter, a pretty, shy girl of about fifteen, joined the company, and despite what Mrs. Maudlin had said about bringing up her daughters to be useful, the girl sat at the grand pianoforte and played a sonata with execution and taste.

The young Maudlin escorted her back to her hotel in their carriage, and as Octavia undressed and got ready for bed in her comfortable hotel room, she thought rather wistfully of how different her life would have been had her mother married not a baronet, but a merchant, a man such as Mr. John Maudlin. She would have grown up in a world very different from the one she knew. No landed squire and rising parliamentarian for brothers, no grand ladies for sisters. But she must not be sentimental about it, doubtless there was as much lust for power and ambition and folly here in York as in London.

She lay back against the soft feather pillows, reflecting on what her life had brought her; loneliness, yes, but the rare experience of her sea voyages, and the chance to see another country, so far removed, so very different from settled, green, complacent England. She remembered the brilliant colours of an Indian sunset, the vivid plants and birds, the teeming life, the strange temples, and knew that she would not have foregone that, not for all the comfort and security of these people from whom her mother had come.

She was too sensible to have any regrets, and too self-aware not to know that perhaps a life of the familiar mercantile round would not suit her temperament. Perhaps that was the touch of the gambler she had inherited from her feckless grandfather, a liking for excitement. He had found it in gambling; she relied on life itself to provide it.

But not the life of the country; no, to be busy and occupied was the road to happiness, but not the occupation of Mrs. Ackworth with her last-century devotion to her manor house, nor the buying and making and selling of these new Yorkshire acquaintances.

She did not feel inclined to sleep, so instead of extinguishing her candle, she opened the first volume of a lurid tale she had bought for her journey, hot off the Minerva Press, entitled *The Prisoner of Castle Porphyry,* and settled down to make her flesh creep.

Chapter Nineteen

The next morning, after a night untroubled by the fantastic dangers and alarms of her novel, Octavia rose early, breakfasted, paid her bill, and climbed into the hired carriage that was to take her on the next part of her Yorkshire odyssey, Axby Hall.

She looked out eagerly as they passed through the large village of Axby, a prosperous-looking place, with a broad sandy street. She noticed a baker, a butcher, a general store. Axby Hall lay about a mile beyond the village, Mr. Forsyte had said, and as they drove along a deep leafy lane, she pictured the house in her mind. It would be much like many of the houses she had seen here in Yorkshire, she supposed: red-brick and square, a solid, sensible house.

So she was astonished when the carriage climbed up a slope with a broad sweep overlooking a hilly ridge and the driver called out to her, "That is Axby Hall." There before her was a magnificent house, built in the classical style, with pillars beneath a fine pediment, set around with a landscaped park, green swaths leading down to a lake.

She had no idea it was so large, nor so fine. Was she truly the owner of all this?

For the first time, the solid substance of what she had inherited came home to her. Until now it had been on paper: lists of jewels, land, tea plantations, title deeds, rent rolls. And the only tangible aspect had been the wad of paper money which the lawyer had pressed on her, saying that she would need it for expenses, that on her return to town he would, if she would permit, introduce her to Mr. Hoare. Hoare's were the bankers who dealt with the late Mr. and Mrs. Worthington's affairs, and he would strongly advise that she continue to bank with them.

"You need not worry about your money if you bank with them; there is no danger of Hoare's failing." Mr. Wilkinson had said with a thin-lipped smile; a bank breaking was too serious a matter for more than the mildest jest.

Here was a house, the kind of house she had constructed in miniature, the epitome of great English style, perfectly balanced, the proportions of the ancient world renewed and fitting snugly and serenely into an English landscape—and it belonged to her.

Mr. John Forsyte was at the door to welcome her. Behind him stood his wife, with two or three shy children peeping round her skirts, who skipped forward as they saw Octavia's warm smile to curtsy and make a leg.

The house was as fine inside as it was from the outside. A lofty hall had matching stairs turning up to meet at a landing. The floor was tiled in black and white marble, the perfectly placed niches were graced with classical busts, the house smelt fresh and perfumed with flowers that stood in bowls on every side.

Octavia was taken into the splendid drawing room, and then, after refreshments were offered and accepted—"peaches and pines from our succession house," said Mrs. Forsyte—she was taken on a tour of the house by Mr. Forsyte.

He was a man of medium height, with fashionably cut brown hair, very much the country gentleman, and both he and his wife, Octavia decided, were pleasant, intelligent, well-bred people.

They were indeed excellent tenants. The house was in perfect order, inside and out. Mrs. Forsyte showed off the improvements they had made in the kitchen, the closed stove which had replaced the old-fashioned range, and Mr. Forsyte was eager to talk about the drainage, and the work he had done in that direction.

The servants were a clean, cheerful, active set. Octavia had learned long ago that you might fairly judge people by their servants. Of course it was easier in the country, where families worked generation after generation up at the big house, whereas London servants were notorious for their fickle ways, but even so, it said much for the Forsytes that the whole place was immaculate, within and without: the gardens, the Home Farm, the public and the private rooms, the kitchens, and even the attics, which were piled high with boxes and cast-offs, but all neatly arranged and covered with sheets against the dust.

Octavia was loud in her praise, but she could sense an undercurrent of concern in both the Forsytes. Of course they would feel uneasy. They had made their home here, and now there was a new owner, a young woman who might choose to come and live here herself; their lease was near its end and it might be that they would be turned out of the home they had lavished so much care and attention on, of which they were so rightly proud.

Octavia wanted to reassure them. Wonderful as it was, a happy, beautiful house that was also a home, she was quite certain by now that country life wouldn't suit her any more in Yorkshire than in Hertfordshire or Dorset.

Mr. Forsyte was not sure, she could tell, as to whether he could discuss his tenancy with her. He made a reference to her man of business, had she met Mr. Apthorpe yet? Would he be looking after her affairs here in the north, he had been Mrs. Worthington's right-hand man, he found him to be a clear-headed, competent person.

Octavia saw no point in beating about the bush. Mr. Forsyte sought reassurance; she was able to give it to him. She had no intention of living in Yorkshire, delightful though the county was. On a May morning, with the countryside unfolding in rich greens and the lark ascending and the cuckoo sounding in the woods, it was another Eden, an Arcadia. But come days of fog and rain, come autumn storms and winter snow and ice—then it was a region that held no charms for her. So she told him frankly that everything she knew of him and had seen made her certain that she would be happy to agree to a new lease; she had not met Mr. Apthorpe, who was presently in

Scotland, but would be seeing him in Leeds before she went back to London, and she would instruct him accordingly.

The bright smiles on the faces of all the Forsytes, knowing that the house that suited them so well was to remain their home, was reward enough for Octavia. Mr. Forsyte would by no means have been homeless had she had other plans; he was a man of substance and standing; a man who could rent one fine house could well rent another, but it would not be the same, he was attached to Axby Hall.

Octavia thought that he might in the course of time like to purchase the property; well, unless her views changed markedly, she would have no real objection. Of course, all her advisers would be bound to counsel her otherwise, since a good property with a good tenant was not lightly to be disposed of. However, that was in the future, and if she allowed her heart to rule her head in such matters, what was wrong with that? It would only be if she made a habit of it, was too conciliating, too ready to lend an ear to stories of hardship and distress, that she would be at fault.

So dinner was a cheerful affair. The Forsytes had invited two or three families from around and about to dine, and they bowled up in their carriages, people very much of the same kind as themselves, and Octavia found them agreeable company.

She realised ruefully that this was an end to her secrecy; Mr. Forsyte was open about her status, they all knew she was heiress to the very great wealth of her great-aunt, even if they had no accurate idea as to the extent of that wealth. One or two of the women attempted to sound her out, saying that Mrs. Worthington had property and interests in the East, did she not? but they were too well bred to persist when she was unforthcoming.

Word would quickly fly from here to London; she could expect a sharp welcome from her family on her return to town. Well, that was for another day, and meanwhile she ate the excellent food, more fine cuts of meat, more vegetables fresh from the Hall's own vegetable gardens, more fruit from the pinery, which Mrs. Forsyte had shown her with considerable and justified pride.

Mrs. Forsyte loved growing things, it transpired. She had green thumbs, her husband said with fond affection. "She can coax any seedling; anything green that will grow will do so under her care. We have exotic fruits here that I dare say you will not find in the whole of Yorkshire. You will be familiar with many of them, I expect, after your time in India."

The talk at the dinner table turned to politics. There was much local interest and excitement; the small town of Axby, although it had only a handful of voters, returned an MP to Westminster. This was the Mr. Urquhart who had celebrated his recent victory—his tenth—at the general election the previous month by drinking himself into a stupor, and being overcome with a fatal apoplexy as a result.

"It is not surprising," said Mr. Forsyte. "He was the size of one of Cooper Joe's biggest barrels, and a man who indulged himself. It was bound to get to him in the end."

"What will happen?" said Octavia. "Will there have to be another election?"

The table fell silent, and the guests with one accord stared at her.

"Why, of course there will," said Mr. Forsyte. "There has been no reform act passed, more's the pity, and so London will send word to the Castle as to whom they wish to be elected. Strictly speaking," he went on, "the seat is in your hands, Mrs. Darcy, but for many years, since Mrs. Worthington took no interest whatsoever in politics, and indeed never lived in this part of the world, preferring her house in Leeds, it has been part of the Castle interest."

"Which castle is that?"

"Why, Rutherford Castle, seat of the Earl of Rutherford."

"Lord Rutherford's seat is here? I had no idea," said Octavia.

They were amazed at such ignorance, it seemed inconceivable that anyone should not know all about Rutherford Castle.

"Lord Rutherford is rarely here, not as often as we should like. And of course, there is another parliamentary seat there, the Castle seat, a member of the Rutherford family always holds that seat. The Whigs will have a candidate lined up for Axby, you will find it is all a matter of form."

The next morning, waylaying Mr. Forsyte before he set out for his chambers in Leeds, Octavia asked him some more questions about the seat. Would the electorate—all twenty-six of them—automatically vote for the Castle choice? Was he ever opposed?

"No, never."

"But if I chose to put up another candidate—"

"You?" Mr. Forsyte looked thunderstruck. "It would be . . . But there is nothing . . . You own most of the village, you will find; most of the inhabitants are your tenants, and the householders, who are of course the only men with the vote, are your tenants, too, all but one of them, I believe. What you say must go; that is the nature of rotten boroughs. They will be done away with in the end, it is stark wrong that a small town like this sends its man to Parliament whereas cities with a population of fifty thousand people have no representation. It will be righted in the end; Pitt tried for reform in the last century but to no avail, the vested interests were too strongly ranged against him. And the Tories will never reform, they are afraid of change, they work on a principle of what was good enough for their forefathers is good enough for them. They are secure in office, but things change, and the Whigs will have their day, and then we will see some action on this front."

"You are a Whig yourself, Mr. Forsyte?"

He hesitated. "I am something of a Radical persuasion, although I know that these days to be considered a Radical is to be considered by many to be unsound if not dangerous. I am Whiggish, definitely Whiggish, never a Tory, despite my country background—but yet I am still Radically minded."

"Would not you like to sit in Parliament?"

"I, Mrs. Darcy?"

"Yes. Why should Lord Rutherford, who may live nearby, but is not of this neighbourhood, have the choice of Axby's MP? If the choice is mine, as you say it is, why should I not choose you?"

Mr. Forsyte's jaw dropped. "You cannot be serious!"

"I would hardly make a joke of such a matter. I find the seat is, despite appearances to the contrary, mine to bestow. I am expected to have no say in the matter; the candidate is chosen by the Party—whether a Party I support or not. I find I do not care for this."

"Are you a Tory, to go against the Whig interest in such a way?"

"To be truthful, Mr. Forsyte, I am only now beginning to form political opinions of my own. My family are Tory, through and through, but from what I have heard and seen since I came back to England, I rather think I share many Whiggish views. I may even wake up one day to find myself a Radical!"

She saw from Mr. Forsyte's countenance that he was struggling between delight and apprehension.

"I should like nothing better than to have a seat in Parliament," he said finally. "Only, think what you are about; to antagonise the Castle interest might not be wise."

"Oh, you will have to bear the brunt of that, for I shan't be here, and I don't give a fig for what the Castle thinks or wants. And," she added shrewdly, "I do not believe you are quaking in your boots at the prospect of upsetting Lord Rutherford."

"He will be annoyed, he is not, from what I know of him, a man who cares to be thwarted, but he will get over the disappointment. If you mean it, Mrs. Darcy, if you really mean to offer me the seat, then I accept. I must consult my wife, naturally, but I am sure she will support me; she is well aware of my political ambitions."

"Then it is settled." She held out her hand, and he shook it warmly. "I shall look forward to seeing you in London when you come up to take your seat."

Chapter Twenty

Lord Rutherford had not planned to make the journey north, not at this time of the year. He had a sense of duty to the vast castle which was his family home, but he never had any desire to spend more time there than he had to. It was a duty, a responsibility, not a pleasure; he was of a modern cast of mind, and although he would not dream of selling even a square yard of his land, nor neglecting the upkeep of every one of the numerous walls and battlements and towers, still, he was never happy there.

His steward was an experienced, competent man, who was glad to see him, and who at once made an appointment for him to go through any number of papers the next morning.

"You have come upon parliamentary business, I feel sure," the steward said. "You will want to go over to Axby this afternoon, to meet the electors and introduce them to Mr. Stanley."

Rutherford had brought Septimus Stanley with him, not a man he greatly cared for, but considered a rising star in the Party; he was to fill the seat at Axby. He was a thin man with a supercilious lip, and Sholto had taken no great pleasure in his company on the journey north. Rutherford had driven himself, changing the horses of his curricle along the road, and so he had not had to endure so much of his companion's dull conversation; the evenings when they put up at an inn one night and at a friend's house the next had been rather more of a trial.

The steward was hovering, having been about to take his leave.

"What is it, Shuttleforth?" Lord Rutherford asked. "Out with it."

"The late owner of Axby Hall died last year. A Mrs. Worthington. You will not have known her, my lord, she never lived in these parts."

"So I heard. And?"

"The new owner of Axby Hall—and therefore the owner of most of the houses in the town of Axby—is here at the moment."

"Is he, by God? Do you mean I shall have to call on him? What a bore."

"It is a her."

"Oh, a woman. Well, and where is she staying?"

"With the Forsytes."

"Then I'll pay a duty visit when I go over there with Stanley. We can introduce him to Forsyte at the same time."

Shuttleforth coughed. "Begging your lordship's pardon, but it isn't so simple."

"Why not?"

"It seems that this new owner wants to put up her own candidate. And it is to be Mr. Forsyte."

"Mr. Forsyte? Impossible. The Party will never stand for it."

But when he met his political agent, who had overseen the election in both Axby and the Castle seats, Lord Rutherford swiftly realised that the Party would have no say.

"It has been an understood thing that we choose the candidate for Axby, with the late Mrs. Worthington taking no interest at all in politics. However, in law—well, if she chooses a candidate, the voters will put him in, they can't well do otherwise. They are not going to be setting themselves up in defiance of their landlord. Same as the voters here wouldn't go against your lordship's choice."

"We'll see about this," said Lord Rutherford. "Who is this interfering woman who thinks she can come meddling in matters she knows nothing about?"

"She is a stranger to these parts, perhaps that's why she doesn't quite understand how we do this. She is a widow, a Mrs. Darcy. Member of the same family as the Darcys of Derbyshire, I dare say. She is a great-niece of the Worthingtons and I understand has inherited a substantial fortune from them, of which Axby and Axby Hall are only a small part."

Rutherford was speechless. "Mrs. Darcy? Are you serious? Do you mean the Mrs. Darcy who is a tall, fair woman, recently arrived from India, sister to the Melburys? I don't believe it. She's no money, no fortune; you must be mistaken. I know her family well, unfortunately, and they would not keep such an inheritance quiet, I assure you. She is here on false pretences. I shall have to find out what kind of a game she is playing."

Rutherford rode to Axby, a distance of some five miles across country, and he was glad of the ride on a fresh, active horse, well up to his weight, a hunter he himself had bought only the previous year, but hadn't yet ridden to hounds. He was not particularly keen on hunting; he went out from time to time, usually when staying with friends in Leicestershire or the other great hunting counties. His was essentially an urban life, despite his vast estates, and he preferred it that way; he was at home in the clubs and salons of London, and most of all in Parliament; for the long months when the House wasn't in session, he was still active in the business of politics. He held no high government position, being a Whig, but he was a close associate of Castlereagh's, knowledgeable about foreign affairs, and often acting on his lordship's behalf when that active statesman was abroad, conducting delicate negotiations in the aftermath of the Napoleonic wars.

Rutherford let his horse have its head, taking little notice of the countryside around him; familiar to him from his boyhood, it held no novelty to draw his eye away from his internal musings.

Until his attention was attracted by the sight of another horseman, galloping in the distance under the long shadow of Axby Fell. No, he was out, it was a woman. He frowned. Riding alone, at a headlong pace. It must be one of the Henty girls, who were for ever careering about the countryside on their ponies and horses, instead of sitting at home and minding their stitches and attending to their music lessons. Still, he had to admit that their unusual upbringing did make them into more pleasant companions than most of their sex; the eldest girl had married a friend of his, and it was an unusual but a happy match, and Julia Henty, as she had been before her marriage, was shaping up as an excellent political hostess, an asset to her husband in his political life, for all she'd probably never produced so much as a single sampler in her girlhood.

He lost sight of the other rider as he topped the hill and reined in his horse to make his way down the steep path that would bring him out behind Axby Hall. From there he could take a tack into the village, skirting the Hall; he had no intention of calling upon Mr. Forsyte until he had spoken to his agent, who should be waiting for him in Axby.

Damn Urquhart for being so gross in his habits, and celebrating his victory—his undisputed victory—too well. If he had restrained himself, he, Rutherford, would not have had to leave London at a most inconvenient time and certainly would not have found himself having to sort out this stupid tangle.

As he set his horse at the gate that would take him on to the track, he heard the beat of hooves behind him. He drew aside into the lane as the rider set the horse at the gate and went over it perfectly.

It was Mrs. Darcy. Riding a raking bay, far too big and strong a ride for any woman, although she certainly was a good horsewoman, handling him with a light hand.

"Your servant, ma'am," he said, removing his hat.

Her cheeks were tipped with colour, and she had an exultant look in her eye; how he disliked an emotional woman.

"Lord Rutherford," she said, nodding her head at him. "I have had such a capital gallop."

"I saw you. Where is your groom?"

"Oh, I did not bring a groom with me. I was riding on Mr. Forsyte's land, I could come to no harm."

"Had your horse stumbled, or—"

"Then they would have sent a search party out for me in due

course, and if I had broke my neck, then it would not have mattered whether there was a groom about or not. You look as though you would like to break someone's neck for them, Lord Rutherford. Are you here to call upon Mr. Forsyte?"

"Not at present."

Drat the woman for her insouciance, had she no sense of decorum? "I have business in the town of Axby."

"Parliamentary business?" she asked.

Was she laughing at him?

"As it happens, yes. And since I have met you, perhaps I might mention—"

"You do not like my candidate for the seat, I can see it in your face. Is that based upon rational grounds, or do you merely choose not to have anyone treading on your toes?"

"My dear Mrs. Darcy, I hardly think you are a proper person to discuss this with. I shall talk to my agent and to some people in Axby and then I shall call upon Mr. Forsyte. But first of all, I—"

"It is quite true that I have offered him the seat, if that is what you wish to ascertain."

"You have offered him the seat—upon my word, I cannot think what game you think you are playing."

"It is no game. I have discovered that, as owner more or less of the village of Axby, and landlord to most of its voters, the seat lies in my gift, as it were. I had no idea parliamentary seats were thus allotted. I have been in India, you know, and I paid little attention to such things when I was a girl in Dorset. However, Axby is to have a new MP, and I have decided that Mr. Forsyte is the man."

"The choice of a candidate in such a case is made in London. There are political issues involved, which I dare say you do not properly understand."

"I am very sure you are right."

"Axby returns a Whig, it has always returned a Whig."

"Well, you must argue it out with Mr. Forsyte as to exactly what his political allegiance is; I understand that he is more a Whig than a Tory, and more a Radical than either."

"A Radical! Well, that is exactly my point . . ."

"He is a sensible man, a lawyer, he seems to me just the sort you need in the House. Much more so than the drunken buffoon whom I gather has represented this borough these last ten years. Mr. Forsyte can only be an improvement."

"I have nothing against Mr. Forsyte, an estimable man, I dare say, and a veritable Cicero among lawyers, however—"

"However, you want to put up your own candidate. Well, you may do so, but I am reliably informed that, great though your power and influence is, mine is the greater here, locally. It is all a matter of rents and so on, you will understand that better than I do."

He wasn't going to give her the satisfaction of seeing how angry he was. How could this young woman, this nobody, as Snipe had rightly called her, be sitting here on that horse whom she could hardly control—he knew he was being unfair, she had the animal well in hand—defying him like this?

"I feel sure, Mrs. Darcy, that your brother Arthur Melbury—"

"My half brother, Lord Rutherford."

"Very well, your half brother, will be as alarmed by your impetuous action as I am."

"Is that a threat, Lord Rutherford? I do not care for threats."

"A threat? I threaten you? I merely wish to warn you—"

"Stop there, or you will later wish that you had done so. After being bullied and harassed by my brother Arthur for most of my life, I am now in the delightful position of finding myself an independent woman in charge of my own fortune and life, and I do not give a jot for Arthur's opinion. Nor whether you have sufficient influence to hinder the advancement in Parliament he so keenly longs for."

"Family feeling—"

"I have little family feeling. My mind is made up. Nothing you say or do will alter it. If you choose to vent your temper at being thwarted on my brother, then so be it, and I shall think the less of you for it. Good day to you, my lord."

With which words she turned her horse's head, gave his flank a light tap with her whip, and cantered down the rutted track towards the Hall.

Octavia was ruffled by her encounter with Rutherford, more so than she admitted to Mr. Forsyte when she told him of the outcome of her ride.

"Lord Rutherford is not a man to cross," said Mr. Forsyte. "I told you so when you offered me the seat."

"It is I who am crossing him, not you. You are surely not going to let him have his way," cried Octavia. "You are surely not going to submit to this kind of overriding of what anyone else's wishes may be." Then she recollected herself. "I am sorry, I forgot, you are a neighbour, it might make for awkwardness."

"I should not exactly call Lord Rutherford a neighbour," said Mr. Forsyte. "Apart from the fact that he is rarely in this country, we are too small fry for him, he does not visit in Axby."

"But you have not changed your mind? You won't turn down the seat?" said Octavia, surprised at how keenly disappointed she would feel if he had.

"Not at all," replied Mr. Forsyte, and his wife was quick to agree. "It is a matter of what one believes in, one's views cannot be swayed by whether Lord Rutherford approves or disapproves," he said seriously. "If I sit for Axby, I shall be a thorn in the side of Whigs, for I disagree with them on many points, but I shall be an even bigger thorn in the flesh of the Tories, for I disagree with them upon practically every subject."

Octavia was relieved, and they passed a most agreeable evening, Octavia gaining some insight into Radical thinking, and Mr. and Mrs. Forsyte discussing how a parliamentary career would affect their lives, given that Mr. Forsyte would have to spend many days in London.

It transpired, when Mrs. Forsyte and Octavia were sitting together after dinner, while the children were outside on the terrace annoying the peacocks, and they were all enjoying the unusual warmth of an early summer evening, that Mrs. Forsyte held very much the same views on absent husbands as did Harriet Thurloe.

"I shall go with him, when he has to spend any length of time in town. The children are in the care of a kind nurse and a competent governess, and I have been thinking that I shall ask my sister, my unmarried sister, who lives in Leeds, to come and live with us. The children are very fond of her, and she of them, and she is more than capable of looking after the house while I am away."

"Is that not a cause for conflict? When you return and she has to hand over the reins of the house? Might not this prove a difficulty?"

Mrs. Forsyte laughed. "I think your sisters must be very different creatures to mine. Agnes is not a person to attempt to usurp my position as a mother or as mistress of the house. At present she lives with my brother's family; she was disappointed in love, and content to remain a spinster, so she says. She paints and loves music, and I think would like to spend more time here with these nephews and nieces, if my brother can spare her."

Again Octavia marvelled at the picture of family life so removed from most of her own experience, but she said nothing about this, and instead fell to discussing whereabouts in London it might be possible to find suitable lodgings. "Although it may not be necessary, for Mr. Forsyte's elder brother lives in town, in a big house, and we are always welcome there."

Where to live in London was a subject uppermost in Octavia's mind, as, after several days at Axby Hall, and two days in Leeds talking to her late great-aunt's man of business, Mr. Apthorpe, who was clearly an utterly reliable and capable person, she set off on the long journey south to London.

Once the news got about, she would find life in Lothian Street very uncomfortable; she knew her sister well enough to be sure of that. And she was quite right, for she had barely stepped across the threshold, weary after nine long hours in the carriage, when her sister pounced on her, full of indignation and fury.

Chapter Twenty-one

"What is this I hear, what is this extraordinary rumour that is flying around town? And where have you been, who are these Darcy relations in Yorkshire you were supposedly visiting? There are no Darcys or Darcy connections in Yorkshire, no one who could possibly have anything to do with you, I am sure of that, I had it from Lady Mordaunt, and she must know, she was born a Darcy, which you are not. Ah, you colour up, you have been caught out in a lie. I knew it!"

"Theodosia, calm down, you will do yourself a mischief. There are always rumours, you should not listen to them."

Her sister paid no attention. "People are saying you have inherited a fortune. I tell you, it will do you no good to spread such tales, for it must have come from you, who else would put such nonsense about? You will be found out, you will be the laughing-stock of London. 'Who is there to leave Mrs. Darcy a fortune?' I said to Lady Barchester, when she called round, quivering with curiosity, to see what she could find out. I told her that there was no truth in it, that I had no notion where such an idea could have come from; had you inherited anything, so much as another sixpence, then we, your family, would be the first to know, and I could assure her that it was all a hum. She went away satisfied, but the story has not been quelled, on all sides people ask me impertinent questions. It was always so, you have been nothing but trouble to us from the moment you were born!"

It was only as Octavia had expected. The cat was out of the bag, and she must come clean. "It is true," she said calmly. "A relation on my mother's side has left property and money to me in her will. It is not a cause for dismay, Theodosia, and if you continue to work yourself up into a state, you will need your smelling salts; shall I ring for Icken?"

"A relation? On your mother's side? You have no relations."

"Not any longer, no, but it turns out that I did, without ever knowing about them. I am very glad for this inheritance, and so should you be; only consider, there is no need for me ever again to be a burden on any of my brothers or sisters."

"What property, how much money? A vast inheritance is spoken of, enormous sums, plantations in India, jewels, tens of thousands of pounds in gilts, a large estate in the north of England—" She paused, and shook her finger at Octavia. "Ha, of course, that is where you have been! I should never have believed you could be so sly! And where exactly in Yorkshire is this house and land, pray? I shall find out from Drusilla, make no doubt of it, so you may as well tell me."

"Oh, for heaven's sake, Theodosia, what a fuss about nothing. Are you not glad that instead of being poor, I am rich?"

"It is the ungratefulness I mind so much. The ungratefulness and the untruthfulness. You must have known of this for some time, before you even arrived in England; you knew in India, that is why you came home!"

Since this was all perfectly true, Octavia found herself unable to say anything to rebut her sister's accusations; all she wanted was to escape from Theodosia's increasing rage, to go upstairs and wash off the dust of her journey and compose herself.

Theodosia had no intention of letting her off so easily, and her probing interrogation was only ended by the arrival of Arthur, whose anger at his sister becoming an heiress was only exceeded by what he had heard of her defiance of Lord Rutherford: "To offend a man of his standing and influence, have you taken leave of your senses? And meddling in politics; my word, Octavia, your arrogance is beyond all bearing!"

A knock at the door, and Augusta was announced, sailing into the room even as the butler was speaking her name. She moved straight into the attack, but even as she spoke, Theodosia was keeping up her thread of ill-humour, and Arthur, raising his voice in an attempt to silence his sisters, was booming away.

"There is to be no obstinacy in this on your part, Octavia. I and Adderley need to have all the details, we need to ascertain at once just how large this fortune of yours is; no, I do not ask you for the information, how can you possibly have a grasp of values and financial matters? If your inheritance is even a fraction of what is being bruited about, we must step in immediately. Who is the lawyer in the case?"

Octavia, a headache buzzing behind her eyes, looked at the three enraged figures of her sisters and brother, words streaming from them like a scene in the opera, or more likely a farce, and didn't know whether to laugh or lose her temper. Temper won.

"Yes, I have inherited a fortune, a considerable fortune, and no, Arthur, I do not need any assistance from you, nor from Adderley, nor from Mr. Cartland, in managing my affairs. I have a good lawyer and a first-rate man of business, thank you, and if I am foolish and lose every penny, then I shall have no one to blame but myself."

"Lose every penny?" Augusta shrieked, turning pale at the thought; money and property were sacred, they were not a fit subject for jesting.

"I am not going to lose any of it, Augusta," Octavia said wearily.

"This settles it," said Theodosia, a scheming light coming into her sharp eyes. "It makes it even more imperative that we find you a husband. Of course, it will be much easier, men will be prepared to overlook your height and your ungovernable tongue when there is a fortune involved. You must and can marry a lord, a man of substance, an influential man. Augusta, let you and I put our heads together and discuss what is to be done."

It was too much. Octavia pressed her hand against her burning eyes, and with a firm step headed for the door. Deaf to her siblings' instructions to stay where she was, there was still so much to say, she almost ran out of the room and upstairs to her bedchamber.

In a moment, Alice was there, and after one look at Octavia, she hurried away to make a tisane, advising Mrs. Darcy to lie down upon the bed, she could see she had the headache as bad as ever so. She pulled the curtains across the windows to shut out the slanting evening sunlight, and then whisked herself out of the room.

"Not surprising that she has the headache," she said to herself as she ran nimbly down the back stairs to the kitchen quarters. "The way they were going on at her in there, Lordy, what's she done to deserve that?"

Coxley the butler was on hand to tell her. "Mrs. Darcy is an ungrateful woman and a disloyal sister," he pronounced. "A vast great fortune, and never a word to them, leading them all up the garden path, thinking as how she didn't have two pennies to rub together. They say"—he lowered his voice to a sepulchral whisper—"they say she's rich enough to buy an abbey. Chests of gold coins and jewels, all from India."

"Why should she want to buy an abbey?" said Alice. "It seems an unnatural thing to do."

"You play your cards right," said Hannah, the sullen head housemaid, "and you'll get taken on when Mrs. Darcy sets up her own establishment. Lucky for some."

"If you ever had a smile on your face, she might employ you," Alice retorted, heaving the heavy kettle off the fire.

"Own establishment?" said the butler. "Ho, that's not very likely, she'll be married in a trice, to one of the royal dukes, like as not, if her fortune's as big as they say it is."

"No more scrimping and saving for her," said the cook. She was a wiry woman, with muscular arms. She thumped the pastry she was working with extra force. "Some folk have all the luck. And don't they say this money comes from trade? It's not the same as real wealth, it's not land or old money."

"Money's money," said the butler sagely, "and when there's enough of it, people, however grand, won't be too particular where it came from. She was a Melbury before she married, and Darcy's a good enough name for anyone, so no one's going to start asking questions about her mother's origins. Oh, she'll find London society treats her very different now, bowing and scraping they'll be."

"It couldn't happen to a nicer lady," said Alice. She finished stirring the brew she had made, and poured it from the jug into a delicate porcelain cup. "And her family have no need to go turning on her like that."

"She deceived them," said the butler.

"Kept her mouth shut, that's all," said the cook. "Like a sensible woman. Look a' them now the cat's out of the bag, she'll be wishing she stayed in Yorkshire, I reckon. Look lively with that tisane now, Alice, or it'll be stone cold by the time you get it upstairs."

Coxley was quite right; London did treat Mrs. Darcy very differently, as soon as the word spread that the rumours were true; a rich, a very rich Mrs. Darcy was not at all the same person as the Melburys' indigent widowed sister. Somehow, a fair approximation of her wealth was arrived at, and Theodosia could barely restrain her anger when one of her oldest friends addressed her on the subject—taunted her, she said to Mr. Cartland later.

"Well, Theodosia, you must rejoice in her good fortune, I think she deserves it as well as any woman. Upon my word, it is a fairy tale come true for your despised younger sister. Unmarriageable at nineteen, London at her feet at twenty-five!"

All this was a red rag to a bull, and Mr. Cartland regretted the words the moment they were spoken.

"You may sit there, high and mighty, and pretending not to mind. She is richer than we are, how can she deserve that? It seems that she will have getting on for a hundred thousand in gilts and funds, and jewellery worth nearly as much. The income from the India tea gardens is substantial. Pagoda Portal will know how much, but one can get nothing out of him, he's like a Trappist monk when he wants to be, I always said he was a disagreeable man. And the estate in Yorkshire, all those acres, and a fine house. Then there are shops in Leeds, and some in London, good tenants, long leases, more income; oh, I can't bear it."

"Compose yourself, my dear. What is it to you? I am not a whit the poorer for her wealth and nor are you."

George Warren heard the news from his stepmother. He stared at her in disbelief, and drummed his fingers on her marble mantelpiece. "It's all a hum, Caroline, where would she get that kind of fortune from? Her mother was a grocer's daughter, and he went bust, I am sure of that."

"It was the grocer's brother who made the fortune, he was a younger son, sent off to India in disgrace—an old story, but one that rarely turns out so well. He died, left everything to his widow, no children—she named Octavia Darcy as her heir, and there you are."

George's eyes narrowed. "I wonder exactly when this widowed aunt of hers—"

"Great-aunt."

"Great-aunt, then—I wonder when she died. For, if by any chance it was before Christopher snuffed it, then the money would be his, would have to be, as Octavia's husband. And under his will, I inherit everything except her little capital sum of three thousand pounds. I shall make some investigations as to dates and times, as to the accuracy of reports of Christopher Darcy's death; we may have been misled or misinformed, the man who was supposedly with him might have been mistaken, or could be encouraged to remember that he was mistaken—"

"I cannot bear to think of her with all that money and property," said Caroline with vigour. "Nabobs! India has a lot to answer for, enriching people of a class who could never in the normal run of things expect to have two pennies to rub together!"

Chapter Twenty-two

One thing was certain: Octavia must move out of Lothian Street as soon as ever she could. She was longing for a home of her own; Theodosia was being tiresome in the extreme, and she had Arthur hounding and haranguing her. He was a strong-willed, forceful man, a bully, as he had always been, and she longed to be free of him. Which she might be in her own house, but could not when she was living with Theodosia.

Even Mr. Cartland was finding it wearing; he risked his wife's fury by expostulating with her about Arthur, saying, "Your brother treats this house as if it were his own, and he is wasting his time, Octavia will not budge."

Mrs. Cartland was not standing for a breath of criticism of Arthur, and told her spouse so in no uncertain terms.

"Next we shall have Sir James arriving, spluttering and harrumphing," Henry Cartland was heard to observe to Penelope as he left the house to find solace in his club.

Alone of her family, Penelope was delighted by Octavia's new wealth. It seemed exactly like a fairy tale to her, and she told her aunt so, her eyes sparkling at how annoyed all kinds of people would be. And, she added casually, did Octavia perhaps have any livings at her disposal now? For Mr. Poyntz was a most deserving case, an excellent clergyman, would adorn any parish in the land.

Octavia didn't know the answer to that; perhaps she had, she would make enquiries, although surely Mr. Poyntz's friend Lord Rutherford was the person to approach on that front.

"Oh, Lord Rutherford has promised him the living of Meryton whenever it should become vacant, and it is a good living, but of course a clergyman cannot have too many livings."

"How would he serve his parishioners in Hertfordshire at the same time as those in Yorkshire, pray?"

"There is no problem with that, he would appoint a curate, you know, and give him a stipend to do the work. But Mr. Poyntz will not remain a parish priest for long, he is too clever and amiable and well-connected for that; I am quite certain he will advance very rapidly, do not you agree?"

"I am sure of it," said Octavia, privately thinking that it would have to be a remarkably swift advancement to further Penelope's hopes, since Theodosia would hardly countenance a match with anyone less than a fully fledged bishop.

And Camilla Wytton, like Penelope, was delighted at the news. She called on Octavia, mercifully during Theodosia's absence, with an invitation to accompany her to a bookshop in Leadenhall to purchase some frivolous novels to occupy her time during the rest that the physician was obliging her to take every afternoon.

"It is all nonsense, I am in the rudest health, but Dr. Molloy is an old woman, and Alexander is another, so I do as I am bid, lest I be nagged into distraction by the pair of them. Only it is the most tedious thing to be lying with one's feet up in the daytime, I have never wanted to rest in the day. So I want some exciting tales to while away the time. Do come, have you ever been there?"

No, Octavia hadn't, she had purchased the novel for her journey north from Sam's bookshop in Bond Street.

"I am a good customer there as well, but for the novels from the Minerva Press it is best to go to Leadenhall Street, where you may find everything in print. And if I come with you, I can tell you which ones I possess, and you can borrow them from me, and save the expense. Although of course," she went on merrily, "you could buy the whole press yourself, I dare say, never mind the odd three guineas for the novels! How delightful you must find it to be so rich."

"I have not got used to it yet," said Octavia. "After spending so many years of my life having to watch every penny, it is strange to know that I can buy as many books as I please, and fashionable clothes. Besides being able to be as generous with my purse as is necessary for charitable concerns. I am looking into funding orphanages in Yorkshire."

"Fellow feeling?" said Camilla, quick on the uptake as ever. "I plan to interest you in a scheme I have of my own, to help country girls who are stranded in London and are forced on to the streets and into brothels. We women must stand by our own sex, even the most unfortunate members of it."

"Certainly I will help. And on a more selfish note, I want to buy a horse, although that will have to wait until I have found a house."

"As to the house," said Camilla, settled comfortably in her open carriage, "I have some ideas on that. For the horse, let Alexander assist you in the purchase, for women, however rich, cannot so easily be buying horses. I am of no use to you there, I do not care for riding."

Octavia and Camilla passed a very happy couple of hours in Mr. Lane's establishment, coming away with several mottle-covered volumes. They went from there back to Harte Street, "to eat a nuncheon, for I am always hungry these days, and cannot go without food in the middle of the day," Camilla said.

What had Camilla to say about the house? Octavia ate her cold meats and fruit, while Camilla talked about her family, passed on absurd snippets of London gossip, and related the plot of the book that her former governess, Miss Griffiths, was presently writing—"She has had half a dozen novels published now, and they are a great success."

"Now," said Camilla, when they had finished the light repast, "let us go to the drawing room, where I may lie down upon the sofa, and I shall tell you my great idea."

Octavia watched, amused, as Camilla's maid bustled about with cushions and shawls and smelling salts—"horrible stuff," said Camilla, "I can't imagine why she thinks I need them on the table here, I never ever use them. Now, go away, Sackree, I am quite at my ease."

"Do not let her get up, if you please, ma'am," Sackree said to Octavia.

"Goodness, how they all do fuss," said Camilla. "You would think no one had ever produced a child before. Now, have you ever heard of Lady Susan Threlford?"

Octavia had not, although she had a vague recollection of hearing the name Lord Threlford mentioned.

"You might very well have, but you will not have met him, for he never comes to London. He and his wife and half the rest of the family all live perfectly happily in a rambling great house in Shropshire. Lady Susan is his youngest daughter, he had about five of them, I believe, and she alone of her family felt that the remoter parts of England were not where she wanted to spend her life. So, having some money put by, she decamped with her maid to America, where she became an actress."

"An actress?"

"Yes, it is incredible, is it not? But it was what she chose to be, and while she was there, she married a fellow Thespian. However, that ended unhappy, for he turned out to already have a wife, in Chicago or Minnesota, I can't remember, and it doesn't matter. The upshot was, she has returned to England, to be reunited with her family."

"You mean they didn't cast her off?"

"No, no. She is the apple of her father's eye, and they think nothing of her escapades, they are those sort of people. And so grand, you see, that it is difficult for people to criticise them, and it doesn't bother them one jot if they do. But Lady Susan is no happier in Shropshire than ever she was, and longs to be in London. She is older than you, past thirty, but the greatest fun. However, she does not have a great deal of money, very little in fact, and so cannot be setting up her own establishment in London. And nor, to be frank with you, Octavia, can you."

Octavia did not agree at all with Camilla on that. Why should she not have her own house? She was a widow, not an unmarried girl, why should it be the least kind of a problem?

"Because of the way the world is. Of course, since you are now so rich, you can choose to do as you like, and I know that you do not give a button for the opinion of the polite world, but I assure you, it matters more than you think it does. Besides, it is lonely living on one's own, and I think you have had more than your fair share of loneliness."

That struck home, that was all too true.

"Lady Susan is the best company in the world. She will never bore you, will not impose her company on you when you do not want it, for she has a great number of friends of her own, excluded though she is from some circles on account of her having trodden the boards. At least let me introduce you, she is paying a visit to London next week, and see how you like one another. Oh, and I forgot to mention, she is a poetess, she has a volume of poetry preparing this very moment, that is what brings her to London, to discuss the work with Mr. Murray."

Octavia didn't want to say so, but she privately thought that Lady Susan sounded not only eccentric, but far too formidable to make a comfortable companion. But yes, she would dine with the Wyttons next Tuesday, and make the acquaintance of Lady Susan.

Meanwhile, Pagoda Portal had been busy on her behalf. There were half a dozen houses, he said, which might be suitable, let her name her time, and, if she wished, he would go with her to view them. Much to Octavia's pleasure, Mrs. Rowan came with Mr. Portal. "For I love looking at houses," she said.

Two of the houses were to be let unfurnished, and it was those Octavia wanted to see first. "I should so much enjoy seeing to everything myself, and buying furniture and fitting it all out," she said. "Perhaps Mrs. Rowan will help me to purchase some Turkey rugs, for I love those rich colours."

Octavia found the first house unsatisfactory. Her keen eye spotted many deficiencies which she said would have to be put right; the prospect was a dark one, the kitchen quarters inconvenient, and, she said, there had been some internal alterations which had been carried out in a shoddy manner.

"Upon my word, you seem to know a great deal about it all," said Mr. Portal.

"I like houses, and have always been interested in their design and construction. When I lived with my stepmother, she had a great deal of work done on the house, and the architect and builder were kind enough to answer all my questions."

"In which case," said Mr. Portal, "I think that this next house we are to see will take your fancy. It is new built, and just the right size for your purposes, I would venture to say. It was designed by Mr. Quintus Dance, have you heard of him?"

"I have indeed," said Octavia. And, when she saw the house, she exclaimed with pleasure and admiration, "It is perfect."

Fitting snugly in between the neighbouring houses, and built entirely in the modern style, it was a creamy stucco on the outside, with wrought-iron balconies. Inside, the house was light and airy, with the traditional two rooms on each floor. The fine drawing room on the first floor pleased Octavia particularly. It had a wide, curved balcony outside the deep sash windows, and looked out on to a small front garden through elegant wrought-iron arches.

"Everything in just the right proportion, the rooms are all a good size, and the servants could never complain about their quarters."

"I agree," said Henrietta Rowan, inspecting some cupboards. "It is as neat a house as I have seen. Three bedchambers; should you want to invite guests, there is room, and look, there is a modern water closet installed, what could be more convenient?"

"It is a fashionable street," said Mr. Portal, throwing up a sash and peering out to look up at the guttering. "Mr. Oliver, the painter, lives at number 15, and the Macauleys have number 9."

"Will you be setting up your carriage?" said Henrietta. "We should go and look at the mews, to see what stabling there is."

That was also just right, a small coach house, with stabling for four horses, room for a carriage, and accommodation above for a coachman and groom.

"You may want to ask your sister's advice on hiring staff," said Mr. Portal, when Octavia told him that she was very happy to take the house, "but if I and Mrs. Rowan can be of any assistance . . ."

Octavia thanked him; no, she did not share her sister's ideas of what made a good servant. She would hope to bring her maid from her sister's house, if her sister would agree, for the girl suited her; otherwise, she would hardly know where to begin.

"And hiring London servants is not so easy, if you are not used to it," said Mrs. Rowan. "You will need a housekeeper, a cook, a kitchen and scullery maid, your maid, a chambermaid, a footman, or perhaps two. And a butler. As well, of course, as the stable staff."

"So many?" said Octavia, for although she had been used to a large household in India, such a number seemed unnecessary.

"For a house this size, you can do with no less," said Mrs. Rowan. "You do not want to be working your servants into the ground, for it never pays."

Octavia was feeling slightly daunted; perhaps she should have thought of taking some rooms, where she would manage with a much smaller staff.

"Nonsense," said Mrs. Rowan. "You are used to running a house, you did so in India without any difficulty. The staff I suggest will do you well; nothing extravagant or extreme, but in keeping with the house and with your position."

Her position! She was still not used to having any position at all, and then her heart gave a leap at the prospect of furnishing and equipping this enchanting, pristine house. She went round the rooms again, and looking into the bedrooms found herself hoping that she did like Lady Susan, for she might indeed find it lonely here, with only the troop of servants for company.

"Mrs. Wytton has suggested that I should have a friend of hers to live with me," she said to Mrs. Rowan as they drove back to Lothian Street.

"That is a sensible notion," said Mr. Portal. "Who is it she has in mind?"

"Lady Susan Threlford."

"Susie!" cried Mrs. Rowan. "Oh, what a capital idea, how clever of Camilla to suggest it. She is one of my oldest friends, we went to the same boarding school, only she ran away, she was always running away. And now she wants to run away from Shropshire again, and live in London. I do so hope you like one another. I am sure you will."

Octavia wondered about this; she had found that when people said they were certain you would like such-and-such a person, you usually found it was no such thing. So she set off for the Wyttons' house on the following Tuesday in a doubtful mood, quite ready to find Lady Susan not at all the kind of person she could live with. She had formed an idea of what Lady Susan Threlford would be like. A dramatic kind of a woman, she supposed, perhaps something of a tragedy queen, a Hamlet's mother, with a ringing voice and affected manners.

So nothing had prepared her for a rather plain woman with a humorous mouth, expressive dark eyes, and a beautiful speaking voice. Far from being dramatic, she struck Octavia as being a restful person, although not in the least dull. She had a droll turn of wit, and, Octavia judged, a kind nature.

Camilla had invited Mr. Portal and Mrs. Rowan, and the numbers were made up by her brother-in-law, Mr. Barcombe, in London on business, who was staying with the Wyttons. He had heard, in Yorkshire, about her bestowal of the parliamentary seat upon Mr. Forsyte. "He will make a first-rate MP," he said. "I am glad you defied the Party powerfuls, and insisted on your own candidate."

"It has caused a good deal of talk," said Mr. Wytton, helping Lady Susan to some beef and peas. "Lord Rutherford is reported to be very much annoyed."

"What, did you defy Sholto?" said Lady Susan. "You brave creature, but I am glad to hear it, for of course he is used to having everything his own way, and it is very bad for him."

"He is a cousin of yours, is he not?" said Mr. Barcombe.

"Oh, yes; everyone is a cousin of ours," said Lady Susan. "But of course he is a London man, and wrapped up in the House and political intrigues; they say he is becoming quite a statesman, so none of my family ever see anything of him, buried in Shropshire as they are. Besides, the Threlfords are Tories, they always have been, so they disapprove of Rutherford; you should hear my father's view on Metternich and the treaty!"

It was Lady Susan who broached the subject of her coming to live in Octavia's house, which she did in the easiest way. "Pray, do not feel under any obligation, because it is Camilla who made the plan. I shan't take the least offence if you feel it would not do."

Octavia had already made up her mind. "If you would care to, I think it would be a very good arrangement," she said.

Mr. Wytton raised his glass. "I drink to you, Mrs. Darcy. I like a woman to be decisive. I think you two will get on famously, and I dare say you will form a salon to which the whole of London will flock."

"I do hope not," said Octavia. "Only think of the bores who would be filling the drawing room."

"No danger of that," said Lady Susan. "My name is my protection, but the dullest part of London finds my life so far to be nothing short of scandalous, so we shall be spared their company, thank goodness."

Chapter Twenty-three

The next few weeks were as busy as any Octavia had ever known, and she wondered how she would have managed without Lady Susan, who stayed on in London, and went with her to warehouses, drapers, furniture makers, examining and choosing; a delight to Octavia, who revelled in being able to buy what she wanted, instead of what she could afford.

Theodosia was scathing, she had been in a huff ever since she realised that it was indeed Octavia's intention to move into her own house.

"You will set all London by the ears, although I do not suppose you care about that, you take a positive pleasure in going against the wishes of all those concerned for your well-being."

Octavia might have retorted that she was not sure who such people might be, but was sure they did not include her sisters Theodosia or Augusta, nor her brother Arthur.

There was another reason for Theodosia's ill nature. Her sister Augusta was in triumph; her daughter Louisa had received a very eligible offer from a young viscount, everything perfect about him: breeding, fortune, appearance. It was aggravating for Theodosia that Penelope, "who has far more charm than Louisa, you must agree," she said peevishly to Octavia, "has not had the hint of an offer."

That was, Octavia suspected, because her niece cold-shouldered any young man who chose to make her the object of his attentions;

she had eyes for no one but Henry Poyntz. Theodosia could not see it; the young couple were circumspect in her presence, and careful at public functions, Penelope never dancing more than one dance with him, and having the good sense and self-control not to let her eyes wander in his direction or linger on his handsome person.

Octavia admired her for it, but felt sorry for her; it was bound to end in tears.

"Penelope is still very young," she said to Theodosia, "barely eighteen, while Louisa is a good year her senior."

"It was a mistake to bring Penelope out this year, I knew it would be. When the old King died in January, I knew it would not be a good season."

Octavia dutifully attended her niece's betrothal party and found Louisa's affianced to be an ordinary young man, small and pale and colourless, looking diminished as he stood next to the buxom glowing beauty of Louisa Adderley. It was easy to see who would wear the breeches in that household, Octavia said to herself, although she was annoyed to hear that odious Snipe Woodhead utter much the same sentiments to a friend a few minutes later.

Octavia did not go about much in the circles favoured by her family, to Theodosia's further dismay. She had accompanied her sister, under pressure, to another political gathering, and had a taste of how it would be, now that the news of her fortune had got around. Theodosia played it down; uncertain of just what Octavia had inherited, she turned it off with talk of modest sums, a few jewels, Indian property not worth tuppence an acre.

Which meant she was considerably annoyed when Octavia chose to wear some of her great-aunt's jewels, nothing ostentatious, but they were diamonds of the finest water, which added a glow to her complexion; demanding stones for a young woman, but her height made her able to carry them off; that and a most elegant gown from Madame Lilly.

Lady Susan had been loud in her praise of this dressmaker, and wholly concurred with Octavia's plan to set her up in her own business in Old Bond Street.

"She will do very well, but mind you arrange to have the most advantageous terms from her for all your future gowns," said Lady Susan.

Lady Susan had a good eye for clothes. She insisted that Octavia should buy hats from Mrs. Bell's establishment as well as Millicent's, and told her that her gloves must come from Paris, but parasols were best bought from English makers. "You will need several for the summer," Lady Susan pronounced. "You cannot walk or drive out without you are carrying a parasol."

At the reception, which was being given for a visiting dignitary, with Arthur much in evidence, Octavia found her situation was very different from that of her first London party a few weeks earlier. Now she had the great men of the moment brought up for an introduction, including Lord Liverpool, who gazed at her dispassionately, and Lord Castlereagh, with his soft mouth and long nose. It was a varied gathering, Whigs as much as Tories in evidence, and Octavia saw Lord Rutherford, in the company of a very beautiful woman with a decidedly fashionable air, deep in discussion with a portly gentleman with sleek black hair.

"The Russian ambassador," a passing acquaintance whispered in her ear.

"And who is the woman with the animated countenance and the magnificent sapphires?"

"Oh, my dear, that is Lady Langton, Lord Rutherford's constant companion."

"She is extremely handsome," Octavia said, striving to conceal the instant dislike she had taken to Lady Langton.

That brought a sniff. "Handsome is as handsome does. Still, one has to admit that Lord Rutherford is as well able to look after himself as any man in London."

Arthur was at her shoulder, frowning, drawing her away to make yet another introduction. "For it does not do for you to be standing around like this, you must mingle, you must not look as though you would rather be anywhere than here."

There was a gallantry about many of the men, they were eyeing her up, deliberating over exactly what she might be worth, and she was mortified to find herself looked over and summed up exactly as a prize racehorse might be. She had been used to that, when she did her season, although then she was far from being the centre of attention, or considered in any way a prize, but she liked it no more now, when she was considered a great catch, than she had then. Men flocked to be introduced, their mamas and sisters set out to make themselves agreeable; there was a predatory air to many of them, and Octavia was glad when her carriage was called, and she could make her escape.

"It was bound to happen," said Lady Susan. "I shall write a poem about it, on the vanity of men, the resemblance of these gatherings to a raree-show, all display and gossip. I enjoy it, for my part, because I may stand aloof. No one suspects me of being on the lookout for a husband, and they are quite right, I am not."

"Nor am I," said Octavia. "What, hand over my fortune to one of those men who were ogling me this evening?"

"You are twenty-five, I am two and thirty, that is the difference. I am supposed to be at my last prayers, besides having a doubtful past. My name carries it off, but I rank very low in the matrimonial stakes. You, however, are now floating very high."

"Well, I care little for the season. I find these parties dull, I shall accept no further invitations, except to private parties where I know I will be among friends."

"Oh, friends may turn out to be the most dangerous of people," said Lady Susan.

Octavia was longing to move into her own house at once, but it was not possible, would not be possible for some time. Plasterers and decorators had to finish their work, hangings and carpets and everything to fit out a house from top to bottom had to be made and delivered and put up or arranged. Mrs. Rowan had engaged a housekeeper, a bony woman with a long neck, a genteel but practical widow, relict of a poor curate, who was glad of the position. She at once took over much of the detailed work to be done on the house, and said that she would attend to the engaging of the rest of the female staff.

Theodosia, unwilling to oblige Octavia in anything, reluctantly agreed to release Alice, saying that she was a lazy girl that she'd been intending to turn off in any case; Octavia was welcome to her; it was all of a piece, stealing her servants from under her very nose; Octavia would soon find herself with a house full of idle servants, not attending to their duties and eating her out of house and home.

The weather was warm, and London was emptying of company as the season drew to a close. The Wyttons went down to their house in Shillingford. They invited Octavia to stay with them at Shillingford Abbey, but she declined. "I do not greatly care for country life, as Camilla knows. I may perhaps go to the seaside, I should enjoy that."

So, with Mrs. Reeves in full command in Firth Street, Octavia and Lady Susan set off for the four-hour drive to Brighton, where Lady Susan's contacts had procured for them a pretty little house to lodge in, not on the Steyne, but a little way further along the front.

Octavia had never been to Brighton, and she loved it from the first, relishing the sparkling sea, the salty air, the vast throng of fashionable people parading up and down, the sea bathing with the ladies in the careful hands of the dippers, leisurely hours spent in the libraries looking at new books and periodicals, drinking coffee, exchanging news with her growing acquaintance, some of whom, she felt, might actually like her for herself and not for the tens of thousands of pounds she was known to have in the funds.

In the evening there were balls in the Assembly Rooms, much more easy-going than the kind of dances Theodosia had frequented in London. Octavia would never want for a partner, and since she loved to dance, she took the compliments and the more persistent advances of some of her suitors with a lightness of touch that amused her well-wishers.

"Lord, I do not know how you keep it up," said Mrs. Rowan, who had taken a house in Brighton for the summer. She was yawning as they left the ballroom. "You danced every dance, are not your feet quite wore out?"

"I like the exercise," said Octavia, and that was true, just as she liked her early morning rides out of Brighton when she went up on to the downs to have a good gallop. The quiet strolls along the front, which were considered more than adequate exercise for young women, were not enough for her, and she found that she was being laughed at for taking vigorous strides instead of neat little steps, and for her habit of riding before the fashionables were up.

Unkind wags were heard to say that she and Lady Susan would make a fine couple, which made Lady Susan laugh. "When men are scared of a woman, they always accuse her of being mannish, pay no attention."

Lady Susan had set up a flirt of her own, a dashing hussar with fine side whiskers, lively company. "He makes me laugh, and I like a strong arm to lean on when I go for a walk."

Octavia did not envy Lady Susan's conquest; she hadn't met a man who could touch her heart, she told herself, and she had to confess, in the dark watches of the night, when the sound of the sea on the gravel beach should have shushed her to sleep, that fond as she had been of Christopher, it had really not been a love match, at least not on her part. She never had been in love; perhaps she was one of those people who was too level-headed ever to lose his or her heart.

People talked a lot about the first Mrs. Darcy; she was the great love of Christopher Darcy's life, they said, look how grief-stricken he was when she died, he could never care so deeply for any other woman after that.

Octavia found that these remarks bothered her more than they should. They brought back the feelings of inadequacy which she had hoped she had left behind her, the time when any mention of the dazzling first Mrs. Darcy carried a message that the second Mrs. Darcy was a second-best wife. A second-best daughter, a second-best wife, and therefore, by implication, a second-best person.

She envied Penelope her attachment to Henry Poyntz. Penelope had no doubts about herself or the place she held in Mr. Poyntz's affections. She had contrived to be in Brighton while her parents were gone to Melbury, staying as the guest of Lord and Lady Barchester, whose daughter Sarah was Penelope's age and her particular friend. Octavia had seen her niece and Mr. Poyntz on more than one occasion, walking together in quiet parts of town, where they might not be noticed.

Penelope was not such an intrepid horsewoman as her aunt, but when she heard of Octavia's morning rides, she begged to be allowed to join her. The stables had a suitable hack; and Penelope's riding habit was sent down from London. "I shall have to face Mama when she returns from Melbury and learns I have been riding in Brighton," said Penelope.

"Are not you allowed to ride? You ride sometimes in London."

"Only a gentle outing in the park."

"Your mama is concerned for your safety, she fears you may have a fall."

"No, she considers that riding at more than an amble is too exhilarating to the spirits, and not appropriate for a young woman. When I am married, she says, I may ride out if I wish, although she also says that it will be at the discretion of my husband. Mama is Gothic and old-fashioned in some of her views," she added dispiritedly, "and it is not as though Papa laid down the law for her, she never pays any attention to him; why should she suppose that my marriage will be any different?"

She saw the expression on Octavia's face. "Oh, you are thinking it is very wrong of me to criticise Mama, but she seems bent on making my life as difficult as possible. Besides, I do not want to have a husband that— Well, never mind. What time shall I be ready for our ride?"

She was prompt the next morning, running down the stairs of the Barchesters' house as soon as she heard the clip-clop of hooves outside the door. Octavia was mounted on the raking chestnut she always rode, and the groom was leading a pretty mare, the horse which Octavia, in consultation with the stables, had chosen as being the right ride for her niece.

The groom held his hands for Penelope to mount, and she bounced into the saddle, arranging her long skirts, and settling herself on the high pommel. They rode off, heading for the broad uplands behind the town where Octavia usually rode, although she knew she would have to forego her gallop this morning. A canter would be all that she would allow Penelope. She was surprised at this sudden enthusiasm for a ride, and suspected a motive.

Half an hour later, as they made their way along a broad grassy track, the motive came into sight. Two horsemen were cantering towards them: Mr. Poyntz on a neat grey, and with him, Lord Rutherford astride a black horse—it must be one of his own, Octavia thought instantly; no livery stable ever provided a horse like that.

She had found herself in Lord Rutherford's company two or three times and knew that he had not forgotten their encounter about the Axby election. She had taxed him with it, and he smiled, and shook his head, saying that politics was always an uncertain game, and if she chose to dip her toe into those waters, she must be prepared to take no prisoners. "Never admit a wrong, that is the first rule of political life, Mrs. Darcy."

"I have not done so; I believe Mr. Forsyte will make an admirable MP."

Greetings, expressions of surprise from Poyntz and Penelope that they should meet out here on the downs, a sardonic look from Lord Rutherford, and then, by unspoken consent, the gentlemen turned and joined the ladies.

Penelope and Poyntz soon fell behind, and Rutherford brought his big horse alongside Octavia. "Would that horse of yours like to stretch his legs?" he asked courteously. "I confess I find this modest pace doesn't suit Pluto here. I do not think Poyntz and Miss Cartland would miss our company were we to take a canter."

Octavia smiled, and nodded her head, and reined back to tell the groom to stay with the others. Then she flicked her whip against her horse's flank, and was off.

Her horse was no match for Rutherford's, but it was not a race, merely an exhilaratingly fast ride across the green, springy turf. It was a breezy day, with puffs of cloud drifting across the sky, a day when it gladdened the heart to be up there, with the sea twinkling and gleaming to one side, and to the other the English landscape stretched out, dotted with woolly sheep.

Lord Rutherford slowed his pace to a canter, and then to a walk. "They will need time to come up with us," he said. "Or we can head back towards them."

"Let us go on," said Octavia, sniffing the air and relishing the warm breeze on her face. "We have not been out so long."

Rutherford glanced at her, and then rode silently for a few minutes beside her.

"You are a fine horsewoman, Mrs. Darcy," he ventured after a while. "Did you ride much in India? Do you care for hunting?"

"I rode on the Maidan, as one does there. And no, I have never hunted."

"Ah, then we cannot bore one another with extravagant accounts of long runs we have had."

"I am sure you are never boring, Lord Rutherford, although I can hardly answer for myself."

He smiled. "Boring is not an adjective I would use to describe you, Mrs. Darcy." Then, abruptly, he changed the subject. "Miss Cartland, who is your niece—does she care for Mr. Poyntz?"

She gave him a quizzical look, hiding her surprise that he should ask her such a question.

"It would be impertinent for me to venture an opinion as to the feelings that anyone else has. You can be the judge as well as I; I should say that she is very happy in his company. As to the gentleman's feelings, you are his friend, you should know him better than I."

"I have no doubt about his attachment, not because I presume to judge his feelings, as you put it, but because he has spoken to me of them. I believe him to be very sincerely in love with Miss Cartland, so I ask you if you can tell me how her family would view a possible match."

Octavia felt her horse's mouth, and gazed distractedly at the gorse bushes, as though with the idea that one of them might be more comfortable than the situation she now found herself in.

She was annoyed with Lord Rutherford for raising this, and in an abrupt way, so directly, with no opportunity for her to turn the conversation before it came close to this subject.

What could she say that was not disloyal to her sister, to her brother-in-law, what business was it of hers, what business of Lord Rutherford's?

"You are silent. You consider I should not have asked this question, and I dare say you are right, but I have an idea that you are sometimes impatient with the conventions that tie us as creatures of the world we live in. Come, Mrs. Darcy. We are, as it were, alone here. There is no one but the rabbits and the sheep to catch our words. What you say will go no further than me, I am not known as a gabster, I know how to respect a confidence."

And Octavia was sure this was so. Although in her previous encounters with Lord Rutherford, she had met with anger, exasperation, indifference, even hostility, she had formed an impression of a man with steel in his conscience. He was not a man to lie, nor to pass on tales when it would do harm. And now she sensed a kindness of heart that she would not have expected.

"You are concerned for Mr. Poyntz," she said at last. "You are a close friend of his, I believe."

"He is the best friend I have," said Lord Rutherford. "We were neighbours as children, we went away to school together and then to the university. I value him and his friendship more than I can say. That is why I am concerned to know whether he has a chance with Miss Cartland."

"I am sure that she cares for him, but she has never spoken to me about him in any direct terms. She is a reserved girl, for all her lively ways, and she, too, knows how to be discreet. I think also, given the circumstances of her upbringing, she is careful not to reveal her sentiments or even thoughts to her parents or anyone else." Octavia hesitated. "She would be nervous of revealing such an attachment to her mother."

"Your sister."

"My half sister."

"I am sorry, half sister. You are much younger than Mrs. Cartland, and I understand you were an orphan. Did Mrs. Cartland bring you up, do you have personal experience of a—how shall I put it—a harsh regime at home? From what I know of Mrs. Cartland, I can believe it."

"No, I was brought up by my stepmother; I did not come to London until I was eighteen, for my come-out." Another silence; he seemed to be waiting for her to say more.

"You wrong my sister if you think she doesn't have my niece's best interests at heart. However, her idea of what are Penelope's best interests may be different from—"

"From yours, or, indeed, mine."

"From Penelope's. Do I think the Cartlands would consent to a match with Mr. Poyntz, is that what you want to know?" She saw no point in shirking the question. Lord Rutherford had been very open with her; he knew Theodosia, knew Henry Cartland, and he was far, very far, from being a fool.

"Penelope's cousin, Louisa Adderley, has just contracted what the family considers an excellent match."

"Louisa Adderley? Oh, yes, she is to marry Buxton. The man's a fool, and weak to boot, and I doubt if any female ever called him handsome, but I suppose there is the viscountcy." There was a world of disdain in his voice; from the lofty heights of an earldom that went back through several centuries, a mere viscountcy, and a recent creation at that, although the family were old enough, was hardly anything to get excited about. "He is a rich man, with a good estate. Is Miss Adderley attached to him?"

"One must hope so."

"Yes, for there would have to be some compensation for rising in the morning to behold that rabbity countenance."

Lord Rutherford had a reputation for a scathing tongue; Octavia could tell that it was fairly earned.

"The point is," she said, trying to control a quivering lip; she must not laugh, "that Mrs. Cartland is very envious of her sister's triumph, and therefore all the keener to achieve some great catch for her daughter. I do not think that Mr. Poyntz would count as a great catch."

"Then she is a stupid woman, he is the best of fellows and will be an admirable husband."

"I am sure of it, I like Mr. Poyntz, but a younger son, a man in holy orders, even with prospects of rising high in the Church, is not to be compared with a viscount."

"Who does your sister have in her eye? An earl, a marquis, a duke? I find Miss Cartland perfectly charming, and of course to Poyntz, she is perfection, but as to beauty and rank, she doesn't rival her dull cousin."

"There is a younger sister," said Octavia. Out of the corner of her eye, she saw that the others were catching up with them, the groom leading the way at a steady canter. "I have not seen her since she was a child; she is away at boarding school, being only just seventeen, but I understand from Penelope, who is not at all vain, that she casts Louisa Adderley into the shade, Penelope tells me cheerfully that she is the loveliest creature imaginable, and very sweet-natured."

"What are you saying?"

"Only that if Penelope is not turned off this season, and there is the second, more dazzling sister waiting in the wings, as it were, then Mrs. Cartland might be more ready to agree to a match with Mr. Poyntz. But tell me, Lord Rutherford, quickly if you please, or they will be within earshot, can Mr. Poyntz support a wife?"

"Certainly he can. He may be a younger son, and come rather late into holy orders, but he has a modest income of his own, and as soon as the Rector at Meryton decides to retire from the parish and devote himself to finishing a great work he has on hand on the history of the Druids—a work of scholarship which I take every opportunity to encourage—then Mr. Poyntz will step into a good living."

"And my niece should have a good portion; Mr. Cartland is a wealthy man."

They exchanged a swift, conspiratorial look as the others joined them. Octavia, not wishing it to seem that they had been discussing their companions, recollected that there were important events in the wider world, and turned the conversation to the subject of Queen Caroline's trial.

Estranged for many years, Queen Caroline had returned to England in June, hoping to claim her rightful place as Queen alongside her husband, King George IV, only to find herself accused of adultery by a royal husband eager for a divorce and the chance to remarry.

"It is a most shocking affair and has been shockingly mismanaged," said Lord Rutherford. "I don't intend to be in the House for the second reading of the Bill, the whole thing rests in the hands of the Tories. Few of the Whigs in the House of Peers will have anything to do with it. We find the proceedings pure hypocrisy, but who knows, it could bring the government down."

Octavia told Lady Susan something of Lord Rutherford's remarks about the Queen's trial later that morning, as they ate breakfast in the pretty parlour overlooking the front.

"Sholto is a political animal through and through," said Lady Susan. "He is a formidable performer in the House, you must go and watch him in action one of these days. He is not one of your lounging, drawling speakers; no, he is full of controlled power, he is considered a dangerous man in the House, an opponent not to be taken on lightly. He would do well with an office of state, it is the most dreadful shame that the Tories are there apparently for ever, wanting nothing changed, the status quo to be preserved at all costs."

"Lord Rutherford thinks this affair of the Queen could drive the Tories out of office."

"Does he? Well, if he says so, it may come to that, for he has an instinct in these things. However, he would be the first to say that the essence of politics is unpredictability, even though Old Jenky would disagree. One of these days the Whigs will regain power, if not because of the Queen's trial, then simply because the country will grow weary with them."

"Do you think the Queen guilty?"

Lady Susan gave one of her sidelong looks. "Of adultery with that Italian?" She laughed, and repeated the catchphrase that was on everyone's lips, *"Non mi ricordo,"* which was what the Queen's putative lover had replied to no less than eighty-seven of the questions that Brougham, her counsel, had put to him.

"Sholto Rutherford did hear Brougham's speech," she went on. "He told me it was a brilliant, insolent showing. Is the Queen an adulteress? Who am I to judge? And if she has let a handsome man creep into her bed, I shouldn't blame her, for she has no pleasure from her husband, not now, nor at any time, if truth be told."

Octavia was used to Lady Susan's outspokenness, and her robust and unfeminine attitude to such a subject as the Queen's adultery. Theodosia, she reflected, would never speak in that easy way on such a topic.

"Your family value respectability," said Lady Susan. "My family have to worry about no man's opinion, and so we express our own pretty freely, I will admit. You do not mind it, I hope? You are not inclined to take offence."

"I like it," said Octavia. "I hate pretence."

Chapter Twenty-four

Octavia and Lady Susan returned to town before the end of August, since there were queries relating to the house, and Lady Susan's poems were soon to be printed.

The house in Firth Street was ready, or near enough that they were able to move in, and the architect, Mr. Dance, was among their first visitors.

Octavia took to him at once, liking him for his well-bred ease and his tone, which was not at all patronising. He was very ready to enter into a lively conversation on the subject of the classical in architecture and perfectly happy to go with her from room to room explaining why he had chosen this moulding or that architrave.

"You ladies have a vast deal of taste," he said approvingly, as he looked around the drawing room, which seemed full of sunlight with its yellow paint and wallpaper. "I could not have done better myself. How comfortable this room is, and yet it is as elegant as you could wish. That Greek vase in the niche there is a nice touch."

"It was found for me by Mr. Wytton," said Octavia. She had a love of antiquities, and Mr. Wytton, who knew a great deal about them, and had spent a good deal of his time travelling abroad, in Egypt and Turkey and Greece, helping with excavations, was very happy to advise and guide her in her acquisitions.

"Buy what pleases you, and then you will get pleasure from what you have around you," he advised. "And, when it comes to value, should you ever wish or need to sell, it is my experience that objects chosen with the heart, with instinct rather than purely with the rational part of oneself, have in the end the greater value in the market."

Such objects of vertu did not come cheap, and Octavia was not yet quite used to having the money to indulge her taste, but she was growing more accustomed to her situation, and bolder in what she felt she could do.

"I hope your fortune is as large as they say it is," remarked Lady Susan, admiring a particularly fine porcelain bowl, which Octavia had acquired at Mr. Christie's auction house. "Otherwise, we shall find ourselves out on the street."

"The tea harvest was good this last season," Octavia said. "A crop of the very finest quality. And there are the rents, apart from the money in the funds. According to Mr. Portal, it grows beyond what I spend."

"Money begets money," said Lady Susan. "I have no false sense of morality with regard to money, having been poor at certain periods of my life, just as you have. Riches which are attained honestly are a great aid to happiness, I find. Only think of the good you may do with them. Enjoy your wealth, and just take care you do not gamble away your fortune as the first Mrs. Darcy did."

Octavia thought she had not heard aright. "Gambled? The first Mrs. Darcy? What can you mean?"

"You mean you did not know? Lord, I had no idea Christopher Darcy had managed to cover it up so well, but to hide it from you, that is surprising. I suppose he did so from pride. Yes, she was a gambler, she could not keep away from the tables, and would engage on private bets upon anything, the weather the next day, the turn of a coin, two ants running along the terrace. It is a masculine trait, generally, but she was insatiable in her longing for a bet."

"Christopher never mentioned it. But then he rarely spoke of his first wife; I imagined that he still felt grief for her."

"Grief? He must have heaved a sigh of relief when she died. She was ruining him. That is why he left you so little money; why, if your own family hadn't been so remarkably good at amassing the wealth of the Indies, you were left almost destitute. I cannot believe he never spoke of it to you."

"Good heavens, I have always heard her spoken of as the sum of all the virtues! No one ever said anything about gambling."

"It was generally known that she gambled, but Christopher managed to keep the extent of her depredations from the ears of the world. She went through all the income from Dalcombe, and he even mortgaged some of his land, what he could, that is, with the entail. I know this, because his agent came afterwards to work for my father. If it hadn't been for the entail, in fact, the whole estate, house and land, would all have gone. Certainly she cost him all his prize money, and he made a good deal in prize money, many thousands of pounds."

Octavia was stunned at these revelations. Christopher's wife a gambler who had nearly ruined him! Oh, why had he never said? That was his nice sense of honour, of course, but should he have kept it a secret from her, his wife? Poor Christopher, not weighed down by grief for his lost love, as she had thought, but simply oppressed by the financial legacy she had left him.

Lady Susan got up and stretched, then went over to the window, and looked down into the street. "Here is Mrs. Trumpington's carriage going by, with her perched in it. I never saw so many feathers on a hat in my life, she looks as though she has had a fight in her poultry yard." She turned back to look at Octavia. "Does it distress you to hear about the first Mrs. Darcy's bad habits?"

"No, no. I never knew her—but it distresses me that I did not know—it must have been a heavy burden for Christopher to carry. I wish he had felt able to tell me."

"That is why he was still in the navy, for a naval career is not at all what it was during the war. He would have liked to live at Dalcombe, I am sure, but of course he could not afford to do so."

A thought struck Octavia, and she laughed. "Ha, George Warren must be discomfited to find his inheritance a good deal less than he supposed."

"He is furious about it," said Lady Susan frankly. "He is not a man to keep his grievances to himself, and he finds the estate in very poor order, with no money to spend on essential repairs, and he will lose a lot of the land if he cannot redeem the mortgages, which he can ill afford to do. He resents your good fortune exceedingly, although I do not see why, your money has nothing to do with him, it comes from your family and not from Christopher; only a mean-spirited man would take it upon himself to bear a grudge because your great-uncle was a nabob! Don't I wish I had a great-uncle who was a nabob; people may pretend to look down their noses at money obtained in that way, but in truth, everyone has a sneaking admiration for the little gold pieces that accumulate in the nabobs' chests at the bank. Take dear Mr. Portal, such a delightful man, he is worth a million they say, and all obtained by his own diligence and intelligence; he came from an old and respected family, but they were as poor as can be. He set out to restore the family fortunes, and succeeded beyond what anyone could have expected."

"I wish I could have been a nabob," said Octavia, her eyes gleaming. "There we are women despatched in an East India boat in the fishing fleet, our goal a husband, and travelling alongside us are men setting off to earn their fortunes by activity and hard work."

"It takes activity and hard work to catch a husband these days," said Lady Susan with an exaggerated sigh. "How lucky we are to have withdrawn from the running. You have lost a husband, and it turned out that mine was no such thing, but it is great fun to stand at the sidelines and watch the merry-go-round."

Chapter Twenty-five

The last, lingering shadows of the day were fading into twilight. Sholto Rutherford, driving back to London in his curricle after a day spent in Oxford, decided to make a stop at the Crown, to take some coffee. In half an hour or so, the full moon would be rising, and he could finish his journey by moonlight; he was a fast but not a reckless driver, and the semi-darkness of dusk was just the time when you could hurtle into who knew what obstacle, or miss the road in the dim light and cause an accident.

He had been in Oxford to visit the dean of his old college, a man rich in years and experience, an influential man in the Church. He had hoped to interest him in Poyntz, and persuade him to use some of his influence in that direction. He had dined in hall; the dons did themselves well at his ancient and rich college, very well indeed, and their cellars were famous for the port. Coffee would clear his head.

The Venerable Francis Wilbraham, who knew Poyntz from his college days, had listened to what Sholto had to say. He pursed his lips, joined the tips of his thin fingers together—the man was exactly like a spider, Rutherford thought, sitting there behind his desk, weaving webs, watching; an inhuman man, although one he liked, respected, and had, in earlier days, feared.

"Marry, eh?" said Wilbraham. "I am not a marrying man myself, but there are those who speak well of the state. Henry Poyntz wishes to marry, you say, and therefore seeks advancement. He is the kind of man who can advance on his own merits, I believe. An able scholar, a likeable man, popular among his peers, I recollect."

"I can give him the living at Meryton in due course, but a country parish . . ."

"Ah. For a man like Poyntz, there needs to be more than emoluments. Does he know you are paying me this visit?"

"No," said Rutherford.

"Would he object?"

Rutherford shrugged. "He might, but if he wants to marry—"

"Marry, yes, marry," Wilbraham repeated. "Time you thought of marrying, Rutherford. Poyntz will marry and produce a brood of clergyman's children, all to be provided for, a sore trial to any man; a celibate clergyman has a much easier time of it. But you, with an ancient title, large estates, a position in the world; you have to marry. You need a wife, a successful politician needs a wife."

Rutherford raised an eyebrow, but said nothing.

"Ah, you will say I sound like your mother, or your sister, or your aunts. The women are always pressing a single man to find him a wife."

"My mother is not concerned as to my matrimonial status," said Rutherford.

"Lady Rutherford . . . is an original. And your sister, Lady Sophronia, she is not married, either. Or is she? Living so out of the world, I don't keep up with all the *on dits* and gossip of town, as you Londoners do."

Another raised eyebrow, this time accompanied by a wry smile. Living out of the world indeed; if ever there were a man in the thick of things, it was the dean.

"Sophronia is hard to please."

"She'll die an old maid if she don't look out."

"She is exactly my age, being my twin, as you know. She would consider herself well past the age of marrying; it is different for a woman."

"Perhaps if you marry, then so will she. Or does she consider it her duty to spend her life looking after Lady Rutherford?"

"Hardly. But there are worse fates than spinsterhood. Such as being married to a disagreeable man, or a stupid one, or a bore—Sophronia would find all of those hard to bear."

"Then she is a deal too fussy, since you describe the main part of the masculine sex."

"It is, however, Poyntz's situation that I have come to Oxford to discuss with you."

A wave of the dean's long, lanky arm and hand. "Oh, that, dear boy. I'll do what I can. It's no hardship. Is he as handsome as ever?"

"Most women would call him a fine-looking man, I believe."

"Ah," said the dean with a long sigh. And then, "Find yourself a wife, Rutherford. And soon. You will be the happier for it, there comes a time when a man needs more than a mistress, however desirable and beautiful. Of course, the wife does not preclude the mistress, no wife of a man in your position, no woman of breeding, that is, would do other than turn a blind eye to a mistress or two, it is the natural order of things. But you need a wife, and to be setting up your nursery."

What an immoral old devil Wilbraham was. Sholto jumped down from the curricle, handing the reins to the groom who had come running out to attend to him.

"You have dined, my lord?" said Mr. Sandham, the landlord of the Crown, an old acquaintance of Rutherford's. "A glass of wine, port, brandy, I have a fine French brandy."

"Smuggled, I dare say," said Rutherford. "Coffee will do. Hot and strong."

"Go into the little parlour, my lord, and I will bring it to you directly. There is no one in there, you will have it to yourself, I will see that you are not disturbed."

Rutherford wasn't bothered about being disturbed, he didn't care whether he brushed shoulders with his fellow men or not. But he went into the little parlour and flung himself down on one of the stiffly upholstered chairs, feeling a vague sense of dissatisfaction.

The dissatisfaction was caused, as he knew, by old Wilbraham.

Damn him for harping on about wives; he was losing his touch, it was a very sentimental view for so cynical and worldly a man.

The parlour was empty, but through the partition which separated the room from another small parlour, a less-favoured room, came the clear sound of voices.

Who the devil was it? He knew that voice. Warren, George Warren. What was he doing out here at this time of night? Not his usual patch; he was a man for the more seedy side of London life, unless he had ventured out of town for a prize-fight, but there was nothing of the kind taking place, not that Sholto had heard of.

Rutherford was far from being any kind of an eavesdropper, and having identified one of the speakers—the other was unfamiliar, he did not recognise the voice at all—he dismissed Warren and his companion from his mind.

Coffee was brought, hot, strong coffee. As he began to drink it, the voices next door grew louder, and he heard a name that made him put his coffee down and listen. Mrs. Darcy, he had definitely heard Mrs. Darcy mentioned. There were several Mrs. Darcys, and Rutherford knew that Warren had little love for any of them. He listened more attentively.

They were talking now about India, the navy, a journey up country. In that case, the Mrs. Darcy under discussion was the rich widow, Christopher Darcy's second wife. Rutherford considered. Warren had been Christopher Darcy's heir, an inheritance that had left Mrs. Darcy almost penniless, and Warren, in his usual graceless way, had refused to make any restitution, no annuity, no capital sum. And now, so he had heard, Warren had discovered that the estate he had inherited was grossly encumbered, that Dalcombe needed money spent on it rather than his being able to draw a comfortable income from it as he had hoped. That was due to the recklessness of the first Mrs. Darcy's gambling.

That was what a wife could do to you.

And then the second Mrs. Darcy had inherited a nabob's fortune, from her mother's family, merchants or shopkeepers; he hadn't paid a great deal of attention as rumours and counter-rumours had flown around London, finally settling down to the indisputable fact that there was a great Indian fortune, made even more handsome by the addition of jewels and an estate in Yorkshire.

Lord Rutherford had taken a sardonic pleasure in seeing the attitude of London society change overnight towards the formerly ignored and despised widow, whose outlook had been so bleak: another marriage, if she were lucky; very lucky, for she was not precisely a cosy armful. In Sholto's opinion, anyone who took on the second Mrs. Darcy would need to have his wits about him, a marriage to such a woman would keep any man on his toes, no bed of roses there. Not even the large fortune would make her an easy helpmeet, although that much money must make a quick tongue and more independence of mind than was right for a woman rather more palatable.

It irked him, this brief contact with Warren. Warren was a man he disliked and mistrusted, a Tory, but a Tory without integrity, the worst kind of a Tory. He would be interested to know who the other man was, and hearing the men open their door, he strolled out of the parlour, not calling yet for his carriage, but moving with quiet speed to observe without being noticed himself. He kept to the shadows and caught a glimpse of the man's face as a stable hand held a torch aloft. A fair young man, no one he knew; there was a look of nervousness about him. Warren was up to something, no question about it.

It was no affair of his, he told himself; neither Warren nor Mrs. Darcy were any part of his life. He climbed into the driver's seat of his curricle, took up the reins, felt his horses' mouths, told the groom to stand clear, and was briskly away, back on the London road.

Chapter Twenty-six

Octavia's days were full. She was making new friends, finding herself happiest among the numerous circle of Henrietta Rowan and Mr. Portal's friends; clever men and women who led interesting lives and talked about books and paintings and music and travel, as well as politics, a circle far removed from the generally stuffy set of her sisters and brother, which was all the people she had formerly known in London.

Her life was hardly a round of pleasure, though. She had to spend a great deal of time managing her affairs, and she began to despair of ever mastering the details of her inheritance. "My great-aunt must have been a remarkable woman," she said to Lady Susan as she sat at her desk, surrounded by papers and figures. "I find I am woefully ignorant about tea. I have never seen a tea plant, I can barely distinguish between one tea and another when I drink it, let alone make any sense of it in its original state." She took up a sheet of paper. "I am constantly asked to make decisions, to sign this or that, and yet Mr. Portal and Mr. Wilkinson are both definite that I must sign nothing unless I understand it."

"You are lucky that they are such capable, honest men. Of course, you could always eat humble pie, and ask for Mr. Melbury's help."

Octavia sighed and returned to her figures.

"You could make an expedition to India," suggested Lady Susan, "to visit the tea plantations; were you to spend some time there, you would have a far firmer grasp of the business."

Octavia had dreamed of going back to India, but now she found the idea of it held no charm for her. "At some time in the future, perhaps," she said with a sigh. She didn't care to examine too deeply why she had no inclination to leave England at present, telling herself that she needed to get settled, there was still a lot to do in the house. Tomorrow she would go to Broadwood's and have a look at the instruments on sale, she had promised herself a pianoforte. Her mind drifted into a reverie, until Lady Susan told her sharply that if she did not attend to what she was doing, she would incur the wrath of her lawyer.

Lady Susan took Octavia to the House of Lords, to watch some of the proceedings against the Queen, which were still going on. There in the lofty red chamber, they saw the Queen dozing in her seat.

"She doesn't seem greatly concerned," said Octavia.

"No, the trial will last for months, I dare say, there is no point in her getting het up. Did you hear Lord Holland's quip?

"'Her conduct at present no censure affords/She sins not with peasants but sleeps with the Lords.'"

Octavia was still laughing at this when they put their heads into the House of Commons, which sat in St. Stephen's Chapel. She was amazed at how small it was. "They must be very cramped in here."

"Oh, there is rarely a full house, only for an important debate. Members mostly stay in the country or are away at sea or serving abroad, if they are naval or military men. It smells dreadful when it is full, with the oil lamps, and so many men crammed in where there is not room for the half of them, and then there is a lot of animal excitement. The Lords are more stately, but there you do not find the same vehemence and savagery. Although Parliament is dull these days; my uncle, who has been an MP since he was nineteen, speaks longingly of the days of Pitt and Fox, and Lord Grey thundering in the upper House. But we were at war in those times, and the atmosphere was quite different, war lends an urgency to a nation's affairs."

"Who is that woman in the elegant green dress?" Octavia asked as they walked through the lobby.

"That is Lady Framlingham. One of the great Whig ladies, her salon is the meeting place of all the important Whigs. I shall take you there one day, you will like it. Make no mistake," she said, as they were in the carriage and on their way back to Firth Street, "the Tories may have the majority in the House, but the real work is done in the drawing rooms and dining rooms of London, and it is there that the Whigs rule supreme. They have brains and influence, and you can never underestimate the effect of those."

They returned to Firth Street to receive happy news from Shillingford, announcing the birth of a child to the Wyttons; Camilla had been safely delivered of a daughter with whom the parents were duly besotted, so the new mama wrote in a joyful letter to her friends. The Wytton family returned to town soon afterwards, and Octavia was summoned to their house to admire the many virtues of the infant Hermione Elizabeth, a plump, rosy baby, of whom her doting father said gloomily that he already saw the gleam of authority in her infant eye.

Chapter Twenty-seven

November brought its customary fogs and damp, windy weather that made Lady Susan cough and declare how much she hated the English climate. "There is nowhere you can go," she said. "The country is worse, far worse, than any town, everything drips, and chimneys smoke, and one is never, ever warm."

"Well, at least you are warm here," said Octavia, "with all the fires drawing well, and thick curtains to keep out the worst of the draughts, although we are not at all draughty. I must say that Mr. Dance has an eye for the details as well as the appearance of a house."

Octavia was in her riding habit, and Lady Susan shook her head at her. "It isn't wise to go out on such a raw day."

"I feel uncomfortable if I am indoors all day. I shall have a short ride, to get rid of the fidgets, and then I shall stay in and enjoy being so snug."

"Mr. Dance is to build the new Chauntry, did you hear that?" said Lady Susan, taking up her embroidery frame, and then setting it aside. "I had it from Poyntz, it is all decided, the work clearing the old house is all finished, and the plans are being drawn even as we speak."

"I hope Lord Rutherford is not going to erect a Gothic palace, but I am sure he has too much sense to do that."

"And taste; he has a good eye, Sholto Rutherford, for a house, a picture, a horse. Not for a woman, though. I do wish he'd get rid of that dreadful Kitty Langton, I can't bear the woman. She is grown even more careful of him, now that poor Philip Effingham is ailing."

Octavia frowned. Philip Effingham? Who was he? Ailing? And what had it to do with Rutherford and Lady Langton?

"Of course you wouldn't know," said Lady Susan. She gave a prodigious yawn. "Oh, how dull I feel this morning. It is terrible being shut up indoors all day."

"If you go out before the fog lifts, your cough will be twice as bad."

"I know, but why doesn't anyone call on us?"

"They, too, want to avoid a cough. Tell me about this Philip Effingham."

"It is an old scandal. Lord Rutherford was engaged to Eliza Hawtrey, this was years and years ago, in his salad days. He was head over heels in love with her, and she was quite exquisite. But a week before their wedding day, poor Sholto received a letter from her saying that she was ending the engagement, and was off to marry this Philip Effingham. Who was, incidentally, going to have been groomsman to Rutherford."

"Good gracious," said Octavia, feeling a quite unreasonable surge of dislike for the unknown Eliza Hawtrey. "Why?"

"It seemed that while Sholto was so much in love with her, she was all the time desperately in love with Philip. But Rutherford was by far the better match, no comparison; Philip has a comfortable income, but nothing more, it couldn't compare with the title and castle and all the rest of it. I think, deep down, Eliza was afraid of Sholto, and knew she wasn't up to his weight."

"For heaven's sake, Susan, the woman isn't a horse!"

"If men chose their wives with as much care and attention as they do their horses, there would be fewer unhappy marriages. So, no wedding. Sholto was left looking the fool—which of course no man can bear, let alone a man like Rutherford, he is very proud, you know—and the Effinghams went off to the Peninsula."

Octavia was puzzled for a moment, then realised what Susan was talking about. "The war, you mean; Mr. Effingham was a soldier."

"Yes, but it didn't answer for Eliza, she hated being with the army; you have to be a particular kind of woman to accompany your husband on campaigns abroad, to follow the drum, and she liked her creature comforts too well. Within a few months she was bitterly regretting that she had made that fateful decision, and she came back to England, full of woe, and complaining to anyone who would listen what a bad husband Philip was."

"Was he?"

"No. He was a good soldier, and a gallant one, and he had to have his mind on his job, he couldn't be dancing attention on a demanding Eliza day and night."

"Of course not."

"I have a suspicion that she tried to resume her friendship with Sholto Rutherford, her amorous friendship, that is; she wanted a divorce, so it was said, but she had picked the wrong man to jilt, and Sholto, who was still very hurt, I think, would have none of it. They wouldn't have suited at all, in my opinion, and Rutherford was well out of it, but then he never married, and so people said he was carrying a candle for her all these years."

"Oh, nonsense," said Octavia, with a good deal of feeling, which made Lady Susan give her a swift, appraising glance.

"I have no patience with all these heartrending tales of lost love," Octavia went on. "It is nothing but fancy."

"She may have caused him to become rather cynical where the opposite sex are concerned."

"I dare say his mother might have done that, should he look closer to home," said Octavia.

"I like Lady Rutherford. She was the greatest beauty of her generation; my papa told me that all the men were in love with her when she was a girl. She was an heiress, impeccably well bred and carefully brought up; how could old Lord Rutherford have had any idea that his lovely, dutiful wife would turn into such a wily, eccentric person?"

"Surely the eccentricity only came with age."

"Not a bit of it; the minute she was away from her oppressive parents, her true nature unfolded, and she became much what she is now.

I find her delightful, but I know she irritates and upsets most of her acquaintance. She is really very odd. She drives Rutherford to distraction, and yet I believe he is more fond of her than he shows. I think he is rather exasperated than irritated by her whimsical ways. They make life very difficult for him, and he is worried about Lady Sophronia, that she is dwindling into an old maid, dancing attendance on her mother, and perhaps becoming equally eccentric. It is a pity she never married, but she is hard to please, as hard as Rutherford is."

Octavia went out into the grey cold world. She hadn't yet bought a horse; Mr. Wytton had had other calls on his attention, and though any of her male admirers would have leapt to her service, she had no wish to encourage them, nor would she have trusted most of them to find her the kind of horse she wanted.

Instead, she rode a horse from a livery stable, not one of the tired hacks they hired out, but one of a handful they kept for more favoured riders, who were mostly gentlemen up from the country and wanting a good horse while in London.

It wasn't far to the park. She and the attendant groom picked their way through the traffic, moving quite slowly on such a foggy day. When she got to the park, it was quiet and eerie, like riding through cobwebs. Perhaps Lady Susan was right, and she had better have stayed at home; however, her horse was fresh, and snatching at the bit to be off. A brisk canter soon improved her spirits and warmed her up.

The figure of another rider appeared in the distance and Octavia knew it at once for Lord Rutherford. He trotted up to her, sweeping off his hat and bowing over the pommel of his saddle.

"That is a very pretty mare you are riding," she said, looking with admiration at the spirited chestnut with her dished nose, small, attentive ears, and elegant tail held high and to one side. "She is too small for you, however."

"She is an Arabian, of my mother's breeding. I have brought her because she needs exercise and I wanted to try her. This is a most fortunate meeting, Mrs. Darcy, for I hear from Lady Susan that you are on the lookout for a horse."

"Mr. Wytton is going to find me one."

"He is a good judge of a horse, but I doubt if he will find you better than this one."

"That one! Is she for sale?"

"In the ordinary way, no, for Lady Rutherford is attached to all her horses and will only let them go to people she approves of."

"Why should she approve of me? She hardly knows me."

"She has a kindness for you, for helping to rescue both books and chaplain when Chauntry caught fire. And she has seen you ride, I believe; she says you have light hands and are a natural horsewoman, which I can confirm."

Octavia laughed. "As to the horsemanship, I cannot say, but I don't think you have a kindness for me on account of the night that Chauntry burnt. Interference, I think, was the word you used."

"I was somewhat overwrought," he said.

"As well you might be. Come, Lord Rutherford, I bear you no grudge. And I hear from Lady Susan that you are to employ Mr. Quintus Dance as your architect. He built the house I have taken, you know, I think you will be pleased with him."

"He is a friend of yours?"

"He has become one, both Lady Susan and I take pleasure in his company."

"I see."

They rode on together in silence, and then Lord Rutherford, somewhat abruptly, said that he must go, was her most obliging servant, and would have the mare sent round for Octavia to try her paces.

With that, he was gone, leaving Octavia feeling that she had in some way offended him.

For some reason she hesitated to tell Lady Susan of her meeting in the park, but then there would be questions when the horse was brought round, so she mentioned, casually, that Lord Rutherford had been exercising one of his mother's horses in the park. "I think I said something to offend him, he turned and went off with hardly a word."

"I expect he had some appointment; you would know if you had offended him, for Sholto is never one to hold his tongue."

The knocker sounded below, and Lady Susan brightened. "A caller! Some kind creature has ventured out in the fog, come to raise our spirits with news of the world beyond the dismal grey one we look out upon."

The caller, who was welcomed with real enthusiasm, turned out to be Lady Sophronia. "I am spending a few days in London," she said. "What a charming house! How I envy you, such a neat little place and in the best part of town. No parrots nor monkeys, either, which makes a refreshing change."

The bell was rung, a tray of fruit and sandwiches was brought in, and a cup of steaming peppermint for Lady Susan, who was talking so much that she had succumbed to a paroxysm of coughing.

Octavia sat slightly withdrawn as Sophronia and Susan, who had known one another since childhood, busily exchanged news and gossip about friends and family, people Octavia had perhaps heard of, but didn't know. Scandals, appointments, political activity, births, deaths, and marriages were presented, discussed, exclaimed at, laughed at, dismissed. Octavia felt a momentary stab of envy for the two women with their web of family and connections and acquaintances, the kind of relationships she had never known.

Lady Sophronia had moved into Netherfield House with her mother, in time for her mother to retire for the winter months. "Heavens, Sholto was so eager to see us go that I almost left a few birds behind, just to annoy him. Netherfield House is one of the reasons I have called upon you, apart from just wishing to see you again. I want to invite you both to Netherfield for Christmas, for the whole Christmas season. Now, do say you can come. I have carte blanche. Mama is hibernating, we shall probably not see her until March, or later if it is a severe winter, and Sholto, who comes to Hertfordshire for the festivities, only stipulates that I must ask Henry Poyntz, which I would do in any case, and Pagoda Portal and Henrietta Rowan, who would be welcome guests at any time."

Octavia was pleased, and expressed her pleasure openly and

instantly. Lady Susan, who had been wavering as to whether to brave the bad roads and worse weather of a journey to her ancestral home, brightened immediately, and managed to stop coughing for long enough to thank Sophronia and accept her kind invitation.

Another knock on the front door, another visitor, but this time it was a stranger who was shown into the room. "Mr. Forsyte, ma'am," the butler announced.

Octavia stood up, expecting to see Mr. Forsyte from Yorkshire, but it was a complete stranger who entered the room, a big man in his early forties. He had a full mouth, a pair of humorous and penetrating dark eyes, and a considerable air.

He bowed, and explained. "I am Mr. John Forsyte's brother, just come back to town after a visit to Yorkshire, and I promised Mrs. Forsyte that I would do myself the honour of calling upon you, and bring you some of her plums. I left them downstairs and told the footman to take them down into the kitchen."

Octavia smiled and said what was proper, and introduced him to Lady Sophronia and Lady Susan, both of whom were looking over the newcomer with appraising eyes. There was a watchfulness to Lady Susan, Octavia felt, but the moment passed, Mr. Forsyte was seated, and Lady Sophronia was asking him if he lived in London.

"I do. I have a house not so far from here, I walked round, in fact, although it's an unpleasant day to be out and about. I am a banker," he added.

Lady Susan gave a little cry of recognition. "Of course you are, I have heard of you. They say you are the cleverest man with money in London."

He smiled, a smile with a great deal of charm, but like a well-bred man did not talk about money but about the dismal weather, the pleasant aspect of Octavia's house, and the inconveniences of there being so much building presently going on in London. He stayed for a half hour, then rose politely to take his leave. Sophronia also got to her feet, exclaiming that she must be on her way, she had a thousand things to do before she went back to Netherfield.

"I heard that Lord Rutherford had taken a house in Hertfordshire, near Chauntry," Mr. Forsyte said. "Are you to spend the festive season there?"

They left together, and when the door had closed behind them, Lady Susan and Octavia looked at one another, each of them uncertain where to begin.

"I think that is a remarkable man," said Lady Susan finally.

Another glance exchanged.

"He seems to me to be a man of an ardent temperament," Lady Susan continued. "An attractive man."

"Yes."

"I wonder if he is married, he did not mention a wife. I shall find out easily enough."

"Why are you interested?" said Octavia with a flash of suspicion; surely Lady Susan wasn't turning matchmaker, that would be quite out of character.

"Not for you, he would not do for you. But did you see the way Sophronia looked at him? Sophronia knows a vigorous man when she sees one, that's clear. Good heavens, though, a banker, quite out of her world."

Octavia was laughing. "You build a great deal upon a look."

"I am right, you will see. I have an unerring instinct for such matters. Lord, if it came to anything, what would Sholto say? My goodness, we may be in for some fun!"

Octavia was taken aback by Lady Susan's words. "There is no reason for them to become further acquainted."

"There is every reason. He has already found out where she spends Christmas. I'll wager my new silk stockings that he remembers a friend or relation in Hertfordshire. We haven't seen the last of Mr. Forsyte. Is his brother like him?"

"Not in appearance, no. Nor does he have, what shall I call it, the masculine energy of this Mr. Forsyte. I fancy they are alike in intellect and strength of character, however."

Chapter Twenty-eight

"Good heavens, Mr. Wilkinson," said Octavia, who hadn't expected a visit from her lawyer, and was taken aback by his grave looks.

"Come into the library," she said. "You will be surprised, I dare say, that I have a library, but it is quite my favourite room; in the evening, with the curtains drawn and a good fire in the hearth, I love to sit here and read."

She was talking almost at random, simply to fill the space with words, for she could see that Mr. Wilkinson had something important to say, and by the look of him, it wasn't good news.

"Mrs. Darcy, I have come myself to— Upon my word, I hardly know how to begin."

"Pray, take a seat," said Octavia, sitting down herself on a seat near the fire.

Mr. Wilkinson did not sit, but stood before the window, his impassive countenance stirred by something approaching emotion.

"Are you acquainted with one Lieutenant Gresham?"

"Why, yes. He was a fellow officer of my husband, indeed, Lieutenant Gresham was with him when he died. He accompanied him on that fateful expedition; like Captain Darcy, he was a keen naturalist."

"Ah, well, that at least is true. Now, as to the exact date of your husband's tragic death, was that solely based on the word of Lieutenant Gresham?"

Octavia looked at him uncomprehendingly. "What do you mean? What are you saying?" Her heart was thumping and her throat was dry; what had happened to make Mr. Wilkinson look like this?

"To put it in a nutshell, the late Captain Darcy's cousin and heir, Mr. Warren, has made a claim on the estate of your great-aunt, Mrs. Worthington."

"George Warren?" Octavia felt nothing but relief. "There is some mistake, Mr. Warren has nothing to do with my family, with the Worthingtons, nothing at all."

"I mentioned when you first came to my office that it was fortunate that your husband predeceased Mrs. Worthington. Otherwise it might be possible that your inheritance would form part of his estate. And that is precisely what Mr. Warren is maintaining."

Octavia frowned, trying to make sense of what Mr. Wilkinson was saying. "How can he, when Captain Darcy died before my aunt?"

"Ah, that is where the situation has changed. Lieutenant Gresham is back in England, and he has now sworn an affidavit saying that Captain Darcy died not on the fifteenth of April, but ten days later, on the twenty-fifth of April."

Octavia's mind was in a whirl. "On the twenty-fifth?"

"Mrs. Worthington died on the twenty-first of April."

"Even so, how can he claim my great-aunt's estate? It was left to me, and he has no connection with the family, none whatsoever."

"In law, a wife can hold no property, no assets of any kind. It belongs to her husband. If your husband were still alive when your great-aunt died, it is possible that your inheritance should form part of his estate."

"Why does Lieutenant Gresham come forward now with this change of date?"

"I will be blunt. He says that you paid him to say that your husband died on April fifteenth."

"And why should I do any such thing?"

"In order to inherit."

"But I had no idea that I had a great-aunt, let alone that I was her heir! I had no notion that she had ever existed, until the lawyer in Calcutta told me, and how, therefore, was I supposed to know when she died?"

"Can you prove it?"

Octavia stared at the lawyer. How could you prove that you didn't know something?

"This is a serious business, Mrs. Darcy. Firstly, the whole of your inheritance is at stake. Secondly, to have bribed Lieutenant Gresham would make you liable for a criminal charge—"

"A criminal charge? You cannot be serious."

"Mrs. Darcy, the situation is one of the utmost seriousness."

This was a scheme devised by George Warren; it must be. He had found his inheritance paltry in comparison to her huge fortune, and so had worked out this way of depriving her of it. The audacity of his plan took her breath away. She knew the truth, but who would believe her? Did Mr. Wilkinson believe her?

She took a deep breath. "Lieutenant Gresham arrived in Calcutta with the news of my husband's death. He was clear as to the date, he never, at any time, revised the date he gave me, and told others. Indeed, a memorial plaque was put up to my husband in the cathedral, and there it was, April the fifteenth."

"That is no proof of anything. He says he very much regrets taking the bribe from you, and now that he is back in England he is eager to right the wrong."

"Very convenient for Mr. Warren."

"He claims never to have met Mr. Warren. He ascertained who the lawyers were who handled your husband's affairs, and says that he went straight to them to make a clean breast of it."

Octavia's eyes were alight with anger. "It is all a monstrous farrago of lies," she cried. "Don't you see that Mr. Warren has put him up to this? Mr. Warren is the man handing out bribes, not me!"

"I am inclined to agree with you," said Mr. Wilkinson. "Mr. Warren does not have a good reputation; however, his father sits in the Lords, he has what one might call a position in society, he denies having ever had any contact with Lieutenant Gresham, says the first he knew about the matter was when his lawyers were in touch with him."

"Dear God, what am I to do?" An old feeling of helplessness threatened to overcome her, but she pushed it away; this was not a time for any weakness. "What will happen?"

"Mr. Warren is inclined to be generous. For your acknowledging his entitlement to the inheritance, he offers to grant you a handsome annuity."

"He offers me a small portion of what is rightfully mine, and calls it generous! I think not."

"Then he will take the matter to law, and I am afraid that will be a slow and expensive business."

Octavia was thinking. "I wonder if Lieutenant Gresham's story can be challenged by anyone in India? It will have to be more than his word in such a case as this."

"I hope so, for if that is what it comes to, the word of a naval officer of good standing will count for a good deal."

"Whereas I am nothing but a scheming widow," Octavia said bitterly.

"I shall send to India for information, and at once," said the lawyer. "It cannot be quick, however, for even with the overland route, we are talking many weeks. And meanwhile—"

"Meanwhile?"

"Mr. Warren's lawyers will make it impossible for you to continue to enjoy the use of your inheritance."

"What do you mean?"

"Control of your fortune passes into the hands of the lawyers. You will be allowed a small income, perhaps, but otherwise—"

"Otherwise?"

Her house, her new life, her income, her plans, all in ruins, all because of a lie, a falsehood, that might be upheld by the slow processes of an indifferent justice.

Justice indeed.

"I will fight this every inch of the way, Mr. Wilkinson."

He allowed himself a thin smile. "You are right to do so. If you want my personal opinion, I think you have the right of it, and Mr. Warren is at the bottom of this. However, I most strongly advise you never to say so, for Mr. Warren is of a litigious disposition, and you might find yourself facing an additional charge of slander. Leave it to others to blacken his name; I think you will find that they will do so, he is not greatly liked, from what I hear."

After he had gone, Octavia sat in the library, staring into the fire, unable to face Lady Susan and the inevitable questions.

As it turned out, she had no need to tell Lady Susan; another visitor had braved the fog, and brought this exciting piece of gossip with him.

"Snipe Woodhead was here," Lady Susan said. "Coming with the news and wanting to weasel his way into my confidence. He said that George Warren, that despicable man, has laid claim to your fortune, and also that you will be had up on a charge of bribery and corruption and false pretences and heaven knows what else."

"Witchcraft, I shouldn't be surprised," said Octavia. "Dear God, Susan, what am I to do? I shall be virtually penniless, we can't stay in this house, it seems—"

Lady Susan took it all very calmly. "I am quite used to reversal of fortune, you know, and let us trust that this will only be a temporary one. Why must we leave this house?"

"Because I shall have no money to pay the servants' wages, to keep up the house. And as for expenses I have already incurred, but have not had the bills for, I don't know what will happen about those."

Octavia, tears stinging her eyes, hardly took notice of what Lady Susan was saying. Alice came, smelling salts were wafted under her nose, making her eyes run, but clearing her head.

"Susan, where are you going?"

For Lady Susan was directing the butler to have the carriage brought round.

"I am going to pay a call on Caroline Warren. She is the only person who has any influence on that dreadful son of hers. No, I will not be able to convince her that she should persuade him to withdraw the case, she will be cock a hoop at the prospect of George getting his hands on such an immense fortune. But I shall make her put pressure on him to moderate his lawyers' demands, so that at least you may keep this roof over your head. Our heads, as it happens."

"Will she listen to you?"

"I know things about Mr. Warren's private life that she and he would much prefer were not made public. Don't fret, it isn't honourable or ladylike, but it will be effective. In a prize-fight, you know, the gloves must come off!"

Chapter Twenty-nine

It was Sophronia who brought Lord Rutherford's attention to Octavia's plight. He had been out of town, visiting Rutherford Castle before going on to stay with friends in Scotland. He had returned to London in a gloomy mood, which wasn't at all lightened by a note from Lady Langton demanding his company that evening, and decided instead to drive straight down to Netherfield House.

"Warren has laid claim to her fortune?" he said to Sophronia. "And everything is now in the hands of the lawyers? Well, there could not be a worse place for it to be. I pity Mrs. Darcy. To go from being a poor widow to a female Croesus and back to penury in the space of a few short months must be taxing to the spirit."

Sophronia was not deceived by his air of indifference. She had noticed the sudden alertness when she had mentioned Octavia's name.

"I have invited Mrs. Darcy and Susan to join us at Netherfield for Christmas," she went on.

"You have, have you? I suppose Susan will make a happy addition to our theatricals. Well, I gave you free rein with the invitations. Tell me whom else I shall have the honour of entertaining over the festive season?"

Sophronia handed him the list, and he ran his eye over it.

"I didn't invite the Langtons," Sophronia said calmly. "I thought you would not wish it."

He gave her a quizzical look.

"Besides," she went on, "I do not care for Kitty, as you know. She has a voice that trills; there are enough birds in our house without having her chirrup, chirrup, all day long."

Sholto had to laugh, and he raised a hand to acknowledge the hit.

"And," with a sidelong glance, "I have not invited Eliza, although she has been angling for an invitation."

This time there was a long silence. Then Sholto said, "Philip has not been in his grave these three weeks, and she wants to come to Netherfield for Christmas? It's hardly seemly."

"Eliza never was seemly. I lied to her," Sophronia said matter-of-factly. "I wrote and said you were only going to be here for a few days and would be spending the rest of the time in Yorkshire. Eliza does not care for Yorkshire."

"Nonsense, she cares for anywhere she may live in state," said Rutherford abruptly. "I am sorry for Philip. I liked him, but with that terrible wound he received in Spain, he was never going to make old bones. And now Eliza . . ." He paused and looked into the flames.

"Is hoping to pick up the threads of your long friendship," Sophronia said drily.

"Just so."

"Now, as to the theatricals," Sophronia said, changing the subject abruptly. "The ballroom will be the best for our stage, unless we are to have a dance."

Sholto followed his sister into the pretty ballroom, ghostly now, with its crystal chandeliers swathed in muslin and the floor squeaky with sand.

"Perhaps we should have a dance," said Sholto, almost to himself. "Will many families be in the country for Christmas?"

"Yes, but we shall take a party to the assembly in Meryton, that will be enough dancing, I suppose. And if not, if our guests want to dance, why, there is room in the drawing room for five or six couples."

"Have you decided on our play?"

"Why, yes. I am in the mood for Shakespeare this year. We are to put on *Twelfth Night*."

"Very appropriate."

"Isn't it?"

It was a family tradition, theatricals at Christmas, although for several years now, Rutherford had avoided Chauntry, unwilling to foist its inconveniences on more than a few guests who might be prepared to put up with the cold, the damp, the smoking chimneys, the animals. But Netherfield was much more comfortable; the house could accommodate twenty guests with ease.

"Who is to play Orsino?" Sholto asked.

"Why, you, dear brother, of course. And I hope Susan will oblige with Olivia. Poyntz, who is among those invited, of course, has agreed to take the part of Malvolio, while our neighbour Mr. Harrison will be Andrew Aguecheek."

"And Viola? Will you play Viola?"

"I am too old for Viola, and as you know, I prefer to be behind the scenes, as players say. I will organise, and chivvy, but I shall not act. Charlotte Goulding might do, she is just of an age."

"But not a natural actress."

"No, however, she will do as her mama tells her. She will be among friends, so will not find taking a role beyond her powers."

After they had dined, they went into the library, a handsome room with more comfortable chairs than in the drawing room. A roaring fire kept away the wintry chill, and they settled themselves in front of it.

Sholto watched his sister's face, warmed by the glow of a crackling log fire. Damn it, why had she never married? He had been remiss to let her stay to look after their mother. A companion could have been found, and no one could pretend that Lady Rutherford would be bothered to lose the company of her daughter, provided it did not inconvenience her.

Sophronia looked up at him with the blue eyes that were an uncanny reflection of his own, both in colour, and in the glint of humour that lurked there.

"I know what you are thinking, brother."

"You so often do," he said, sitting back and closing his eyes.

"It is not unusual to reach the age of five-and-thirty without meeting the man one wishes to marry. I am more fortunate than most women, I am in no danger of being forced to scrape a living for myself, I have all the ease and comfort and company I could wish. Unlike Mrs. Darcy, if Warren succeeds in wresting her fortune from her."

"What is the basis of his claim? I had understood the inheritance came from her own family, not through her marriage."

"I am not sure of all the details, but it is more than a dispute over a will; she is accused of bribery, and the buzz around town is that she may face a trial."

Rutherford sat up, his ease quite gone. "Trial? What trial? What are you saying?"

"She is supposed to have bribed a naval officer to lie about the date of her husband's death. She denies it, of course, is horrified at the very idea."

"It is impossible, she is not a woman to scheme and manipulate and lie, anyone with half their wits can see that. If any bribery has been done, you may be sure Warren is at the bottom of it."

"You are right, of course. Warren would bribe the dark gentleman himself to get his hands on a fortune half the size of Mrs. Darcy's," said Sophronia. "He is up to some wickedness, you may be sure of it."

"Who is this naval officer? Why has it taken this long for Warren to come up with this preposterous accusation?"

"One Lieutenant Gresham. He was with Christopher Darcy when he died. He has been at sea ever since, only just returned to this country. That is what Warren says."

"Lieutenant Gresham? Never heard of him."

"He is one of the Suffolk Greshams. The younger son of a younger son. I don't suppose your paths have ever crossed. He went to sea when he was twelve, he has no influence, he will never be more than a lieutenant. Particularly now with this scandal hanging over him; the navy does not care for that kind of thing among their officers. If Warren bribed him, he must have paid him a princely sum.

Which he can afford to do, if he can wrench her fortune from Mrs. Darcy."

Rutherford was prowling up and down the room. He stopped and turned on his heel. "What does this Gresham look like?"

"I have no idea. I have never set eyes on him. You sound annoyed, Sholto. Why?"

"I can't stand Warren. And it will be hard for Mrs. Darcy, to lose her fortune."

"She hasn't lost it yet. I would put her down as a fighter."

"Oh, I am sure she will not give in so meekly, but the law will not be on her side. The judges, if it comes to that, will take a man's word against a woman's, and in their minds will be the thought that such an enormous fortune will be much better in the hands of a man. It is a pity she has not married again, she could have had the pick of a dozen men, she has had half the men in London at her feet."

"All after her money," said Sophronia cynically.

"Perhaps not, she is hardly squint-eyed or in any way disagreeable. She likes to have her own way, men do not like that," he said shortly.

They sat in silence, watching the fire, Sholto still not quite at his ease, his fingers drumming on the arm of his chair.

"You should marry, Sholto," Sophronia said. "It is time you finished with Kitty Langton, she is beginning to bore you, and what is the point of setting up another mistress, when you should be thinking of the title and an heir? Besides, if you aren't careful, Eliza will have you. Is there no one you might fall in love with, no woman who tugs at your heartstrings?"

"Like you, Sophronia, I do not deal much in love. It is an overvalued commodity." He stood up and went over to the fire to kick a log back into place, then leant his tall frame against the marble fireplace. "I am thinking of offering for Charlotte Goulding."

"Charlotte? Are you sure—?" She checked herself. "She is a very lovely girl."

"Oh, as for that . . ."

"She is very young."

"As are all the debutantes."

"Her parents will be exultant, but do you care for her, or she for you?"

"We will understand one another. She will learn my ways, she is a biddable girl. No, don't look like that, Sophronia. Left to my own inclination, I wouldn't marry, but then Cousin Phineas would inherit the title, or that idiotic son of his, and I don't relish the prospect."

"If he should inherit, you won't be around to know about it."

"Very true. Should you like to have Charlotte for a sister?"

"No," said Sophronia. "She is a feather-brained creature. And I would have said a domestic one, who would be happiest running a neat little household. I suppose she will accustom herself to a political life in London and learn to take on the responsibilities that go with becoming a countess. However, you don't marry to please me, and you won't care what Mama says. Let me propose a better idea. Why don't you marry Octavia Darcy? You need not care whether she has a fortune or not, you are so rich it doesn't matter."

Rutherford was examining the shiny surface of his boot. "I can't think what put such a ridiculous notion into your head. Even if—I dare say she would not have me. You will find that she has other plans, I think. Or did have, before this blow. I have no wish to marry her, in any case, we only meet to disagree."

"That would make for a livelier marriage than with Charlotte."

"I'm not looking for liveliness. Octavia Darcy! When I wanted her, I'd find she was off galloping about the countryside, and when I hoped for soothing agreement to my opinion of some political issue, she would argue every inch of the way. Captain Darcy was a braver man than I am."

"He was in love with her."

"And she with him," Rutherford said impatiently. "I do not think she is hanging out for another husband."

"Hanging out, indeed! How vulgar you are, brother. And she liked Captain Darcy well enough, but she was never in love with him."

Rutherford gave her a frowning look. "You do say the most extraordinary things, how can you possibly know that?"

"From Susan," said Sophronia.

"Lady Susan," he said in tones of strong displeasure, "should keep her mouth shut and her tongue from wagging."

Sophronia retired early, leaving Rutherford to prowl about the public rooms, finally settling with a book in the library and a fine old brandy to soothe his nerves. Then he called for his candle and went upstairs to his bedchamber, where his slumbers were disturbed not by visions of Charlotte's beautiful face and figure, but by a tall graceful woman with no claim to beauty beyond eyes that a man could drown in.

And, just as he was falling asleep, by the memory of the stranger at the inn on the road from Oxford.

Chapter Thirty

By the time the date of their departure for Netherfield arrived, Octavia was more thankful than she would have believed possible to leave London. Hertfordshire might have all the disadvantages of country life, but there she would be among friends, and would not, she hoped, have to face the whispering and cold shoulders that had been her lot in London ever since Warren, with undue malevolence, had spread the tale about of her underhand and dishonest corruption of Gresham.

Some stood by her, such as Mr. Portal and Mrs. Rowan among them, but others proved fair-weather friends. Invitations ceased, and more than one former acquaintance crossed a street to avoid greeting her. Lady Langton, looking down her elegant nose, had cut her dead at the library, following this by declaring in her fluting, carrying voice that Mr. Hookham should be more careful about whom he let in through the doors, or she would change her subscription to Eber's library.

Lady Susan had responded swiftly, advising her to do just that. "It can make little difference to you, Kitty, for you are so busy listening to tittle-tattle and passing it on that I am sure you never have time to open or read a book."

Once again, Octavia found herself in Meryton, this time in her own carriage—but her own carriage for how much longer? She had been awakening at night, hot and unhappy, her future once again uncertain, and with the dreadful persistence of the law hanging over her.

Lady Susan noted the dark rings under Octavia's eyes, and admired her friend's attempts to keep up a good front, but the worry was there, and no comforting words or distractions could remove it. Many weeks and months had to be lived through before the lawyer's agent could return with information from India—and that might be no help at all.

Octavia remembered quite clearly the day she had heard the news in Calcutta, and there had been no hesitation in the details which a white-faced Gresham had given her. She had been at divine service at the moment of Christopher's demise; he had died on a Sunday, Lieutenant Gresham said, at eleven in the morning. Sunday the fifteenth of April, a date engraved in her mind.

She had attempted to make contact with Gresham over the last few weeks, because she was sure that if she could meet him face-to-face, he would have great difficulty in standing by his preposterous story, his out-and-out lie—but Mr. Gresham was not in London. Mr. Gresham, it appeared, was not even in England. He had gone to France, was in Paris or Toulouse, or possibly Dijon; no one could be sure where.

"Fishy," said Portal, when he heard this. He was brisk in Octavia's defence, spoke of the refutation of Gresham's lie as being a certainty, as did Mrs. Rowan, and Octavia was heartened and touched by his belief in her.

Gresham's father was a clergyman; Octavia had a wild notion of travelling to Suffolk to ask him to intercede with his son, but Lady Susan convinced her it would be a wasted journey. Father and son were not on good terms, and apparently, clergyman or no, the Reverend Gresham was not a model of Christian probity.

So it was with relief that she sat back against the squabs as the carriage turned into the long drive leading up to Netherfield House. Dusk was falling on the chill December evening; it was two days before Christmas and there was frost in the air. The house had a welcoming look, with soft lines showing behind the shutters, and before the carriage had come to a standstill, the front door was opening, servants were hurrying out, and there was Lady Sophronia, greeting Lady Susan with an embrace and shaking Octavia's hand with great warmth.

Octavia's room was a pleasant chamber, with long windows, heavily curtained against the winter night. A maid brought her water, and Alice, flushed with excitement at the visit to a grand country house, was unpacking her trunks, and asking Octavia what she wished to wear for dinner.

Octavia met Lady Susan on the stairs. Octavia was resplendent in a silk dress the colour of old claret, with a very dashing feather in her hair, and looked as though she were prepared for an evening of enjoyment. They went down arm in arm, Lady Susan calling out to Lady Sophronia and Lord Rutherford, who were standing in the hall below, wrangling about seating arrangements for dinner.

Lady Susan kissed Rutherford on both cheeks; Octavia hung back a little, feeling almost nervous, and annoyed with herself for it. Only a slight colour in her cheeks betrayed her emotion, and she looked perfectly calm as she shook hands and exchanged the usual conversation about the journey—swift, changed horses at the Swan, raining in London, snow forecast . . .

The truth was, she found that Lord Rutherford disturbed her thoughts and even her dreams more than was quite right. He unsettled her, threw her off balance. She was too experienced not to recognise how much he attracted her, and too sensible to imagine for a moment that he had any such inclination towards her. Was she in love with him? Good gracious no, she was beyond the age of that kind of folly. A handsome figure, a lively mind, a quick wit, a kind disposition—not to mention a good seat on a horse—were excellent qualities, but she didn't deceive herself; Lord Rutherford's affections were not so easily engaged, and she must not let her liking for his company betray her into the least indication of her feelings.

And then it was into the handsome drawing room, with its yellow and old gold hangings. There was quite a little crowd of guests gathered before the large fireplace, appreciating the merry blaze from the heaped logs. Octavia was happy to see Mr. Portal and Henrietta already there; they had told her in London that they would be joining her at Netherfield. And Mr. Quintus Dance, smiling at her and crossing at once to her side, drawing her attention to the panelling—"of another age, but admirable in its way." Yes, he was here as a guest, but also on a professional basis; he had all the preliminary plans for the new Chauntry to be discussed with Lord Rutherford, he was sure she would be interested to see them, in the morning, perhaps.

Octavia found herself relaxing among people who neither stared nor passed whispered comments, such as she had endured over these last two or three weeks. She was able to smile and laugh in a perfectly natural way, and was delighted, when they presently went into the dining room, to find herself seated at the dinner table between Mr. Poyntz and Mr. Quintus Dance.

"Your niece will be in Hertfordshire in a few days," said Poyntz, with undisguised satisfaction in his voice.

"Penelope? I had no idea she was invited."

"She is to join her cousins the Ackworths after Christmas."

Octavia had seen little of her sisters and brothers recently. She had had an unpleasant encounter with Arthur, who had paid a call at Firth Street a few days after she had heard the news from the lawyer.

"Well, sister, and now you have got yourself into a fine mess. Had you let me handle your affairs, I am sure none of this would have happened, Warren would not have dared to make this claim had I been looking after your fortune; this is what comes of your headstrong ways."

What irked her most was that Arthur was quite ready to believe her guilty of bribing Gresham, and he confided to her that he would have done just the same in her shoes. "For Warren has no moral right to Mrs. Worthington's estate, none whatsoever, and nothing could be more aggravating than to see family money ending up in quite another quarter. You were right to do as you did, but you should have been more careful, more discreet, and you were mean, you did not pay Gresham handsomely enough, every man has his price, and you obviously bought him too cheap, so that now Warren has outbid you."

She could say nothing to convince her brother that there had been no conspiracy, no bribery. She was speaking the truth; Gresham was not, and that was the end of it.

"You are obliged to say so, but it is not easy to believe that you were in such perfect ignorance of your relationship to Mrs. Worthington, a woman in the same country as you, a close relation. Your case would sound better if you did not insist that you were unaware of even having a great-uncle; people do not lose relations, especially when, as in your case, they have so few of them. No, no, Octavia, it will not do, and you will have to come down off your high horse and come to terms with Warren. You have bungled and must pay the price. I dare say he will settle for perhaps half or three-quarters of the inheritance, you cannot reasonably expect to come away with more."

And Octavia had responded with sudden wrath and a sharp tongue, so that Arthur went away in a considerable huff, and Octavia received a note from Augusta the next morning saying that in view of her stubborn refusal to see reason, it would be better for all family contact to be avoided for the present.

"I know Penelope was reluctant to be immured, as she put it, with my brothers and sisters at Melbury. They are a hunting set, and it is a cold and uncomfortable house. She will be much happier with the Ackworths."

Octavia didn't say, as she might have done, that comfort had nothing to do with it, the superior charm of Ackworth Manor was a human one, nothing to do with bricks and mortar and hunting.

"Now, tell me, Mrs. Darcy," Mr. Poyntz was saying, "what part do you take in the theatricals? For we are to put on a play, you know, we shall perform *Twelfth Night* by William Shakespeare. Viola, perhaps, or even Olivia?"

"I very much look forward to seeing the play, but I have no talent nor ambition in the Thespian line, so I shall be content with forming part of the admiring audience. Lady Susan is to take the role of Olivia, but as to Viola, I have no idea who plays her."

"It is a pity, you would make an excellent Viola. To take a man's part, an actress should be tall, I always think. Would you care to dress as a man, and wear breeches?"

Octavia laughed, and said that she preferred her skirts. "I rode astride sometimes, as a girl, when there was no one to notice me, but I took some terrible tumbles. Skirts have their advantages, as do side saddles."

Rehearsals began on Christmas Eve, with the actors assembled to read through the first act after a light luncheon. Lady Sophronia handed a copy of the play to Octavia when she came down in the morning. "I have decided that you shall prompt."

Lord Rutherford was passing by just at that moment, and after bidding Octavia a civil good morning, he told her that Sophronia had the habit of directing people to do as she wished, and that she must feel free to assert her will if she preferred not to prompt.

"Nonsense, Sholto," said Sophronia. "If you encourage people to argue, we shall never get anywhere."

"I am more than happy to prompt," said Octavia. "It is all new to me, I have never been involved in any play before, and I am looking forward to it. I shall be glad to be of use."

Lord Rutherford smiled and moved away to talk to Mr. Portal. For a second Octavia's eyes followed him, and then she looked down at the book in her hand and began to riffle through the pages, aware that Sophronia was watching her.

The Rutherford she had met during the fire had been overpowering in his anger and authority. The man she had crossed swords with in Yorkshire had been formidable and forceful. The man who had talked to her about his friend's love for Penelope had been a different person, direct, thoughtful, but still with some distance and reserve.

Now she saw yet another facet of his personality, a man among his friends, at ease, an affectionate brother, and with more charm than she would have credited him with, she reflected as she saw him bowing over the hand of Charlotte Goulding, who had arrived with her mother to take her place among the actors.

She turned to find Mr. Quintus Dance at her elbow. "You mentioned that you would like to see the plans for Chauntry," he said.

"I would indeed."

"I am using the library, they are spread out on a table there."

Octavia enjoyed every minute of Christmas Day, which began with a walk across glistening frosty fields to church and ended with mummers performing in the hall. The Christmases of her childhood had been lonely ones, and the one she had spent at Melbury Hall had been a damp and depressing time in the company of hearty hunting men, sleeping in a small and chilly bedroom in the attics, finding herself among women who stared at her as though she had been a chicken in a cage, passed over for the pot. She felt she had been judged and found wanting yet again, and only her sense of humour carried her through the days of hard riding and hard drinking; it had been a relief to go back to the chilly formality of Theodosia's London house and life, for the last few weeks before she set sail for India.

And Christmas in India was a different kind of feast, with regimental displays in the hot sunshine and a meal of scraggy birds doing duty for the traditional goose or turkey. It was too hot to relish eating the rich Christmas pudding that was so often dutifully ordered in the English houses, although the men set about it with a will.

Christmas at Netherfield was entirely different, with the house warm and enchanting with boughs of evergreen and bunches of holly, ribbons fluttering from them, hot punch and delicious food, from the tiny spicy mince pies served in the hall to the feast served in the dining room. When they came back from church, a cheerful group of them set about cutting up gold paper and making tassels and ornaments to add to the greenery.

Dinner was a long and splendid affair, with the wassailers appearing at the same time as the pudding, to sing and wind their way around the rooms in the customary way. Then all the guests and the servants stood in the hall while the mummers put on their play, their efforts rewarded with loud applause and substantial plates of mince pies and hot punch.

Octavia went tired and happy to bed, too tired to do anything but fall asleep the moment her head touched the pillow.

Chapter Thirty-one

Rehearsals for *Twelfth Night* resumed the day after Christmas. The wind had turned to the northeast, blowing away the damp clouds, but bringing a biting frost. The ground was too hard for hunting, and the gentlemen had to resign themselves to no more exercise than could be afforded by taking out a gun after breakfast.

"They are glad to be back," said Lady Sophronia when they came in, bringing gusts of icy air into the hall and stamping their feet to warm frozen feet. "Go into the dining room," she told them, "where there is a good fire, and food set out."

They tucked into the cold pies and brawn and ham with a will, washed down with mugs of ale, and then pronounced themselves quite ready to participate in the gentler activity of the drama.

The estate carpenter had brought up some of the wood saved from Chauntry, part of the Elizabethan gallery that had been in the great hall, together with its supports and some of the panelling that had, miraculously, not burnt. This had been erected at the end of the ballroom, giving a very convincing Shakespearean look and providing the structure of a stage.

The huge wicker baskets containing the costumes and heavy red velvet curtains from the Chauntry plays had also been rescued.

"Without that, we could not have contemplated putting on a play," Lady Sophronia told Rutherford. "What a stroke of luck,

Mama deciding that the baskets were to be brought down from the attics in the spring."

"It was time they were sorted and cleaned," said Rutherford. "Some of the costumes were looking distinctly shabby, I remember thinking."

The contents of the baskets were laid out on trestle tables in a parlour off the ballroom, and those of the housemaids who were adept with their needles were hard at work altering and trimming sufficient robes and breeches and ruffs for the performance of *Twelfth Night*. Lord Rutherford and Lady Sophronia fell on the garments with cries of delight and exclamations as they recalled past performances.

"Do you remember the year we put on scenes from *Henry VIII*?" Lord Rutherford said, picking up a heavily embroidered gold robe with crimson slashes in its sleeves.

"And this was what I wore as Amelia in *Lover's Vows.*"

Lord Rutherford had found a long sword. "Macbeth's sword, I'd forgotten how long it was."

"Here's the coat you wore when we did *The Rivals,* that was one of our best productions."

"And this was the yellow robe Poyntz had for Prospero."

"When Eliza played Miranda, and you were Ferdinand," said Sophronia with a sly glance at her brother. "You wore this cloak."

Rutherford folded the cloak up and put it to one side. "It was all a long time ago."

"Ten years at least."

"This will do for me as Orsino," he said, holding up a set of black velvet doublet and hose, slashed with gold. "We had this for *Hamlet,* did we not?"

"Lady Susan will be perfect in this." Sophronia pulled out a dress in crimson silk with an embroidered fronter and a gold filigree ruff. "I am so happy that our costumes escaped the fire, they are a part of Chauntry."

"Make-believe, our theatricals, just as Chauntry was."

"There was nothing make-believe about the smoking fires and draughts and stone floors running with damp," said Sophronia tartly.

"Well, we are agreed on that. It was a house that outlived its usefulness, and was a mere facsimile of its original self," said Lord Rutherford, suddenly serious. "I shall build a new house to suit the new age."

"With plumbing for the new age as well, I hope, dear brother; the smells at Chauntry on hot days in the summer were something I shall be glad to forget," said Sophronia, pulling out a pair of baggy yellow breeches. "Yellow for Malvolio, to go with his cross gartering. Henry will have his work cut out to appear a glum Puritan, it is one of his most delightful characteristics that he smiles so readily. He'll have to practise making his mouth turn down and his brow furrow. Now, what have we for Viola? And Sir Toby Belch, we shall need padding for him."

"I shall leave it to you," said Lord Rutherford. "Mama was right, they could do with a clean, most of them."

"Mrs. Sandford will see to it, so that by the time everyone arrives, there is nothing to be done but to fit the costumes and make final adjustments."

Mrs. Sandford, the housekeeper, had duly carried out her task, and now, instead of untidy heaps of costumes, everything was in order, a costume for each member of the cast, with its own place on the trestle or on the racks set up behind, and a label pinned to every dress and hat and the other accoutrements.

Octavia found Lady Susan in the wardrobe, as Lady Sophronia had dubbed it. She stood there, standing stock-still while Alice, who was a notable needlewoman, crawled around her feet, pinning up the hem of her dress with the assistance of one of the Netherfield housemaids.

Lady Sophronia watched with a critical eye, and then said to the plump maid whom Mrs. Sandford had put in charge of the costumes, "The breeches we put out for Viola will not do, Lady Goulding will not permit Miss Goulding to wear breeches. We shall have to find her a robe of some kind that she can wear instead."

"Those breeches you picked out would have needed shortening in any case, my lady, for all that Miss Goulding's a tall young lady. I'll go through the baskets again, and see what I can find."

Sophronia, who had a keen eye for colour, was thinking aloud. "Black, gold, scarlet, yellow—there is a purple robe, my brother wore it once, I think, for Shylock. That would do. Purple with green trimmings, I seem to remember."

Another housemaid was in charge of hats, and was trimming a black velvet cap with curling golden feathers. "For his lordship," she said, showing her work with pride to Lady Sophronia.

The first rehearsal took place at the far end of the ballroom, while the workmen were still busy about the stage, talking in loud whispers as they set up an intricate arrangement of pulleys for the heavy curtains.

Octavia took her place to one side, a copy of the play in her hand, but at the moment most of the actors were still reading their parts, no prompting was called for, and she could listen and enjoy.

Octavia had seen very few plays until these last few months, when she had gone several times to the theatre. It still held novelty for her; she was like a child when the curtain went up and the action began. Now she was backstage, she felt the magic in the air; even in a country house production, even with a play staged in a ballroom, the promise of enchantment was there.

And even to her inexperienced eye, it was obvious that this was going to be a far from amateurish production. For a start, there was Lady Susan, already line perfect, transformed the moment she stepped forward from the aristocratic daughter of an ancient house into a professional actress. Her voice, always expressive and beautiful, was exact in its modulation, pitch, and projection, and every gesture, every expression, was considered and effective, although, Octavia noticed, nothing was set in stone; Lady Susan would try a phrasing, a movement, and then run through it again in a different way.

She commanded the stage, which put both Lord Rutherford and Henry Poyntz on their mettle. Lord Rutherford's voice, deep and resonant, would have graced any stage, and he knew how to use it to the best effect. Octavia loved listening to his speeches; he had an ear for poetry, and his verse speaking brought out both the meaning and rhythm of his lines.

Henry Poyntz, a natural tenor, shed his clerical nature entirely and threw himself ably into his part. He would preach an excellent sermon, Octavia thought. She had heard it said that all the best preachers had something of the actor in them, and in Poyntz's case this was certainly so. Gone was the lively, amiable man, and in his place was the vain, self-absorbed, sad character of Malvolio.

Among the main characters, only Charlotte Goulding was something of a disappointment. She spoke her lines clearly and well, she had been well schooled in elocution by her governess, but there was little life to her, none of the passionate feeling and ardour that was in the role of Viola. Still, she would look well, and moved gracefully; it might be enough.

"She is a sweet little cabbage, and full of pretty smiles," said Lady Susan when a halt was called for refreshments to be brought for the hard-working cast. "However, she is no actress. We must be glad that we have such a good Orsino and Malvolio. Who is seeing to the scenery, Sophronia?"

"Mr. Dance, who is also to play Sebastian. He should be here, but I'm told he went out earlier on horseback and hasn't yet returned. He has shown me his sketches, which are very good indeed, and he will supervise all the work."

Charlotte was glad when Sir Toby and Maria, played by a lively young Miss Amelia Lucas, came on for their scene, and she could sit at the side and watch.

"I am not to wear breeches," she confided to Octavia. "Mama will not permit it. I am to wear a kind of robe. Lady Sophronia is to see to it. Who is the man who plays Sebastian?" she added.

Quintus Dance had come in late, full of apologies; he had ridden over to Chauntry to check something on the site, and had quite lost track of time.

"That is Mr. Dance, the architect, who is to build Lord Rutherford's new house."

"An architect? Oh," Charlotte said, "I took him for a gentleman."

"And so he is. He is a younger son, with his way to make in the world, and he chose to be an architect rather than go into the law or the military or the Church, as he tells me his brothers have done. As you can tell from his name, he has four elder brothers."

"Does he? Four, and sisters as well, I dare say, he comes of a large family. But why does his name tell you that?"

"Quintus means five, he is a fifth son. Just as I am called Octavia because I am an eighth child."

"It is Latin, I suppose," said Charlotte. "My brothers study Latin, but of course I never did, girls do not need to know Latin. He is very handsome, do not you think so?" she said, lowering her voice.

"Mr. Dance?" Octavia would not have described him as handsome; he had a good figure and a lively countenance, but his features were unremarkable.

"I should not say so," said Charlotte, colour flaring into her cheeks. "It is impolite to make personal comments, I know."

"I think there is no harm in noticing whether a man is handsome or no," said Octavia, smiling.

"Sebastian is Viola's twin brother in the play, is he not? My governess read it through with me. I don't care much for Shakespeare. And a girl dressing up as a boy, it is like something out of a novel, and I don't think I make at all a good boy. I don't know why Shakespeare had women disguised as men; my governess told me he did it in other plays as well."

"You must remember that in Shakespeare's day, women were not allowed to act on the public stage, and all the women's parts were played by boy actors."

Charlotte was too well mannered to protest at this extraordinary idea, but her incredulity was obvious. "Mama says that Lady Susan was an actress in America, although she is a great lady. Is that not very shocking? And yet she is received everywhere."

"She is a very good actress," said Octavia, knowing that she was being evasive, but she found Charlotte's artless questions difficult to respond to. "Now, that scene is finished, turn over your pages, look, we are here, and there is your cue. On you go!"

Octavia watched for a few minutes, and then, deciding that she was not needed among the actors for the moment, took herself off to the other end of the ballroom, where Quintus Dance was deep in discussion with the carpenter, a gnome of a man in his leather apron, who listened attentively and intelligently to what Mr. Dance was saying.

"There's a gent as knows what he's doing," the carpenter said appreciatively to Octavia, and Mr. Dance, after acknowledging her presence with a smile, went over to talk to the man who was putting together the curved wooden staircase that led up to the gallery.

"It's a pleasure to work with him, and he's going to be a marvel with the new Chauntry, mark my words. These architects mostly have their heads in the clouds, with no more notion of how their fancy drawings can be built in bricks and mortar than my old ma has; less, I reckon. But Mr. Dance is a man who knows his houses and his building materials through and through."

"You are right," said Octavia. "I live in London in a house built by Mr. Dance, and it is a most practical and well-built house."

Her house! Every time she forgot her predicament, she or someone else said something which brought it to the forefront of her mind. She had resolved to put her concerns to one side for the Christmas season, and not allow herself to consider the prospect that the new year would bring, of her losing everything, including her London house that she felt so at home in.

She turned her mind to the designs for the set. Worrying would do no good, and to brood would be to make herself uncongenial company. There was nothing she could do about her affairs at the moment, neither here nor if she had remained in London.

As far as the possibility of criminal charges went, her reason told her that she need not worry. Both Mr. Wilkinson and Mr. Portal had reassured her on that point, when she had seen them the day before coming down to Netherfield.

"It will never come to that, however much Warren blusters and threatens," Mr. Portal said, and Mr. Wilkinson nodded his head in silent agreement. "He could not attempt it, not without becoming an outcast from society. Your brothers and sisters, and therefore you also, have too much standing in the world for that, and then the Darcys are very much on your side; Mrs. Wytton has been very active in your favour, she has altogether no doubts about your innocence, and as for any prosecution, she says that the Darcy clan have quite enough influence to scotch any attempts in that direction—although Wytton agrees with me," Mr. Portal added, "that Warren will not be such a fool as to press for charges. He is a greedy man, an unscrupulous man, certainly not too nice in his morals, but he is not a stupid man. He will go for the money and the property, but will not lay charges."

Octavia wrenched her thoughts back to the present moment. If she lived each minute as it came, if she concentrated her attention on what was in front of her, then there was no room in her mind for anything else. As to the silent watches of the night, when the fire in her room burned low, and fears and worries came weaselling out of the darkness, she could light a candle and lose herself in a book; no good could come of lying there and brooding and frightening herself with apprehension about the future.

She offered her services to Mr. Dance. "I'm not wanted at present at the other end, and I like to be busy."

"Can you paint?" he asked. "Here are the sketches of the scenery, but as you see they are only drawn in line. They must be coloured, so that the paints can be mixed to the right shades."

"You are very trusting," she said. "I may have little skill in that direction."

Mr. Dance at Netherfield, purposeful about his work on the scenery, was not the urbanely courteous gentleman he was when paying calls in London; here he was the professional, a man with more edge to him, competent and authoritative.

"I can soon be the judge of that. Have you your sketchbook with you?"

She had. She had brought several of her sketchbooks from India with her, for Lady Sophronia had asked to see them. "I shall fetch it directly," she said.

She crossed to the main door which led to the hall and the staircase, walking on silent feet so as not to disturb the actors. Orsino's words sounded in her ears:

"And the free maids that weave their thread with bones,
Do use to chant it: it is sooth—"

Lord Rutherford's attention faltered for a moment. "Damn it, all these sibilants."

"—it is silly sooth,
And dallies with the innocence of love,"

Octavia came back downstairs in a few minutes, but she took care this time to walk through to the other doors at the far end of the ballroom, where her return would be unmarked by the actors. She handed her sketchbooks to Mr. Dance. He flicked through the pages, raising his eyebrows, and pausing on some of them. "I was quite right, your eye for colour is extremely good. I may say these are remarkable, you paint a vivid and vital picture of India. I have never been there, but I should like to look through your books at my leisure, if you will permit it, for I feel that will be as good as making the journey there myself."

Octavia coloured slightly at the compliment, produced the paint box she had brought down with her, and sat herself at one of the trestles to colour at Mr. Dance's designs. She painted quickly and deftly, following Mr. Dance's instructions not to strive for too natural an appearance, but to be mindful that this was theatre, there would be lights shining on the scenery, and the whole nature of the stage was to present an illusion, not a sense of reality.

She enjoyed herself, and added some touches of her own, suitable for the season: a pair of partridges in one of the trees, garlands of evergreen entwined with red and gold ribbons, and, in one wintry outdoors scene, a snowman in a gentleman's tall hat. These additions made Mr. Dance laugh when he saw them.

"They may be omitted, if you wish," she said, swirling her brush in the tub of water.

"I would not dream of it, they are charming, and quite in keeping with the setting of the play."

"Are these the drawings of the sets?" said a voice behind them, and Octavia looked up, startled, straight into Lord Rutherford's enigmatic blue eyes. "You are making the devil of a noise up here, with your laughter," he said, holding up one of the drawings and looking at it at arm's length.

"Rather fanciful," was his comment, and Mr. Dance looked surprised at the coldness of his lordship's voice. "I hope all this does not take you away from your work on Chauntry, Mr. Dance."

"Indeed it does not, I am well ahead with my plans, as you know."

"I think your new house will be a model of its kind, Lord Rutherford," said Octavia, made uneasy by the tension in the air.

Lord Rutherford bowed. "I am glad it meets with your approval, ma'am," he said, and turned abruptly away. "Ah, Jenkins, you are doing a good job there with that staircase, but we do not need to rebuild Chauntry entirely in this ballroom."

Mr. Jenkins gave a guffaw. "No, my lord, I'll make sure of that."

Lord Rutherford was on such easy terms with his estate workers, and yet so stiff with Mr. Dance. Odd, thought Octavia, as she bent her head over her painting once more.

The next few days passed in a whirl of activity. The actors, all of them brought up from childhood to memorise verse, had no trouble learning their parts and they were all soon word perfect, needing only occasional reminders from Octavia. And even Charlotte was managing, with some careful coaching from Lady Susan, to put some expression into her lines.

She was brought over to Netherfield every day by her mama, and Lady Goulding sat in on all the rehearsals. Octavia had been slightly wary of her at first, fearing that she would cold-shoulder her, as so many matrons in London had done when Warren's attack became public, but Lady Goulding went out of her way to condole with Octavia on the unfortunate situation she had found herself in.

"You should be sanguine about the outcome," she told her comfortably. "I find these things so often turn out to be a storm in a teacup. Sir Joseph is very indignant on your behalf, he says he would not trust George Warren further than he could see him, and he holds that in the end, justice will be done, and something will happen to show the world that it is just Warren up to his tricks again. Of course, Mr. Warren has the ear of the King, and he presumes rather on that; however, the King's influence is not near so great as he thinks it is, so Sir Joseph says."

Octavia wasn't sure whether to be consoled or alarmed by these words, but she decided just to be grateful that Lady Goulding wasn't inclined to shun her company. In fact, after a while she began to feel it might almost be preferable if she had kept her distance, as Lady Goulding sat beside her, keeping up a gentle flow of conversation which made it hard for Octavia to attend to the actors, who, however, needed little help from her.

The main topic of Lady Goulding's prattle was her hopes for her daughter, her growing confidence that Lord Rutherford was going to make her an offer, and Octavia found herself obscurely annoyed by this. At first, she dismissed it as a mama's fancy, but then Lady Sophronia said, in a casual aside when the ladies were in the drawing room after dinner, that her brother had formed the intention of ending his single status, and had Miss Goulding in mind.

Octavia had so far forgotten herself as to let out an exclamation of disbelief, which she had hastily retracted, saying that it was merely that Miss Goulding was very young, not yet out, and that Lord Rutherford—

"Is . . . ?" said Lady Sophronia, looking at Octavia expectantly, but Octavia shook her head. "It is only that he can be a formidable person, and Charlotte has no character," Lady Sophronia finished calmly. "It is not the match I would have chosen for him, far from it, but one thing I have learned in thirty-five years, Mrs. Darcy, is that one has to leave other people to fall into the pits they have dug for themselves. If my brother thinks he needs to marry, is feeling oppressed by Kitty Langton, and now sees a cloud on the horizon in the shapely form of Eliza Effingham—ah, I see Susan has told you about her—then he may make the mistake of turning to the insipid peace of a Charlotte Goulding. Of course, if he does any such thing, then when the inconveniences of a Kitty Langton and Mrs. Effingham have passed into memory, he will be left shackled to a ninny," she went on.

"She is a beautiful girl, she will make somebody a good wife," said Octavia.

"She is not in love with Sholto and never will be."

No, thought Octavia, but she is falling in love with Mr. Dance; however, she kept her thoughts to herself. If the others hadn't noticed the warmth with which Charlotte looked at Mr. Dance, and the careful way he refrained from looking at her when they were in company together, then she wasn't going to say anything about it. It was an impossible match, at least in the eyes of Lady Goulding; the prospects for Charlotte in that direction were worse than Penelope and Poyntz.

Chapter Thirty-two

If no one had noticed Charlotte's interest in Mr. Dance, Lord Rutherford had noticed how much attention Mr. Dance was paying to Octavia, and how much she seemed to enjoy his company.

"A fine thing for a woman in her position to flirt with a Mr. Dance," he said irritably to his sister and Susan. They were in the breakfast parlour, first down; Sophronia because she was naturally an early riser, Susan because a cockerel had chosen for some unknown reason to perch itself in the lower branches of a tree directly outside her room and set up a joyful crowing at the first hint of a frosty dawn, and Lord Rutherford because he made a point of being up to welcome such of his guests as chose to come down to breakfast.

"Flirt?" Sophronia was scornful. "Mrs. Darcy does not flirt with Mr. Dance, and if she did, what is wrong with that? She is a widow, true, but out of mourning; is she supposed not to take any pleasure in male company, as though she had taken the veil?"

"Mr. Dance—he is a good architect, I grant you, and a man I like; however, he is hardly of the same world as Mrs. Darcy."

"He is a gentleman, she is a gentleman's daughter," said Susan. "Pour me some more coffee, if you will be so good, Sholto, and stop talking fustian. Mr. Dance is not of your world, no, and you could say not of the world of the Threlfords, either, but where does that leave me, a runaway, an actress? Why, I am amazed you let me into your house. Besides, Mrs. Darcy may be the daughter of a baronet, but he allied himself with the daughter of a grocer. She could do worse than Mr. Dance, who will obviously make a great name for himself; on the other hand, she has no interest in Mr. Dance in that way, none at all."

"How do you know? You women are so absolute in your judgements, so sure that you see everything with greater insight and clarity than anyone else."

"And your judgement, any judgement that begins 'You women,' is clouded by your feelings," said Sophronia calmly. "Susan, you have ate up all the plum jam, I shall have to ring for some more. Ah, I hear voices, yes, Mr. Poyntz is joining us, and Pagoda. Good morning to you both, you have arrived in the nick of time to prevent poor Sholto being quite overrun by us mere women."

"What was all that about?" said Susan, when she was alone with Sophronia for a moment before the rehearsal began.

"Sholto's feathers are ruffled. His rational mind tells him he should marry Charlotte Goulding, with whom he has nothing in common, and who will bore him into fits within six months; his heart is inclined towards Octavia, but his dignity tells him it is not a suitable match, and his rational response, as is so often the case with a man where the emotions are involved, is to bury his head in the sand and take no action."

Susan laughed. "Sholto is the most active and decisive man I know. He never had any trouble in shedding a mistress nor taking on a new one, why should acquiring a wife cause him such anguish? I agree he had better not marry Charlotte Goulding, but surely he will come to his senses as far as that is concerned."

"He must take care. Lady Goulding is beginning to count on the match, and a mama can force a man, even a man like Sholto, into a position from which he will find it very difficult to escape."

"Octavia is the very wife for him, I have thought so for many weeks now."

"He is afraid she does not care for him."

"He has made no effort to woo her. She has a good deal of reserve, she is wary, which is not surprising, given the blows which she has endured. She felt she was entering upon a period of happiness, and now it seems that the independence she values is about to be snatched away. And while this whole Warren business hangs over her, she won't give way to her feelings for any man."

"Is she in love with Sholto?"

Susan shrugged her elegant shoulders. "Who knows? We do not talk about it; if she is, she may not even admit it to herself. Well, they are a fine pair. They will be thrown much into one another's company between now and *Twelfth Night,* so perhaps that will bring them to an understanding."

Unaware of her friends' interest in the state of her heart, Octavia busied herself with her role as prompter, and, as it turned out, a kind of stage manager, noting down what Lady Sophronia and the actors decided as to entrances and exits and where they were to stand on the stage. They were rehearsing on stage now, and several times in every rehearsal, Octavia would find herself appealed to.

"You have come on from the left, Sholto," said Lady Sophronia, "and last time you entered from the right. Mrs. Darcy, what say you?"

"No, Charlotte, you stand behind Olivia here, so that you may make your exit there."

"Poyntz, consider what you are about, you should not be walking across there."

"Excuse me, Lady Susan, this is exactly where I should be."

And Octavia would hastily look at the scribbles she had made on the side of her copy of the play, and tell Lady Sophronia that Sholto's entrance was from the left, that Charlotte was indeed in the wrong place—too busy looking around to see if Mr. Dance was come into the room, in Octavia's view—and that Lady Susan was, in this rare instance, in the wrong.

With such a lively bunch of people, and with all the high spirits that naturally went with the putting on of the play, the atmosphere was full of gaiety and pleasure. Only Lord Rutherford could sometimes be seen with a frown on his face, chiefly when he saw Octavia, yet again, enjoying a joke or a discussion with Mr. Dance. He had taken to avoiding Lady Goulding as much as he could; he knew quite as well as Susan how determined mothers could be, and he had not outmanoeuvred them for years without getting the trick of it. He felt obscurely ashamed of himself for the way he was behaving, but he had the comfort, if comfort it was, of knowing that Charlotte, who had taken to shying like a frightened horse whenever he came near her, had no warm feelings at all for him.

A voice rang in his ears, a whining voice that warned him not to have any high expectations of matrimony, reminding him that the lovely bride of today could turn into a hibernating ladyship of tomorrow, or that even, should he become engaged a second time, this bride-to-be might treat him as had Eliza Hawtrey. A siren voice, the implication of its words being that it might not really much matter which woman he became engaged to, since any marriage was doomed to disappointment.

Women were not to be trusted. The only woman he had any faith in was Sophronia, who never behaved out of character or deceitfully. She was not a flirt, she didn't spend hours in the library with plans and maps; what a pretence. Who would be taken in by this supposed passion for house building and architecture? No, it was the architect that caught Mrs. Darcy's fancy, not drainage systems and the type of beam necessary for a roof of a certain pitch.

In fact, as Octavia's apparent interest in the house grew, his own liking for the new Chauntry diminished. It had been a mistake to employ Mr. Dance. Sophronia had erred, inviting him to be among their number over Christmas—on this, he conveniently forgot that he had requested that Sophronia invite the architect, so that they could look over the plans and site together. Did he really want to build a house here in Hertfordshire? The owners of Netherfield House would willingly grant him a long lease, it was a good-enough house, why go to the trouble and expense of rebuilding? It was not as though he planned to spend much time in Hertfordshire.

Sophronia laughed at him for his new attitude, and laughed at him in company, on more than one occasion, for being so dull.

"Why should I not be dull if I want to be? Not that I am at all dull, it is just a fancy of yours to say so."

Their company was soon further enlivened by the arrival at Ackworth Manor of Penelope Cartland; the very next day after her journey, she persuaded her cousins to drive her over for a visit to Netherfield. "You will want to wish them the compliments of the season," she told them. "And Mrs. Darcy is there, you have told me how much you enjoyed her company when she was at Ackworth."

Since the cold weather, frost turning to sleety rain which then froze again at night, precluded Mr. Ackworth's hunting or shooting or doing anything useful about the farm, he agreed to have the horses put to so that they could drive over to Netherfield House.

"She has a motive, the hussy," he grumbled to his wife as he finished his breakfast.

"Of course she has, she is in love with Henry Poyntz, had you not noticed when she was here last winter?"

"I thought it a passing fancy."

"Well, it is clearly not so, if it has endured for a year."

"Theodosia will have none of it."

"I suppose the couple may take matters into their own hands."

"Elope?" Mr. Ackworth shook his head. "You are out there, my dear, it would never do for a man in Poyntz's position, a clergyman cannot be seen to make a runaway marriage. Nor can they anticipate the married state, which might frighten Theodosia into agreeing to a wedding; again, it will not do for a clergyman."

"Clergymen have much the same in their breeches as other men," said Mrs. Ackworth robustly.

"Not if they're Dr. Rawleigh," said Mr. Ackworth. "You are very coarse, I find, you will offend the young people if you do not mind your tongue."

"Dr. Rawleigh suffers more than usual from the rheumatism this year," said Mrs. Ackworth thoughtfully. "If he could be encouraged to retire . . ."

"I do not think that Shropshire will be of benefit to aching joints."

"No, but when he no longer has a parish to take care of, he will not have to be out and about in all weathers."

"Out and about in all weathers? Since when was old Rawleigh out and about in any weather, unless it is to be visiting his henges in distant parts of the country? Besides, even if he retired tomorrow, and Mr. Poyntz stepped into his shoes, it will still not be the grand match Theodosia is longing for."

Mrs. Ackworth rose from her chair. "I shall write to her, and express my concern that Penelope is not improving in looks, and asking how Eleanor is. I shall say how hard it will be for Penelope to be seen alongside her ravishing sister—perhaps something along those lines will give Theodosia pause for thought."

"Well, I leave all this cunning and contrivance to you, my dear. We men concern ourselves with greater issues."

"Yes, such as the roof flying off the pigsty."

"And have you considered," said Mr. Ackworth, ignoring the unkind thrust about the pigsty, for he was in fact more of a gossip than his wife had ever been, "that Penelope may have formed a lasting attachment to Henry Poyntz, but he may not care for her anymore?"

"That is why we shall go over with her to Netherfield. I shall know in an instant how things stand between them."

The Ackworths' doubts were set at rest by their visit to Netherfield; the attachment between the couple was evident, however carefully they still tried to hide it. Although here, among friends, they could be more open about spending welcome time in one another's company than was possible in London.

"They had better be married," said Pagoda Portal in his expansive way. "My dear Mrs. Darcy, cannot you convince your sister to give her permission? Indeed, has Mr. Poyntz approached Miss Cartland's parents and asked for her hand?"

"No," said Octavia. "Penelope will not let him do so, she feels that he would be met with a flat no, and she would thereafter be kept under such rigorous supervision that they could never meet."

"What is she hoping for? A miracle? Your sister will not change her spots. Miss Cartland had much better try the tactics young women employ in such cases: tears, sulks, not eating, going about with a miserable face, making her parents' life a misery until they give in."

"Theodosia would take not the slightest notice, she cares very little for how happy or not Penelope is, nor indeed if she is pining away. She is so ambitious for Penelope's that her life would truly be unbearable, and Mr. Poyntz is well aware of how things stand there."

Mr. Portal looked at her with some amusement. "You represent your sister as something of an ogre."

"My family do rather resemble something out of a fairy tale, Mr. Portal, but I fear that this fairy tale does not have a happy ending. Not a one that is brought about by any direct means, at least. But we have a scheme. I have been thinking hard how it may be brought to a happy conclusion for the couple, and I now discover Mrs. Ackworth has much the same idea in mind as I have."

Mrs. Ackworth sat down that very evening to write to Theodosia. It was a difficult letter, one that was scratched out and rewritten several times, with Mr. Ackworth adding not altogether helpful advice as to its tone and wording.

The gist of it was that they were shocked to find Penelope out of sorts and out of looks. Perhaps she had not recovered from her spell of illness the previous winter, but it would be hard for Theodosia to turn her off, looking the way she was. "For she is a pretty child," Mrs. Ackworth cunningly wrote, "although not the equal of Louisa in looks. She tells me that Eleanor outshines Louisa by a long chalk; would it not be possible to make some match, any match for Penelope, so that the way may be clear for her sister to contract the kind of marriage that her beauty, fortune, and position would achieve for her? Penelope is not cut out to be a great London hostess, a leader of fashion, as you would like to see a daughter, but is there not someone among the ranks of her admirers and well-wishers—a country squire, a clergyman, a soldier—with whom she might be happy enough, and you could feel that she had made a respectable if not a brilliant match?"

Weasel words, each one planted to make its mark; Mrs. Ackworth could only sigh at her own duplicity, as she signed the letter, folded the paper, and sealed it with a wafer. "I shall take it over to Netherfield tomorrow. Penelope is eager to go there again, and I can ask Lord Rutherford to frank it for me."

"I am quite able to afford the cost of postage, my dear," said Mr. Ackworth.

"Of course you are, but it will be a good notion to make Lord Rutherford aware of what we are up to; Octavia tells me he is very keen on the match for his friend."

"A cunning plan," said Octavia, taking the letter from Mrs. Ackworth and looking at it as though it might burst open and reveal a furious Theodosia. "I do hope our plan works."

"What plan, may I ask?" said Lord Rutherford, coming into the room. He glanced from her face to Mrs. Ackworth's. "You have a guilty look about you."

"Mrs. Ackworth has written to my sister, to Mrs. Cartland, a letter that we hope will pave the way for Mr. Poyntz to be able to marry Penelope."

"Tell me."

Mrs. Ackworth told him, and he listened without interrupting, a rare grace in a man, Octavia thought.

"You want it franked," he said at once, taking the letter and scrawling his signature across it. "I will put it with the rest of the post, it will be on its way today."

"Do you think it will serve?" said Mrs. Ackworth.

"It may, but what if Mrs. Cartland has some possible suitor of her own up her sleeve, some tiresome country gentleman with interest in the Party? I think I shall be underhand myself. I shall write to Cartland—stay, no. Poyntz must contrive a meeting with Cartland, propose himself, ask for Miss Cartland's hand. At the same time I shall write, saying how much I will approve the match. Will that carry any weight with your brother-in-law?" he said to Octavia.

"Mr. Cartland does, I believe, sincerely care about his daughter, and would be happy to see her marry the man she loves. But his word or opinion counts for little in their household, it is no secret that he lives under the cat's foot. Now, if there were anything you could do for my brother, that might have a great effect. It is a shame you are such a great Whig, and not a Tory."

Rutherford gave Octavia a swift, knowing look; she was mocking him, and he knew it.

"Ah, Mrs. Darcy, inexperienced in political matters as you are, you perhaps don't appreciate that even a Whig such as myself can have some influence in parliamentary matters, Tory government notwithstanding. A word in the right quarter would do wonders for your brother. How may this information be conveyed to Mrs. Cartland? We cannot state it baldly; we cannot say, 'Consent to Miss Cartland's marriage to Mr. Poyntz, and Mr. Arthur Melbury will find he has the office he has long sought'—a minor post, I do hope you will be content with a minor post, Mrs. Darcy, since I don't care to see the country in the hands of such men as your brother."

"He is not a bad man, nor a corrupt one," said Octavia fairly. "I have little affection for him, but I don't think he will be any worse than any of the other men who fill such positions. Your conscience may be easy on that point."

"You put my mind wonderfully at ease," he said.

Mrs. Ackworth looked from one to the other of them, and made an interesting discovery, which she imparted that night to her husband.

"Lord Rutherford and Octavia? Make a match of it? You cannot be serious."

"I am certain there is a powerfully strong feeling between them. Unacknowledged as yet, I am not saying they are about to announce their engagement, but the attraction and affection is there on his side; I am not so sure of Octavia, yet—"

"If she wishes to marry him, she would be the greatest fool on earth to turn him down. The loss of her fortune, if it turns out that it is the case, will be of no moment at all if she married Rutherford, who is one of the richest men in the country."

Mrs. Ackworth adjusted her husband's nightcap, which had slid down his forehead.

"It would solve her problems at a stroke," Mr. Ackworth continued. "With Rutherford's wealth and influence on her side, her situation would be quite different. George Warren may take on a mere widowed Mrs. Darcy, he would never dare to try his tricks on a Lady Rutherford. Should such a marriage take place, we will hear no more of Lieutenant Gresham."

"That is all very well, but while there is this vile accusation, the charge of behaving in such a way, Octavia will never accept the hand of Rutherford, no, nor anyone else."

"You are probably right. She is too nice, too careful and scrupulous for that. Her name will have to be cleared, openly and with Warren's complete agreement that he was mistaken. Nothing less will serve."

"Warren mistaken?" said Mrs. Ackworth, as her husband blew out the candle and drew the covers comfortably around himself. She tugged at the eiderdown. "There is no mistake, it is sheer wicked skulduggery, and if there is any justice in the world, it will be shown up as exactly that!"

"There isn't, my dear," Mr. Ackworth murmured.

"Any what?"

"Justice."

She lay there as his snores grew from a gentle rumble to a resounding thunderous noise. She poked him in the ribs, forcing him to turn over, and lay back against the pillows, with thoughts of nuptials floating through her brain.

Chapter Thirty-three

The house party at Netherfield were very glad when Lord Rutherford announced a brief suspension in the rehearsals. "With my sister's consent, we are all to have one day off, for she has made plans for us to go, such of us as are inclined, to make a party for the Meryton assembly. We go every year, it is expected of us, but at Christmas it is always a merry occasion."

In the event, it was a large party that gathered in the hall as the carriages were brought round. Lord Rutherford and Lady Sophronia, Lady Susan and Octavia, the Portals, Henry Poyntz and Mr. Quintus Dance, together with five or six other guests who were looking forward to an evening's dancing.

To Octavia's great joy, when they arrived and had unburdened themselves of cloaks and coats and muffs and gloves and the other appurtenances of travelling on a cold winter's night, there were several other friends in the ballroom. The Ackworths were there with Penelope, Mrs. Ackworth looking very fine in a bronze satin ball dress, Mr. Ackworth pretending to find it all a great bore, but deceiving no one, not with his bright eyes, and his joyful greeting of numerous acquaintances. Sir Joseph and Lady Goulding were present, keeping a watchful eye on Charlotte, who was a picture in pink, and Octavia was particularly happy when soon afterwards Mr. and Mrs. Wytton came into the room. They were staying with Mr.

Bennet at Longbourn until after the new year. And yes, they had heard about the play; the Rutherford theatricals were famous and they would be driving over to Netherfield on the sixth, weather permitting, to see it.

Octavia enquired after young Hermione, who was, Camilla told her, thriving. "Mr. Bennet dotes on his new great-granddaughter, she is clearly destined to have shoals of admirers, starting at so early an age. We are always glad to come to the assembly here, where we meet old friends and make new ones. It has a special place in the family's affections for another reason, for it was at an assembly here that my papa first met my mother. Of course, the place is not exactly the same, for they have built a new ballroom since then; there was a fire a few years ago, and they improved the rooms and enlarged the ballroom when they rebuilt."

"It seems that this part of the country is prone to houses and buildings burning down," said Octavia.

"It was a chimney caught fire at Chauntry, was it not? At this inn, I believe, a candle was left too near a hanging in one of the bedchambers, and several rooms were gutted. Anyhow, now it is all to the good, for there is more room for dancing, it was rather cramped before. Now, I shall point out several of the local worthies, should you be interested. There are the Darleys, who live in the great house at Stoke. That is Mrs. Collins; her husband, who is a self-important bishop, may be here also, they are spending the Christmas season at Lucas Lodge; Mrs. Collins was Charlotte Lucas before her marriage and was my mama's closest friend when she was a girl. There are a regular troop of Lucases here. And there is a good joke about the bishop, for Mr. Bennet's estate at Longbourn is entailed—of course, you know all about entails—and the Collinses have been waiting for my grandfather to die any time these last twenty years. But as you see, although he is now sixty-seven, he is still spry and full of life. I dare say he may outlive Mr. Collins, just to spite him. Now, how goes it with the love affair between your niece Penelope and Mr. Poyntz?"

Octavia, knowing she could trust her not to spread the tale around, told her what had been done.

"Good gracious, I call that excellent staff work. So all we need is for old Dr. Rawleigh to give up his parish."

Mrs. Ackworth, who happened to be passing, heard these words. "Yes, Mrs. Wytton, and we have hopes in that direction. Lord Rutherford has been too tender-hearted, not wanting to push the rector into retirement, but to tell the truth, it has been a mistake. The parish is falling apart, for all Mr. Poyntz does what he can. Dr. Rawleigh not only neglects his duties, but he does not care for Mr. Poyntz to take over any but the most minor of them; he frustrates him at every turn, and if things go on as they are, no one will be christened, married, or buried, and things will be in a sad way and so I have told Lord Rutherford. Now he says he will prevail upon Dr. Rawleigh to depart; he believes he can obtain for him a canonry in Shropshire or some such place, where he may retire with honour and dignity intact, and, more importantly as far as he is concerned, continue to unearth the secrets of those tiresome Druids."

"Whereupon Mr. Poyntz steps into the living, and a young couple are made very happy," wound up Octavia.

"I wish all difficulties might be so easily surmounted," said Mr. Ackworth with a sly look at Octavia. "Now, tell me, who is that surprising and handsome man who is leading Lady Sophronia into the dance?"

At that moment, Mr. Portal came up to beg Octavia's hand in the dance, but she just had time to say over her shoulder, "That is Mr. Richard Forsyte, the banker," and to see Camilla and Mrs. Ackworth putting their heads together after several keen looks in the direction of Mr. Forsyte and his partner.

"I was surprised to see Mr. Forsyte here," said Mr. Portal.

"You know him well?" said Octavia.

"Oh, anyone who has any connection with the City knows and admires Mr. Richard Forsyte. An impressive man, with a name for being honest and honourable, which is not always the case among the money men of London, let me tell you. I see that he is a friend of Lady Sophronia's."

Octavia was about to tell him that as far as she knew, Lady

Sophronia had met him only once before, at her house in Firth Street, but the dance separated them just then. Octavia took steps to the right, to the left, and then behind, which brought her closer to where Mr. Forsyte and Lady Sophronia were waiting their turn. The warmth in their eyes as they looked at each other startled her; she blinked, looked again, and became aware that she wasn't the only one to have noticed the rapport there was between them; Lord Rutherford, who was partnering Charlotte Goulding, had lost his place in the dance for watching his sister and her partner.

He made a quick apology and caught up, but Octavia was amused to see him look back over his shoulder to where Lady Sophronia was now twirling round on Mr. Forsyte's strong arm.

To Octavia, the two men dominated the room: Lord Rutherford, tall, eagle-nosed, dark, with those astonishing eyes, and Mr. Forsyte, nearly as tall, but of a much broader build, older, balding, yet with something of the same vigour and vitality that was present in his lordship.

The dance finished. Octavia walked over to where Lady Susan had just been delivered by her partner, and Mr. Portal went off to fetch them glasses of lemonade. Lady Susan's face was alight with mischief. "My dear, have you seen Sophronia and Mr. Forsyte? And, vastly more amusing, Rutherford, who is full of alarm to see his sister capering away with the dashing banker."

"Why should not Lady Sophronia dance and enjoy herself?"

"Lord Rutherford is no fool, he has eyes in his head, anyone can see that those two are smitten with one another, it is as plain as the nose on your face."

"Is Lord Rutherford such a jealous brother?"

"He has never had occasion to be so. I think this has come as a complete surprise and shock to him. Look, Sophronia is sitting down with Mr. Forsyte; it is a joy to see her looking so alive and happy. My word, I never saw a man have such an effect on a woman. Sophronia has been out in society for more than fifteen years, and in all that time she has never met a man who could please her. And into her life walks this Mr. Forsyte, by the merest chance, and there you are."

"Where are we?" said Octavia. "You are making too much of it."

"I am not. You felt yourself the attraction of the man, and Sophronia recognised it instantly. I think her feelings are as strong as her brother's, but the world being as it is, she has not had the opportunity to find an outlet for them, as he has done. But now—well, you have started something here, bringing Mr. Forsyte to Firth Street."

"It was the merest chance that he called when Lady Sophronia was there. Do you think that he is here tonight by chance?"

"Of course not! He will have found where Netherfield House is situated, and made the reasonable guess that a party would come to the assembly tonight; it is the custom of the Rutherfords to do so, after all; that is well known here. And now he will call at Netherfield House, and then we shall see what happens."

"If he is serious, will Lord Rutherford be displeased?"

"What, that his sister has fallen for a man from a completely other world to that in which she was born and bred? I should think it will alarm him greatly, but there is little he can do about it. Sophronia is of age, she may bestow her affections and her hand where she likes. He may disapprove and try to dissuade her from any rash steps, but she is as strong-willed as he is. If she has a particle of sense, she will seize this chance of happiness with both hands; she will not meet such a man again, men like Mr. Forsyte do not grow on trees. I only marvel that he was not snatched up years ago."

"It is early days, they barely know one another."

"It is a *coup de foudre,* you know what that is."

"That is the stuff of novels." Even as she said it, Octavia chided herself for the sharp envy she felt; how could she be envious of Lady Sophronia, whose happiness must be the wish of everyone who knew her? It was not as though she had fallen for Mr. Forsyte herself; although aware of how attractive a man he was, he did not have the effect on her that he so clearly had on Lady Sophronia.

No, it was quite another man who made her heart beat faster, and he, laughing and smiling, too well-bred not to hide any disturbed feelings he had about his sister, was on the other side of the room, standing next to Charlotte.

Mr. Quintus Dance approached to ask her for the next dance, and she rose with a smile to put her hand in his. She didn't see the reaction of those two people she had just been watching; Charlotte Goulding's head flew up, and for a moment a stricken look passed over her face, while Lord Rutherford frowned and missed what Poyntz, standing on his other side with Penelope on his arm, was saying to him.

Mr. Dance lived up to his name, and Octavia, who was always able to lose herself in the movement and activity of the dance, put the complicated and tangled cross-currents of feeling in the ballroom out of her mind and concentrated on her steps.

She danced one dance with Lord Rutherford that evening. He came up to her as the musicians struck up for a waltz, and a moment later, she was whirling round the ballroom with his arm about her waist. He was an excellent dancer, and the exhilaration she felt brought an extra colour to her cheeks and a sparkle to her eyes. But when the dance was over, he left her with a civil bow and a thank-you, before going off to dance with one of the Miss Lucases.

"Nothing in it, I told you so," said Mr. Ackworth to his wife as they went in to supper.

"You're a fool," she said with great affection, and settled down to drink her soup.

The Netherfield party were not back at the house and in their beds until the early hours of the morning. The others might be wrapped in slumber, but as the church clock in the distance struck three, Octavia found herself still awake, thinking about Lady Sophronia and Mr. Forsyte, of Penelope and Henry Poyntz, and with a sad weariness of heart, of Lord Rutherford and Charlotte Goulding. The rumours had been buzzing about the ballroom that his lordship was indeed going to offer for Miss Goulding. Poor Charlotte, who had eyes for no one but Mr. Dance; did Lord Rutherford not realise that she cared nothing for him, that she would go unhappy to the altar, driven there by her parents, who no doubt thought they were acting in their daughter's best interests? Or did he know and think nothing of it, coming from the aristocratic tradition of marriages being as much a matter of arrangement and convenience as affection?

Why Charlotte, though? She was not from one of the great aristocratic families where Lord Rutherford might be expected to seek a bride. It could only be that he wanted to hold even more sway over his wife than was usual, and that might be easier with a girl from the Gouldings' rank of society.

Octavia took no comfort in this reasoning, and as a consequence of her restless night, came down the next morning in far from her best looks, with dark rings under her eyes, a slight headache, and a reluctance to attend to her duties beside the stage.

She was not the only one in a languid mood. Charlotte looked as though she had been crying—it was the smoke from the fire that made her eyes red, her mother declared—while Lady Susan gave in to prodigious yawns whenever she had finished speaking her part.

Lady Sophronia had not, it seemed, suffered at all from lack of sleep. She was in glowing looks, although her mind did not seem on the play; she let several slips go past without comment, and called an early end to the rehearsal—"Since most of you look half asleep," she said.

"Speak for yourself, sister," said Lord Rutherford, who looked his normal self. And after dinner, he had the card tables set up in one corner of the room and invited those who did not care for cards to indulge themselves in a game of Speculation. Mr. Portal joined this group, and showed how he had gained his enormous fortune by winning effortlessly, although the wild bids of the rest of the players caused a great deal of merriment, their mirth causing the card players to turn disapproving heads towards their end of the room.

Lord Rutherford played neither cards nor speculation, but went away to attend to some business. When he returned, he went over to a table on which lay some books, and where Octavia had left her sketchbooks. He took one up, and began to look through it. Then he came to a particular page, and paused. He carried the book over to a set of branched candles to cast a stronger light upon it.

"What are you doing, Sholto?" his sister called out to him. "Why do you not join us here?"

"I have no desire to be fleeced by Portal," he said easily. "It is always the same with him, he cannot help but win."

"What are you looking at?"

"This sketchbook. My apologies, Mrs. Darcy, for I realise it is yours, and I should not go peeking and prying without your consent."

"Oh, look as much as you like," said Octavia cheerfully, and then let out a groan as Mr. Portal won more of her fish. "There are no secrets in it."

"Charming drawings, however," said Lord Rutherford politely. "That is how I knew it must be yours, all these scenes of Indian life are quite fascinating." He took the book over to the table where she was sitting with the others and found the page that had caught his attention. "You have drawn a portrait here, who is this man?"

Octavia glanced at him, and the smile faded from her face. "Oh," she said wryly. "That is my nemesis, that is a likeness of Lieutenant Gresham."

"Is it indeed? You interest me strangely."

"Do you know him?"

"I do not."

The next day Lady Sophronia was dismayed to learn, when she came down to breakfast, that Lord Rutherford was not in the house, that he had left at first light to drive to London.

"Are you sure?" she said to the footman who imparted this news.

"He ordered his curricle, my lady, and I heard him say to his groom as how he was going to town. He set off at a cracking pace," he added, with a gleam of enthusiasm, swiftly suppressed as he saw the look in her ladyship's eye.

"Did he leave word as to when he will be back?" she said.

"I don't believe so, my lady, but I will make enquiries if you wish."

"It is too bad," Lady Sophronia said to Lady Susan. "Here we are, only three days until the performance, and our Orsino has done a flit."

"I expect he will be back this evening, it will be some matter of business, I dare say. Let Octavia stand in for him, she knows his part inside out, we can manage perfectly well without him."

The rehearsal did not go well, however. Charlotte was in a hopeless mood, forgetting her lines, missing her entrances, and seemingly lost in another world. When Lady Sophronia told her, quite sharply for her, to attend, she went pink and hung her pretty head and apologised, but it brought no improvement in her performance. Her mother was indulgent. "She is in love," she confided to Mrs. Rowan, who wasn't in the play, but who liked to come to the rehearsals.

"That is very nice, who is the fortunate man?" said Mrs. Rowan.

"She has eyes for no one but his lordship, we are in daily expectation of a declaration. Indeed, it seems that he may have gone to town to fetch a ring."

Satisfaction oozed out of Lady Goulding, but Mrs. Rowan felt uneasy. The word was that Rutherford and Charlotte were to make a match of it; but she had noticed the change that came over Charlotte when Mr. Dance entered a room. Charlotte's face never lit up at the sight of Lord Rutherford; indeed she seemed to take care not to look at him. Which might be bashfulness, but there was no bashfulness in the quick, secretive smiles she exchanged with Mr. Dance when she thought she was unobserved.

"I told her what I suspect," went on Lady Goulding. "I have told her that she must contrive to be alone with Lord Rutherford when he returns, so that he may ask her. Of course, he should approach Sir Joseph first, but these days the young people are impatient of convention."

Chapter Thirty-four

The next morning brought a message from Haye Park, with extraordinary news. Charlotte had eloped, stolen out of the house in the dead of night, and been driven away.

The messenger was followed in short order by Sir Joseph himself, anxiety etched on to his usually rubicund and amiable face. Lady Sophronia greeted him with words of comfort and consolation, which, however, he was too distressed to pay much attention to. She led him firmly to the dining room, ordered coffee, and almost pushed him down on to a chair, and listened to what he had to say about his daughter's disappearance. "I shall summon my brother directly," she said.

"Lord Rutherford is here?"

"He is. He returned late last night, he was in town for the day. I hear his voice."

Sir Joseph gave a deep sigh. "It is as I feared. Lady Goulding had some slight hopes that perhaps Charlotte and his lordship— I told her it could be no such thing."

"Good morning, Sir Joseph," said Rutherford. "You honour us with an early visit. Is Miss Goulding not with you?"

Sophronia shot him a warning glance. "Here is Sir Joseph come in a great state of worry to see if we have any idea where Charlotte may be. It appears that she has eloped, but the note she left with Sir

Joseph and Lady Goulding isn't clear, and they are not at all sure with whom she has run away."

"I brought her note," said Sir Joseph, producing a sorry-looking piece of notepaper. "It was written in haste, I suppose, and"—his voice caught—"I think she was weeping when she wrote it, look how the ink has run."

"May I read it?" said Lord Rutherford, and took the letter. He ran his eye down the almost illegible words. "Not very coherent," he said.

"How could she be, she must have known what distress she was causing Lady Goulding and myself, how could she do such a thing?"

"More to the point," said Rutherford, "who has whisked her off in this unseemly way? But, my dear sir, rather than coming here, would you not be better employed going after your daughter? She cannot have got so far. I assume she will be heading for the border, since she is not of age."

"I have sent men out along the Great North Road to make enquiries. I am not sure when—that is, Charlotte retired early, saying she had the headache, and indeed, she did not look at all well. Lady Goulding put her head round the door of her bedchamber before we went to bed, that was at about midnight, and she was there then, fast asleep. I have no idea how she woke up, or by what means she contrived to leave the house. Her maid, a stupid creature, just weeps into her apron and declares that she knows nothing, which is probably the truth. I came to Netherfield because this is where Charlotte has spent all her time these last few days. Is it someone here, or has she received some clandestine correspondence at Netherfield? She could not do so at Haye Park, she could not have received any letter without our knowing about it."

Octavia had come into the dining room halfway through this conversation, and Lady Sophronia drew her aside to fill her in on the events of the night at Haye Park.

Octavia thought for a moment, and then said in a low voice to Lady Sophronia, "Has anyone seen Mr. Dance this morning?"

"I have not, but it is early. Do you think—?"

Octavia nodded. Lady Sophronia at once rang the bell, and told the footman who answered it to go up to find Mr. Dance and ask him to come to the dining room. "He might be in the library, working, or in his room."

"Neither of those, my lady," said the footman. "Mr. Dance seems not to have slept in his room last night; the maid who took up his chocolate this morning found the room empty. She says that Mr. Dance is usually an early riser, but she is sure he didn't sleep there last night. The curtains on the bed were drawn back, and the bed has not been disturbed. And his bags have gone. I should say," he finished in a burst of importance, "that he's done a flit!"

"Go to the stables, Thomas," Lord Rutherford said. "Ask if any of the horses are missing."

Silence reigned in the dining room while Thomas was gone. Lord Rutherford stood by the window, looking out at the thin drizzle that had set in that morning. Lady Sophronia and Octavia brought coffee for Sir Joseph, and pressed food on him. "I am sure you left Haye Park without eating," Lady Sophronia said.

Thomas came back into the room, big with news. "Just as I got to the stables, my lord, there was the groom from the inn at Meryton coming into the yard, leading the brown hack. He says a gentleman from the house here left the horse there in the early hours of the morning, with the request that it be returned to Netherfield House."

"The gentleman in question would be Mr. Dance, I suppose?"

"It seems so," said Thomas. "The groom said the gentleman had arranged to have a chaise waiting in the yard, and he was off the horse and into the chaise directly he reached the inn."

"Well, there is your answer," said Lord Rutherford, giving Sir Joseph a sympathetic look. "Miss Goulding has run off with Mr. Quintus Dance."

Sir Joseph was nearly apoplectic. "Mr. Quintus Dance, who is this Mr. Dance?"

"You will have seen him at the assembly," said Octavia. "He danced with Charlotte. He is an architect, the architect who is building Lord Rutherford's new house."

"Architect! An architect! Charlotte has eloped with Mr. Dance the architect! This is far, far worse— Whatever am I to tell Lady Goulding?"

"Well, if they are apprehended and brought back, then no great harm is done," said Lord Rutherford. "You may be sure that the story will go no further than the walls of this room; we are not a set of gossips, and I believe we know how to hold our tongues."

"The shame," cried Sir Joseph. "The impropriety of it!"

"If you cannot catch the runaway couple, then all I can say to comfort you is that Mr. Dance is a talented young man, of a respectable family, a clergyman's son, and that he has a great future ahead of him. Wealthy he is not, but he may acquire riches through his abilities, which are considerable."

"After such a scandal as this, who will employ him?" said Sir Joseph. "What an unequal match; how came Charlotte, who was clearly destined for a great marriage, to have sunk so low—" He put his head in his hands, and the others looked at each other. Lord Rutherford shrugged his shoulders.

"It seems that Miss Goulding found my company hard to bear," he said quietly to his sister.

"Oh, stuff, don't try to pretend you cared tuppence for Charlotte."

"She has only done what Eliza did all those years ago, fled so as not to marry me."

"She has done nothing of the kind. You were in love with Eliza, you are not in the least in love with Charlotte. Mr. Dance has done you a great favour, brother, and you know it."

Octavia was trying to convince Sir Joseph that Mr. Quintus Dance was no fortune hunter, that he and Charlotte were in love, and that he would make her a good husband, if they reached Scotland and found a clergyman who would marry them.

Sir Joseph let out a moan at the mention of a clergyman and marriage, and Lady Sophronia said, somewhat sharply, Octavia thought, that marriage would be the best that could be hoped for, and that the alternative would be far worse.

"No, no, do not upset yourself, sir," Octavia cried, giving Lady

Sophronia an exasperated look. "Mr. Dance is an honourable man."

"If he's so honourable," said Lord Rutherford, who seemed to be in a most cheerful frame of mind, ill suited to Sir Joseph's evident woe, "why did he not approach Sir Joseph and ask for Miss Goulding's hand?"

"Ask me for her hand! When it was the dearest hope of myself and Lady Goulding— I think, Lord Rutherford, we were not indulging in any false fancies when I say— Well, the long and the short of it is, we thought you and Charlotte might make a match of it, that is all."

"Yes, and so did many other people," said Lady Sophronia. "You need not reproach yourself with that, Sir Joseph, and let me assure you that Charlotte is likely to be a good deal happier with Quintus Dance than ever she would be with my brother."

"But the difference, a mere Mrs. Dance, when she might have been a countess," said Sir Joseph despairingly. "Even if his lordship hadn't proposed, with her beauty and fortune and breeding, she could have married a duke, even!"

"She would have made a beautiful countess," said Lady Sophronia, "but only consider, would she have been happy? Did she love my brother? I never saw any sign of it, only duty and a willingness to please you. Charlotte does not care for the kind of life Rutherford leads in London; you know that she is shy, and she finds large groups of people intimidating."

"And I shall have to support them for ever. After this, who will employ Mr. Dance?"

"Well, I shall," said Lord Rutherford. "His plans for Chauntry are excellent, he is a most gifted architect, I would not dream of replacing him."

"There, sir," said Octavia. "With Lord Rutherford's patronage, he will be much in demand, and making a good income."

"With that and Charlotte's fortune, they may live more than comfortably," said Lady Sophronia. "Mr. Dance can build a fine house in a good part of town for himself, and Charlotte will be far more content running such a household than she would be at Rutherford

Castle, or in Rutherford's London house, full of arguing politicians and clever, talkative people, and intriguing Whigs!"

"Thank you, Sophronia, for your interesting insights into my life," said Lord Rutherford.

Octavia was not at all sure, as Sir Joseph took his rather mournful leave, shaking his head and declaring he did not know how he was to break this news to Lady Goulding, that the bracing company of the Rutherfords had been much use to him.

"Could you not have been a little kinder, more sympathetic?" she said to Lady Sophronia.

"Sophronia is more concerned about the play, and how she will manage without a Viola and a Sebastian, than about Sir Joseph's feelings," said Lord Rutherford.

"Well, they are a silly pair, going off in that dramatic way. I suppose her mama had persuaded him that you were about to propose—were you, Sholto?"

"A pointless question," said Lord Rutherford, "since it's clear that Charlotte preferred Dance to me. A blow to my self-esteem, but I dare say I shall recover."

"At least you are too honest to pretend it is a blow to your heart. As to the play, I shall ask one of the young Lucas boys to play Sebastian, they all do theatricals at school, and of course Octavia will have to take the part of Viola."

Octavia didn't think she had heard aright. "I? I have never acted in my life!"

"Then it's time you began," said Lord Rutherford. "Sophronia, summon the rest of the cast, I don't care if they're asleep or awake or what they are doing. Mrs. Darcy must have the whole play by heart, but she will need to rehearse the role, there's not a moment to lose."

There was no asking or inviting her, Octavia told herself, it was simply assumed by both the Rutherfords that she would step into the breach. She did not want in the least to play Viola, the very thought of being up on the stage, in front of an audience, filled her with dismay. She would forget her lines, miss her entrances, make her exits on the wrong side of the stage, stand in the wrong place.

Lord Rutherford was looking amused. "I know what you are feeling, and you are quite wrong to be alarmed."

"Alarmed? Panic-stricken would be nearer the mark."

"There is no need to be. You will manage splendidly, you will carry off the part with aplomb, and everyone will be grateful to you. Come, Mrs. Darcy, it would be such a shame to call off the performance at this stage, when we have worked so hard."

"Surely there is someone else—"

"To take over the prompting? Certainly. I am sure Mrs. Rowan will oblige, I have noticed a stage-struck gleam in her eyes."

"Someone else to take the part. Perhaps Mrs. Rowan—"

"No, we need a more youthful Viola. You will be splendid," said Lady Sophronia, coming briskly back into the room after sending directions to her Thespians to assemble in the ballroom. "Now, before we begin, let us go and find you a costume. You can wear breeches, you will not object to breeches."

"Good," said Lord Rutherford. "Charlotte in that robe looked more like a lawyer than Viola. And find Mrs. Darcy a more dashing hat than Charlotte had."

"What if Sir Joseph's men catch up with Charlotte, and she is brought back to Hertfordshire? It may happen, and then she can play Viola," said Octavia, clutching at a straw.

"In that case, Dance is more of a fool than I take him for," Lord Rutherford said. "If he hasn't stinted himself, and I believe it is the first rule of an elopement to do things in style, then he will have a coach and four, and they will not be able to catch up with him. And should Charlotte be brought back an unmarried woman, then I am sure the Gouldings will be far too full of reproaches and lectures for her to be spared for a drama which will seem much less exciting than the one she is enacting for herself."

The breeches which had originally been put out for Charlotte, only to be rejected by Lady Goulding, were brought out once more, and Octavia was thrust behind a screen by Lady Sophronia to try them on.

Octavia had a tussle, trying to hold up the skirts of her morning dress so that she could pull on the breeches, but she managed it with help from Alice, who had peered round the screen to see how she was getting on and stepped in to assist her. It felt extremely odd to be wearing breeches; Lady Sophronia laughed at her when she said so.

"I know exactly how you feel. I have taken breeches parts, but after a little while you will find you grow perfectly used to them, and will be strutting around in a most masculine style. Those are a good fit. Alice will see to a shirt and jerkin for you, and there are the shoes to be considered. Never mind those for now, the important task of the morning is to have you on stage, going through the play."

Octavia found there was a world of difference between sitting to one side, with the play in her hand, and taking a role. Lady Susan, Lady Sophronia, and Lord Rutherford were hard taskmasters; Mr. Portal begged for them to have some pity on her, but Lord Rutherford said in his ruthless way that she would need their pity if she fumbled her lines or missed a cue, for then she would be a laughing-stock.

Which did nothing to calm Octavia's nerves; however, as the morning went on, she found herself calmed by the words themselves. As she spoke her lines, the poetry took over, and she found herself becoming Viola, with Octavia receding into the background of her consciousness.

"How very strange it is," she said to Lady Susan, when they were allowed a brief respite to eat the nuncheon that was laid out in the dining room.

"We will make an actress of you yet," said Lady Susan. "Your breathing is at fault, however; this evening I shall show you how to breathe, otherwise there is a danger that you will lose your voice; we can lose one Viola, but not two."

"Two days to go," said Rutherford at the end of an exhausting day. "Sophronia, we shall need the musicians." And the next morning, there they were, two bassoonists, one a scrawny man, who looked almost too weak to hold his hefty bassoon, the other a burly individual, the local baker. One of the guests had brought his fiddle with him, another his cello, and a young Lucas, a younger brother of the one who was to play Sebastian, came over from Lucas Lodge with his flute.

To Octavia, the world of the play, of make-believe, was seeping into her normal self. She was confused, now Octavia, now Cesario, now Viola, but when she found herself saying Viola's lines, she was suddenly, acutely aware of the feelings that were echoed in the words.

Orsino, still the melancholy duke, sat on a stool, in the attitude of an Elizabethan consumed with hopeless love. Octavia sat at his feet, and when he said, "And what's her history?" her heart was in her mouth, and she picked up her cue to say,

> *"A blank, my lord. She never told her love,*
> *But let concealment, like a worm i' the bud,*
> *Feed on her damask cheek."*

Lord Rutherford broke in on her words. "When you reply, you must look up at me, into my eyes. I see you as a boy, you see me as a man. Now, try again."

Octavia's head swam as she brought out the lines. Her breath was wrong; not surprising, she could hardly breathe, overcome with the realisation that had swept over her, the feelings that she had so resolutely refused to give in to.

Lady Susan's voice rang in her ears. "Octavia, please pay attention. You have forgotten all I taught you. Now, breathe, from here—" She held her rib cage with both her hands. "Control your breath, let it flow out through the line. Then you breathe again after the break."

Octavia forced herself to attend to nothing except the breathing and the words, but looking up at Lord Rutherford, whose dark blue eyes held more than a gleam of amusement, she once again faltered. Then, with an effort of will, forcing herself to think only of the poetry and not at all of Lord Rutherford, she spoke the words smoothly and easily.

Chapter Thirty-five

The sixth of January, the Feast of the Epiphany, dawned to a magical frost sparkling over the trees and fields. Octavia looked out of her window through the spun crystal of a frozen spider's web into a blue sky. The gardener, Lady Sophronia told her when she came down to breakfast, was the best weather seer in the district, and he had promised them a fine, clear day, and a milder one than of late, so that with the moon full, all the families from round about would feel happy to make the journey to dine and watch the play at Netherfield House.

"And then," said Penelope, who had arrived early in the day—to help with costumes, she said, but in truth to be near Poyntz—"Christmas will be over." She gave a heartfelt sigh. "And I shall go back to London."

Mrs. Ackworth and Lord Rutherford exchanged conspiratorial smiles.

"What have I said that is so amusing?" Penelope asked peevishly, and while her cousin hastened to assure her that she knew her to be enjoying herself in Hertfordshire, Lord Rutherford asked his sister if the post had been brought up yet.

"My dear Sholto, what are you expecting? That is the third time you have asked me. Do not you know how busy all the servants are today? The man who usually collects the post has a dozen other errands in the town. Now, I must see to the lights. I fear that Mr. Jenkins will set fire to Netherfield if we are not careful; he is fascinated by the limelights, and I am sure we shall end up dazzled by the footlights he is setting up for us."

"Limelights!" said Octavia. "You know, Lord Rutherford, when I first heard Lady Sophronia talk about a play, I imagined that a country-house performance would be more akin to an evening of charades, not anything so intense and accomplished as what is planned here."

"Ah, well, we have our reputation to look to. We have to show our neighbours that although Chauntry has gone, the traditions remain."

The play was to be performed at dusk and followed by a magnificent supper for all the guests. So the house was in turmoil as the final preparations were made for hospitality that would be worthy of the occasion.

As Lady Sophronia predicted, it was late in the morning when the manservant returned from Meryton with the post. The letters were taken at once to Lord Rutherford's room, and when his lordship was told that they have arrived, he broke off at once from a spirited conversation he was having with Pagoda Portal as to a Bill to be brought in during the next session of Parliament, and went to attend to his correspondence.

Octavia had no time to wonder what letter Lord Rutherford might be so eagerly awaiting. Lady Susan, serene, but with an excitement about her, had instructed Alice to make up Viola in good time, and Octavia, whose excellent complexion needed no enhancement, found herself being painted to within an inch of her life. "Good gracious, whatever do I look like?" she exclaimed when her maid handed her a looking-glass for her to inspect her face.

Lady Susan cast a critical eye over her. "Like an impure, or alternatively, an actress. To most of the English, they are the same thing. You should visit America, my dear Octavia, and then you would find yourself in a different world, with many of the truths and shibboleths you have grown up with quite ignored, or considered plain wrong."

"Do you miss America?" Octavia asked, putting down the mirror.

"I confess that I do," said Lady Susan with a sigh. "It's a young country, and full of a sense of adventure which I don't find in London. However, fate has decided that I am once again an Englishwoman, so I must make the best of it."

A footman came into the room. "A letter for you, my lady," he said.

Lady Susan took it without looking at it, and tucked it into her reticule. Her mind was on the present moment and on the play; she didn't have time to read a letter now, she remarked, as she picked up the velvet cap that Viola wore in the first act and directed Alice to pin up Octavia's hair to go under it.

Carriages were soon bowling up the drive, disgorging guests all in a happy mood of expectation. The Wyttons and Mr. Bennet were early arrivals, and Camilla put her head round the door of the room set aside as a dressing room to exclaim at Octavia's appearance and to wish her luck.

"You must not do that," said Lady Susan, driving her out of the room. "Do you not know that you must never wish an actor or actress luck before a performance? Ill wish her if you like, that is considered much more fortunate."

Octavia's mouth was dry, her lines had flown from her head, and she turned a desperate face to Lady Susan, who laughed at her in a most unfeeling way.

"Never look at me with that tragic face. You will do very well, as soon as you are out there on stage, you will be a shipwrecked girl cast up on the shores of Illyria, and Shakespeare will do the rest."

With her Elizabethan skirts heavy and clumsy over her boy's costume, Octavia went to the ballroom. Lord Rutherford was already on stage, hidden from the gathering, chattering audience by the great fall of curtain, issuing directions to Mr. Jenkins, who was wrestling with a tree that formed part of the scenery.

When he saw Octavia, his eyebrows rose, and he swept her an elegant bow. "How does Viola, my queen, my mistress?"

Octavia felt her rouged cheeks flaring into more vivid colour, and annoyed with herself, tried to turn off his greeting with a smile. There was something more than the usual amusement in Rutherford's expressive eyes this evening. Laughter, yes, but also a tenderness that made her heart thump; a sensation that had the effect of driving away her theatrical nerves, but left her feeling peculiarly defenceless standing there in front of him. However would she get through the performance with even a modicum of credit if she couldn't control her feelings better than this?

Lord Rutherford disconcerted her by changing the subject. "I have news for you that will put a lilt into your step and joy into your voice," he said. "Mr. Warren has withdrawn his claim."

Octavia couldn't believe her ears.

"Mr. Warren has done what?"

"Withdrawn his claim to your inheritance. Absolutely, without reservation, he agrees he has no claim."

"But how—when did you hear this." And then, "How came *you* to have this news; and what has it to do with you?"

Then Lady Sophronia was there, telling Octavia to go off to the side and chivvying Mr. Jenkins to finish his work.

"The two of you must not stand here gossiping; the performance will begin very soon, and there is Mr. Jenkins, listening hard. I don't know what you think you are about, Sholto!"

Octavia made to follow Lady Sophronia to the side, but Lord Rutherford laid his hand on her arm to hold her back for a moment. "It is true, I wouldn't tease you on such a subject. I will tell you everything afterwards."

As they came off the stage, he paused to twitch the edge of the curtain so that he could look out into the ballroom. "Let us make sure that we are to have an audience for our efforts," he said.

"You must be deaf if you think we have not," said Octavia. "It sounds as though half of Hertfordshire is present; let us trust that they stop talking when the musicians strike up."

Lord Rutherford wasn't listening. "What the devil is that Mr. Richard Forsyte doing here? Who invited the man, why is he in my house?"

Lady Sophronia was at his side, mocking him. "Your house, your invitation; you are not the only person in the world, Sholto. Mr. Forsyte is here by my invitation, and I am very happy that he is able to attend."

With which she whisked herself round the curtain and into the ballroom, where in a moment she was beside Mr. Forsyte, greeting him with evident delight. Octavia, peeking through a gap in the curtain left by the indignant Lord Rutherford, saw the warmth in Mr. Forsyte's eyes as he stood looking down at Lady Sophronia.

"Well, I will be damned," said Lord Rutherford, even more wrathfully. "If Sophronia thinks—" Then he caught Octavia's eye; it was her turn to look amused, and for a moment his mouth tightened before he relaxed, laughing. "I make too much of it, Sophronia is of course entitled to her friends, although I would have thought a fellow like that—"

"If you are talking about Mr. Richard Forsyte, Rutherford," said Mr. Portal, who had come up behind them. He was swelled to quite twice his normal size by the stuffing in his doublet and made a startling figure. "I have to tell you that you are being absurd. He is a man I would welcome to my house at any time, and before you retort that I am another cit, I beg you to refrain from making any such remark."

"Of course I would not say any such thing," said Lord Rutherford. "What do you take me for? It is just that he seems very forward, very free and easy with my sister."

"If you have eyes in your head, Rutherford, which I sometimes doubt, you would see that your sister and Mr. Forsyte are in love."

"In love?"

"It happens to people, Sholto. Even you," and with a roguish glance at Octavia, and a quick pressure on her arm, he moved away to where he would make his first entrance.

The lights in the ballroom were extinguished at Lady Sophronia's bidding. The actors heard the chattering voices of the audience die down and fade away as the musicians began to play, and then the curtains drew apart to reveal Duke Orsino, dashing and insouciant in his black and gold, to speak his opening lines:

> *"If music be the food of love, play on . . ."*

Octavia, intensely moved, knew with sudden awareness that there was no difficulty in playing her part as Viola, no difficulty at all. Viola was young and deeply in love with the Duke Orsino, and here she was, inhabiting Viola's persona and sharing all her character's emotions. She had never seen Lord Rutherford look more handsome than in his extravagant costume, and the sound of his voice speaking the golden poetry sent shivers up and down her spine.

She went through the play almost in a dream. The words were Shakespeare's, but she spoke them from her own heart, with an ardour that made up for her inexperience as an actress. She did well, she knew she had done well, although there was no question but that Lord Rutherford and Lady Susan were the hit of the evening. The audience were attentive and responsive, and burst into joyful applause as Octavia put her hand in Orsino's, and the duke said,

> *"Here is my hand: you shall from this time be*
> *Your master's mistress."*

As his eyes looked intently into hers, Octavia felt as though the world stood still; the audience, the applause, the other actors faded from her senses, as though only she and Rutherford existed.

Mr. Ackworth, who loved his Shakespeare, was all attention, and at this he turned to his wife, sitting demurely beside him, and said, in a loud whisper, "Well, you were quite right, my dear. You so often are in affairs of the heart; they will make a match of it, his lordship and Mrs. Darcy."

Such was the effect of this spontaneous and indiscreet utterance that the audience hardly attended to the closing song, instead breaking into a flurry of whispers, interrupted only by the need for enthusiastic and sustained applause as the curtain was drawn across, and the actors and actresses came out to take their bows.

The cast stayed in their costumes, with the exception of Octavia, who had no intention of wandering about Netherfield in her breeches, despite Lord Rutherford's provocative remark of how well she looked in them. She hurried upstairs to put on a more conventional evening dress, while Mr. Portal, proclaiming that his own girth was quite substantial enough for any man, put aside his padding in favour of his own coat.

It was a very happy gathering, with friends and neighbours delighted to celebrate this last day of Christmas in one another's company. News was flying round about Charlotte and Mr. Dance. They had been apprehended in Scotland, where they were not yet married, and had agreed to come back to Hertfordshire for a more seemly ceremony than one over the anvil. Sir Joseph was reported as becoming more and more pleased with his new son-in-law, and Lady Goulding, joyfully reunited with her daughter, had shed tears of mingled joy and fury, before admitting that she thought Charlotte might do very well with her Mr. Dance.

Penelope was radiant, and as soon as Octavia came down, she took her to one side to confide in breathless tones that no one had ever been so happy. At Lord Rutherford's urging, Mr. Poyntz had written to Mr. Cartland and had received a letter giving his consent to the match and requesting him to present himself in Lothian Street as soon as he was in town.

"I don't know how Papa persuaded Mama. He enclosed a note from her; he must have made her write it. It is all so strange, for normally— She is very displeased with me; she is quite outspoken, but she is prepared to let me marry Mr. Poyntz at such a time as he is in a position to support a wife. And Dr. Rawleigh is to become a canon of somewhere or other, and so he will give up the living of Meryton. But I think it is all due to Lord Rutherford; Mr. Poyntz declares it is, at all events. He is the kindest man imaginable to go for so much trouble on our behalf. Oh," and her eyes took on a mischievous twinkle, "I do not need to tell you how kind he is, since you are going to marry him. Oh, how cross Mama will be, when you are a countess!"

Octavia, who had been listening to her niece with only half an ear, her own thoughts running on Lord Rutherford's extraordinary words about Warren, blinked. "I do not know where you got such an idea from."

"I have eyes in my head, and being in love myself, I recognise all the signs in other people; a cold and love cannot be hid, Aunt. That is what they say."

"Minx," said Lord Rutherford, appearing beside her. "A glass of wine, Mrs. Darcy, to restore your nerves after such a fine performance."

"Thank you," she said, all dignity. And then, abandoning her lofty air, she said urgently, "Please do tell me what you meant about Warren. Can it really be so? Can he have given up his claim?"

"Let us go where we cannot be overheard. The library will do."

He ushered her in and closed the door behind them. "Come over to the fire."

She refused a seat and stood before the blazing logs, stretching her hands out to the warmth, not trusting herself to look at him.

"It all came about by chance," he began, and told her, swiftly and succinctly, of his journey back from Oxford. "As soon as I saw the likeness you had drawn of Lieutenant Gresham, I recognised him as the man I had seen at the inn with Warren. Not only had I seen him, but I had also overheard some of the conversation that passed between them. So I went to London to tax Warren with what I knew. He tried to bluster his way out of it, even had the damned cheek to suggest I had hatched up this story with you to discredit him, but I pointed out that while his word might prevail against yours, it certainly would not do so against mine."

"So I owe the restoration of my fortune to you, Lord Rutherford. How can I ever thank you?"

"You owe me no thanks," he said, his voice low and definite. "I want no thanks; it was a pleasure to thwart Warren's wicked and unjust scheme. One might comprehend, although not forgive, a man's attempts to get his hands on a fortune, but to blacken your name and threaten you as he did was outrageous." He paused. "I like to think that I would have acted with similar enthusiasm against him had anyone been the victim, but I have to confess that my determination was sharpened by knowing that you were the one to suffer from his nefarious activities."

Only a few days ago, the knowledge that she could return to take up the threads of her life in her small London house would have filled Octavia with joy. Now it hardly seemed to matter; she was glad it was all over, but her concern for her future and her fortune had paled into insignificance in comparison to what had happened to her here at Netherfield House.

Rutherford was standing very close to her now, and she turned to find herself in his arms; overcome by a blazing sense of happiness and rightness, she responded without hesitation to his passionate embrace.

"Of course," he said, when he freed his lips from hers, "Warren may say that I acted from self-interest, desirous of adding your fortune to my own."

"What, do you think he will dare? I should not venture a second round with you, were I in his shoes."

"In any case, I intend to settle all your fortune upon you, and upon our children, so you need not suspect I am any kind of a fortune hunter."

She laughed and drew him closer to her. "I was never in love like this before," she murmured. "It makes me feel giddy."

"Never in love?" he said, looking down at her.

"I loved Christopher, but it was not the same. Is that disloyal?"

"No, honest. I love you for your honesty and courage."

"You did not think so when I acted honestly and courageously over the seat at Axby."

"You were dabbling in affairs about which you knew nothing, which is quite different."

"Ah, but my political education has continued apace, and now I know I was right to do as I did."

"Just you wait, you will have so much of politics when you are Lady Rutherford that you will cry for mercy."

"Is this a proposal, Lord Rutherford?" she said, laughing. "I find you are not at all romantic."

"My own love," he began, and then his voice, husky with emotion, changed, as the door to the library was flung open. "Now what the devil— Sophronia!"

Lady Sophronia stood at the door, her hand still on the handle, her face alight with amusement. "My word, Orsino, I find you in a compromising position. You will have to marry your Viola."

"That is precisely what I intend to do."

"Well, I am most heartily glad of it, and I wish you both joy. I always wanted a sister, Octavia," she went on, going over to her and kissing her warmly, "and you will be the best one I could wish for."

Octavia took Sophronia's hands in hers, searching for the words to express her pleasure in Sophronia's felicitations.

Lady Sophronia stood back and gave Lord Rutherford a wicked look. "And now you may wish me joy, brother, for I know you will be delighted to hear that Mr. Forsyte has proposed to me, and I have accepted him. We can have a double ceremony, Octavia; we shall accompany one another to church!"

Lord Rutherford's countenance darkened, and Octavia, giving him a swift look, took his hand, pressing it warningly. "Oh, I am so glad! I must tell you how much I like Mr. Forsyte!" she said. "And I can see you are the happiest creature in the world, except for me. Lord Rutherford, you must say something. Do you not share in your sister's delight?"

"I hardly know the man, although I know Portal thinks well of him." He gave Sophronia a shrewd glance. "You are all aglow, Sophronia. Do you really care for Mr. Forsyte? It is not that you simply wish for a different life, with a home of your own? I should not like to think of you marrying simply for the sake of an establishment."

"Don't you dare suggest such a thing to me!" she said, with considerable indignation.

Octavia was laughing up at him. "You are a fool if you can't see that your sister is head over ears in love with her Mr. Forsyte, and he is the same; they have been a case from the moment they met."

"I wish you joy in return, then, Sophronia, with great satisfaction, since Octavia is sure of your mutual affections; she must be right. Tell Forsyte to come and speak to me— No, do not bristle. I know that you are of age and do not need my permission, but there will be settlements to discuss, someone must take care of your interests; you have too many stars in your eyes to think of practical matters."

Lady Sophronia had left the library door open, and now, in a whirl of skirts, her eyes sparkling, Lady Susan appeared in the room. "Dear me," she said looking from one to the other of them. "What is going on in here? Octavia, Sholto, you do not need to tell me your news; it is written all over you. I saw it coming weeks ago, did not I, Sophronia? And you are to marry your banker, and I am so very happy for you."

Octavia, her awareness of others' feelings heightened by her own joy, looked intently at Lady Susan.

"Something has happened to you," she said. And then, in a flash of insight, "That letter, it contained good news, did it not?"

Lady Susan laughed. "You have sharp eyes. Yes, I have had some very good news from America. My husband, the wretch who turned out to have a wife living, has finally obtained a divorce. No, do not look so shocked. He and his former wife have been estranged for many years; indeed he had quite lost touch with her. But now everything has been put in order; he is a free man, and he has written begging me to return to America. What an amusing idea, to be married twice to the same man."

Cries of astonishment, congratulations, and a good deal of kissing and hugging were watched with a sardonic eye by Lord Rutherford and also by Mr. Forsyte, who had come looking for Sophronia.

"Pray come in," said Lord Rutherford, as he stood at the door. "Join the throng."

"I should have asked your permission to pay my address to your sister, I dare say," Mr. Forsyte said to Lord Rutherford, his eyes fixed on Sophronia. "But with or without your blessing, we shall be married."

"I wish you happy," said Lord Rutherford. "You may well be. It is not the marriage I ever envisaged for Sophronia, but she knows her own mind."

"And heart," said Octavia reprovingly.

"Yes," he said, putting an arm around her waist and pressing her close to him. "No, you do as you please, Forsyte; I shan't stand in your way. And, Susan, do you really want to go back to America?"

"Oh, indeed I do. My husband is no plaster saint, but I am strangely fond of him, and we shall have an interesting life together, I am sure. I shall stay only long enough to see my good friends here to the altar, and then I shall sail away to the new world once more."

"Now," said Rutherford, "if everything is arranged among you, perhaps I might have my library to myself."

"To yourself, Sholto?" said Lady Sophronia, quizzing him. "You want us to take Octavia away?"

"I do not want any such thing, as you very well know."

They left, laughing and talking, and shut the door behind them. A log flared up with a sudden crackle of sparks, and Octavia, for an instant overcome with a ridiculous shyness, told Lord Rutherford that he should tend to the fire before Netherfield, like Chauntry, went up in flames.

"I should not mind," he said, taking her hand and sinking dramatically on to one knee as he pressed her hand to his lips, a gesture that set her tingling from head to toe. "You could carry out all these volumes, and I could make my proposal to a woman with a smut on her nose. Now, dear heart, my own love, will you do me the very great honour of accepting my hand in marriage?"

A TOUCHSTONE READING GROUP GUIDE

The Second Mrs. Darcy

SUMMARY

Octavia Darcy's friends and relatives keep telling her that a single woman is always in want of a husband, especially an impoverished widow whose late husband's estate has all gone to a pinchpenny male relative. But to Octavia, an orphan whose half siblings have always bullied her and whose husband was kind, but not the love of her life, the idea of giving herself up to the control of another is anathema. When she unexpectedly inherits a fortune, she is overjoyed and looks forward to a new life of independence. Escaping from the efforts of her half brothers and sisters to marry her off, Octavia goes to Yorkshire to find out more about the family she never knew, and while she is there she meets and crosses swords with landowner and politician Sholto Rutherford. And her encounters with him, unbeknownst to her, are destined to continue.

After her time in Yorkshire, Octavia returns to London and shares a house with the dashing Lady Susan. Although she is now secure in her new life as a wealthy heiress, Octavia is quickly caught up in the romantic problems of her young niece and the confusing, but pleasant, meetings with Lord Rutherford. But when the shadow of her loathsome relative, and her late husband's heir, George Warren, falls over her, she is threatened with the loss of both inheritance and reputation. Octavia seeks relief from Warren's intrigue by spending Christmas as a guest of the Rutherfords at Netherfield House (the same house that Bingley rented in *Pride and Prejudice*), which brings not only festivities and theatricals but also unexpected solutions and happiness for more than one member of the party.

DISCUSSION POINTS

1. Elizabeth Aston creates a number of unusual character names in *The Second Mrs. Darcy,* such as Octavia, Dance, and Forsyte. Make a list of these names, and discuss with your group why you think she chose them and how they relate to the story.

2. On page 70, Sophronia Rutherford says to her brother, "I have no more desire to attend all day long to household trivia than you have. Simply being born a woman does not mean that I am naturally domestic, all women are not that way inclined, however convenient it is for the male sex to believe it is the case." Were you surprised by this comment? Did Sholto assume his sister should tend to the household because of the time period, his own beliefs about women, or another reason?

3. During the hey-day of the British Empire, many English expatriates made their lives and fortunes in India. The result left these expats with a fascinating blend of East and West culture and lifestyle all their own. How does Octavia compare her life in Calcutta with her life in London?

4. Compare Octavia's Melbury stepfamily and relations with the Darcy side of the family, as introduced in this and other Aston novels. What characters in *The Second Mrs. Darcy* remind you of characters from previous novels in the series, or in *Pride and Prejudice* itself, and why?

5. Octavia's marriage to Christopher Darcy, though brief, was amiable. She found pleasure in her husband's company and came to care for him enough to truly mourn his death. Why, then, is Octavia so set against another marriage?

6. What is Sholto's first impression of Octavia? How and why does his opinion of her change with each encounter? When does his heart first seem to warm to her?

7. Why do you think Sholto didn't tell anyone he'd witnessed George Warren scheming with Lieutenant Gresham? When did you begin to suspect what he was up to?

8. As part of their family Christmas tradition, the Rutherfords direct their guests in a performance of Shakespeare's *Twelfth Night.* Do you think this is an apt choice, given the various situations of the characters involved both in the play and in the novel? Why or why not? What other plays might also be appropriate?

9. Why, in the end, is Sholto Rutherford still not completely happy about his sister's engagement to Mr. Forsyte?

10. There are certain elements of Jane Austen's novels that writers have respectfully put to their own use throughout the years. If you have read *Pride and Prejudice* or any Austen books, what elements of *The Second Mrs. Darcy* are familiar to you?

11. Have you read any of the first three novels in this Darcy series *(Mr. Darcy's Daughters, The Exploits & Adventures of Miss Alethea Darcy,* and *The True Darcy Spirit)*? If so, did you find it helpful to know those chapters of the story before reading *The Second Mrs. Darcy*?

12. What other Jane Austen novels would you like to see Elizabeth Aston tackle? If you were to write a spin-off, which novel or series would you choose and why?

ENHANCE YOUR BOOK CLUB EXPERIENCE

1. Throw an Indian-style book club gathering, complete with ripe mangoes, Darjeeling tea, and the *nimbu pani* drink that Octavia's servants bring her lawyer guest, Mr. Gurney. You can find a great recipe for *nimbu pani,* along with other Indian delicacies, at *www.Indianfoodforever.com* and *www.cuisinecuisine.com*.

2. William Shakespeare's works are performed with regularity throughout the United States. Find a local performance of *Twelfth Night,* or rent Trevor Nunn's 1996 film rendition to watch the folly of lovers who ignore, or hesitate to reveal, their hearts.

3. Spend some time browsing the author's website, *www.elizabeth-aston.com*. Check out the reviews listed there, or search the Internet for other reviews. Share your findings at your next book club meeting, and discuss whether or not you agree with the critics and why.

AUTHOR Q & A

1. What first gave you the idea to create a series of novels about the trials and tribulations of the extended Darcy family members?

I was musing about the world that the children of, for example, Emma and Mr. Knightley would grow up in—Emma's daughter would be the age Emma is in the book just as the young Queen Victoria came to the throne. Which made me think back to the first draft of *Pride and Prejudice,* written in about 1797, and I realized that any Darcy children would be growing up towards the end of the Regency period, just after Jane Austen died. That set me to wondering how different the life of the Darcy daughters, with fortunes and the grandeur of Pemberley behind them, would be from that of their mother, Lizzy Bennet, and her sisters.

Only the privilege and money might create their own problems . . .

2. Writing historical fiction seems like a vast enterprise. What kind of research did you do to prepare yourself for creating this series?

Part of the research comes from the reading I've done over the years and my studies at university. I like to draw on the writing of the period—letters, journals, novels and nonfiction, to get the flavour of the times and the language right. I also did a lot of research on the situation of women at this time and attitudes to sexuality and marriage.

Apart from that, social and political history provides the facts and framework for the stories.

3. There are several intersections of military and political history with the events of *The Second Mrs. Darcy.* Was this a conscious effort to ground readers in the historical time period?

It's important for historical novels, even light-hearted ones, to be based on the wider world that the characters move in. And I felt that Octavia, destined to be a political hostess, would take a keen interest in everything that was going on.

4. Octavia does an awful lot of travelling in this novel—from Calcutta, India, to London, Yorkshire, and Hertfordshire, England. Have you ever visited India? If so, what was your most memorable experience?

I lived in India as a child and went to school in Calcutta—as well as living in London, Yorkshire, and Hertfordshire; I like to place my books in places I know. My most memorable experience in India? A snake in the bathroom, perhaps, or the scorpion in my slipper—but on a grander scale, the drama of the monsoon.

5. There are several Jane Austen–inspired novels and films. Do you have any favorites you'd like to share with your readers?

Like many lovers of the novels of Jane Austen, I never feel that the actors and actresses match the picture I have of the characters! From way back, the old film of *Pride and Prejudice* had a terrific Darcy in Laurence Olivier. I think *Clueless* really caught the feeling of Emma, and I loved the dances in the BBC version of *Pride and Prejudice.*

6. Jane Austen is often celebrated as one of the original "women's fiction" writers. Which Austen novel is your favorite, and why?

I hate to hear Jane Austen described as a women's fiction writer. You can read her for the romance and escapism, but to do that is to be short-changed. She is one of the very greatest of the English novelists, and that's because the humanity, the wit, and the insight into the workings of the head and heart are so powerful in her novels.

7. *The Second Mrs. Darcy,* like your other Darcy novels, concerns characters and events that never grace the pages of Austen's original, thus creating a spin-off that is really quite a departure. Were there cues in *Pride and Prejudice* that inspired or helped direct you? Can you tell us a little about your process for writing *The Second Mrs. Darcy?*

I took one of the basic situations of *Pride and Prejudice*—five sisters of marriageable age wanting to meet and marry the right men—as the starting point for *Mr. Darcy's Daughters,* the first of the novels. And I chose to write about characters who share some of the virtues and faults of the Bennet girls, which meant that I had to create heroes who were worthy of them, as Mr. Darcy is of Elizabeth.

I began *The Second Mrs. Darcy* with the premise and question: "What if an impoverished young woman inherited a huge fortune?" Then the unsympathetic family sprang up to add to her woes; but of course she had to have friends and well-wishers as well!

8. All four of your Darcy novels have been warmly received by fans of Jane Austen and by new readers alike. To what do you attribute your success?

That's a tough question. I think it's because I don't try to rewrite or do a pastiche of Jane Austen, which would leave readers dissatisfied, but instead create new characters within the world that Jane Austen knew and lived in. And, like Jane Austen, I love to amuse and entertain while writing about things that matter as much now as they did two centuries ago.